WATERS FALL

A NOVEL

BECKY DOUGHTY

Create in me a clean heart, O God
And renew a steadfast spirit within me.
Psalm 51:10 NASB

ONE

Nora's bones ached in the frigid water, and her lungs thrummed in desperation for oxygen, but she resisted the urge to push to the surface. She tipped her head back and gazed up at the warped glow above her, the sunlight flaunting its promise of warmth. The water roared as it flung itself over the stacked boulders of the falls and into the pool where she was submerged; the cacophony surrounded her, shutting out all sounds from above. The kids would be calling for her by now, and if she stayed under much longer, Jake would come after her. She'd long ago breathed out the last of her air so she could sink to the rocky bed of the pool. Her long dark hair drifted up around her head, reminding her of mermaid stories, and her arms floated out to her sides of their own volition. If she could just keep from kicking her legs, she might be able to stay there...longer.

It had started out as a game to see who could hold their breath the longest, and Nora knew she'd win, hands down, even against Jake. A choir girl—first school, then church—her lung capacity was in tip-top condition because she worked to keep it that way. On the third round, though, something tripped inside her head, like a live wire sending a string of sparks skittering across her thoughts, and she was suddenly and acutely aware of the thrill of this watery cocoon, of being out of breath, of the cold, and of the churning chaos just a few feet away from where she waited in a strange state of suspended animation.

They'd stumbled across the huge pool with its waterfall a few years ago while on their annual family camping trip to Kennedy Meadows in the Sierras. It was a bit of a hike up from their actual campsite, and some distance down a tributary of the main river, but they made the trek almost daily during their week-long stay.

They called it Anderson Hollow, and there was never anyone around to challenge their claim to it. The falls made it less than ideal for the hardcore fishing fanatics, and the hike made it less than ideal for waders and sunbathers.

The banks along the west side of the stream were cut away where the water ran swift and deep, but on the east side it was sandy and wide, and they picnicked in the shade or napped in the sun after swimming in the chilled mountain water. The kids collected pretty stones, quartz crystals, and shiny bits of pyrite they were certain was gold.

"The California Gold Rush did happen in California, Mom," Felix reminded her with wide, hopeful eyes. Leslie gathered wildflowers and seedpods to make peace offerings to the local water sprites, and they both learned to weave tall reeds together to form little rafts for boat races.

"This way, if we lose one down the stream, we're not littering." Leslie had participated in an Earth Day Campaign at her school and won a contest for her artwork depicting children putting flowers in the tailpipes of black cloud emitting vehicles. For a while, she'd driven everyone crazy with her activist behavior, but her fervor waned over time to "healthy awareness," much to the relief of her family and friends.

Today was the first time Nora had ever intentionally opened her eyes under the water here without her goggles on. The torrent from the falls kept the pool stirred up and cloudy, and she'd always been afraid of debris blinding her.

But the swirling specks of silt and sand, glittering and pale, added to the other world sensation that held her in its grip. What would happen if she just opened her mouth and drew the fairy dust water into her lungs?

Suddenly the very thought of breathing had her clamoring for the surface, bursting up out of the water with a great gulp that left her coughing and gasping. She looked up to find she'd drifted to the far side of the waterhole where there was no easy place to climb out. Across from her, Leslie scrambled from the top of the large boulder where she'd obviously been perched to try to locate Nora. Felix, tears of panic streaming down his face, stood ankle deep at the edge of the pool, helpless in his youth. Jake, treading water out where she'd first gone under, couldn't seem to make up his mind whether to come to her aid or go back to comfort the kids.

Nora waved him off, and he grimaced at her before making his way to Felix. She read both fear and condemnation in his eyes, but she was too busy trying to catch her breath to respond. She was trembling a little, and her side felt like it wanted to cramp; she wasn't sure if it was from the cold or the depletion of oxygen. She'd have some explaining to do, and she sighed in frustration, knowing nothing she could say would make sense to them. At least not to Jake.

The kids would probably accept that she'd been swept under by the rushing water, even if they didn't like it, because they'd never ventured too close to the falls for fear of just that.

Jake, however, wasn't going to be so easy to appease. He stood with his arm around Felix, his other hand up to shield his eyes from the glint of the sun off the water as he watched her, waiting for her to come back to them.

TWO

Lashing out at her husband never made for a good start to a family outing. Nora knew that from experience. But the bags were not packed. They were not sitting in the driveway waiting to be loaded into the back of Jake's truck.

The morning was nearly over, and they still had a six hour drive ahead of them to their favorite campsite, Kennedy Meadows, on the South Fork of the Kern River. Fortunately, it would be light until almost eight o'clock tonight, so if they got on the road by noon, they'd still be able to set up camp in daylight. They might even have time to take a dip in the river before the sun set behind the peaks, making it too chilly to enjoy the water.

Jake sauntered into the kitchen from the garage, his arm around Felix, regaling the boy with fishing stories from his own childhood. Nora stood at the kitchen sink, washing the last of the breakfast dishes, trying to force her mounting frustration down the drain with the dirty water. As they passed behind her, Jake reached over and ran a hand along the curve of her waist, his fingers drifting across her low back, and she clenched her jaw to keep from flinching.

She did not want him touching her right now.

She usually loved camping with the family, but it was getting increasingly more difficult to take time away from her business. She had calls to make, orders to place, shipments to process, two new clients to book, and a miscellaneous to-do list a mile long.

And Jake had waited until the last minute to pack him and the kids up.

"It's only four days, Nor." So he *had* noticed her less-than-warm response. But then, what did he expect? She'd asked him every day this week how the packing was going, and his noncommittal answers didn't bode well with her. And she'd been right to ask—he'd done nothing but stock the tackle boxes and junk food supply.

"We can wear the same clothes the whole time. Just toss some clean underwear in a grocery bag, and we're good to go, right guys?" He and Felix high-fived across the counter behind Nora.

Leslie sat at the table sorting her change, her long brown hair, so like her mother's, pulled back into a ponytail. There was a quaint little general store near the campground, and the kids collected coins for weeks in anticipation of the homemade goodies at the snack bar. At her father's words, she stopped counting, and rolled her eyes.

"That's so gross, Dad." Looking to Nora, who was now filling the old red and white cooler with perishable food items she'd frozen overnight, she said, "You don't have to worry about me, Mom. I'm packed. Clothes, toothbrush, deodorant, my hairbrush. And my sketchbook and pencils, of course."

"Of course. Thank you, Les." Nora, too, wanted to roll her eyes over Jake's incompetence, but she refrained. "Would you do me a favor?"

"Sure." Leslie, still young enough to be excited about camping, was also old enough to be aware that there was more to it than just showing up for the fun.

"Will you make a list of everything you've packed and give a copy to each of the boys? Then when they're finished packing their bags, please do an inspection to make sure they haven't forgotten anything."

"I don't want her touching my underwear," Felix quipped, a nine-year-old boy with bouts of teenage attitude. "That's just wrong."

"I don't *want* to touch your underwear, freak."

"I'll count your underwear, Felix," Jake laughed, ruffling the boy's hair.

"No, you won't. You'll be too busy counting your own." Nora eyed her capricious husband over the kids' heads, making sure he understood that he'd been categorized with Felix in his ineptitude. Jake had the decency to mouth an apology before reaching over to smack her backside as he left the kitchen.

The three of them headed down the hall toward the bedrooms while Nora finished up alone, a reluctant smile softening the edges of her discontent.

· · · ● · ● · ● · · ·

"It's too much for me to handle on my own," she murmured, responding to his sideways glances across the silence between them; the unspoken questions in his eyes.

"You could have just asked for a pair of floaties, you know." He grinned and nudged her shoulder with his own. "They probably sell them down at the General Store."

She frowned at his effort to make light of things. She wanted him to listen, to really hear what she was trying to say. The way she'd felt today had scared her, too, and she needed to talk about it without him turning it into a joke so they could brush it under the carpet along with all their other unaddressed issues.

"I need your help, Jake." She dragged in a slow breath, then continued, not looking at him. "I need you to contribute more. It doesn't have to be equal amounts. I don't care about the 'his money, her money' thing, so please don't make this about that, but I'm sinking here." She tried to pick up a piece of curled gray ash that had landed on the cuff of her flannel shirt. The delicate flake disintegrated between her thumb and finger, leaving behind only smudged traces of itself. "I need your help," she repeated, her voice barely more than a whisper.

The kids were tucked into their sleeping bags in the tent, and she and Jake sat close to each other on a blanket by the campfire, a second one wrapped around their shoulders. This was usually her favorite part about camping; the two of them alone by the fire at the end of the day. Away from the cares and concerns of reality, they talked late into the night, snuggling closer and closer under a starry sky in the middle of nowhere.

Usually, there was nothing more romantic.

Jake, wide awake even after a long day of hiking, fishing, and swimming, looked over at her. "Sorry if I seem a little confused, or surprised, but I thought we were doing okay, that things were going well."

"Going well? For whom?"

"For the family. For you and me. I mean, we're just doing better all around. We both have jobs we love, and the money's good." He pulled her close to his side, his arm around her waist. "I know it's not perfect, but we're making it work, right?"

She leaned away a little and turned to look at him, taking in his handsome features made rugged by the firelight and the wilderness around them. She wanted to reach over and run a caressing finger down the crooked line of his nose, but his insensitive response to her needs wouldn't let her. "Really, Jake? Making it work? I'm the one *doing* all the work, *making* all the money, *paying* all the bills. You're living the life of a... of a kept man. Of course it's working for you."

Even in the flickering glow cast by the flames, she could see the tightening of his mouth; the lines between his brows deepen. "A kept man? Wow." He stared into the fire as though pondering some disturbing revelation. "You know, I was under the impression that I was doing some work, too. Maybe I'm not making tons of cash, but I'm certainly not sitting around in my smoking jacket and bedroom slippers all day."

His feelings were hurt, and she squeezed his thigh where her hand rested. "I shouldn't have said that. I'm sorry." Why did the words with the sharpest barbs always slip out at the worst time? "Try to see things from my angle, okay? This isn't the way we planned it. I was going to work some extra hours, take on a few more clients for a while, just until your business was up and running. Remember?"

He didn't say anything, so she continued. "It's been almost two years since you got your license, and I'm still working 'extra hours.'" She made quotation marks with her fingers to emphasize the words. "But your business hasn't...." She shrugged her shoulders, letting her sentence go unfinished. Her voice dropped. "When, Jake? When are you going to get this thing off the ground? I need to know."

He continued to stare into the fire, not saying a word. The silence between them filled with the sounds of the wilderness at night; scrabbling little claws in the scrub brush around the perimeter of their site, the rustle in the trees above as life hurried by in the shadows. There was the whup-whup-whup of a set of large wings; perhaps an owl, or even a bat, she didn't know.

Finally she stood up, leaving the warmth of the blanket still draped around his shoulders. "I need a little hope, Jake. I need to know what you're thinking, what you're planning for our future. I don't even need specific answers right now, but I do need to know what the plan is, if it's changed. I can't keep going at this pace."

When he still didn't speak, she sighed heavily. "I'm tired. We've got a full day tomorrow; I think I'll turn in. You take care of the fire, okay?"

"I thought you liked your job." He blurted out the words without looking up at her. "You're so good at what you do. And how can you argue being paid so well for doing something you like doing?"

"Like my job? I *love* my job, Jake. And it's not about the money." With her booted toe, she nudged one of the blackened logs jutting from the fire's stone ring, making sparks shoot up into the sky. A balloon cloud of smoke gusted up toward her face, making her eyes burn. "I love my clients. I love helping people get their homes in order." She wrapped her arms around her chilled body, hunching her shoulders up to her ears.

"But I love being a mom even more," she said, her words throbbing with longing as she continued. "And I miss it. I love being a wife, and I miss that, too. I love being a friend, but I feel guilty for spending any more time away from home than I already do, so I don't have many of those left, either. I'm too busy for any of it." She looked sideways at him, holding her hands out to the fire. Even in May, the nights were cold in the Sierras once the sun went down.

"Don't say that, Nor. You're a great mom, and a great wife. We couldn't ask for any better." He rose and came to stand behind her, wrapping the blanket around them both. She didn't pull away from the heat his body offered. "I wouldn't mind if you spent an evening or two out with your friends. I know I'll still be the one you come home to at the end of the day." He bent and planted a kiss in the curve of her neck, nuzzling her ear in a way that made her shiver with pleasure. "Come back to the blanket, baby. I'll help you warm up."

They lay on their backs, close together beneath their cover, gazing up at the brilliant stars twinkling in the canopy above their heads. She tried to relax, to simply enjoy their time away from the busyness of life.

She tried. But she couldn't. He just didn't get it.

Finally, she sat up again and looked down at him. Her voice was quiet, but firm. "You've got to get yourself some work, Jake. Call your brother; he's always hiring. Drive a forklift. Get an office job. I don't care. Just do something, so I feel like we're still a team."

"Can I ask you something?" He stared off over her left shoulder, and it bothered her that he didn't look her in the eye.

She nodded.

"How would you feel if the tables were turned? What if you were, as you put it, a *kept* woman, and I was the primary bread winner?"

She'd asked herself this same question many times. It was one of the reasons she'd let things go on so long. But she'd worked their whole marriage. Even after leaving her receptionist job when Leslie was born, she'd turned her stay-at-home status into a work-from-home career, successfully launching SoNora Décor with a baby on her hip. She'd always contributed financially. She couldn't imagine what it would be like not to.

Besides, the question didn't seem fair in these circumstances, and she responded with a flippant rebuttal. "I wouldn't know. Unlike you, I've never had the chance to find out, have I?"

"Ah. Is that what this is about? You want your turn to stay home in your robe and slippers?" He propped his elbows up underneath him. Now he did meet her gaze, and his was slightly hostile.

Even with her thigh still pressed against his, she felt the chasm of unaddressed frustration widening between them. What kind of man asked his wife a question like that? She brought her knees up, wrapping her arms around them, her voice tight. "You've always said the man should be the provider. I'm happy to contribute to our finances, but that's not what I'm doing anymore. I'm providing, Jake. And I'm doing so with very little help from you."

"That's not true," he declared. He was sitting up now, absently snapping a twig into tiny pieces and flicking each one into the fire. "We wouldn't be where we are today if I wasn't providing in one way or another. It may not be financially right now, but I still provide my services. The house is clean, dinner is cooked, dishes are washed, the kids are happy. And I certainly don't hear any complaints in the bedroom. If I'm a kept man, then I'm doing a pretty good job earning my keep."

Nora sighed. She didn't want to play tit-for-tat. She pushed up to her feet and put distance between them again, standing so she could hold her hands out over the fire and still look at him; making certain he could see her face.

"Actually, Jake, *I* finish the dishes at the end of the night, so you have a clean slate to work with every day. *I* sort the whites, because you stubbornly refuse to pair the right socks together." Her head begin to bobble, emphasizing her words like a teenage drama queen, and she tried to control it. "And *I* fold the towels, since no matter how many times I've shown you how to fold them so they fit in the bathroom cupboard, you fold them wrong, and the cupboard door won't close." Now she was jabbing her chest with every *I*. "And speaking of the bathroom, it's clean because *I* clean it. Have you ever, even once in our entire marriage, cleaned the bathtub? Or the toilet, for that matter?" Her cheeks felt hot against the cool caress of the mountain breeze. She had to stop, get her emotions under control, or he would just glaze over.

She tucked a strand of hair behind her ear, took a deep breath, and spoke quietly to soften the blow of her words. "Jake, you need to remember that you're supposed to be working from home, not just staying home. You're at the house because that's where your office is, not so you can be our housekeeper."

"What about the kids? I'm a great dad." He was understandably defensive, and now he was on his feet as well. He didn't come near her, but stood on the other side of the fire from her, their communal blanket abandoned on the ground.

"Yes, you are!" She nodded emphatically. "You're a great dad, Jake."

He shoved his hands in the pockets of his jeans, but remained silent, eyes squinted, shadowed in the flickering firelight. It was as if he could already hear the *but* coming.

"But have you considered what kind of example you're setting for your children, as a husband and a father? What kind of man do you want your daughter to marry? One who takes care of her and provides for her, or one who allows her to provide for him?" She paused briefly, but he didn't speak. She pushed harder, an edge of desperation in her voice. "Would you prefer that your son grew up learning to keep a house, or learning to provide a house for his family?"

The fire was beginning to die down, but instead of drawing them together as it usually did, it only formed a chilled void between them. Finally, more to himself than to her, he said, "Let me see if I got this straight." His arms hung loosely at his sides, as though he was unsure what to do with them. "I don't make a very good house-wife, and apparently I haven't been a very good husband or father, either. I'm obviously not a very good business man, by your standards. So, I guess I'm not very good at anything, besides being a kept man, am I?"

His gaze swept back up to hers, his eyes dark and deep. Nora shivered, her mind pulling her back to Anderson Hollow and the embrace of the icy water as it swirled around her.

THREE

Four months later...

"I'm dying here. I can't stand it, Jo. I just can't." Nora sat in her silver Altima with the windows rolled up, the end-of-summer sun making the temperature inside the vehicle skyrocket. Sweat beaded at her hairline and along her upper lip, but she hardly noticed.

"Nora, you need to pull yourself together. It's time to draw a real line. No more bargaining, you hear?" Her friend's voice on the other end of the line was calm, but firm. "Besides, you're running out of time. School will be out in an hour and your kids—"

"I know. I didn't forget about them." Nora's voice shook. "I just don't know if I'm ready to play the ultimatum card. Or if he's ready to hear it."

"When is anyone ever ready for stuff like this? But the longer you wait, the worse it's going to get." Jo paused. "You know that, right?"

Nora's left hand gripped the steering wheel, and she tried not to stare at the diamond on her wedding ring, mocking her as it glittered in the afternoon sun.

"Nora? Stop with the excuses. I'm tired of hearing them. It's time. Give him your ultimatum, if you must, but this needs to be his last chance. If it were me, I would have kicked him to the curb a long time ago." She paused, and Nora could hear a phone ring in the background. "Besides, I need to go. I have a client on the other line." Jo didn't wait for her response; the line went silent in Nora's ear. She leaned forward and rested her forehead on her knuckles.

Jo Simpson was one of the few women with whom she still spent any time, mainly because the two of them worked out of offices in the same downtown building, and their friendship had developed out of the convenience of proximity. They shared many lunch hours, and a few after-hours together, and although they had little in common, they'd reached an understanding about each other that didn't require either of them to wear masks.

Jo was divorced. "And it will happen, I'm telling you. Your Jake is exactly like Henry and you'll get to the end of your rope exactly like I did. I was fooled for a while. I thought he was being supportive of me and my dreams. But then I realized he was just lazy and unmotivated and was glad to hand over the reins because it let him off the hook. He didn't *want* to lead. Well, I got tired of dragging his weight around. And believe me, you can't change him. No matter how hard you try, how much you encourage or beg, no matter how many temper tantrums you throw, he won't change. Think about it, honey. Have you ever been able to trust him to take care of things, or does it scare the living daylights out of you to even think about giving him the pants to wear?"

She seemed the only one who understood Nora's frustration. Jo didn't judge her for her marital dissatisfaction. In fact, she assured Nora she was perfectly justified in feeling the way she did.

Nor did she put her up on a pedestal like the women at church did.

During Bible study each Wednesday night, Nora sat in mute misery, listening to Jake advise the other couples on how to keep the romance alive between them. "Guys, it's the little things that make her melt. Cut a single rose or flower from the garden—even a dandelion would work in a pinch, right Nor?—and take it to her while she's in the bathtub. Something that tells her you're thinking about her even when she's not right there with you." Then all the ladies would sigh, look longingly at their husbands, and the questions for the marriage veterans would begin in earnest. It was like that every meeting anymore, the group racing through the scheduled study, right into discussion and prayer, where marital problems and solutions were bandied about like a game of egg-toss. Nora usually found herself giving advice she knew didn't work, desperately hoping her words, wrapped in their fragile shells, wouldn't fall to the floor, messy contents splattered for all to see.

Was it possible Jake still believed things were working between them? Either he believed it, or he was trying awfully hard to convince everyone he did, including himself.

"Nora?" She lifted her head to see her husband's concerned face peering through the closed window at her. He looked crisp and cool in his faded jeans and white t-shirt, in complete contrast to the way she felt, and it irritated her. "Are you okay?"

Why, oh *why*, did he always ask her that? And what would he do if she told him she was *not* okay? If she told him just how *not* okay she really was. No, not if; when she told him.

Instead, she nodded, pointed at her phone, and mimed that she'd been on it. He motioned for her to roll down her window. She opened the door instead, forcing him to step back.

"What on earth are you doing? It's a thousand degrees in there! How long have you been sitting out here?" He leaned against the outside of the door, ducking his head a little so he could see her. Then he grinned and pointed at her mouth, reminding her of pictures she'd seen of him as a little boy, the same precocious look in his eyes. "You have a sweat mustache."

She didn't bother responding, but leaned over the console to grab her portfolio off the floor on the passenger side.

"Why didn't you come inside? The air is on, and the house feels great." No wonder he looked so refreshed. Nora thought of last month's terrible electric bill, but didn't say anything. "You'll get heat exhaustion or something."

"I won't get heat exhaustion, Jake. Don't be ridiculous. I just needed to finish my conversation. You know I don't like to be on the phone when I walk in the house."

"I'm not one of the kids, Nor. I would have respected your privacy." He thrust his chin forward. "Unless you don't want me to know who you're talking to." He was gripping the top of the open door, and Nora had a wild urge to slam it on all of his fingers. So much for respecting her privacy.

"I was talking to Jo. Do you want to see for yourself?" He did not approve of their friendship. A bad influence, he called her. Jo only laughed when Nora apologized for his often tactless behavior around her. She said it was just fear talking, that Jake was afraid of her, and afraid of Nora when she was with her.

"Don't be silly." He snorted, making a point to not look at the screen she held up for him to see. "I trust you."

"Mm-hm." Nora slid out of the driver's seat, stepped back, and slammed the car door, a little harder than necessary. He snatched his fingers out of the way, just in time. "Oh, sorry," she said, as she headed toward the front of the house.

She knew he followed closely by the sound of his sloppy footsteps on the cobbled stones behind her. Flip flops. That irritated her too, as her feet complained inside the sharply-angled toes of her three-inch pumps.

Once inside, she decided against kicking off her shoes the way she usually did. Crossing the tile, she let her heels clip purposefully, reminding him which of them was the grown-up in the house. She dropped her things on a chair at the table, then went to the cupboard for a glass. She was parched, the heat outside combining with the frustration burning just under her skin. Jake beat her to it, taking down a green glass tumbler, and filling it with ice and water from the refrigerator door before handing it to her.

She hated the way she felt as she watched him attempting to appease her. He'd been trying way too hard since their camping trip in May. He just didn't get it. She hadn't asked him to spend more time doting on her. She'd asked him to do his part in contributing to the welfare of the family so that she could spend less time away from them. Come up with a solid plan, at least...but no. She got chocolates and love notes in her packed lunch instead. He washed her car more often, cooked more often, mowed the lawn more often, vacuumed more often.

From somewhere inside, a small voice piped up. Most women she knew would give anything to have husbands who did those things for them. And honestly, she would have loved those things beyond measure if they didn't come with the price tag of her sacrifice. Most women she knew didn't put in the hours she did trying to keep all the loose ends from unraveling...freeing him up to do all those things for her.

"Peace, okay?" He leaned against the counter and studied her as he spoke, the spicy aroma of his aftershave strong. He must have just taken a shower. Her eyes drifted along his jaw line to the lobe of his left ear where a dab of shaving cream had been overlooked. He even shaved more often. "Sorry I got a little parental out there. I actually came out to meet you because I have some good news. I'm glad you're home early. I didn't think I'd get to tell you about it until this evening."

She drank her cold water in silence, wondering if it would even occur to him to ask her *why* she was home early. He just smiled expectantly, so she took the bait.

"What's your news, Jake?"

"It's a good possibility that I just landed an exclusive contract with Granlund and Gray Real Estate, that company you hooked me up with several months ago. They refer me to their clients already, so it works out great for both of us."

She kept her antennae up for Jake; he was very diligent when he had work, and she had no qualms about referring him to anyone. "That *is* good news. So what's in it for you? Give me details. Is it payroll or commission? And will you be eligible for benefits?" Benefits were always the question of the hour, since they were both self-employed.

"They assure me I can get an average of three or four home inspections a month to start out. It'll increase from there." He absentmindedly picked up the sponge in the sink and began wiping down the counter beside him. It was already spotless; he seemed full of nervous energy.

Nora frowned. "Isn't that about what you're doing with them now? And what if their clients already have someone they want to use? Will that affect your pay?" He seemed awfully confident, but something about the whole setup didn't sit well with her.

"I'll still only get paid for the inspections I actually do, but G and G will offer my services as part of their promo package."

"Wait." She frowned into her glass, then looked askance at him. "Does that mean you'll have to offer their clients a promotional discount?"

"I'll be giving their clients a discount, yes, but it will eventually turn into more work."

Nora sighed. She seemed to do a lot of that lately. "I'm sorry. I'm not trying to be thick, but I don't understand. The company already refers you to their clients, and you're getting paid the full amount for inspections.

The only change I see is that you'll be paid *less* for the same amount of work. Am I missing something?"

Jake's face fell a little as he tried to defend himself. The sponge went still under his hand. "It sounds bad at first, I know. But there's potential for a lot more work if this deal goes through."

It did sound bad. It sounded to her like a raw deal for him. "Jake. Think about what you're saying. There's no way they can guarantee you anything, but apparently, they want you to guarantee them everything. And at a discount rate. I don't see how this can be a good thing for you." She set her glass down and rubbed the back of her neck with her cool, damp hand. "Who designed this contract anyway?"

"I designed it, okay? Geez, Nor." Jake pushed away from the counter and tossed the sponge into the sink. "Don't get too excited for me." Then he turned and left them room, his sandals slapping the tiled floor indignantly.

Nora dropped into a chair at the dining table, her still-damp fingertips making dark circles on the leather portfolio in the seat beside her. Maybe she should go after him and tell him *her* news. Why not? He was already angry with her.

But she just sat there, her words trapped inside.

• • • • • • • • • • •

"Mom? You're home!" Leslie pushed open the door that led from the garage, and Felix came charging past his sister, vying to reach Nora first. She sat at the table, several fabric sampler books opened in front of her, matching paint chips from two different color palettes. Leslie slowed down to let her younger brother win, and snorted derisively when he turned in his mother's embrace to shoot her a triumphant grin.

"You're such a goob, Squealy-Feely."

"Don't call me that, Messy-Lessy."

Nora reached out to touch fingers with her daughter, noticing the delicate line of her cheekbones in the slanting afternoon light that streamed through the kitchen blinds. She was growing up so quickly.

"Don't call you what? Goob or Squealy-Feely?"

"Mom," Felix whined. "Les is calling me names."

"And hello to you, too," Nora cut in, smiling at their sibling banter.

"So I got an A on my Picasso today." Leslie offered nonchalantly, tossing her backpack over the back of the sofa, and dropping into a chair to sit close to Nora at the table. "Mr. Larsen wants me to let him use it as an example for his other classes."

"Wow! I'm very proud of you. Congratulations." Nora turned to her son who had wandered over to the fridge. "Felix, do you have something to say to your sister?"

"Um," He looked confused; he hadn't really been paying attention. "I'm sorry? But what did I do?" Nora laughed out loud at his assumption that he should apologize for something.

Leslie rolled her eyes again. "It's not what you did, it's what you *are*," she taunted.

"Congratulate your sister, Felix."

He still looked confused. "What for?"

"My Picasso, Goob." Leslie stated. "Don't you hear anything with those flaps on the side of your head?"

"I don't know what a Picasso is, so why should I congratulate you? For all I know, it's a mutant booger you pulled out of your nose, and your teacher named Mr. Larsen wants to keep it in his class for other kids to get grossed out over." He brought an apple to the table with him, sitting across from the girls. "See? My flaps work fine."

"Nice save, Felix." Nora acknowledged him with a high-five. "But just so you know, Picasso is an artist, and Les had to do a Picasso-style painting for her art class."

"Isn't that plagiarism?" He'd recently discovered the hard way that copying someone else's work, even from a report posted online, and calling it his own, was cheating, but with a fancy name.

"Geez, Felix. Don't get too excited for me." Leslie's words, though directed at her brother, reverberated inside Nora's mind. She could hear Jake saying the exact same thing to her not more than an hour ago.

Speak of the devil. Jake stood in the doorway, and shot her a smug look behind the children's backs. He'd recalled his words, too. "Come on, kids. Your mother has work to do. And you have homework, too, I'm sure."

"No, actually, I think I'm done for the day." Nora stood and began stacking her things into neat piles. "Let's go celebrate the artist. How about dinner at Pepe's?" Leslie grinned proudly, while Felix ran around in a tight circle, his fist in the air, chanting like a football player. Nora turned to face her husband.

"I'm sorry for being negative today, Jake. Congratulations on your contract. I mean it."

He hesitated just long enough for the children to take notice. Leslie looked from one parent to the other, her face carefully blank, and Felix stopped whooping, but kept spinning in a circle. He didn't fool Nora, though. She could see his flaps were tuned in.

"Well, thank you. It isn't quite in the bag yet, but Robert's pretty confident that the board will sign off on it." He shoved his hands in his pockets, but only came a few steps inside the kitchen. "He's presenting it at their meeting tonight and will call me in the morning."

"Are you going to get a job, Daddy?" Felix stopped spinning and looked over at his father.

"I have a job." Nora tried not to watch the flush creeping up Jake's neck. "I'm just getting more work."

"Oh. Is that a good thing? I'd rather get less work."

"Congratulations, Dad." Leslie cut in, crossing the room to hug her father. Nora's heart sank as she realized just exactly how aware her daughter had become of things. "I hope you get it."

"Me, too," Felix agreed, although he still didn't look convinced. "Can we go eat now?" He grabbed Jake's forearm and started tugging him back toward the garage door.

"Wait a minute, Mister." Jake pulled Felix to a stop, placed both hands on his shoulders, and turned him to face Leslie. "Now that you know what a Picasso is, don't you think you ought to congratulate your sister for real?"

"Sure. Congratulations, Lester the Lion."

Leslie raised both hands like claws and growled deep in her throat, but she grinned at his use of her favorite nickname.

· · · · · ● · ● · · · ·

IN HIS OFFICE, JAKE stared at the phone sitting on the glass-topped desk in front of him. Why couldn't things go his way just once? It had taken G & G nearly a month to make a decision on his proposal before opting to keep things as they were. A whole month of him assuring his wife that things were going to start happening, he just knew it; that by the holidays, she'd be able to cut back her hours significantly. He knew that was what she really wanted—the love notes, the chocolate, and the extra care he took in bed with her were his way of telling her that he was trying.

He should call Nora, but he didn't think he could bear to hear her voice right now; her disappointment, both for him, and in him.

Nora often seemed sad these days, even though she refused to acknowledge it. A few weeks ago, when he came out to the driveway to see what was keeping her, he was shocked to find her sitting in her car, bent over the steering wheel. He thought she was crying, but he was even more concerned when he realized she was just sitting in the sweltering heat, pink-faced, and sweating, as though enduring some self-inflicted punishment. She assured him she was fine, but inside the closed up car in the middle of an uncharacteristically warm September afternoon? Who does that?

He'd been trying so hard these last few months, and in many ways, things were greatly improved. But Jake couldn't help noticing Nora's smiles rarely lasted once the kids left the room, that everything seemed forced and unnatural when she was alone with him.

"Are you okay?" He asked her that question almost every night, certain she wasn't, but her answer was always the same.

"I'm fine, Jake. Just tired. It's been a long day."

Was her day any longer than his? Any longer than Felix's or Leslie's? When he probed, though, she only grew impatient with him.

Nora's work load was one of the things that hadn't improved. It had gotten worse.

She used to bring a file or two home every once in a while, stuff she had to finish in time for a client meeting the next morning, but now it was her nightly routine; dinner, dishes, and decorating. In fact, more often than not anymore, instead of bringing work home, she headed back to the office after putting the kids to bed, explaining, "It's hard for me to concentrate here, and everything takes twice as long. It's like a mental block. It just works better for me to go back to the office."

Well, it didn't work better for him, especially since it meant he went to bed alone.

"At least sex is still good," he muttered to himself. He lifted his gaze in a halfhearted prayer. "Yeah, I know. Spoken like a true man. But it seems like the only thing I can do right for her. Don't get me wrong," he added quickly, lifting a hand in a halting gesture. "I'm not complaining. Don't know what I'd do if that wasn't happening, either."

He leaned back in his chair and closed his eyes, imagining his wife standing in the doorway, crossing the room to him, brushing her fingertips along his jaw, lifting his face to hers. He loved thinking about her; about her curves, her silky auburn hair, her eyes, her full mouth. His skin tingled when she said his name; the special way she answered her cell phone when she knew it was him. At least, he reminded himself with a grimace, the way she *used* to answer it. Anymore, he got her voice mail more often than not, and when he did catch her, she was always in the middle of something, or in a hurry to get somewhere...besides home to him.

It was days like this that made him seriously consider going back to working for someone else. He didn't miss driving a forklift. He didn't miss the warehouse atmosphere. He didn't miss the early and long hours. But he missed coming home at the end of the day. There was something rewarding about flexing his arms and straining his back to provide for his family.

And there was something soft and feminine about Nora after she'd spent a few hours puttering around her nest and nurturing her children. He especially missed that.

"No. I can't go back," he asserted aloud. "I can't. I deserve better. I can't quit now." Today was just a little bump in the road he had to get past. So what if it wasn't happening as quickly they'd planned? That didn't mean it wasn't happening at all.

He scrubbed his shadowed jaw with his fingers—he'd need to shave before she got home—then flicked his phone so that it spun across the slick desktop and bumped up against the miniature sand garden Leslie had given him for Christmas last year, complete with rake, shovel, and a red pail. The sound of canned clapping, his text message ring tone, had him raising his fists in triumph, as though all those tiny cheering people in the phone still believed in him. "Who's the man? I'm the man. That's right."

Then he saw the sender's name. Nora.

Need to put in a late night at the office - sorry. Coming home for early supper, then back to work for me. Bringing Antonio's family meal unless you have something else planned. Love you.

FOUR

The glowing windows seemed to glare at Nora as she pulled into the driveway, angry at her for making them wait up. It was after midnight, and Jake had left all the lights on again.

Slipping out of her heels just inside the door, she systematically made her way through the kitchen, dining room, family room, and the hall, shutting things down as she went. She poked her head into the kids' rooms, smiling at the sight of each rumpled head in the glow of night lights. She wrinkled her nose at the sweaty boy smell in Felix's room; it seemed to be losing its charm these days.

"Good. You're home." Jake's voice spoke out of the darkness as she crept into their bedroom. No matter how quietly she came through the house, she always woke him up.

"I'm home."

"What time is it?" Jake knew exactly what time it was—his clock with its bright blue numbers faced him on his bedside table. This was a game they played almost every night, even those when she didn't stay late at her office. If she came to bed after he did, it was how he greeted her. Not "Come snuggle with me," not "Where have you been all my life, Baby," but the badly played part of the neglected husband who'd been rudely awakened out of a sound sleep.

Nora responded the way she always did. "It's late. Sorry I woke you." She quickly retrieved her nightgown from the top drawer of her dresser, and tucked her shoes under the bed so she wouldn't trip on them in the dark. She would get ready for bed in the bathroom.

Just as she was closing the door behind her, he spoke. "Did you finish what you needed to tonight?"

Nora stopped, and turned slightly to answer him. "I did. I'm going to take my shower now. Go back to sleep."

"Who are you working for right now?"

"The Carlsons, remember? I told you at supper."

"Yeah. The Carlsons. Are you meeting with them in the morning?"

"What is this, Jake? Twenty questions?" Nora peered through the darkness toward the shadowy shape of their bed. She pressed her tight spine against the door frame, her muscles protesting, but the pain bringing relief and loosening her tongue. "Or are you asking me something you're not really asking?"

"What does that mean?"

"I don't know. You tell me."

"No, you tell me, Nor. Is there something I should be asking you? Or is there something you should be telling me?" She could see him moving, pushing himself upright into a sitting position. His shape was now silhouetted by the pale moonlight slipping in through the blinds at the window, and she could see him cross his arms. She crossed hers in response.

"What would you like to know, Jake?" She was exhausted; too tired for this. Her feet hurt, her head hurt, and her heart hurt at the sound of accusation in her husband's voice. All she'd wanted was to wash away the day and crawl into bed next to him, to have him take her in his arms and hold her, comfort her, assure her that things would change soon.

Not anymore. Now her weariness turned her sour, and once the words started spilling out, she couldn't pull them back in. "Do you want me to tell you about the undercover prostitution ring I run from my little hole-in-the-wall office? Or are you asking about the pole-dancing job? Don't worry. I quit that last month. I found a better night gig. Now I'm a highly-paid escort to the stars. Not nearly so seedy." She turned to leave, then spun around and came right back in, not quite finished. "Wait! Maybe you're referring to my Latin lover who comes to my office at night; who calls me *mi corazon* and does all my paperwork for me in between bouts of passionate love-making. I almost forgot about him." Indignation burned her cheeks. "Is that what you wanted to hear?"

"Overreacting a little, aren't you? I just asked a simple question."

"No, Jake. No, you *never* just ask a simple question. There's always so much more than a simple question in your questions." She pulled the door closed behind her, just shy of slamming it, so as not to wake the children, and made her way to the bathroom across the hall.

By the time she stood beneath the blistering flow of hot water in the shower, she was crying. "Why do I have to cry over everything?" she berated herself. "I hate crying!"

Nora ran her water extremely hot. Even as a child, she loved baths that turned her skin pink and tingly. Tonight she let the water cascade over her body, washing away the tension in her neck and shoulders while her hands kneaded her low back. She couldn't quite get rid of the dull pain that settled there every night.

When she was pregnant, Jake used the heel of his hand to push against her sacrum as she lay on her side in bed, relieving the strain her swollen belly put on her back just enough that she could fall asleep.

It had been a long time since he'd touched her without expecting anything in return.

As her body began to relax, and her tears dried up, she closed her eyes and made a concerted effort to think good things about her husband.

"Every night before you go to bed, remind yourself how blessed you are," Vicky's voice prodded. "Be thankful for a man who loves you, who loves your children, who takes your family to church. Thank God for giving you someone who is kind to your parents, who supports your dreams, who thinks you're incredible."

After she chickened out on giving Jake his ultimatum, Nora started therapy. He didn't know she'd been seeing Vicky Johanson for the last several weeks, and the longer she put it off, the harder it was to tell him.

"We don't need counseling, Nor," he argued, every time she suggested they try it. "We're good together, you and me. This is just a rough season for us, but it's not so bad we need a shrink. We can figure it out on our own; do our own therapy."

But Jake's idea of therapy consisted of a little conversation, a lot of sex, and enough sleep to get up and do it all again. Besides, there was no way he'd admit they were having problems to a complete stranger if he couldn't even acknowledge it to himself.

"Find things to be thankful for, Nora, and do not climb in bed next to Jake until you can do so with a thankful heart." Vicky's expectations seemed idealistic, but the woman was absolutely unrelenting about positive thinking, in a biblical sense of the word. "Stop focusing on the things you want to change about him, and pay attention to the things you love about him."

The first visit had been the "rant" session, and Vicky allowed her forty-five minutes to say anything and everything she wanted to say, without interference. Through tears that developed into stomach-wrenching hiccups, pacing that included flailing hands and raised fists, Nora unloaded on the counselor all the weight she'd been carrying on her shoulders for the past sixteen years of marriage.

"Okay. Time's up, Nora." Vicky tapped the timer she'd set. Nora was shocked to see she'd used every last second. "Do you feel any better?"

"Yes. I do." Nora spoke quickly, certain the overwhelming sense of relief washing over her was because she'd been allowed to release all the things she'd kept bottled up for so long. Vicky didn't respond. The silence settled between them until Nora began to feel uncomfortable and she reached for a tissue from the box on the end table beside her to dab at her puffy eyes. Meeting Vicky's gaze, she saw a question there.

"I do feel better. I really do," she assured the counselor again. When Vicky still didn't speak, Nora felt her eyes began to well up again. "At least I think I do." Then she covered her face with her hands. "Actually, I feel terrible. No, worse. I feel *wretched*. My head is throbbing, my stomach hurts, my sinuses are so plugged I can hardly breathe, and I feel like I didn't accomplish anything." A sob escaped when she took a deep breath. "In fact, I think the relief I feel is because I finally shut up."

Vicky reached out and laid a hand on Nora's shoulder. "I'm going to pray for you, Nora." It wasn't a request. "Father, thank you for bringing Nora to my office today. We come to you, now, and lay these things that Nora has spoken at your feet. Please take them, sort through them, and help us figure out which of them we should deal with, and which of them we need to leave in your hands. We come in your name, Jesus. Amen."

Nora sat stone still, as a sensation, like fingers fluttering along her skin, washed over her, and the tears flowed in earnest again. They poured from her eyes, down her cheeks, dropping steadily onto her folded hands in her lap. She could not remember the last time anyone had prayed with such fervency over her. Finally, Vicky spoke again.

"Here's the way this works, Nora. This is the only time, I repeat, the *only* time you will be given the freedom to speak negatively about your husband in this office. As you can plainly see, the method of unloading, of venting, of letting off steam, whatever you want to call it, rarely benefits anyone. I know from experience though, that it seems to be a bit of a necessary evil. So I intentionally get it out of the way at the very beginning." She chuckled and patted Nora on the knee. "I'm not surprised you feel like you've just been run over. In fact, freight train comes to mind when I think of what you've just gone through in the last hour. And look. You're still alive."

Vicky stood, rolled her shoulders a few times, and crossed the room where she began flipping through the leather bound appointment book on her desk. "Please take that box of tissue with you. You may be reeling from this session for a couple of hours. And I suggest you do not go straight home to your husband. Go shopping, go watch a movie, go hang out at a friend's house, one who won't require you to explain anything. Just don't go see Jake right now. Wait until your spirit has settled and you can forgive yourself for daring to say all those terrible things about him to me."

Feeling chastised, Nora frowned. "But I... I thought you *wanted* me to—"

"To unload?" Vicky, still standing, braced both palms on the surface of her desk and leaned forward a little, eying Nora across the room. "It's exactly what I wanted you to do. I'm talking about the natural progression of feelings here. You may not feel weird about what's gone on here yet, but I can almost guarantee you, that over the next hour or two, you'll run the gamut of emotions, everything from guilt, shame, embarrassment, resentment and possibly even anger toward me for making you expose yourself this way. It's okay. Just give yourself time to process before you go home. Now, when will I see you back here?"

Nora returned to Vicky's soothing plume and amber hued office five days later. She'd made it home in time for a quick dinner, then told Jake and the kids she was meeting with a client. She hated lying to them, but she didn't know how else to explain Vicky. Besides, who was to say the counselor wouldn't become a client at some point?

Vicky welcomed her with a warm handshake. She waited until Nora was settled into one of the matching over-stuffed armchairs in the room, then handed her a blank spiral notebook and a pen, and sat down in the other chair. She was dressed in a swirl of charcoal-hued flared pants, and a cross-over teal blouse that tied in a floppy bow on one side of her waist. Nora thought it looked sleek and stylish on the slim woman, and as much as she would have liked to don an outfit like that, she could never get away with it, not on her frame. She was like Vicky's counterpart in appearance; petite, a little too curvy, with dark hair and pale skin, while the golden-haired, bronzed beauty sitting across from her, had to be nearly six feet tall in her stocking feet.

"Are you a list person?"

Nora nodded slightly. "I do lists sometimes."

"Good. This is going to be your book of lists. I want you to list twenty things you love about Leslie. Then on a new page, list twenty things you love about your son. His name is," Vicky referred to the contents of the folder in her lap. "Felix. Twenty things about Felix. Can you do that for me?"

"Of course I can. But what does this have to do with Jake and me? Is there a catch somewhere?"

"Yes, there's a catch." Vicky chuckled. "But I'll explain later, I promise. You just get started." She stood up and crossed the room to her desk, retrieving her purse from behind it. "Would you like a cup of coffee? Tea? I'm going to run over to that little cafe while you're working." She tipped her head toward the window where Nora could see a bustling coffee shop across the street, a gargantuan, foam-topped cup and saucer as its beacon on a pole above the outdoor seating. "My treat."

"Oh. Sure. That would be great. Coffee, thank you. Just black." She was still befuddled by the assignment, but she picked up the pen and labeled two pages, one with each child's name. It took her several moments, but once she got started, the reasons she loved her children began to flow from the tip of her pen like water. By the time Vicky returned, the pinched feeling between her eyebrows had dissipated, her jaw was no longer clenched, and her shoulders relaxed. She looked up with a soft smile on her face and accepted the steaming paper cup with its brown cardboard sleeve.

"Careful. That's hot." Vicky sat back down, pulled the lid off her own cup, and blew into it. "So how are the lists coming?"

Nora's smile turned a little sheepish. "I have more than twenty reasons for both. I hope that's okay."

"Of course. Far be it from me to limit your love, especially for your children." The counselor smirked at her own teasing, flipping her shoulder-length blond hair back, so it wouldn't slip into the top of her cup while she drank. "Now comes the next part of the assignment. This might be a little more difficult."

"Is this the catch?"

Vicky's eyes twinkled, but she didn't say yea or nay. She took the notebook from Nora, opened it to the very last blank page, and handed it back. "I'd like you to make me a list of twenty things you love about yourself."

"What? About me?"

"About yourself. And I want it on the last page so you can find it easily and refer to it often."

Nora was skeptical, but still softened by the Utopian feelings of love for her children, she did as she was asked.

Ten minutes later, she looked up at Vicky, who appeared to be catching up on charting notes while she waited in the chair across from her. She had her feet tucked up under her, making her seem a little more accessible to Nora. "This is hard. Can I write stupid stuff, like I love my hair?"

"Of course you can. If you love your hair, write it down! Not many women can say that," Vicky declared. "These lists aren't for anyone to see but you. Even I'm not going to look at them."

It took her nearly the rest of the visit before she reached twenty things she loved about herself; things she was happy about. Nora was quite proud of herself when she closed the notebook and mentally added 'I like twenty things about myself' to the list.

"Done."

Vicky closed the folder she was working in, and folded her hands in her lap. "Good. Now for the final and most difficult part of your assignment. Open to a new page, about halfway through the book, and write down two things you love about Jake. Two things you're thankful for."

"So that's what this is about." There was always a catch.

Vicky leaned back in her chair, elbows on the arm rests, fingers laced together around the large coffee she was still nursing. "In general, making lists of things for which you're thankful about someone is a healthy practice in any kind of a relationship. I had you start with the easy lists, those of your children, so you would get into the mental mode of thinking positively. Then I had you move on to yourself, a little harder, but still doable. And now that you've had some practice, I want you to do the same with Jake."

She leaned forward and held up two fingers. "I do want you to limit it to just two things today. No more, no less. Just two." Vicky waited until Nora nodded. "But I want you to share those things with me."

"Why do I have to write them down, then?" She didn't want to do it. If she was only allowed to write down good things about Jake, wouldn't her reasons for coming here be invalidated? "Can't I just tell you two things if we're going to talk about them anyway?"

Vicky smiled understandingly, "There's a method to my madness, okay? Trust me on this."

"That's what they all say..." Nora muttered from the side of her mouth. This was what she disliked about counseling; the stuff that caught her by surprise. She hated feeling exposed and vulnerable, then judged for feeling that way, and in this plush, tapestried armchair of Vicky's, she felt it all in abundance. She giggled nervously. "What if I can't come up with anything?"

"It's an assignment. You are required to come up with two things. You can do it."

Vicky gave her some scripture references to study. "I know you've heard these before. Maybe you've even memorized some of these. But I want you to really take them to heart and practice them. Philippians 4:6-9 says, *'Be anxious for nothing, but in everything, by prayer and supplication with thanksgiving, let your requests be made known to God. And the peace of*

God which surpasses all comprehension, will guard your hearts and minds in Christ Jesus. 'It's the peace we're after, Nora. And I'm not talking about everything being hunky-dory, a-okay. I'm talking about peace in our spirits, knowing that we're where we're supposed to be, regardless of what's going on around us. Peace even when we don't understand or agree with our circumstances. That's the goal.

"The passage goes on to say that we are to practice thinking about things excellent and worthy of praise. Practice. That means it isn't going to come naturally. We have to *practice* these things. It's the only way to get the results we're after. And what are we after?"

"Peace, man," Nora retorted, drawing her words out, holding two fingers up.

Each time they met together, she was required to come up with two more things about Jake for which she was thankful. Vicky encouraged her to think about what was on her list every night before going to bed.

"I want your primary thoughts about Jake to be positive when you climb under the covers next to him. I want you to sit across the table from him at mealtimes, and only let yourself think on good things. I want you to *practice* thinking good things about him. Make it a habit, Nora."

Well, she tried. She purposed every day and every night to think good things about him. She closed her eyes and visualized her growing list in her head. She ran down that list and poke out each item on it. She thanked God for Jake's attentiveness, for his kindness to their extended family. She thanked God for how much her husband loved their children. She thanked Him for Jake's willingness to put up with her work, even though she knew he was tired of her long hours. She thanked God he was healthy and strong, that Jake was a good and generous lover, that he was both passionate and gentlemanly in bed.

Now she felt horrible for the ugly things she'd said to him in their bedroom. Standing in the shower, her body relaxed and flushed from the hot water, she began to soften toward him. She thought she knew how to make it up to him. It may not bring the peace of God, but there would at least be peace of some kind in their home tonight. She turned off the water, quickly dried and perfumed her body, then slipped back across the hall, her nightclothes still draped over her arm.

FIVE

MORNING ALWAYS CAME. WITHOUT fail, it showed up. And without fail, it delivered a hangover of emotions from the day before. Jake awoke to the echo of Nora's angry words ringing in his ears. Even though she'd come to him so sweetly from her shower, he'd fallen asleep long after she did. Why would she say things like that, even if she was tired or in a bad mood?

She slept with her back to him, pressed up against his side, and he lay still, listening to her breathe, as he contemplated the questions in his head.

What if she was hiding something from him? Some*one*? What if there really was another man? Granted, he probably wasn't some young Spaniard who called her love names in his native tongue, but a client perhaps? One of the distributors she was always on the phone with? She was so distant, so withdrawn; sometimes it seemed like it almost pained her to be around him. When she came to bed naked and smelling so good, it only confused him more.

He rolled over and sat up on the side of the bed, running his fingers through his choppy dark hair. His eyes burned and his stomach felt hollowed out by fatigue, but there was little hope of falling back to sleep, not with his mind in such turmoil.

"Coffee," he mumbled, pressing a palm to his chest. It wasn't quite six, but he knew Nora would be up soon, and she'd be grateful for the caffeine, too.

Several minutes later, he returned to the room, two steaming cups in his hands. She was just beginning to stir as he came around to her side of the bed, and he nudged her over so he could sit beside her. She looked soft and vulnerable in the morning light, all rumpled and mussed from sleep. Eyes still closed, she ran her fingers down his side and over the ridge of his hip bone. Such a dichotomy between this flushed lover in his bed this morning and the woman who'd mocked him from the doorway the night before.

"Good morning." He held her mug where she would see it when she opened her eyes. "I brought you something."

She sighed and smiled, her nose already lifted as she breathed in the rich, earthy fragrance of the Italian roast that was her favorite. "Mmmm. I love you, Jakey."

She didn't call him that very often. He didn't like it, and she knew it, but he rarely felt like she did it to irritate him. It just rolled off her tongue every once in a while, and she almost always apologized for it, so he tried not to let it bother him too much. Today, however, it grated on his already raw nerves.

"Please don't call me that."

She pushed herself up to a sitting position and took the mug from him. "Sorry. It just—"

"Slipped out, I know." *Kinda like the stuff you said last night*, he thought to himself. He let his eyes drift down the contours of her body under the nightgown she'd slipped on sometime in the middle of the night. It was inside out.

Nora didn't say anything. She took a sip of the hot drink and leaned her head back against the bars of the iron headboard behind her.

"Can we talk about last night?" He reached over and touched the exposed seam on her shoulder.

"Please, Jake." She tilted her head to one side, a sexy little smile tugging at the corners of her mouth, slanting her tired eyes. "Wasn't my apology enough for you last night?"

He ignored the question. His head was starting to hurt as the notion of her with another man hammered inside his skull. "I want you to know that I love you, Nora. I don't know what's going on, and I feel like I'm always asking if you're okay even though I don't think you are, but even if you don't want to tell me, you must know that I'm here for you, and I will listen whenever you're ready to talk." He took a deep breath before adding, "No matter what it is, I forgive you, and I want—"

"You forgive me?" Her eyebrows shot up, and she slowly, carefully set her coffee down, folding her hands in her lap. Her gesture, fluid and controlled, warned him that things had just taken a turn into very dangerous territory. Nevertheless, he pressed on.

"Yes. I do. If there's anything you're afraid to tell me, if you've done anything you think might hurt me, well, I've already forgiven you. I still love you. No matter what."

Her eyes, so warm and inviting only moments before, turned icy. Unable to hold her gaze, he looked down into his own cup. "I'm tired of trying to guess what's wrong with you, Nor. I want you to be happy. I want *us* to be happy. I don't care what you've done. I just want to wipe the slate clean and start over again. Is that possible? Can we do that?"

He looked at her again, hoping for a softening, for the return of the warm reception she'd awakened with.

That was not what he saw on her face. Instead, she pressed her lips together in a grim smile, and he could see her knuckles turning white as she clenched her laced fingers together. "Just what is it you think I've done?"

"I—" He stopped, afraid to put his fears into words. "I don't know. I don't know what I think anymore. I just know that you're different. You're distant. You're *always* busy." He grimaced. "You're sad." Leaning forward, he rested his elbows on his knees, gripping his cup with both hands. His stomach was beginning to churn and his next words came out barely above a whisper. "I hear you cry at night when you think I'm already asleep."

"I'm busy? Distant? Different?" Her voice raised in pitch with each word. "Let me see," she said, sarcasm oozing from every syllable. "I *am* busy. I'm busy working my butt off to keep this family clothed and fed, to pay the bills, to put a roof over our heads. I'm busy trying to keep the reputation of my business intact without any help from anyone, because I can't afford an assistant. And I'm busy trying to be an attentive mommy and wife." She was ticking things off on her fingers as she spoke. "I'm distant? Hm. Maybe it's because I'm busy." She sat forward, trying to untangle her legs from the sheets with little success. "And did you ever think that maybe I'm sad because I wish things were different for us? For our family? Did you ever think that maybe I *miss* you and the kids? That maybe I'm so exhausted I can't think straight? I'm working sixty-plus hours a week! I haven't read a book in three months. Three months, Jake! Have you even noticed? Oh no. You sit there on your pompous backside and think the very worst of me, then graciously offer me your forgiveness. How dare you? How *dare* you!"

Her voice broke on the last word, and he saw her eyes well up with tears. Feeling flushed with shame, he reached over to put a hand on her leg.

"*Don't* touch me." She slapped his fingers away, making the hot coffee in his other hand slosh onto his lap. He flinched, and she scooted away from him to get out on the other side of the bed. Slipping her arms into her robe, she stalked out of the room.

Jake said a very bad word.

· · · ● · ● · ● · · ·

"I WILL NOT BE able to make my appointment this evening, Vicky. I'm sorry for the short notice. Felix has an open house tonight that somehow didn't end up on my calendar, and I have to shuffle everything around today."

"That's fine. Can we reschedule for tomorrow?" She sounded concerned, but Nora didn't know if she really was, or if it was just her own guilty conscience projecting her assumptions on the woman.

"Sorry. Bible study."

"You're still going then?"

"Yes."

"Jake is, too?"

"Of course. If I go, he goes."

"And if you don't go?"

"He doesn't either, Vicky. But I'm sure you already knew that."

"Has anything happened, Nora?" Vicky switched tactics. "Anything changed that would keep you from seeing me?"

"Other than a kid's open house? Nope." But the fact that *nothing* had changed was really getting to her, and now, so was this conversation. "Listen Vicky. I'm tired. I'm tired of praying that God will fix things. He's not doing anything. He's ignoring the situation. I need a break. I need... I don't know what I need." She shook her head. "Actually, I need to go now, that's what I need. I have to get some work done before this evening."

"Of course, Nora, but please call me in the morning. According to your file, we've only been meeting for six weeks, Nora. These things take time. Sometimes a lot of time. Don't give up now. The dry places can be disillusioning, but they're to be expected. Let's get you in within the next few days, all right? If you have a spare hour, you call, and I'll see what I can do to squeeze you in."

"All right." Even to her own ears, her clipped answer didn't sound too convincing.

"You'll call?"

"I'll call," she said, knowing she wouldn't.

"Okay. Enjoy the open house."

"We always do." Nora was already dreading it. The week before, at Leslie's open house, the teacher spoke to Jake almost exclusively. Even when Nora asked a question, Ms. Flutter-fingers fluttered her fingers, and her answers, at Jake instead. They seemed to have already established a rapport, and Nora couldn't be absolutely certain, but she thought the woman shot a couple of heated looks her way. She felt decidedly excluded, and when she asked Jake about it later in the car, he hesitated, then admitted he'd asked the teachers to contact him if the need ever arose, because Nora was so busy.

"I didn't think she'd act so ridiculous, though. I saw a couple of those looks she pinned you with." He chuckled, his Adam's apple bobbing up and down, as though he was trying to swallow his laugh.

"You think this is funny?" She turned in her seat to face him, one hand on the dashboard, the other pulling the shoulder strap of the seatbelt away from her neck where it seemed to be strangling her "Why would you do that? Now that woman thinks I'm too busy to be concerned about the welfare of my own daughter, Jake."

"Aren't you overreacting a little?" He glowered at the taillights of the car in front of them, not looking at her.

"No, I'm not overreacting." Was that his favorite word these days? "Let me explain to you what you've done. I am now the absent career parent, and you're the wonderful, practically-single father raising his children without a mother-figure in the home. No wonder she barely spoke to me. I couldn't tell if she was punishing me, hitting on you, or both!"

"Well, now you know how I felt all those years when I worked such long hours." He sounded like a petulant child, and Nora had a nearly uncontrollable urge to reach across the middle console and slap him. She brought her fist down hard, thumping it against her knee as she spoke.

"No! I never, ever, *ever,* asked the teachers to not bother calling you because you were too busy for your own children. I would *never* do that to you." She crossed her arms and shifted in her seat, glaring out the window instead of at him. "Fix it, Jake. Call the school tomorrow and put my number back on the list. On the top of the list." Her breath momentarily steamed the window as if emphasizing her words.

"Fine. I was just trying to help you. I know you actually *are* busy, and I thought it would make things easier for you not to have to trouble yourself about the kids." He had both hands on the steering wheel, and when she glanced back at him, she could see him kneading the soft leather casing, his wrists moving up and down in the moonlight.

"Do you know when I worry about my children, Jake? I worry when I *don't* hear from them or from their teachers. I'm their mother, not their guardian. Not their care-taker. It's my very nature to trouble myself about my children."

"Hey!" He smacked the console between them, and she wondered if he was feeling the same impulse to inflict bodily harm as she was. "They're my children, too, Nora. Stop calling them yours, especially when you're talking to me."

"Then stop acting like they're *not* mine." The rest of the ride home was spent in a thick, murky silence that hadn't let up all week.

Tonight, they had another open house to attend, and they'd barely spoken all week. Granted, they'd had few opportunities to discuss much of anything at all. She had three clients chomping at the bit to spend some money, and for once, she was grateful she was too busy to spend any time alone with her husband.

Nora now bent her head to the task at hand, a pile of paperwork needing her attention. The phone rang and she hesitated before answering it. It was Jake.

"I'm won't be able to go tonight. I have a meeting with a client." He didn't greet her, or ask her how she was doing.

"Oh. Okay."

He continued, his voice tense and his words rushed, as though he'd rehearsed his lines. "I'll need you to be home by six tonight. I'm having dinner out, too."

"I'll see what I can do." Nora wasn't sure whether she should be offended or worried.

"No, I need better than that. I need you to be here. I'm leaving the house at six o'clock this evening. If you're not here, your children will eat their dinner alone."

"Wow, Jake. My children? I thought they were your children, too." She leaned back in her chair and pinched the bridge of her nose between her thumb and finger, eyes closed as she tried to sort out what he was really saying. "What's up with you?"

"Will you be here?" His voice rose, demanding, impatient. "I don't have time to play games, Nora. I have work to do."

"Ohhh. Work." She knew her sarcasm would irk him, but she didn't know how else to respond to his odd behavior. "Well, good. It's about time. Since you're working, of course I'll be there to have dinner with my children, and to attend my son's open house."

"Our children," he growled.

"Oh dear. I can't keep up. My children, your children, our children." Her voice was glacial, even to her own ears, but this was insane, he was insane. He was acting like a crazy man. What was his problem? "I'll be home to care for *the* children. How's that?"

More curious than she wanted to admit, Nora stared at the phone in her hand for several minutes after they hung up. What was he up to? What could possibly be more important than attending Felix's open house? He'd never missed one before. She frowned and returned to the file she'd been compiling, but her mind kept slipping back to Jake's mysterious plans for the evening.

That night, Nora actually missed him sitting beside her at Felix's assigned seat. They enjoyed leafing through the kids' school-books together, perusing the samples of art and writing, and finding out what their children were studying in the months ahead. Being able to report back what their teachers said about them was part of the whole experience. She felt slightly bereft going through the event alone, and when she picked Felix and Leslie up from the neighbor's house afterward, they seemed to sense her emotional state, and were fairly subdued themselves.

Jake arrived home a few minutes after midnight. She was putting away the dinner dishes before heading to bed, when she heard the front door open and close, and his footsteps on the entryway tile. She didn't acknowledge him.

"Well, well. Look at you. Usually, I'm the one in the apron, up to my elbows in soap suds. How does it feel?" From the corner of her eye, she could see Jake lean against the wall at the entrance to the kitchen, apparently waiting for a response.

"Feels great. How was your night?" She took a deep breath and turned around to face her husband.

Wow.

SIX

"You look nice, Jake. Really nice." Sometimes she forgot how handsome her husband was. His hair, a little messy, as though he'd run his fingers through it several times, could use a trim, but she liked it this length, because the ends curled this way and that, even when he tried to slick it back with her hair products.

"Thank you," he replied, his chest swelling slightly under the lapels of his dark gray dinner jacket. The white shirt without a tie looked crisp, but casual, and the skinny cut dress pants gave him a retro look that greatly appealed to her, especially in light of how much she'd missed him this evening.

"So? How was Felix's classroom?" Jake stayed where he was, and it suddenly occurred to her that he often stood in the doorway of whatever room she was in. Through her mind flashed snapshot after snapshot of conversations between them, with her at the kitchen sink, at her desk, in the bed, in the shower, and Jake standing in the doorway, leaning against the wall like he was right now. What did it mean? Was he afraid to get too close to her? Did he feel threatened by her? Was he leaving his options open? Her pulse surged, and she felt her cheeks flush. Caught up in the whirlwind of revelation, she didn't answer him right away.

"Nora? You okay?" Jake pushed away from the wall, took a few steps toward her, then stopped when she blinked. The spell was broken.

"Sorry. Yeah. Just a little spacey. Long day." She chuckled at the direction her thoughts had gone, but she was pretty sure there was some psychological explanation for his doorway leanings. She'd have to mention it to Vicky when she saw her again. *If* she saw her again.

"

"How was the open house?" he asked again.

"It was fine. Felix is doing great, as usual, and the teacher had only nice things to say about him. By the way, she said to say 'hi' to you." Nora couldn't help the slight frown that flitted across her face before she went on, but she hoped he wouldn't notice. The third grade teacher was cute, like a pet mouse was cute, but lacked that certain charisma necessary to tempt any healthy male over the age of ten. "You probably already know this, but Felix's class has a big production coming up the end of this semester. He's going to be narrating a historical drama for the whole school, and he's chosen to do it in the character of Abe Lincoln."

"Yeah. He told me. We were going to talk to you about a costume, but things got a little crazy around here."

Nora nodded, not needing clarification. "He wants you to help with the facial hair, though. He figures you should know better than I do what a beard and mustache look like, seeing as you're a man and I'm not."

"That, I am. And you're definitely not." Jake slowly crossed the kitchen toward her. He was looking at her in a raw way, one that made her uncharacteristically self-conscious.

"And he's helping to write it, too. Did you know that?" Nora picked up a dish from the drainer, turning away from him. Jake reached over her shoulder and took the bowl from her hands, setting it gingerly back in the rack, then turned her around so she was facing him.

"Yeah. He told me that, too. I want to kiss you." He reached up to slide a hand along the column of her neck, his fingers tangling in her hair, his thumb brushing across her cheek. "I've been thinking about kissing you since I walked in the front door."

She released the breath she was holding, took another one... and shoved him away from her. He stumbled, but caught himself on edge of the counter before he went down.

"You're *drunk!*" Nora was stunned. An alcoholic who'd fought a terrible battle for sobriety, Jake reeked of whiskey and cigars. Up close, his eyes had that bleary, unfocused look she hadn't seen in over a decade. No wonder he'd been leaning against the wall. He was probably using it to keep himself upright.

"Drunk? Hardly. A couple shots won't send me over." He reached for her again, but she evaded his grasp, and he laughed. "Come on. Take advantage of me. You said I looked hot."

"I said you looked nice, Jake." She tried to keep her voice steady, even as the ground rolled beneath her feet. "That was until you got up close. You don't look so nice now." Her sentences came out choppy, her breath cutting in and out as she tried to find her footing again. Her lungs pressed against the inside of her ribcage. "I'm...I'm going to go to bed. You're sleeping on the couch."

"Oh no," he leered at her. "No one's sleeping on the couch. Not me. Not you. We share a bed and that's where we're both going."

"Don't be ridiculous. You're not sleeping in my bed tonight." Nora turned off the light as she left the kitchen, her fingers trembling so badly she fumbled a few times before finding the switch.

Her head was filled with the sound of an angry beehive, and everything tingled as though she'd stuck her fingers in an electrical outlet. "Breathe. Breathe. Breathe," she chanted in time to her racing heartbeat, recognizing the old familiar signs of a panic attack in its early stages, something she hadn't experienced since the last of Jake's drinking days. She thought she was going to be sick and ducked into the bathroom, locking the door behind her. Leaning against the wall, she slid to the floor, and wrapped her arms around her knees. She left the light off; the cool darkness of the tiny room helping her focus on getting her body's involuntary response under control.

She forced herself to take slow, deep breaths in through her nose, then blow long exhales out through her mouth. She counted in a soft, sing-song voice to the tune of 'Twinkle, Twinkle Little Star' until her heart rate slowed.

Sitting in the dark stillness, she listened, waiting, certain Jake would come after her.

Finally, she heard his footsteps in the hall. Every muscle in her body tensed, but he turned into the bedroom without even pausing outside the bathroom door. A few minutes later, she heard him pass by again, but his footsteps faded as he headed toward the other end of the house.

Nora stood, blinking away the light-headedness from sitting with her knees bent for so long, and smoothed her hair back behind her ears. She bent over the sink, and using her cupped hands, she swallowed several mouthfuls of water. She brushed her teeth quickly and splashed her face a few times to cool her still flushed cheeks. She didn't bother removing her makeup.

Feeling a little more in control, she opened the door slowly, peering down the hall in the direction Jake had gone. The coast clear, she crossed into the bedroom, leaving the light off in there as well. The dark comforted her tonight, and seemed to help her keep the panic at bay. She didn't need to see what she was doing. She and Jake had shared this room for long enough that she knew exactly where everything was.

Crawling into bed, she curled in on herself, debating whether or not to lock the bedroom door. She decided against it. If Jake wanted to come in, she'd rather deal with him in the privacy of their bedroom than out in the hall where the kids might hear.

"Don't let Felix or Les wake up and see their dad like this, please. Whatever Jake is up to, God, he's your problem to deal with. I can't."

It wasn't much of a prayer, but Nora hoped God would understand. She rolled onto her back, her fingers splayed on Jake's cold pillow. She trembled a little as she slipped into the memories of their first years of marriage. How many nights had she spent like this, her hand reaching for him, finding only emptiness? At least tonight she knew where he was. At least tonight she knew he was home, safe. Alive. She turned back over to her side and lay facing the wall in the dark.

Her body longed for sleep, but her mind would not shut down. Where had he spent the evening? With whom?

She still could hardly believe he would bail on an open house, but by all appearances, that's exactly what he'd done. He'd gone out—alone or not, she didn't know—had some drinks, a cigar or two, then stumbled home. Why? Why after all these years? Ten years last month, in fact. She'd given him an elegant tie pin to commemorate the date, and made his favorite meal. He'd smiled proudly, moved that she'd remembered.

Ten years sober, and suddenly, it was as though the last decade had never existed. In a single moment, it all came rushing back; the anger, the shame, the panic.

I'm not crying. The thought crossed her weary mind, and she drifted off thinking about tears, and wondering if she'd finally run dry.

She didn't know how long she'd been asleep, but she was instantly awake as the door to the bedroom opened, a faint stream of light coming from the night-light in the hallway. Jake stumbled into the room and around to his side of the bed. Already stripped down to his boxers, he slowly lowered himself to the mattress and worked his legs under the covers. Fumbling clumsily with his pillow, he made himself comfortable, then he pulled her up against him. His skin was icy; he must have fallen asleep on the sofa without a blanket. It was unexpectedly chilly tonight, especially for early fall in Southern California, and he was probably beginning to feel the effects of the evening's indulgence. His body relaxed against hers, and he let out a heavy sigh behind her, making the hair on her cheek flutter against her ear. She wrinkled her nose at the rank smell of his breath, and gingerly shoved his arm off of her. Reaching up, she cracked open the window above their heads, breathing deeply of the brisk night air.

· · · ● · ● · ● · · ·

Nora and the children were gone by the time he pushed himself up to sit on the edge of the bed. The room was cold, and he squinted in the undiluted light shining in through the open window. If his breath smelled half as bad as his mouth tasted, he should be thankful she hadn't left him fumigating in his own stench.

"What have I done?" It was only a murmur, but the vibrations his raspy voice sent rumbling through his head had him clutching his stomach.

He didn't remember coming to bed. He barely remembered standing in the middle of the living room, stripping off his clothes, then sitting down on the couch to think about where he might find a blanket.

He had to get to the shower. Slowly, with as little movement as possible, he stood up and braced his hand against the wall. The room was deep and narrow with only a few feet of space on either side of the bed for nightstands. Pretty convenient for drunks, he thought to himself. He made his way along the wall, head down, eyes cracked open only a fraction, and pushed open the bedroom door. The hallway was markedly warmer.

The rush of the shower sounded like Niagara Falls to his ears, and he finally opted for a bath instead. He sat against the wall in the hallway while the tub filled, then crawled back into the bathroom and eased his body into it, dragging the edge of the shower curtain in with him. He left it, already seeing Nora's eyes rolling with disgust. It couldn't be helped.

It was too hot, but that couldn't be helped either. He couldn't move; his body simply refused to listen to his brain. He sat there in the shadows of the darkened bathroom, his flesh prickling sharply from the heat, sweating profusely. Lightheaded and dizzy, he closed his eyes and rested his cheek against the cool tile, praying he wouldn't hurl in his bathwater.

• • • • ● • ● • • •

"JAKE? JAKE! ARE YOU in here?" Nora jerked back the shower curtain, splashing water across the tops of her shoes with the dripping hem of it. Fear clutching at her heart as her eyes fell on his prone figure in the tepid water. "Jake!" Her terrified cry ricocheted around the tiny room.

His foot, resting on the edge of the tub, twitched, then his whole body slipped beneath the surface of the water. He burst up out of it, gasping and sputtering, his hands grasping frantically for something, anything. The language that erupted from his mouth made Nora step back as though struck, and she tripped on his discarded boxers. She flipped the light on, anger and relief vying for position in her heart, then she grabbed his towel from behind the door and tossed it on the floor next to the tub. Her voice came out high and tight, sharp.

"Clean up the water you just sloshed all over the place. You'll slip and crack your head open. We don't want that, do we?" Then she left the room.

Her heart was racing from the sight of him floating so lifelessly in the bathtub. He'd left the light off just like she did the night before, and even in the middle of the day, the bathroom was dark because of the absence of even a single small window. But he'd found comfort from the shadows for different reasons than she had, most likely because the light hurt his eyes.

Apparently, he'd only fallen asleep in the tub, but the shock of finding him like that was subsiding way too slowly.

Nora headed toward the kitchen where she filled the kettle with water and put it on a burner to boil. She'd come home to pick up her lunch she'd forgotten on the kitchen counter, and also to check on Jake. He'd been nearly comatose that morning, and she was worried enough to want to make sure he was okay. Now she wished she had stayed away. *I should have let him drown,* she told herself, anger finally taking precedence over fear.

Knowing he would give anything for some coffee, she deliberately chose to make herself a cup of tea. Pushing the sleeves of her thin sweater up, she crossed her arms over her stomach, and leaned against the counter to wait for the hot water. She was a little afraid that if she sat down, her shaking knees wouldn't let her stand up again.

Several minutes later, Jake made his way into the kitchen and sat gingerly on one of the stools at the counter.

"Is there any coffee?" His raspy voice and accompanying wince caused a wave of guilt to wash over Nora, but only for a very brief moment. Just then, the kettle began its shrill whistling, and she gloated silently as he clutched his head with both hands. She meandered slowly over to the stove, turned the burner off, and the whistle subsided.

"Afraid not. I made coffee this morning, but when you didn't get up, I took the extra to work with me, rather than let it go to waste. I'm making some hot tea if you want some."

Jake, elbows on the counter, still holding his head in his hands, didn't respond. Nora opened a cupboard door, withdrew two ceramic mugs, making certain they knocked together repeatedly, then let the door swing shut with an obnoxious bang.

"Oops!" She apologized brightly, cocking her head and blinking vacuously. "Here you go. Pick your poison." She set his mug down so that it clanked on the counter in front of him, and she had the satisfaction of seeing him flinch. "Oh wait. You already poisoned yourself, didn't you? And now drowning? You aren't by any chance trying to kill yourself, are you, Jakey?" This time, it didn't slip out. This time, she called him that on purpose.

Nora opened a drawer, pulled out a couple spoons, rattling the silverware caddy unnecessarily, and closed the drawer again, with fervor.

"Please," Jake gasped. "Please stop banging things." He lifted his head and looked across the counter at her, his eyes pained and accusing.

She opened another cupboard, yanked out the basket of teabags, and slammed the door again, with as much force as she dared. "You mean *that* banging? That's what you want me to stop?" She shoved the basket across the counter toward him, and he had to grab at it to keep it from sliding right off the edge and onto the floor. "Have some tea, Jakey. A little peppermint might settle your stomach. And it won't kill you, I promise."

"Stop calling me that."

"What? Jakey? Why? I kinda like Jakey. In fact, I kinda like the fact that you don't." She was being mean, but she didn't care. The anger inside of her had found an escape hatch.

"Shut up, Nora."

"Excuse me?" She planted both hands on the counter opposite where he sat, and leaned forward, thrusting her face in front of his. She could feel her lips curling in a snarl, her words coming out ragged and loud. Suddenly, she was the teakettle, shrieking her boiling rage at him. "Did you just tell me to shut up? What's the problem? Am I talking too much? Too loudly? Or is it just that I'm saying something you don't want to hear? Huh? What is it, Jakey?"

"Shut up!" Jake ground out, and pushed away from the counter, away from her.

"Don't tell me to shut up!" Nora ranted. As though she watched from somewhere above them, she saw her hand come up, her still empty mug raised, then she hurled it across the room, barely missing Jake's head. It bounced off the wall behind him, leaving a noticeable gouge in the plaster, and crashed to the floor, where it shattered in an explosion of ceramic pieces.

Silence enveloped the room, and they both stood like statues in the aftermath of her eruption. Finally, Jake moved. Nora stared at him as he tenuously made his way across the minefield of shards to the pantry to get the broom and dustpan. Without a word, he began sweeping the broken pieces into a pile, then scooping them up, and throwing them away. Nora, deflated and shaking, picked up her purse from the table, walked out of the kitchen, out of the house, and climbed into her car. She backed out of the driveway, and was almost at the end of the block before it occurred to her that she had no idea where she was going.

She simply could not face her office right now. She knew nothing would get done, even if she did return to the stack of purchase orders on her desk.

"What's happening to us?" she whispered. There were still no tears.

SEVEN

Nora stopped at a gas station and topped off her tank. She checked her watch; it wasn't even noon yet. Three more hours before she had to be back to pick the kids up from school, since Jake was in no condition to do so himself. The fuel nozzle bucked in her hand, indicating the tank was at capacity, and those three hours seemed to stretch out interminably. She climbed back into her car and sat for several minutes, wondering how she'd fill her time without having to think about what was going on in her home.

A few weeks ago, on the way to a client's house in a neighboring town, she'd driven by an art gallery promoting local artists. In her line of business, the next best thing to a legendary piece of art was a piece of art by a local artist. What better way to use up a few hours today? Soon she was back on the road, a fresh cup of coffee in the console, and some old Seth Adams tunes blaring from the expensive speakers she'd paid a little extra for when she bought the car a few years ago.

She pulled into a parking spot right up close to the entrance, and waited for the song to end before she turned off the engine. It was one of her favorites, a song called *Reckless*, about the kind of love that made you do crazy things. It always made her feel a little pumped up, and she climbed out of her car with a saucy grin on her face, still humming the chorus.

"Good song."

Startled, she spun around, dropping her keys. A man leaned against the wall just outside the doorway of the studio, reminding her a little of Jake leaning against the kitchen wall, and it made her stomach do a quick shimmy. She hadn't noticed him when she pulled in, but obviously he'd been there at least long enough to hear her choice of music.

"Yes. It is. One of my favorites," she said, regaining her composure. She bent over and picked up her keys, wondering why she wasn't even a little embarrassed by her juvenile behavior. How long had it been since she'd driven around with her music as loud as the speakers could handle, singing at the top of her lungs? She'd kept the windows rolled up today, but only because she had paperwork and sampler books in the backseat. She smiled as she straightened up again. Nope. She wasn't embarrassed at all. In fact, she was feeling just a little reckless herself right now, thanks to Mr. Adams.

As though reading her mind, he asked, "*Reckless*, huh?"

"You know Seth Adams?" she asked, looking over at the man. He just stood there, watching her, an appreciative grin on his face. She thought perhaps he was flirting with her.

"I know his music."

"Do you like him as an artist, or just my song in particular?"

"Your song?" He raised a dark eyebrow in question.

"My song," she confirmed, closing her car door behind her. "I've claimed it." She strolled jauntily toward him, daring him to challenge her. She knew she looked good today, in spite of the terrible situation she'd just run from. She was wearing one of her favorite dresses, an apple green vintage Lana dress, with a wide-belted waist and a snug bodice, softened by the periwinkle sweater she layered over the top of it. The skirt was full, the hemline falling just above her knees, and her peep toe sling-backs showed off a flash of bright pink toenail polish. With all the rush of getting the kids to school on her own shoulders this morning, she'd only had time to brush out her hair and leave it hanging in sleek straight lines around her face, but even wind-blown, she knew it was her best look. At least, Jake always said so.

"And how do you go about claiming ownership of a song?"

"Exactly the way I just did," she stated, shrugging one shoulder with a little toss of her hair. "I guarantee you the next time you hear it, you'll think of me."

Where did *that* come from? She could hardly believe those words popped out of her own lips.

"In that case, I like your song in particular." He was definitely flirting with her. "So, what can I do for you today?"

Oh, good grief. Pick up lines? She stepped up onto the sidewalk in front of him, and was somewhat unprepared for how tall he was. Even in her heels, she had to tip her head back to meet his gaze, and she was grateful for the gigantic sunglasses she wore, covering much of her face, and hopefully, most of her blush. The way he was smiling made her think he had a good idea of what was going through her head, glasses or no glasses. She had to get back to business with him, quick, before he misinterpreted her behavior altogether.

"Does that mean you work here?"

He was casually dressed in a pair of jeans, not something she'd expect an art gallery curator to wear. "I saw your sign out front when I was driving by, and it says you show local artists' work. I'm a decorator, and I'm always looking for good art. I'm hoping to find some here," she finished lamely, running out of words.

He looked out across the parking lot toward the sign, as if trying to remember what it said, then nodded. "Sure. I can show you around."

"Well, don't let me take you from your work. I don't have anything in particular I need right now; I just want to see what's available. I have a few hours to use up." She stumbled over her words again. "I'll just wander."

He tipped his head toward the doorway. "Come inside. You're not taking me away from anything. I'm just hanging around here, bugging Janelle, because I have nothing else to do either. I was expecting a shipment this morning, and it still hasn't shown up." He shrugged his shoulders. "Apparently, it's our lucky day. You've got a few hours, so if you'll have me, I'm all yours."

He stuck out a very large hand. "Tristan, at your service."

"And I'm Nora." She shook his hand, her face burning over his suggestive comments, his low voice like a velvet caress, and she wasn't surprised when he didn't immediately release her, but drew her through the door instead.

"Welcome to my world," he said, letting her fingers slip slowly from his grasp. She removed her glasses, her eyes widening with delight.

Sculptures graced the tops of podiums and pillars, wall nooks, and low platforms; water nymphs, botanical creations, geometric shapes in metals and plasters, marble and wood. Hanging from the ceiling, beneath the warm glow of focused lighting, were structures looking as though they'd just floated in from outer space or from deep beneath the ocean. Blues and greens, silvers and purples, shot through with sienna and gold, the colors were organic and unearthly at the same time. It was eclectic and otherworldly, the haunting music of Celtic instruments playing softly in the background.

"Oh, my." Nora's eyes were drawn to one sculpture in particular, a piece full of both movement and stillness. A child, or a young woman, poised with arms extended, hair swept up in a swirling pattern above her head. The remnants of a dress turned in and out around her body, and her feet were tight together, toes pointed. She wasn't standing, she was being lifted off her feet.

No, she was sinking.

"Oh." She said it again as she approached. Something in the posture, in the lines, pulled at her heart, and without thinking, she reached out to run a hand along the curve of the girl's hip.

"This one, hm?"

"Oh, my." They were all the words she could manage.

"What do you like about her?" He asked after several contemplative moments.

Nora considered her answer, trying to understand what moved her so deeply about the creature. "I don't know, really. I feel like I...can relate. But relate to what?" She asked the question more of herself than to the man who stood on the other side of the sculpture studying her reaction. Up close, she could see red- and blue-coated electrical wires woven in and out of scrap metal, forming the girl's neck and face, her arms, and feet. The billowing dress was tattered canvas, painted the color of light shining through water, and her hair looked like it might have been fashioned from the strands of an unraveled mop, crimped and rippling through unseen ocean currents. The upturned face, incomplete features made from pieces of broken pottery, euphoric from a distance; shattered up close.

Could she put any of that into words?

"She's like a perfect combination of pain and pleasure, of suffering and joy. Like she's surfacing and drowning at the same time." She paused before she continued, knowing her words were going to sound silly and formulaic, but she didn't really care. "It's as though she embodies the essence of a woman's soul."

Tristan didn't respond for so long, that Nora finally looked up at him. She was surprised to see him staring at her, a curious expression on his face.

"What?" She tucked her hair behind her ear, self-conscious beneath his unguarded gaze. "Did I say something stupid? I'm no art connoisseur, you know. I just like pretty things."

"Stupid? No." Tristan crossed his arms, and his eyes drifted slowly back to the sculpture. "I think you pegged it. I've just never heard anyone say it quite like that. And I've heard a lot of responses to this piece, believe me." He cocked his head and looked at her again. "Wander around a bit down here, then I want to show you some paintings by the same artist on the second floor. Take your time. I need to check in with Janelle."

At the mention of her name, a tall, well-formed redhead peeked around a corner and waved. "Hello. I'm Janelle, the curator here, but you're in good hands with that one." She nodded toward Tristan and winked. "If you need anything at all, though, you just look for me, all right?"

Nora nodded. "Of course."

"Speaking of your good hands, Tristan, could you help me a minute? I'm doing a bit of rearranging over here and I need to borrow your man power."

Tristan grinned and flexed a bicep for the ladies. Janelle snorted, disappearing back around the corner, and Nora looked away, embarrassed and charmed.

The studio was broken up into several sections. The artwork seemed to have no rhyme or reason to placement, yet each display flowed from one to the other seamlessly. If this was Janelle's doing, the woman had a gift for merchandising. Nora took her time just looking, studying brush strokes and textures, her shoes making no noise on the thickly carpeted floor.

When Tristan rejoined her, he let her meander, speaking quietly, commenting on the different pieces and artists. None, though, touched her like the statue up front. Tristan was directing her up the stairs, explaining the layout of the gallery on the second floor; she'd have to remember to ask him about the drowning woman's creator when they came back down.

The second floor was also divided into sections, this time by artist. They wandered through the rooms with walls painted in deep hues, dramatically offsetting the artwork, and Tristan often stepped back to let her absorb pieces on her own. She appreciated his sensitivity and thoroughly enjoyed his non-aggressive sales technique.

She recognized the work of the artist immediately. The paintings were like a flattened version of the sculpture downstairs. There were three dimensional elements to many of them; recycled odds and ends painted into the scenery. An old-fashioned metal seat-belt was the cinched waist on a shadowy figure leaning against a tree in the moonlight, shards of plywood layered into the side of a building. Some of the work was soft and subtle, mysterious and dreamy; other pieces were darker, shrouded in something that made Nora uncomfortable. She especially liked the paintings with swirling colors and organic structures, but there were a few that almost repulsed her in their heaviness. She couldn't imagine putting one of the darker pieces on anyone's walls, and she said so.

"I hear that quite often. But when the muse hits, what's a man to do?" Tristan was standing behind her as she studied a stunning painting in blues and blacks, streaks of goldleaf rippling through the color like sunlight reflecting off turbulent water. Glancing at the signature of the piece, she saw it; a slashing T with a few squiggles following it like a tail. She spun around, alarmed that she'd spoken so bluntly.

"*You* did this? These are yours?" She pointed toward the staircase. "That... the drowning woman downstairs? You made her?"

"*Isolde*. And she's not really drowning. It's only what she wanted to do in her heart."

"*Isolde*." Nora repeated softly. "Tristan's *Isolde*. Of course." She chewed her lip, not sure whether it was romantic or ridiculously cliché. Except that there was nothing cliché about the drowning Isolde downstairs, and the incredible creature came from somewhere inside this man's head. Something about that was very romantic.

"Yes, my *Isolde*." He grinned proudly. "It's how I think of her. How I think she thinks of herself; as mine."

Nora nodded mutely, still reeling at the idea of this man, with his large, work-roughened hands, creating something so wildly feminine. How could he possibly know what it was like, that feeling of breaking apart, of coming undone from the inside out?

"Your work is incredible, Tristan." She had to say something, even if just to be polite. "You're truly gifted." She turned her back to him again, berating herself for sounding so mundane, and let her eyes rest on the painting again. She reached up and hovered her fingers over the contours of a coiled wire protruding from a thick patch of cerulean blue, not quite touching it. "The way you use... stuff."

"They call it 'trash' these days." He chuckled softly, probably over her hesitance to speak openly anymore.

"The way you use trash to create something so beautiful." She turned toward another painting, this one shadowed and disturbing. "Or so terrible."

"Thank you." Tristan glanced down at his watch. "Do you have some time, Miss Nora? I'd like to show you something."

It was a little after one. "I probably have about an hour." Her heart fluttered inside her chest at her lack of caution. Maybe she should have asked what he wanted to show her first.

"My studio is just a few blocks away. I'd love for you to see it. And Janelle can vouch for me," he added, almost as an after-thought. "I'm not going to kidnap you or anything. In fact, you can follow me in your own car."

Nora hesitated. How inappropriate could it be? His studio was his work place, not his home. It would be like him stopping by her office, wouldn't it? Just business. Besides, she liked his work, and she'd be able to promote him better if she knew more about him.

I'm justifying this, she admitted to herself, and her expression must have given her thoughts away.

"Come on. Be reckless. Make Seth Adams proud that you claim his song." He stepped back to allow her to pass. "In fact, Ms. Reckless, ride with me in my car. I'll have you back in forty-five minutes, I promise."

"I... I should probably get back. I don't want to be late." Red lights were flashing behind her eyes, sirens screaming in her ears.

"Late for what? You said you have an hour. Where do you need to go?"

"I'm picking up my children from school. I can't be late."
"I won't make you late, I promise."

"I'm picking up my children from school. I can't be late."
"I won't make you late, I promise."

EIGHT

SHE DIDN'T RIDE WITH Tristan in his car. She might be reckless, but she wasn't crazy. If she kept telling herself that, maybe she'd start believing it, too.

She did, however, follow his roaring, teal-blue, 1970s Camaro four blocks away, to a lovely old Victorian where he housed his studio. He was out of the car and waiting for her by the time she pulled in the driveway behind him.

Now more curious than afraid, Nora entered the house as he held the door open for her. Just inside the front entry was an ornate circular staircase, and she followed him up two flights to a turret-room that was all windows, darkened by drawn curtains. He pulled open the panels of one section of windows to let the light in, and she gasped as she gazed around the octagonal room. Canvases and easels, pedestals and palettes, all were scattered about in organized chaos. Everywhere she looked, she also saw small piles of trash, pieces of junk in which Tristan saw potential. Half-finished sculptures, incomplete paintings, pages and pages of pencil sketches tacked to what wall space there was.

"Oh, my."

Tristan chuckled. "That's what you said when you saw my *Isolde*. Does that mean you like this, too?" He slowly wandered through the space, rearranging a few things, straightening, adjusting, his fingers drifting over canvases and brushes, as though greeting everything personally. She watched, feeling a tiny bit intrusive, like she was watching a private moment, as he interacted with his tools. He stopped on the other side of the room and propped himself against the ledge of a window, hands braced on either side of him. He gazed at her, his eyes bright, waiting for her reply.

"This room seems made for an artist. You fit perfectly here." Well, that sounded forward and assumptive, she chided herself. But the big man just grinned and nodded, watching her from his perch at the window.

She was just beginning to feel awkward under his scrutiny when he spoke again. "I have a confession. I had an ulterior motive for bringing you here—"

"Oh, no," she interrupted. Her heart began to race, and her hands went instantly damp, as she turned to find the door. What on earth had she been thinking? Here she was, alone with a very large, and very attractive stranger, who had somehow climbed right past all her defenses in the last hour. And no one knew where she was, not even Janelle. Tristan had simply called out "We'll be back!" as they headed out the door of the art studio together, and Nora hadn't insisted on any more than that.

"No! No, Nora. Please don't go." He was across the room in a moment, his hand gentle on her arm. "That didn't come out right. It's not that kind of motive. I'm sorry I alarmed you. Please."

She paused, her back to him, trying to regain her composure before facing him. She was confused and embarrassed, feeling completely out of her element, yet drawn to him in that flushed way she hadn't experienced in many, many years.

Even though she didn't want to admit it, she really liked the way she was feeling. She liked the way her heart was pounding, so differently than it had the night before when her inebriated husband had tried to kiss her. She liked the way Tristan's eyes made her awkward in a newly-aware kind of way. But she knew there was only one place this would all lead if she gave in to her feelings.

"I should go. Now." Her voice sounded much more stable than she felt.

"No. Please don't go," he said again. "I didn't mean to make you feel uncomfortable." Tristan removed his hand from her arm, and she took another step toward the door. "Just hear me out, okay? When you first saw my *Isolde*, there was something in your face, something in the way you were looking at her, and I wanted to try to capture it on paper. I just want to do a quick sketch, okay? You can even stand right by the door, and I'll work over there." He indicated a drafting table across the room. "It will just take a few minutes, I promise."

"I—I don't know. I don't know if I want to be sketched. Especially today. You know, I'm not thinking very clearly. I feel a little... well, a little... lost, I think, and I really should go." She finally looked up at him, only to find his features in shadows, back-lit by the afternoon sun streaming in the window behind him. "I need to leave, Tristan. I'm sorry." She pushed open the door and stepped from the hypnotic embrace of the turret studio, hurrying down the stairs and out the front door.

She was fumbling with her keys, her fingers trembling and clumsy, when she heard his footsteps behind her. He reached around her and covered the car door handle with his hand. She noticed flecks of chartreuse and cobalt paint on the backs of his knuckles. She stepped back, placing enough distance between them so she could breathe her own air. "What are you doing, Tristan?"

"I'm really sorry about how this has all gone down." His voice was low, soothing, and she braced herself against the seductive assault to her senses. "Maybe it was that vulnerability and lost feeling you were talking about up there that caught my eye when we were at the gallery. I wanted to capture that, and I was afraid if you walked away, I'd forget what it looked like. I didn't mean to take advantage of you and whatever you're going through, but I think that's exactly what I've done." He removed his hand and stepped back from the car. "I'm being honest, Nora. I'm not a creep, and I'm not accustomed to having to convince people of that fact. Give me a little grace here, okay?"

She took a deep, steadying breath.

"Okay." Looking up at him finally, she could see sincerity in his face, and his words made her feel a little ashamed she'd assumed the worst of him. "I'm sorry I got all weird on you up there. I thought I was having a bad day, then I thought I was having a good day, now it seems like I'm having a bad day again. I can't keep it straight. I'm all extremes and opposites today." She smiled a little. "I feel like your *Isolde.*"

Neither of them spoke for a few moments, her words hanging between them. Nora desperately wished she could draw them back inside, as her imagination ran wild with what it might mean to belong to this man, to be his. She could only guess what he was thinking. It might have been a while since a man's awareness made her notice, but she knew, beyond the shadow of a doubt, that this man was extremely aware of her as a woman.

She heard Vicky's voice in her head. "Don't for one second think you're safe just because you're a Christian, Nora. Satan is a liar and a deceiver, and he wants to destroy you and your family. Traps are real, my friend. Run like mad in the other direction."

Nora had laughed the advice off. "You don't have to worry about that, Vicky. This isn't about another man. One man is more than enough for me to deal with."

Traps are real. Run like mad. Traps are real. The words paced back and forth through her head.

"Look, Tristan. I'm not very good at games, and I feel like this might be one. I need to leave before I say anything else that might mislead either one of us. Thank you for showing me your art and your studio." She stuck out her hand. "I'm especially glad that I got to... to experience your *Isolde*. She's beautiful. She's exquisite."

He looked at her for a few moments, some internal struggle going on behind his gaze, but he seemed to accept that her mind was made up, and he took her hand in both of his. "Well, I apologize again for my behavior. But I will tell you that I'm even more sorry for how this encounter is ending. If this is a game, then obviously I'm not very good at playing, either. I hope the rest of your day turns good again. I really do." He released her hand and took her car keys from her. "Allow me." He unlocked the door and held it open.

"Thank you." She smiled weakly as she climbed in. "And thank you for the strangely awkward, yet stimulating hour I've spent with you."

He cocked his head, his raised eyebrows making fine lines form across his forehead. "Is that a compliment?"

"Yes, in fact, it is. I haven't been awkwardly stimulated in a long time." Her eyes widened, and she covered her face with her hands to hide her mortification. "You know, I just need to close my mouth and drive away. Give me my keys before I say anything else."

Tristan was laughing out loud now. He gently closed the door for her, waited for her to roll down her window, then handed her the keys. Leaning down so she didn't have to crane her neck to look up at him, he tried one more time.

"Listen, Miss Nora. I was serious about wanting to sketch you. If you ever change your mind, you know where to find me, okay?" He reached into his back pocket for his wallet and pulled out a business card. "Here's my number. Just call and we can schedule a sitting. It doesn't have to be in my studio if it makes you feel uncomfortable. I can meet you at a coffee shop, at your work, wherever you choose. My offer stands. I mean it." He straightened, his eyes squinting in the bright sunlight. "Besides, I've never been accused of being awkwardly stimulating before."

From the safety of her car, Nora felt a bit more composed and slightly reckless again. "Okay, now you're just making fun of me. That's no way to convince a lady of your good intentions."

"Who said anything about good intentions?" He cocked his head and grinned disarmingly. Nora blushed. "Give me another chance, okay?" She hesitated a moment longer, then accepted his card. She glanced at it briefly and smiled up at him.

"Thanks again, Tristan," she said noncommittally. As she backed out, she tried not to pay too much attention to the man in her rear view mirror, who stood in the driveway, hands in his pockets, watching her until she was out of sight.

NINE

"Jake, do not go pick up the kids. I repeat. Do *not* pick up the kids. I've got them. I'm just running a little late and I can't get through to the school. I don't want you driving anywhere with them."

Jake listened to her message on his cell phone as he sat outside the house in his truck. He must have been brushing his teeth when she called. Hearing her tone, he was glad he hadn't picked up. She didn't sound any different than she had when she left; still angry and belligerent.

"Well, what should I do?" He asked the question out loud, testing his ears, the throbbing in his head, to see if he could handle extraneous sounds. "Tolerable, at least."

The school had indeed called his cell phone, then the home phone when he didn't answer. He heard Betty's familiar voice in the answering machine, and he hurried over to pick up before she finished leaving her message.

"Hello, Mr. Anderson. This is just a courtesy call to let you know that Felix is here in the office waiting to be picked up."

"Thank you, Betty. I thought my wife was picking up the kids today. I must have misunderstood her. I'll be right there."

Not one to mince words, the secretary simply said, "We'll see you shortly then, Mr. Anderson," and hung up.

No call yet from Leslie's school, but if Felix was still waiting for a ride, then Les was too. They always picked her up after Felix because she was older and liked it when she was one of the last kids there.

Giving her the benefit of the doubt, Jake dialed Nora's number. His call went straight to voice mail; maybe she was trying to get through to him again.

He continued to sit, debating whether or not to brave the chaos of the school office in his condition. He dialed Nora's number again and held the ringing phone several inches from his ear. This time, she answered.

"Jake. I'm on my way to pick up the kids. Just ran into some unexpected traffic on the freeway." She sounded anxious and defensive. He knew she hated being late to things, especially when it involved the kids.

"Are you sure? I'm sitting in the truck only five minutes away. Do you want me to pick up Leslie at least?" As he said it, it occurred to him that he didn't really want to pick up Leslie, at least not by herself. He wasn't sure he could handle the weight of her questioning stare today, without Felix' nonstop chatter as a buffer. He crossed his fingers, silently begging Nora to say no.

"I'll get them both, Jake. Don't even think about driving around with my children in your condition."

"Our children."

"Not when you're drunk, they're not."

"I'm not drunk, Nor."

"Whatever, Jake. You're not driving around with them today. Not in your condition."

He hated to admit it, but his relief was so great he actually smiled, albeit weakly. "Fine. You pick them up. I'm going back to bed."

"Get a lot done today, I take it?" Nora's snide remark stung, and he did something he'd only done one other time in his life, and that time had been by accident when he dropped the phone into the toilet. He hung up on her and did not call her back to apologize.

Crawling under the covers, he couldn't help but catch a whiff of her familiar fragrance wafting over from her side of the bed. He breathed in deeply, a sense of forlorn longing in his gut. He loved it, her unique smell combined with the perfume that reminded him of coffee cake and morning love-making. She'd worn it since before they met. It made his chest feel tight, thinking of her, and he turned onto his side, facing the wall.

The mess she'd made earlier when she threw the cup at him cleaned up quickly. He deserved a whole lot worse, if he was honest with himself. As he swept up the debris, he considered what it must have been like for her to come home and find him passed out in the bathtub. And he could only imagine what had been going through her mind this morning as she opened windows to clear the stench of his binging that tainted everything in their bedroom, their sanctuary. He even had an idea of how betrayed she must have felt last night when he reached for her, and she realized his drunkenness. He had a snapshot memory of the look on her face at that moment, and he wished the alcohol had taken it from him, too, the way it had taken his good sense.

"Where have you been, Nor?" he muttered to himself. He knew she hadn't gone back to her office. Carl Halston, her landlord, had called looking for her. An electrician was coming in first thing in the morning to install some additional outlets for her, and he wanted to make sure she'd be there a little early to let him in. Jake promised to pass along the information and assured Mr. Halston that she would take care of everything like she always did. The man was more than happy to let Nora handle the service call. She'd rented space from him for almost four years now, and she was his favorite tenant.

Jake's phone jingled on his nightstand, and he lifted his head to look at the number. He didn't recognize it, but it was a local area code, so he answered it. "Hello?"

"Hello. Oh. Hello. I'm looking for Nora Anderson. I must have dialed the wrong number." The woman on the other end of the line sounded a little flustered.

"This is Jake, her husband. Can I help you?"

"Oh. I thought I was calling Nora's phone."

"Her number ends with a 6, mine with a 9. Otherwise, they're the same. You probably just slipped and hit the wrong button." It happened all the time.

"Oh! That's exactly what I did. Well," the woman hesitated a moment as though trying to make up her mind about something. Then she continued. "Can you give your wife a message for me? Let her know that the day is almost over, and I still haven't heard from her. "

"That's it? Kinda cryptic, isn't it?"

"Cryptic, yes." It sounded like she was smiling. "I'm trying to guilt her into calling me. And I'm Vicky."

"Jake. Are you a client of Nora's?"

"No, just a friend."

"Okay. I'll give her your message, Vicky."

"Thank you. Goodbye now."

Nora had never mentioned anyone named Vicky before. Some of Nora's regulars thought they were more like friends. That's why they kept coming back; Nora made them feel special. But why did Nora need to call her by the end of the day?

He put the phone down and tried to relax, but he couldn't stop thinking about all that had happened over the last twenty-four hours.

Drunk again. Even he could hardly believe it. All it had taken was one drink and then there was no reason to stop. They told him it would happen that way at his Alcoholics Anonymous meetings so long ago, but after so many years? Last night, he'd convinced himself that he'd been sober long enough to be able to control his consumption. When the guys ordered that first round, he threw in his card and paid for them all, including one for himself. The cute little waitress smiled sweetly at him, acknowledging his generosity, and it made him feel good.

That first shot made him feel even better.

By the time they all parted ways, Jake was plastered, and even he knew it. He was always good at hiding his condition from other drinkers, especially when the alcohol was just beginning to have its effect on his system, and he convinced everyone he was fine and didn't need a ride. How would he explain the absence of his truck to his wife?

He was fumbling with his keys, trying to fit the wrong key into the door of his Blazer, when the waitress who'd been so attentive all night approached him. "You okay, Jake?"

He wasn't sure how she knew his name, but she was awfully pretty, and her voice poured over him like cool water. "Now that you're here, I am." He reached over and tugged on a strand of hair that had come loose from the clip at the back of her head.

"Can I help you with that?" She came and stood right beside him, blocking the light from the lamppost behind them, her body casting a shadow on the lock.

"I can't see my keys now. You're blinding my light."

"Blinding your light, huh?" She laughed, and Jake put his arm around her shoulder, leaning into her. "I don't think you should be driving, big guy."

"I'm fine," he slurred, squinting down at her, but her face was too close to focus on.

"No, you're not fine," she giggled. "How 'bout I drive you home, and you can call me a cab from your place in the morning?" Jake let his arm fall away from her shoulders, then brought his hand up to her cheek, his thumb caressing her bottom lip.

"I don't think my wife will like that."

"I don't know. Maybe she will." Her voice came from somewhere low and beckoning, and he tipped his head to listen to it, not really caring what words she spoke. "Give me your keys, Jake." She had turned so that she was leaning back against the driver's door, facing him. She reached for the keys dangling from his fingers, but instead of taking them, she grabbed his hand and pulled him up against her. He didn't resist. "Or we could go to my place and I could have you all to myself." Then she reached up and pulled his head down, pressing her pretty lips to his mouth.

He felt a tremor course through his body; it was an unexpected shock to his system, like bumping up against an electric fence. He jerked his head up, staring down at her upturned face.

"I'm married. I love my wife."

"Of course you do. I'm sure she's great. Come here and kiss me again." She slid her fingers into his hair and pulled him toward her again, standing up on tiptoe now to meet him halfway.

The second kiss lasted much longer than the first, her mouth open and wanton under his; the third and fourth one blended together with the fifth as he leaned into her, pinning her up against his truck.

"Come on, Jakey," she murmured. "Let's get out of here."

The name hit him like a bucket of cold water, and Jake lurched backward, stumbling a little in a pothole in the pavement. "Oh, God. Oh, God. What am I doing? Oh, God, help me. I'm sorry. I'm sorry. No, no, no. I can't. Oh, I'm so sorry..." He didn't even know her name. "I'm so sorry for this. I have to go. Please, please forgive me. My wife. I love my wife. Oh, God, forgive me." His throat was tight with shame as he none-too-gently gripped her by the shoulders and moved her aside. He clambered up behind the wheel, scrubbing the back of his hand across his mouth.

Jake pulled his pillow over his head now, his stomach churning as the memories of his night played over and over in his mind. How could he let that girl kiss him like that? How could he kiss her back?

And then he drove home! He didn't remember anything after pulling out of the parking lot. Nothing. How did he get home? How did he make it here alive? Without killing anyone else? Shame washed over him in wave upon wave, and he groaned into the pillow.

If she hadn't called him Jakey, who knows what might have happened.

· · · · ● · ● · · ·

DINNER THAT NIGHT IN the Anderson home was a lighthearted event. Jake stayed in bed, claiming the flu, and the kids were empathetic. Nora, still basking in the after-glow of the surreal afternoon spent with Tristan, was thoroughly enjoying the antics of her children. She glanced at Jake's empty chair a few times, but every time she did, the thought popped into her head that perhaps his absence was the reason it was so pleasant tonight.

Nora had the kids help her clean up after dinner, then they set up a board game on the table. Not having a fourth person determined which games they could play, and she thought there might be a problem when Felix really wanted to play one that required equal teams. But they compromised and played Sorry, a family favorite.

"I don't think it's fair that a guy has to go back home if another one lands on the same square," Felix muttered, having had his game piece sent home for the third time.

"That's the reason it's called 'Sorry' Felix." Leslie had no qualms whatsoever about booting someone else's piece.

"Well, I don't get it. In Candy Land, we share the spot. In this adult game, we fight over it. Doesn't that say something about being an adult?"

"Hm," Nora murmured, nodding her head. "You know, I think you might have a point there."

"Yes. Yes, you do. In fact, I think I see it!" Leslie jabbed at the top of Felix's head. "Right there! It's poking through your hair! Disgusting!"

"Cut it out! Mom, make her stop poking my head."

They read together on the sofa before bed every night, except when Nora didn't get home in time. The latest book, a story about a stow-away on board a pirate ship, was full of adventure and mystery. Even though Leslie claimed she was too old to need a bedtime story, she enjoyed the tradition just as much as Felix did. So did Nora.

She and Jake often read together in the first year of their marriage. He was an avid Tolkien fan, and she was happy to oblige, as Tolkien was a favorite of hers, too. She began reading out loud to her children when they were still in *utero*, and hadn't stopped since.

Leslie and Felix poked their heads in the bedroom door and blew kisses at their father. He told them he loved them, and assured them he was feeling better already. "I'll be fine by morning, I promise. I just needed to rest today."

Nora said their prayers with them, tucked them in, and headed back to the living room to straighten things up for the night. She eyed the couch dubiously, realizing that she, not Jake, would be crashing there tonight.

She was not sleepy at all, though, so she filled the kettle with water, and while she waited for the water to boil, she hurried out to her car to pull her case from the back seat; she would try to get some work done. By the time she got back inside, the kettle began to whistle, and Jake was at the stove turning the burner off.

"Thanks," she muttered. She didn't want to talk to him. She didn't want to look at him. She wanted this time for herself, for her work. She didn't want him around distracting her.

Or making her feel guilty about this afternoon.

Jake, in flannel pajama pants and a white tank top, reached up to pull out two ceramic mugs from the cupboard. Nora stared at the muscles in his shoulders gliding beneath his skin. When he set the cups down on the counter, the clinking sound jarred her out of her reverie, and she experienced a momentary twisted sense of *deja vu*. Any minute now, she almost expected a mug to go flying past her head and shatter on the floor.

"What kind of tea are you having?" If he'd caught her staring, he didn't acknowledge it.

"I'll get it." She didn't want him being nice to her, especially when he was wearing that shirt. He knew she liked it on him, and she thought perhaps he'd put it on for that very reason.

"Don't be silly. I'm right here," he said, indicating the basket of tea bags on the counter beside him. "Which one do you want?"

"Earl Grey, then. Real sugar." She opened her portfolio and began spreading paperwork and prints out on the table top.

"Are you going to stay up for a while?" he asked, pouring steaming water over the teabags.

"Yes. I didn't get much work done today, and I can't afford to take any time off."

She could hear the tinkling sound of Jake stirring their drinks as she organized piles on the table. He brought her tea and set it at a safe distance from her papers, then pulled out a chair for himself.

"I'm sorry for the way I acted last night." He sighed deeply. "I behaved...I was a jerk."

"I don't think it was a behavior problem, Jake. You were drunk." She said it without looking at him.

"Yes. I was drunk. And I'm sorry."

Nora didn't respond.

"I can hardly believe it myself, and I feel terrible."

She really did not want to have this conversation. In fact, as she listened to his words, it occurred to her that no matter how good he looked right now, she didn't really care what he had to say. It just didn't matter. All she wanted was for him to go away and leave her alone.

"Okay."

"Okay?" From her peripheral vision, she could see Jake cock his head to one side. "That's it?"

"I'm not sure what else you want me to say." She still wouldn't look at him.

"So it's okay that I went out and got drunk last night? It's okay that I drove my truck home plastered? It's okay that I passed out in the bathtub, scaring you half to death when you came home for lunch today?"

"Actually, none of that's okay, Jake. I mean that I'm okay with you feeling terrible. You should. But no, I'm not okay with any of what happened last night, or with anything that happened today, for that matter. And because I'm not, a few things are going to change around here. I'm not going to let you and your choices affect me anymore. I'm going to do what I need to do to provide for this family, regardless of what you do. I'm not going to let you disappoint me anymore, because I'm not going to depend on you for anything anymore. And I'm okay with that, too."

"I don't follow you." She could hear the slight tremor in his voice. Was he afraid? *Good.*

"It's not that tough, Jakey. If you are capable of making the decisions you made last night, then you have no right to make decisions for me and the kids. You're on your own." She picked up a pile of client files and began thumbing through them. She tried not to think about the not so great decision she'd made this afternoon.

Jake sat silent for so long that Nora's thoughts wandered of their own accord back to her afternoon with Tristan. The way he studied her had really unnerved her, but at the same time, flattered her. He wasn't begging her to notice him, the way Jake was right now. He stared at her as though there was something fascinating about her, intriguing. *Like a hunter eyes his prey.*

When Jake spoke, she jumped. "I'm not leaving."

Nora snorted derisively, hoping he wouldn't notice her flushed cheeks. "I'm not asking you to leave. I'm just releasing you from the responsibility of your family. Like I said, I'm tired of being disappointed by you, and it's pretty obvious from your decision to ditch your children for a night out at the bar, that you really don't want that kind of responsibility anyway. So, you're free, Jake. You're a free man."

"Look at me, Nora."

Still standing, she eyed him across the length of the table. He looked like he was going to be sick. "Yes?"

"I'm sorry. It won't happen again. What can I do to make it up to you?"

"Nothing. There's nothing that can undo what you've done. In fact, I don't really care if it does or doesn't happen again. But," she leaned forward a little, the chandelier over the table throwing the contours of her face into stark relief. "If you so much as *think* about putting either of my children in a car with you at the wheel at any time in the near future, I will call the police." She glared at him with cold eyes, wanting to make certain he did not misunderstand her. She'd done some thinking this afternoon after she'd left Tristan's studio, angry at her own naiveté and blaming Jake for it. "I will be taking them to school and picking them up from now on. I will be home with them after school, and I will take them where they need to go. You are officially relieved of your childcare duties."

"Good grief, Nora! You can't just 'relieve me' of my duties." He waved a dismissive hand in the air.

"You don't get it, Jake. I'm not the one relieving you. That was your decision. I'm just enforcing it. Put my children in your truck, and I call the police." She sat down, and opened a file, flipping through the invoices inside.

"This is ridiculous!" Now Jake pushed himself up, his chair nearly toppling over, and he scrambled to catch it, sloshing a little hot tea on his hand. He set the cup down on the counter behind him and pushed his chair in. "What about you? Why should I let you anywhere near *my* children with your violent streak? How do I know you're not going to throw a cup at my son's head?"

"Now who's being ridiculous?" Nora's derision emanated from every pore. "By the way, thank you for cleaning that up. I was glad to see it gone when the kids got home. I would not have wanted you to have to explain it to them."

"Argh! This conversation is exhausting! You are so manipulative. I can't tell whether you're grateful or sarcastic, whether you're angry or disappointed. I can't tell whether you care about me or hate my guts! You're impossible!" Jake was pacing now.

"Well, well, well. There's another thing that hasn't happened since your drinking days. I don't think you've called me impossible in over ten years, Jake. Funny how the two seem to go hand-in-hand. You drink, and I'm the one who becomes impossible. Why does that not make any sense to me?"

"Fine. You win." Jake raised both hands in surrender.

"No!" Nora slapped her hand hard on the table. "No, I don't win!" She was yelling again. "I lose! You lose! Your children lose! We *all* lose because of you, Jake!" Fists clenched at her side, her whole body trembled with her anger and frustration. "We all lose."

"Mom?" Leslie stood in the hallway, her hair soft and messy around her face. The innocence there was marred by worry, and Nora's heart twisted inside her.

TEN

"It's okay, honey." She hurried to Leslie's side and slipped an arm around her daughter's shoulders. She tried to steer her back to her room. "We're just working some stuff out."

But Leslie resisted, looking over her shoulder at her father. "Dad? What's going on?"

"It's okay, Les. Go back to bed." He stayed where he was, his arms akimbo, obviously at a loss for words.

"It doesn't sound like it's okay." Leslie was still not convinced. "You were yelling, Mom."

"I got frustrated, honey. I can't seem to catch up with things, and I got impatient. Your dad just stepped in the way of my frustration for a bit."

"Well," Leslie said, walking toward the table where Nora's work was spread about haphazardly, files splayed out like over-sized playing cards. "Why can't you help her, Dad? You seem like you have a lot more time than she does. She's always working. Maybe she'd be around more if you helped her. Look at all this," Leslie indicated the mess on the table. "Can't you pitch in?"

"What is this?" It was more an exclamation than a question. "You, too? Does everyone in this house think I'm a loser?'

"I don't think you're a loser, Daddy. I just thought you might be able to help Mom some more." Leslie scowled, but Nora could see she only did so to hide the hurt from his outburst.

"Les," She touched her daughter's cheek. "Daddy doesn't understand my work. It's not quite that easy."

"I don't get it. You didn't go to school for this, did you? I mean, you taught yourself how to do this, right?" She pointed at the table again.

"But I have a gift for it. It comes naturally to me." She didn't want to have this discussion right now. Not only was it futile suggestion, and filling Leslie with false hope, but Nora had so much she needed to get finished before morning. She longed for the quiet of her office.

"You mean, you took the time to figure it out, right? That's what you always say to us." She looked over at her dad again, her voice rising insistently. "I *hate* algebra, but when I take the time to figure it out, I understand it, and I get it done. Why can't you do that with this stuff?" "Leslie. That's enough." Nora took her hand and pulled her away from the table. "Daddy and I will work this out. You need to go back to bed now. I'm sorry I woke you. We'll be quieter."

Leslie went meekly this time, without a backward glance at Jake.

Nora pulled the covers up and tucked them under the girl's chin like she did when she was little. She kissed her forehead, both eyes, both cheeks, her chin, and lastly, her nose. Leslie giggled softly.

"You haven't done that in a long time."

"Well, you haven't asked me to." Nora smiled back in the orange glow of the nightlight.

"I didn't ask tonight."

"Yes, you did. I heard you. In here." Nora lightly tapped Leslie's forehead, then cupped her cheek.

"You always seem to know things, Mom. I love you."

"I love you, too, Lester the Lion." It was her daughter's "brave name," something she'd christened herself with as a child to help her be brave enough to sleep in her own room.

"Are you... is everything... are you guys going to... to be okay?" Leslie stumbled over her words, unshed tears glistening like jewels in the corners of her eyes.

"We'll work it out, honey. We always do." Nora didn't want to lie, but she didn't know how things were going to turn out.

"I wish Daddy would go get a real job. I miss you. Today was nice having you here after school with us again." Nora saw her frown in the shadows.

"Not that we don't love having Daddy around. It's just... well, he's not you. He's Dad, not Mom. That's all."

"I know, Les." Leslie turned onto her side, tucking her folded hands under her cheek.

"Goodnight, Mom. Sleep tight."

"Don't let the bed bugs bite," Nora finished. "We both love you very much. See you in the morning, honey."

• • • • • • • • • • •

JAKE LEANED AGAINST THE wall at the end of the hallway as he listened to Nora and Leslie talking. The arrow of his daughter's longing pierced his heart, and he felt even worse than he had before she walked in on their argument.

A real job? The kids just didn't understand.

Then again, maybe she was right. Maybe he simply wasn't cut out for running his own business. Maybe he wasn't cut out for much of anything, period. "Except being a kept man," he muttered, his voice just above a whisper.

Nora slipped out of Leslie's room, pulling the door closed behind her. She glanced up and saw him, and the look that crossed her face spoke volumes to him. He turned around and walked back toward the kitchen, listening to make sure she was following him.

He still could hardly believe the events of the last 24 hours. It shocked him to see how quickly things could unravel when you tugged on the right string. Why, oh *why* did he take that first drink? He ran both hands through his hair, lacing his fingers behind his neck. Why did he even go out last night?

And that was really the problem, anyway. He went out to make some stupid point to his wife. He went out to prove to her she couldn't tell him what to do, that he was busy, too; that he had a life, too. And it had all been a lie. He had no business meeting, no one to go out with. He went to the bar completely alone, on a night when he knew she'd have issues with his absence.

He just happened to stumble across a couple of guys he knew from his drinking days. Funny thing, too, finding them still sitting at the same table, at the same bar, just where he'd left them ten years ago. They welcomed him back like he was a long-lost brother, especially when he started paying for drinks.

Leaning his hips against the counter, he rotated his head in wide circles, trying to work out the kinks forming in his neck and shoulders. Paying for drinks. He had absolutely no idea how much money he'd spent. "There goes another row of stitches unraveling around me," he muttered under his breath. "I'm going to be naked in no time."

"What did you say?"

"Nothing. Just talking to myself." Jake refilled his mug with more hot water. "I... I was wondering something."

"What?" Nora gave up on getting any work done, not while he was hovering around the kitchen. She carried her cup to the microwave, then started gathering things up into a few neat piles again while she waited for the tea to reheat. She would just have to work like a madwoman in the morning and hope for the best.

"Why haven't you asked me about last night?"

"What do you mean?"

"Don't you want to know where I was, and who I was with?"

Nora didn't answer right away as she took her cup from the microwave and sipped the steaming drink in silence. When she finally looked up at him, her eyes were dark, impenetrable. The urge to squirm was almost overwhelming, and Jake clenched his fists at his sides.

"No, Jake, I don't want to know where you were and who you were with last night. For you to go out and get drunk again, after all these years, simply blows my mind. You just drew a line in the sand for us. No, I don't want to know. In fact, I no longer care enough to want to know." She hitched one shoulder up in a half-hearted shrug. "Besides, I think you're hoping I'll ask so you can unload your guilt. Exonerate yourself. Sorry, but I'm not going to relieve you of anything."

A mental snapshot of the waitress' face, very close to his own, made him rub his eyes. He could still feel her young body pressed against his. Should he tell Nora about her? Things couldn't possibly get any worse. Besides, he'd said no to the woman. Even drunk, he'd pushed her away and refused her advances. Kinda.

"There was this waitress...."

"Good grief, Jake!" Nora interrupted him, shaking her head. "Do you *want* me to kick you out? Don't come clean for my sake. It's too late. If you've got confessing to do, call a pastor. Call a friend. Go talk to God." She narrowed her eyes at him, and Jake nearly cringed. She'd never looked at him like that before, not even back in his drinking days that he could remember. "Call someone who cares." She finished her drink and set her empty cup in the sink.

"And now that I see you're feeling better, *you* can sleep on the couch. You are not welcome in my room so do not slither in at two in the morning again. I will make a scene. If you need anything, get it now. I'm taking a shower, then I'm going to bed. Alone."

Jake watched her walk away. Tell someone who cares, she'd said, as though she didn't. What made his heart pound in his ears was a mounting fear that it was true.

"What have I done," he groaned despairingly. How many times had he asked himself that question in the last twenty-four hours?

Hearing the shower start, Jake pushed away from the counter and headed toward the bedroom to gather a few items. He grabbed his pillow, the extra blanket from the end of the bed, and his Bible. Then he scooped up his alarm clock; he wasn't about to let the kids wake up before him and catch him sleeping on the couch.

Jake sat down on the edge of the bed, deflated. "God? Can You hear me? Or have I screwed things up with You, too? I don't know what I was thinking. You've got to help me. Help us. I don't want to lose my family." He leaned forward, resting his elbows on his knees, his head down. "I don't know what to do. I don't know how to fix this."

The shower shut off and he knew he'd better not be in the bedroom when Nora came through the door. Clutching his pitiful little pile of necessities, he turned his back on their bed. As he passed the bathroom door, he thought he heard her sniffle, but he wasn't sure. Nora cried over everything, because she felt things so acutely, but he had yet to see her shed a single tear over this whole situation, and that realization only deepened his fears.

•••••••••••

NORA AWOKE FROM A fitful sleep to the sound of the bedroom door opening, the telltale squeak of one hinge giving him away. Instantly alert, and utterly amazed at her husband's audacity, she watched as Jake eased into the room.

"Get out. I'm warning you, Jacob Anderson." She didn't yell...yet.

"Please, Nor. It's almost six, and the kids might wake up. I don't want to have to explain why I'm sleeping on the couch."

"Not my problem. Get out."

"Oh, come on. Don't be ridiculous. It's not like I'm climbing in bed...."

"Get out!" This time she did yell. Jake backed out of the room, pulling the door shut behind him. She heard the bathroom door open and close across the hall.

He looked awful. "About as bad as I feel," she muttered, lying back on her pillow. All she wanted to do was to sink down beneath the covers, and close her eyes again. Was it really morning already?

Ten years ago, when he showed up for what seemed like the millionth time, reeking of whiskey and cigars, smudged make-up traces on his lapels, she was waiting for him. Standing in their little apartment kitchen, her pixie cut sticking on end, distended belly stretched tight around the growing body of their second child, she asked him why. When he couldn't answer her with anything other than 'I don't know,' and 'I'm sorry,' she told him that if he ever got drunk again, not to bother coming home. The doors and windows would be locked to him, and he would be put out of their lives forever. They had three-year-old Leslie and a baby on the way, and she was done cleaning up after him. No more calling in sick for him, no more leaving the security locks off, hoping it would be her husband stumbling into their home at all hours of the night and not some stranger, no more lying awake in the early morning hours wondering where he was, who he was with, waiting; dying while a new life grew inside of her. She calmly slid a packet of papers across the table to him and went to bed.

He wouldn't read them, not in his condition, she knew, but she'd labeled the manila envelope very clearly. With a black, wide-tipped marker, in all capital letters, she'd written on the front, divorce papers. If he bothered to look, he would also find paperwork for a restraining order, but she doubted it would come to that. She knew he had no intention of going anywhere. He loved her, she had no doubt, and he loved his little Leslie. He just loved himself and his alcohol a little more.

Jake made the decision to stay. He put in his time with Alcoholics Anonymous, he sought out accountability at church, and he stayed home at night. The money he wasn't spending at the bars was put into a savings account for a down-payment on a home, and a month before their eighth anniversary, they moved in here.

They'd been full of hope in those days. Jake's sobriety, a new home, a growing family, her business, so many new beginnings. But somewhere along the way, things began to go off course a little at a time. In fact, sometimes it seemed to her that they were struggling even more than when Jake was drinking. Back then, the alcohol was the tangible source of blame. Now, there was nothing solid to put a finger on, or point a finger at, nothing to blame the anger and frustration on.

There was only this prevailing cloud of unsettling discontent and despair.

Next month, they'd be celebrating sixteen years of marriage, but as far as she was concerned, there was little left to celebrate. Even before Jake's unexpected drinking excursion, Nora's disillusionment was overwhelming, and she dreaded the upcoming milestone, especially after the last few weeks. Her mother was already making plans to keep the kids for the weekend, so they could have some time alone, but Nora left things up in the air with her, not wanting to commit to anything. She wasn't making plans to leave Jake, but that didn't mean she felt like going out of her way to spend time alone with him, either.

"I hate my husband," she said into the stillness of their bedroom. At first, the words sounded silly to her, childish. She'd never spoken them out loud before, and flushed with embarrassment. But then she tried them again. "I hate my husband. I really hate my husband." She nodded, now feeling a little proud of herself for being brave enough to say so. "Yep. I hate my husband." She sat up on the edge of the bed and said it again. She told her lamp she hated her husband. To her reflection in the mirror above the dresser, she said, "Do you know that you hate your husband?" She looked up at the ceiling. "God? Are You listening? I hate that man You gave me." Then she had the decency to cover her mouth in shame. But she didn't take it back.

Sobered, she pulled on a pair of leggings, a fluttery skirt with an uneven hemline, and flipped through the hangers in her closet until she found a silky little top with three-quarter sleeves. She'd go without a jacket today. Grabbing a pair of silver sandals, she opened the bedroom door and stepped out into the hall. Jake was apparently still in the bathroom. She knocked, a sharp rap on the hollow door.

"The bedroom's all yours, Jake."

"It's me, Mom." Felix opened the bathroom door, a forlorn look on his face.

"Oh! Well, good morning, sweetheart!" Nora reached out and ruffled his already messy hair. "You're up early."

"I heard you stub your toe, Mom. You yelled like a freak."

"My toe? I didn't stub my toe." She held up her foot for inspection. Jake must have made that one up, but she wasn't letting him off the hook so easily.

"Dad said you did." Felix scowled, and shot a glance toward the kitchen.

"Hm." She leaned down and spoke in a stage whisper. "He's got a good imagination, doesn't he?"

Felix just looked confused. "Well, I heard you yell."

"Oh that. Yeah. Sorry I woke you up. I didn't mean to. Are you okay?"

"No. Dad got up on the wrong side of the bed and is being totally poopy. You might want to stay out of his way."

"Ah. Yes." *He woke up on the couch, Felix. Not the wrong side of the bed.* She forced her smirk into a grimace for Felix' sake. "I think I'll take your advice and steer clear, okay?"

"You seem to be in a good mood in spite of your toe that you didn't stub." Felix was still grumbling, his shoulders slumped as they walked down the hall together.

"Yes, as a matter of fact, I think I am. I didn't start that way, on account of the toe I didn't stub," she hopped on one foot to demonstrate, hoping to cheer him up a little. "But I'm feeling better now. Maybe instead of my toe, I just stubbed the poopy out of me."

Felix couldn't help it. He giggled. "Mom!"

"What?" Her brows arched high above her wide, innocent eyes.

Jake was setting breakfast dishes out on the island when they came into the kitchen. He wouldn't look at either of them, a sure sign that he was feeling badly about the way things were already going this morning. She glanced over at the table, but none of her things had been touched. He must have seen her looking.

"I didn't touch anything."

Nora didn't bother responding. He sounded like a sulking little boy. Felix, either defensive because of the encounter he'd already had with Jake, or because he sensed the tension in the air between his parents, hiked himself up onto a stool and sat quietly, tracing circles in the pattern of the tile on the counter top.

Just then Leslie schlepped out of her room. She usually got up around six; she now styled her hair, and Nora let her wear a little make-up, so she needed the extra time in the mornings to get ready for school.

"Are you guys okay?" She didn't beat around the bush as she came into the kitchen and perched on another stool next to Felix. She looked over at Nora, then back at Jake.

Nora wasn't going to lie to the kids. Jake, on the other hand, seemed to have no qualms about doing so. "We're fine, Les."

Everyone stared at him, but Nora didn't speak. Let him take responsibility for the situation. She wasn't going to make any more excuses for him the way she'd done years ago.

"Dad's in a poopy mood and Mom's not." Felix interjected into the silence that stretched out uncomfortably.

"That's it!" Jake banged a pan down on the stove top. Everyone jumped at the sound. Even Jake winced a little. "What did you say to him, Nora?"

"Excuse me?" Nora was honestly taken aback by his accusation. "I didn't have to say anything. He's not stupid, Jake."

"Great. This is just great." Jake crossed his arms over his chest and glared at his family on the other side of the counter. "So I'm in a crappy mood. Is that a crime?"

"No." Felix continued to move his fingertip along the grout lines and didn't look up at his Dad. "Sorry."

Leslie didn't look too happy either, but she smiled tentatively at Jake. "Maybe you're just not feeling good yet, Daddy. Maybe you should go back to bed."

"Back to bed?" Jake guffawed. "Back to bed? What a novel idea."

"Jake." Nora didn't have to say it, but she did anyway. "Cool it."

"*You* are telling me to cool it?" Jake raised his arm and pointed at her.

"All right. That's enough." Nora was not going to do this right now. "I'm taking over breakfast. You go deal with yourself. In the bedroom." She came around the end of the counter toward him, hoping he would comply before things got ugly in front of the kids.

"I can go to bed now, Mommy? In my own room?" Jake's sarcasm was ugly to hear, but the look on his face was even worse. "Yippy!" He clapped his hands together, three times, hard, then stormed out of the room. Nora opened the fridge and took out the eggs. She began breaking some into the pan that he'd left heating up on the lighted burner.

"What was all that about?" Leslie looked wide-eyed, shocked. Felix kept his head down. When she didn't answer right away, Leslie spoke again, accusation in her voice. "Well? I thought you two were working things out last night. That's what you told me."

"Hey." Nora turned around to look at her daughter. "Watch your tone with me. We are working on things, but some things take longer to process through than others. Your dad is dealing with some stuff right now, and we need to let him."

"Is that why he slept on the couch last night?" Felix asked.

Leslie's head jerked around to look at her brother. "Dad slept on the couch?"

"Yes." Nora sighed, submitting to the inevitable. They were going to do this right now, after all. "Like I said, he has some things he needs to work out, some decisions to make, and sleeping in the same room right now makes it a little confusing."

"So how long has all this been going on?" Leslie was not happy.

"A while, Les."

"He's been sleeping on the couch for a while? How long is a while?" Now she was appalled.

"No. He only slept there last night. And part of the night before."

"You made him sleep on the couch even though he's sick? Or was that a lie, too?" Leslie crossed her arms over her budding chest, the frown on her face making her look just like Jake.

"Actually, Les, he has been sick." She wouldn't tell them why. That was Jake's job.

"And you made him sleep on the couch? Because he was sick?" This time it was Felix who spoke, looking aghast over her cold-hearted treatment of his ailing father. Nora squeezed her eyes shut, just for a moment. If only they knew.

"He was barfing, guys. He didn't want to puke on me."

"Gross, Mom." Leslie wrinkled her nose.

"Exactly. And last night, well, we just needed to spend some time alone. That, my children, is where things stand for now." Nora fleetingly thought about the way she'd spent the afternoon, how charming Tristan had been, how good it felt to be flirted with. But just as she was beginning to feel a twinge of guilt, she heard Jake's words from last night, right before she cut him off; echoes of words she'd heard too many times before, words drenched in remorse and shame.

"There was this waitress...."

ELEVEN

THE DAY OF THEIR anniversary dawned overcast and heavy, much the way Jake felt as he peered through the slats of the window beside the fireplace. He was still sleeping in the living room. The kids knew, but they didn't ask about it. Once they were tucked in bed, he and Nora hardly spoke, even though she rarely went back to her office at night anymore. They seldom used the table for meals because it had become her work space, and she doggedly refused his offer to clear a space for her in his office.

She got up and ready in the mornings before the children, made them breakfast, packed their lunches, dropped them off, and then picked them up after school, just like she said she would. She took them to their events, attending most of them without him.

"Why are you doing this, Nor? I *am* their father, and I'd like to attend school functions, too."

She just pointed at his phone and eyed him across the table. "The school doesn't keep their schedules a secret, Jake. All you have to do is call. The kids write most of the stuff on the calendar anyway. Maybe you should look at it every once in a while."

The calendar was a sore spot for him and he made every effort *not* to look at it. He could not, for the life of him, remember to have the kids write stuff down on it, but now that Nora was Commander-in-Chief, they dutifully marched in the door, made a beeline for the refrigerator, filled in any necessary information, and pulled out the tray of snacks their mother had prepared for them; cheese slices, vegetable sticks, and their favorites, dill pickles.

She also took over making the evening meals. The first time she found him in the kitchen when she and the kids arrived home from school, she acted surprised, staring at him like he'd grown a second head.

"Oh! What are you doing in here, Jake?"

"I'm making dinner."

"Well, that's nice of you, but you need to let me know ahead of time," she said, not unkindly. "I already have plans for dinner. Remember? Feeding the children is my job, not yours. If you would like to provide a meal for the kids, check with me, first, okay?" She spoke to him like he was a presumptuous guest in her house.

"Then what, exactly, *is* my contribution to this household?" He followed her to the table where she was setting out dishes.

"I've been wondering the same thing for years."

He'd walked right into that one.

That was less than a week ago. Now, here it was their anniversary, and the weather couldn't be more appropriate. Nora hadn't said a word about what she wanted to do, and he didn't dare make any plans without consulting her first.

He got up and straightened the couch, folding his bedding up and stuffing it into the bottom drawer of the TV console. He still couldn't believe he'd spent the last two and a half weeks sleeping out here. It wasn't uncomfortable, but he missed his bed, his room, his wife. Oh, how he missed sleeping next to his wife.

"I miss my wife," he muttered. Things were so different now. They conversed only about things like home maintenance and grocery lists. She left with the kids in the morning, not returning, even for lunch like she often used to, until the end of the day when she picked Felix and Leslie up. And since they both had after-school activities right now, the house stayed quiet for a long time.

Jake should have been getting a lot of work done but he couldn't focus. Hours went by in a day without his being aware of time passing. Then he'd scramble to have something to show for his time before everyone got home.

Not that it mattered anyway. It wasn't like she was checking up on him.

Well, today, he was going to make an effort to change things. They couldn't continue on like this indefinitely, and he was just going to have to take the bull by the horns.

He would begin this day with taking her breakfast in bed. Nothing fancy, just things he knew she liked. He put on the coffee, strong the way she preferred it, located her favorite blue mug, and set it on a serving tray he'd found among the cookie sheets. In the breadbox was a new package of cheese bagels, a local bakery specialty. He toasted one and dug around in the fridge until he found the tub of whipped cream cheese. He also discovered some seedless grapes in the fruit drawer and added a bunch of them to the tray.

Jake tapped lightly on the bedroom door but there was no answer. When he pushed it open ahead of him, he held his breath, anticipating the worst. He reached the foot of the bed before he realized she hadn't heard him at all. She was sound asleep, lying so that she faced his side of the bed, one hand spread out on the blanket where his chest would usually be. He could almost feel her fingers resting over his heart.

He set the tray on his nightstand, sat down, and picked up her hand, bringing it to his mouth. Gently, tenderly, he kissed her knuckles. A tremor of pleasure raced through him at the sight of her smiling dreamily as she opened her eyes to look up at him.

The light of recognition dawned on her face as she jerked her hand out of his. "Jake!" She said his name like she'd been expecting someone else. "What are you doing?"

He shook his head, alarm tripping through him. "I'm bringing you breakfast in bed. It's our anniversary."

"Oh." She had the grace to sound a little embarrassed, but Jake didn't feel any better.

"Yeah. Oh. So I take it that wasn't me you were dreaming about?" Why? Why, oh why did he have to open his mouth? Why did stuff like that always come out of him? He would give anything to take those words back. Nora closed her eyes and rolled away from him, pulling the blankets up over her shoulders.

"Go away, Jake. I'm not hungry."

"Come on, Nora. Give me a break. I'm sorry."

"You didn't knock."

"Yes, I did. But you were sound asleep."

"You shouldn't have come in, then."

"It's our anniversary, for crying out loud, Nor! When are you going to forgive me? How long are you going punish me? I screwed up, okay? I'm sorry. I don't know how to be any more sorry than I already am. What else do you want from me?"

The answer was soft, muffled, and he had to lean forward to hear her. "What?"

"I want you to undo it."

"Undo what?" He figured he knew what she meant, but it seemed such a silly thing for her to say. He couldn't just "undo" everything.

"Never mind, Jake. Go away."

He sat there a long time, waiting, hoping she'd say something more, something hopeful. Finally, he stood.

"There's coffee and breakfast. I'm leaving it here. I'll feed the kids this morning."

"Thank you." He was just closing the door behind him when she said it, but he knew he wasn't imagining it. Those two little words stopped him in his tracks.

Hope. Only a flicker, but it was there. Taking a deep breath, he headed to the kitchen to fry up some eggs.

· · • · • · • · ·

THE DAY WAS NO different than any other, and the evening was spent as usual, too. But after the kids were in bed, instead of sitting down to work at the table again, Nora opened a bottle of her favorite sparkling wine. She poured herself a tall glass of the bubbly, amber liquid, and disappeared into the bathroom, humming softly as she walked past the living room where he sat on the couch, pushing buttons on the remote control. He heard the bathtub filling with water, and he breathed in the aroma of sandalwood and tea rose drifting out into the hallway; bath oils she reserved for special occasions.

He turned the television off and sat forward, listening intently to the sounds coming from down the hall. He'd shared this experience with her enough times that he could close his eyes and imagine exactly what the scene would be in there.

...clothes puddle on the floor, one pale foot, then the other, stepping over the side of the tub. The water, way too hot, turning her skin pink as she sinks down into the scented bubbles. Her sigh of pleasure as she leans back against the little blow-up pillow she keeps in there for just this purpose. She's closing her eyes, one hand draped over the lip of the tub, the other holding her chilled glass high....

Jake didn't like taking baths, but he loved it when she did. She used to invite him in with her, but after a few miserable attempts, primarily due to the painfully high water temperature she preferred, he opted to wait his turn until she was almost done. They usually talked quietly, twining fingers, the world completely tuned out, while they tuned in to each other. The night inevitably ended with a session of the kind of love-making that left her purring and curled up against his side, and him a satiated and happy man. Jake never felt more like her hero than he did in those moments.

He needed her tonight. He was going crazy without her. He stood up and began pacing the room. This was insane. She was his wife. He was her husband. Why couldn't they work this out?

The open floor-plan of the living room, dining area, and kitchen, gave him ample space to wander. He opened the fridge door, closed it again. His jaw was beginning to ache from clenching his teeth, and his shoulders were tight, his breathing shallow. Balling his fists, he shoved them in the pockets of his 501s.

He crossed to the sink where he splashed water into a glass. Half of it sloshed over the rim as he brought it to his lips, spilling down the front of his shirt.

His hands were shaking as he set the glass down too close to the edge of the counter, then he cursed as it toppled into the sink, shards of glass skittering around the porcelain basin. He grabbed a paper towel and carelessly swept the pieces together to scoop them out.

"Ouch!" He cursed again as a sliver of glass pierced his finger just below the bend of the first knuckle. He turned on the faucet and ran his finger under the cold water, blood turning the fragments still in the sink into swirled Murano glass. Jake roughly pinched and squeezed his finger, reveling in the pain it was causing—who would have thought one tiny little shard could hurt so badly—until he had forced the sliver out far enough to grab it.

He threw it in the sink with the rest of the pieces and stared at the mess, then smacked both hands flat against the counter, leaving a smear of blood behind.

"Enough!" He was done playing this game. No more. He was going to *his* bedroom, he was going to get undressed, and he was going to wait for *his* wife in *his* bed. He was going to demand *his* conjugal rights, and then they were going to sleep pressed together, right where they both belonged.

He marched down the hall and paused outside the bathroom door, just to ascertain that she was still splashing around in the tub. He heard her singing softly and paused, listening. She had such a pretty voice; it'd been a long time since he'd last heard it. Suddenly she stopped mid-phrase, and there was silence. He had taken one stealthy step away from the door when she called out.

"Jake?"

He closed his eyes, berating himself for lurking outside her door. "Yes?"

"Can you do me a favor?" She sounded very relaxed.

"Of course." As long as it isn't sleeping on the couch anymore.

"Can you bring me my robe, honey?"

TWELVE

NORA COULDN'T CONCENTRATE. MEETING with Renee Nash always set her on edge, but the woman liked to spend money.

"I absolutely adore *everything* you do, Nora, dear." Renee's standard uniform consisted of skin-tight, cleavage-baring outfits, and extremely high heels, hair that looked like it might shatter in the slightest breeze, and enough make-up to stock a high-school girls' dormitory for at least a year.

The first time they'd been introduced, Nora was terrified of what she might ask of her. Her taste in home décor, however, was superb. The woman loved clean lines and antique color schemes, beautiful, quality furniture with classic accents. Her style was a perfect blend of all things elegant, and Nora loved putting ideas together for Renee's home. It was her life-style, and the fact that Renee felt she must discuss every last detail of every party, every event, every affair she put together, that left Nora drained. Today, Renee was sharing with her about another kind of affair in which she was involved.

"You remember Tanya Sharpston, the woman who introduced us? Of course you do. Well, I still can't figure out how it happened, but I'm sleeping with her husband." She giggled like a school-girl, and fluttered her bejeweled fingers over her enormous bosom. "I think I'm in love, Nora, but this really throws a damper on my relationship with Tanya. I mean, we're co-hosting the annual Wine and Dine Gala at the Country Club next month, and every time I look at her I just want to weep. I feel *so* sorry for her, so badly for what Freddy and I are doing to her, and she doesn't even know!"

"You say that like it would be better if she *did* know." Nora was appalled at how reasonably the woman spoke, as though her behavior was nothing out of the ordinary.

"It would be! I wouldn't feel so badly, then!" Renee frowned a little, then she looked up at Nora with a resolute expression, her scarlet-tipped fingers waving decisively in the air in front of her. "I really must tell her. Get it out in the open. That way we can clear the air and get on with things."

Nora just shook her head. Get on with things? How does one just get on with things after news like that?

"Oh, don't look at me like that, Nora, dear. *Everyone* knows I like other women's husbands. And everyone knows that Tanya hates hers. Sleeping with him is one thing. That happens all the time. I mean, him with other women. But now that I'm falling in love with him, I don't think I want to share him with anyone, especially someone I have to work with every day. Besides," Renee winked at Nora, as if divulging a saucy secret. "She's younger than I am."

Nora couldn't come up with anything appropriate to say in that moment. At least not out loud. She's going to talk to the woman? To clear the air between them? How would telling Tanya that Renee was sleeping with her husband clear the air between them? The words were all inside her head, but Renee responded as if she'd spoken them aloud.

"Oh, Nora, dear, I'm not such a monster. I don't expect him to divorce her. She deserves his name and his money after all the years they've had together. And three kids, to boot. She's a great girl, Tanya Sharpston is. She's been a wonderful friend, she's got a creative flair that is so charming, and she's put up with a multitude of Freddy's affairs over the years. I'm sure I'm just the most recent in a long line, just as I'm sure there will be more that come after I'm gone. I'm not stupid. But I do want him all to myself while our little affair lasts, and I hope she'll understand."

"I'm not sure she will, Renee. I don't even understand, and I'm not the one you're doing this to." Nora couldn't keep quiet any longer. "It's really a horrible situation all the way around. Someone has to get hurt, you know?" She shook her head. "I feel sorry for all of you. Especially the kids."

"Goodness, Nora, dear. You don't need to worry about the kids. They're so pampered and protected, the world could blow up around them, and they wouldn't know it. But don't you feel sorry for me, either, not for one moment. I'm having the time of my life! I feel young and alive again. I'm barely sleeping, and I haven't looked better in years! Love is the elixir of youth, Nora, dear." She leaned forward across the table between them, and Nora had to look away just in case the woman's left breast escaped its confines. "I can tell when a woman is in love. Do you know how? She looks like she's had a face lift, that's how. And I," She sat up and jabbed at her chest, inadvertently setting everything into motion. "I ought to know about face lifts."

By the time Nora left Renee's home, she was practically in a stupor, numbed by the woman's ceaseless banter about the lifestyles of the rich, if not famous, her relentless gossip. It was almost two o'clock, and she hadn't eaten since breakfast nearly seven hours earlier. She still had a few hours before she had to pick up kids, so she debated whether to go back to the office and just finish out the day, go home to eat something, or stop somewhere along the way.

She spotted the familiar exit just up ahead. Before she could talk herself out of it, she pulled off and made her way toward the cluster of shops. In the parking lot, she maneuvered her silver car into the same spot she'd parked in the last time. She could get some food when she picked up the kids. Right now, she suddenly wanted to see Tristan's *Isolde* more than anything else in the world. And, since she didn't really feel like lying to herself, she admitted that she wouldn't mind running into the artist himself today either.

It had been exactly one month since she'd been here, and even though she and Jake were sleeping in the same bed again, that was about all that was back to normal. She still refused to allow the children to ride with Jake, and even though he told her she was being paranoid, he didn't really argue. She couldn't decide if that made her more or less confident in the sincerity of his apology.

Revamping her schedule required a major effort on her part, and she often felt more overwhelmed than ever. The rewards of spending those extra hours with her children made up for the exhaustion, but not having those hours to invest in her work was taking its toll on her business. She had turned away a few very influential patrons, not because she didn't want them, but because she couldn't get to them within the time period they requested. All she could do was refer them out to another decorator she knew was both reputable and had great taste. Even though she'd received a lovely gift basket and thank you card from Suzi's Shenanigans, the woman was still her competition, and it riled her up to have to feed Suzi clients who should have been her own.

It was that very gift basket, however, that had her unable to get Paradise Lost Art Gallery off her mind this week. It was a typical gift basket, complete with pretty notepads and pens, fancy teacups, some organic Middle Eastern tea, a tin of butter cookies, and some honey sticks. The card, however, was a piece of art. The image on the front was a print of a piece she'd seen hanging near the front of the gallery, and Nora couldn't help but wonder if Suzi had purchased the set of cards there. Since the moment she'd received it, she couldn't stop thinking of visiting again.

Or the way Tristan had looked at her.

She was not an imbecile. She knew that entertaining thoughts of going back, especially under the volatile condition her marriage was in at the moment, was dangerous. Somehow, though, after hearing Renee's callous description of the love-triangle in which she was involved, Nora felt an even greater need to return. It didn't make sense, really, but she almost felt like she had to prove that her attraction to Tristan was nothing like Renee's vulgar relationship with her friend's husband. It really was only a bit of flirting between two people. It would never go anywhere; she was not like Renee.

Just as she turned off the engine, her phone rang. She dug around in her purse for it and checked the number.

Vicky Johanson.

Nora had avoided the woman's calls for weeks, but she obviously wasn't going to give up. "Sonora Décor. This is Nora."

"Nora! I'm glad I caught you. I know you're busy, but I was just wondering if you had some time to get together with me this evening. I have a cancellation and would love to meet with you."

Nora squeezed her eyes shut and pinched the bridge of her nose in frustration. The last time she spoke with Vicky was a few days after Jake's night out. He'd suddenly remembered that the woman had called, and although Nora wasn't sure what she would say to her, she did return the call. She'd been very vague, explaining that her schedule was changing, and she wouldn't be available for evening appointments any longer. Since then, Vicky attempted to contact her regularly, at least once a week, trying to find a time to work Nora in. She might as well get this over with.

"I just can't commit to evenings anymore, remember?" She was tired of reiterating herself to the woman. Was she daft? Did she not have a family of her own to go home to? "I need to be home with the kids."

"What about Jake? Can he keep the children while we meet?"

"That won't be happening anymore." The snippy remark slipped out before she thought about how it might sound.

Vicky didn't say anything for a few moments, and in the ensuing silence, Nora wondered what would happen if she just hung up on the woman.

"Have you two split up? Is he not living at home anymore? Is that why you're no longer available?"

"No, no, and no. Look Vicky," Nora rolled down her window to let a little of the crispy fall air in. "Things are really tough right now. I can't trust him. I won't trust him, and I'm really having a hard time even praying for him. I'm not leaving him, and I don't think he has any plans to leave me right now, either, but honestly, I don't think I would care if he did."

"Wow."

"Yeah. Wow. And I think you and I meeting right now would be a waste of your time, and of my money. Money that I'm now making less of because of him. And I won't leave the kids in his care, unless it's a dire emergency."

"What happened?"

"He started drinking again. To prove that I can't tell him what to do."

"Wow," Vicky said again. "And he's still at home?"

"Well, like I said, he *started* drinking again. He went out one night—in fact, it was the night I was supposed to meet with you and canceled—and he came home plastered. The next morning he tried to confess to me about his shenanigans with some little waitress. So," Nora shrugged, even though she knew Vicky couldn't see her. "I don't think he's had anything since, but I'm not going back to the way things were. I'm not giving him any chances."

"What are you going to do?"

"Exactly what I'm doing. He's living in my house, eating my food, and sharing in family time with my children, only because he also happens to be my husband. I'm taking care of all the responsibilities. I'm working, I'm paying the bills, and I'm making sure that the children's lives aren't turned upside down by his selfishness."

"He's working then?"

"I don't really know. But I don't care, Vicky."

"Wow."

"I wish you'd stop saying that."

"Sorry, Nora. That was insensitive of me." Vicky apologized sincerely, then she continued. "Can we perhaps get together another time? Maybe in the morning, sometime next week?"

Nora clenched her jaw and leaned back in her seat. The woman was tenacious, she'd give her that. "I don't think so. I think I need to just let things go for a bit. I know where you are and how to get a hold of you if I change my mind, Vicky." She sighed, realizing how her words sounded. "This isn't a brush-off, really," she lied. "I just don't think it will be very productive for either of us."

"No offense taken, Nora. I just have two things to ask of you."

"Shoot."

"I want you to try, I mean, *really* try, to put aside these feelings and pray for your husband, Nora. It is imperative to hold him up, especially after he has fallen so hard, and you may be the only one doing so. Can you do that?"

"I can try."

"Okay. The other question. Would you mind if I called you periodically? Just to make sure you're not imploding or falling apart?"

"Sure, that's fine. I think I can handle that." Nora half-heartedly smiled into the phone. She said her good-byes and dropped the device back into her purse. Just as she opened the door, it rang again.

"Gah!" She plucked it out of her purse again; this time is was Jake. She couldn't help feeling the surge of guilt over not one, but two phone calls from people who would not be thrilled with where she was at that moment. Taking a deep breath, she pushed the send button and answered.

"Sonora Décor. This is Nora." She used her professional greeting.

"Hey, Nor." He obviously didn't get the subtle snub. "I've got dinner covered for tonight, but I have to run to the store. Do you need anything?"

"I'm good, Jake." She didn't expound.

"Okay. Um, do you want me to pick up the kids while I'm out?"

"Nope. I'll get them." She was getting impatient.

"Are you sure? I can plan picking them up around the grocery store, and you can get some more time in at the office. You were saying you needed more time last night."

"Jake, you're not driving the kids around. Is that all you need?"

Now he was miffed; she could hear it in his voice. "Yep. That's all I need." He spoke in a clipped tone. "I'll let you get back to whatever it is you're doing that's so important. See ya." He hung up without waiting for her to answer. Nora stared at the flashing screen on her phone, rolled her eyes, and dropped it back into her purse.

THIRTEEN

Nora slid out of her seat, stretched a little in the open door of her car, then headed inside Paradise Lost. The name sounded more like a cheesy lounge than an art gallery to her, but somehow it worked. Once again, she was swept away by the intensity of the artwork around her, but her eyes instantly scanned the room for Isolde. Things had been moved around, but she still easily recognized Tristan's work.

Isolde, however, was nowhere to be seen.

"Welcome. Let me know if you need any help, okay?" It was Janelle, the same woman manning the desk the last time. "Oh, hello! You were here several weeks ago! Welcome back, then." Nora caught a hint of a slight Scottish accent, something she'd not noticed before.

"You remember me?" She was a little surprised the woman recognized her. They'd barely spoken; she'd spent most of her time wandering the gallery with Tristan, and she hadn't even said goodbye when they left for Tristan's studio.

"I try to remember everyone who comes in here." Janelle smiled warmly, her eyes studying Nora in a way that made her feel like she was being measured. "Usually once you've been, you keep coming back, and I want to make sure you feel welcome. Remembering faces really helps. Names, now, that's a bit of a different story."

The curator waved a clutch of receipts in her direction. "But yours, I remember. Nora, right? Tristan asks about you all the time, wondering if you've been back in. He'll be thrilled to find you here today." She said it so matter-of-factly that Nora couldn't tell if she was teasing her or not. But she was secretly flattered to hear that he'd asked about her.

"Oh. Well, yes, I'm Nora. And I'm still surprised you remembered." She reached into her purse to for the card she'd received from Suzi, prepared to ask Janelle about them. She hesitated when she saw the way she was still being studied, as though Janelle was trying to find some answers. Then she spoke, slowly at first, carefully choosing her words.

"Well, I'm not surprised to see you again, but I must admit, I did think it would be sooner than this. He's quite a charmer, our Tristan, isn't he?"

"Um. Yes. Charming." She was beginning to be embarrassed in a way that wasn't quite so flattering. "That he is. But I didn't really come to see him." Now she just sounded silly, but at least she had evidence. She handed the beautiful card to Janelle, who took it, glanced at it quickly, and looked at her with questions in her eyes. "Did this come from your gallery? I thought I recognized the artwork."

"I'm fairly certain it did. We periodically put out card sets, especially around gift holidays like Christmas, Valentine's Day, Mother's and Father's Days, you see? If you look around, you'll notice our Christmas sets are on display, featuring all new artwork. They're dispersed around the gallery, near the corresponding pieces. They are lovely, aren't they?" Janelle went on for a few more minutes about how the cards are one of many methods they use to boost sales for the artists. "We also encourage them to change their pieces around on a regular basis to keep clients' interest. That means the artists must stay fairly prolific, or at least have an ample supply of their work already on hand, if they are to have a place in the showroom here. In fact, I'm expecting Tristan in some time this afternoon with more of his work. If you hadn't noticed, his area is a wee bit sparse. He's sold a few pieces recently, and it's long past time for him to restock." She swept a hand in the general direction of his work and Nora looked again, hoping to see the swaying curves of his *Isolde,* perhaps hiding in a corner or some other unassuming spot.

"I'm sorry. I'm just babbling on and on, aren't I? Is there anything specific I can help you with, or are you just here to wander a bit?"

"Well, the card, of course, and actually, you may have already answered my other question." There was a hollow place forming in the pit of her belly at the thought of *Isolde* being sold to some stranger, and she was almost afraid to ask. "Did he sell the statue of the girl, *Isolde*?"

"You liked that one, did you, now?" Janelle's voice softened, making her accent more noticeable. "She was a beauty, wasn't she? No, she didn't sell, at least not that I know. Tristan took her back to his studio to work on her a bit, or so he told me. He sometimes does that. I've come to accept the frustrating fact that artists are never satisfied with their finished products." She smiled brightly. "You might find something else of his you like, though. I know he has several smaller pieces that are similar in style and form. You look around and let me know if you need anything, all right?" The curator tapped the image on the card, then handed it back to Nora. "If you're interested in this artist, Rhonaad's work, you'll find more of his pieces upstairs."

"Thank you, Janelle." She tucked the card from Suzi back inside its envelope, and slipped it in the side pocket of her purse as she made her way slowly around the gallery, taking in all the new artwork. Just relocating the artists to different parts of the showroom, and shuffling their pieces around, seemed to change the whole atmosphere of the gallery, and she almost felt like she was seeing it for the first time. She finally made her way to Tristan's work and lingered a little longer, seeing a few things she remembered, and many she thought were new since she'd been in. His style was quite recognizable to her, almost as though having been inside his studio had given her an inside connection to him. She shivered a little at the intimacy of the notion.

She headed upstairs, but this time, instead of perusing everything again, she went straight to his corner. He had several new pieces on display, but she was especially intrigued by a series called *Drowning*. There were five large canvases on one wall, and she stood before them in rapt appreciation. The movement and the colors, each one was so unique that they could be sold separately, and the individual owners would be fully satisfied. Yet displayed together, the effect was incredibly powerful, and it seemed almost criminal to even consider separating them. The constant theme was water, flowing, rushing, falling water, and Nora believed if she touched one of the paintings, her fingers would come away wet.

She stood there for several minutes before pulling away to look at some of his other pieces. On another wall were several of his darker, disturbing paintings, and this time, since no one was with her, she reached out to touch one with shards of glass protruding from a man's open mouth. The way he utilized trash still intrigued her, and when she noted the price tag on this horrible piece, she realized that his work must intrigue others, too; others with far more money than she had.

"Yikes," she muttered to herself, withdrawing her hand, suddenly afraid to even stand too closely, lest her very presence send something tumbling to the floor. She meandered from painting to painting, taking her time at each one, imagining Tristan wielding his brushes and palette knives, and odd pieces of trash.

Nora came up short in front of one of the smaller framed canvases in the room, her sharp gasp at a discord with the soft ambient music. She brought a hand up to her mouth, a mixture of dismay and pleasure coursing through her.

The painting was perched on a tall pedestal, set in a way that forced the viewer to come closer to look fully on it. Although the woman in the painting was turned away from the artist, everything about her sparked recognition in Nora. The dress was a replica of the one she wore the day she met Tristan. The way her hair fell long and loose down her back, even down to the over-full curve of her hips she made a point to look at in her mirror every morning; it was all her. What was so lovely about the painting was the way Tristan had blurred all the lines of her body, as though not quite sure he could keep her captive in a painting. Her skirt, all shades of blues and greens, swept out into the same hues in the background, tendrils of long hair wisped away into nothing, and her profile, soft and subtle, looked almost smudged, like the memory of her features was beginning to fade from the artist's mind. But there was no doubt, even without looking at the name on the placard, that this was a painting of her.

"Oh my." She spoke in a hushed murmur behind her fingers.

"Did you find yourself?" Tristan's voice, soft from behind her, startled her, but she didn't turn around. She couldn't, not yet. How on earth was she supposed to react in front of him? She'd wondered if he'd thought of her at all since they'd met, but this was far more than fleeting thoughts.

"You said you were a little lost that day, remember?"

She had to move. She had to speak, to break the spell he was casting. His words, uttered in a low rumble, seemed to reach out and wrap themselves around her.

"I had to capture something of you before I lost you altogether."

"It's beautiful," she said simply, dropping her hand and glancing over her shoulder at him. Her gaze landed in the middle of his chest covered in gray cable knit, then traveled up, up, up to his chin, his mouth, his eyes…. But he was studying the painting, not her, and she swallowed the lump in her throat so she could speak. "I'm amazed. And flattered."

She eyed the painting again, a little askance, embarrassed to seem too intrigued with the image of herself. "That's actually how I felt that day; blurry around the edges. A strong breeze probably could have swept me away. You captured me, I must admit."

"Did I?" He turned to face her now. "Is that why you came back?"

She knew what he was asking, but she faked ignorance. "Actually, I wanted to see your *Isolde,* but she's gone." She glanced around the room as though searching for signs of the missing girl. "When Janelle told me you'd sold some of your pieces, I was very sad to think she was one of them. I pictured her stuck in the middle of the foyer of some austere, cold mansion, and it broke my heart."

"Well, then you'll be relieved to know she's stuck in the middle of my studio awaiting a change of clothes. And I'm glad to be the one to mend your broken heart." He smiled at her in a way that made it hard to breathe. She looked away; no, it wasn't the smile. He was taking up all the air just by standing so close to her. "You can come visit my *Isolde* any time you like. You still have my number, don't you?"

She ignored the invitation. "Janelle told me you were working on her. But what do you mean, she's getting a change of clothes? Can you do that? Should you do that? I thought her tattered gown was beautiful." She stopped abruptly and clamped her lips shut, crossing her arms loosely in front or her.

"What? What's the matter?" He reached out, but didn't quite touch her. She saw his eyes dart to the ring on her left hand where it rested on her right bicep. Her fingers curled into a fist of their accord.

"You can stop me at any time, Tristan. I'm sorry. You're the artist. Who am I to tell you what you can, and can't, or should, and shouldn't do to your own creations? I'm sorry." She shook her head at her own presumptuousness.

"No, don't be sorry. It's good for me to get feedback, especially when I'm considering altering a piece I thought was finished. Just because no one is interested in it, doesn't necessarily mean there's something wrong with it, right? I value your opinion. I appreciate your honesty." He paused momentarily for effect. "I appreciate you." He ran his fingers along the frame of the painting, slowly, gently, and Nora felt a small tremor race up her spine. She could almost feel his hand following the curve of her back, touching her skin the way he touched the artwork. She took a small step away from him.

"Why didn't you call me?" He spoke without looking at her, but she could tell it wasn't because he was insecure. In fact, Nora was pretty sure he was teasing her, challenging her, as though he knew full well how often she'd considered doing just that. She didn't reply.

"I've thought about you every day since we met, Nora. Have you thought about me at all?"

Nora still didn't answer. How could she? How could she tell him not a day had gone by when she didn't catch herself daydreaming, replaying that one short afternoon over and over in her imagination. How could she tell him that she wished everything was different, that she wanted nothing more than to relive that afternoon with him, only this time without the awkward goodbye.

Finally, her voice a little shaky, she answered him. "Yes, I have. I shouldn't think about you, but I do." She turned to walk away, the admission causing her to flush with shame. She only made it as far as the series of water paintings on the large wall.

Tristan followed her and stopped right behind her; she was certain she could feel the heat of his body against her back, and she took a step forward. His voice caressed her neck, her ears, making her cheeks warm.

"Drowning," he murmured. "Do you remember? When you stood there with that look on your face, that look that made me want to... to... capture you, you said *Isolde* was drowning. The way the word flowed out of you made me feel like these paintings." His voice dropped even lower, his words like cool water over her flushed skin. "But like I was the one drowning."

She spun around and glared up at him. "Enough. Enough, Tristan. Okay? Stop, please."

He was so close, she could see flecks of charcoal in his umber eyes. He stared down at her, hungry, potent. She put both hands up between them, stopping just short of touching his chest. "I'm sorry. I can't do this. I shouldn't have come back. I need to go."

Before she could slip around him, he grabbed both her wrists, and held her there, not letting her go. She tried to pull away, suddenly afraid. "Why do you always have to go? Why did you come back, only to run away again?" He brought one of her hands up and pressed a warm kiss into her palm. Her fingers relaxed against the curve of his cheek before she caught herself, and she jerked her hand away.

Skirting pedestals and sculptures, she made her way to the stairs, fleeing him on trembling legs. At the bottom, she slowed long enough to say goodbye to Janelle, then she hurried out the door to her car. This time, she had her keys out and ready, and she was locked inside before he stepped out of the gallery, her card from Suzi in his hands. It must have fallen from her purse when she pulled away to escape him. He walked toward her, and she hesitated, not sure whether to ignore him and pull out, or acknowledge him from the safety of her vehicle. Her indecision gave him the time he needed with his long stride. He stood just outside her window and waited.

When she rolled down the window, he smiled, a little sadly, a little teasingly. "SoNora Décor. I like it. Here you go." He handed her the card, its envelope bearing her business name and address, giving him more information than she wanted him to have. "May I call you?"

"No, Tristan." She couldn't believe how proper he sounded over something so inappropriate. He'd seen her wedding band; she made no attempt to hide it.

"Well, may I hire you then?"

"Hire me? For what? You're an artist. You don't need me."

"You're wrong there, Nora. I think I do need you." He dropped his gaze to his feet and Nora rolled her eyes at the postured embarrassment.

"Well, so do my husband and children, Tristan. They need me, too."

"Ah." He stepped back, and crossed his arms over his chest, his expression closed. Then he spoke again, words that came out a little too smoothly, as though he'd used them before. "Maybe you're going about this all wrong. Maybe this isn't about who needs you, but about who *you* need."

She clutched the steering wheel with both hands, holding on for dear life. His forwardness made her feel off balance and juvenile and... and so alive. As though he could read her thoughts, he spoke again, his voice smooth; sensitive.

"Who do *you* need, Nora?" Everything thrummed inside of her, a bundle of live wires. Finally, she opened her mouth and the words spilled out.

"I don't know, okay? I don't know what I want, or who I want. I thought I came back here today because I wanted to see your *Isolde,* but now I don't even know that." She smiled bitter-sweetly and met his gaze. "Honestly, I don't seem to know anything right now. Which means I need to go. Now."

As she rolled up her window, she heard him say, "Come to my studio if you want to see *Isolde.*"

FOURTEEN

She still had some time before picking up the kids, so she headed back to the office. She desperately wanted to go home and crawl under the covers, but with Jake there, she couldn't.

"Why did you come back, only to run away again?' Tristan asked, over and over in her head.

Yes, why? Why did she feel compelled to visit Paradise Lost and *Isolde* after leaving Renee's company, her sordid tales burning in Nora's ears?

Tristan. Why did he have this pull on her? Nora didn't flirt and tease; she didn't have time for it. Jake was the one in their marriage who couldn't control himself, not her. She was the strong one...and yet, around Tristan, she felt vulnerable, exposed, and intrigued all at the same time.

The way she'd felt around Jake when they'd first met.

The way she hadn't felt around Jake in a long time.

She pulled into her designated parking spot leaned back in her seat, closing her eyes and pinching the bridge of her nose in exasperation. "Get a grip, Nor," she muttered. "You don't need this right now."

Who do you need, Nora? Tristan wouldn't be silent.

Who did she need? That question was much more difficult to answer than it should be.

"I suppose I need You, God," she whispered. "But You don't seem to show up much anymore." She shook her head and climbed out of the car, the sound of her closing door echoing loudly in the parking structure. She opened the door and slammed it again, simply for the satisfaction of the racket it made.

Just as she stepped through the front door of her office building, Jo came out of the restroom in the small lobby. She took one look at Nora's face and snorted. "Oh dear. You look like you've been slapped by your mother. Let's get you inside where you can unload a little."

"Thanks, I think." But Nora smiled, grateful for Jo's tough girl exterior that harbored a kind heart. She flopped down on the client sofa in her showroom while Jo started a fresh pot of coffee in the little kitchenette adjacent to it. Laying her head back against the cushions behind her, she closed her eyes.

I need you. She heard his voice inside her head. *Who do you need?* She shivered as she remembered the way his fingers caressed the painting of her, as though he, too, imagined her body beneath his touch.

She opened her eyes abruptly and sat forward. "Stop it, Nora."

Jo leaned against the open door of the kitchenette and studied her. "You still dying, honey?"

Nora sighed heavily. "Don't tease me, Jo. I'm feeling pretty fragile today."

"So what's up? Jake? The kids?"

Nora groaned this time. "Tristan."

Jo crossed the room and pulled up a chair so that she sat facing her. Her chopped blonde hair stuck out all over her head like wind-blown wheat, and Nora knew it required a lot of expensive hair products to stand at attention like that. "Who on earth is Tristan? As in Tristan and Isolde?"

Nora couldn't help but laugh. "Yeah. Exactly."

"I don't think you're dying, girlfriend. I think you're just going crazy. What are you talking about?" Jo's legs were crossed, and she began jostling the foot that dangled in the air. "You got something to tell me, Toots?"

Nora looked down at her watch. "I have almost an hour. How much time do you have?"

"Oh. I see. Well, let me lock my office first. You pour us some coffee." Jo stood up and patted Nora on the head. "I'll be right back. You need anything? A little something medicinal to put in your coffee?" Jo had a small liquor cabinet she kept stocked for special occasions. Nora laughed and reminded her that she had to pick up her kids.

"But go ahead if you want some. You might need it when you hear what I've been up to."

"Up to, huh? This sounds yummy. I'll be right back. Coffee," she reminded Nora with a nod toward the kitchenette.

By the time Nora had finished her tale, Jo was frowning. "Nora, Nora. This is not good. You know how I feel about Jake, honey, but what you're playing at isn't the answer to that problem. You don't take on another man while you still have one at home."

"But I'm not taking him on, Jo. That's why I'm so miserable."

"Ah, but you are, Nora. And that's why you're so miserable." Jo used Nora's words against her. She put a hand over her heart. "I know these things, honey. I've been around the block a few times, and I *know* these things. I can see it in your eyes. You're trying to figure out how you can have your cake and eat it, too. Well, you can't. It never works. That, I can guarantee you." Jo clucked at her a few times, then took a sip of her coffee, her eyes never leaving Nora's face.

"I walked away, though," Nora defended herself. "I drove away. I told him not to call."

"But you went back to him once. What's to keep you from going back again?"

"I didn't go back to him. I went back to the studio and his sculpture. But I'm not going back; don't worry." Nora shook her head emphatically. "I just can't."

Jo rolled her eyes. "Mm-hm. And what's to keep him from calling you? Or even coming here, now that he knows where you work?" She voiced the question that Nora had been afraid to put into words.

"I don't know. I would hope that he'd have enough respect—"

Her friend cut her off. "Respect? Did he show respect when he tried to hit on a married lady?"

"He didn't know I was married until today."

Jo waved a hand at Nora's ring finger and raised her eyebrows, obvious she wasn't falling for the excuse

"He probably didn't notice it that first time. He seemed surprised today when he saw it."

"Was he wearing a ring the first time you two met?"

"No." She had checked.

"Huh. You noticed, why wouldn't he?" Jo was shaking her porcupine head back and forth repeatedly, and Nora wanted to reach over and grab her chin to hold it steady. "Stop kidding yourself, Nora. He noticed. He also noticed that you came back for him. He also noticed when you admitted that you think about him all the time. He also noticed—"

"Okay!" Nora interrupted. "I get it. He noticed. What was I saying before you interrupted me?"

"Respect, Nora. The man doesn't respect your decision to be married."

"Well maybe it's because I don't respect it either," she said flippantly, defiantly. "You know, I think I hate you right now."

"Good. That means I'm probably right, and you're probably wrong." Jo tipped her mug back, drinking down the last of its contents, then set it on the floor beside her chair. She stood up and came over to sit beside Nora on the sofa, putting an arm around her. "Besides all that respect stuff, honey, I'm wondering about your faith. Is this something you're really going to be able to live with? Are you going to be able to show up in church on Sunday, and in your Bible classes on Wednesday, and talk about Jesus while you're screwing some hunky artist across town all the other days of the week?"

"Jo!" Nora was appalled by how crude it all sounded.

"I've got a point, don't I? This goes against everything you believe in. That's why you're still with Jake, right?" She paused and leaned forward, turning in order to look Nora in the eye. "So do you not believe in all that anymore?"

Unable to sit still any longer, Nora began pacing the floor. "I don't know, Jo. I always thought I was so sure about my faith, about my beliefs. But lately I feel like I've been abandoned. You know I've been meeting with a counselor, right?"

"Vicky someone."

"Yes. She has me praying for my husband and writing lists, things about Jake I'm thankful for. But I'm beginning to despair. For every one thing that I'm thankful, a million other things come to mind I want to change about him. It's almost making things worse. And God? Well, I haven't heard from Him in so long I don't think I'd recognize Him if He walked up to me and slapped me." She covered her heart with her hands and stopped pacing. "It's like He's turned His back on me. I can't feel Him here anymore." Her eyes glistened, but she didn't cry.

Now Jo leaned back into the cushions behind her and closed her eyes for a few moments. When she finally opened them, she looked straight into Nora's, and said, "You've changed, honey. Do you know that? You're a wreck. You've lost weight, you're jumpy, you're just not you. It's like you're a little bit see through, I think. I'm not so sure God went anywhere, Toots. I think you've wandered away from Him." She stood up, put both hands on Nora's cheeks, and made her look at her up close.

"You listen here. You stay away from that place, you understand me? I want you to give me his card, and I want you to call me immediately if he shows up here. He is off limits because you are off limits, got it? I want the old Nora back, and you, my fine replica, simply won't cut it. Now go fetch your children, and the four of you spend some quality family time together tonight, okay?"

Nora nodded mutely. Jo must be worried about her, to the point of encouraging her to spend time with Jake.

"I didn't hear you."

"Yes, Mother."

"That's better."

It helped to talk to Jo. It always did. She was so down-to-earth and real. Nora couldn't help but compare her counsel to Vicky's, and she wondered how Vicky might have advised her today. Pray. Pray. And pray some more. Nora was getting tired of praying. No, she thought to herself, I'm not tired of praying. I'm tired of asking for help and not getting any. I'm tired of being ignored by God. I'm tired of feeling like I'm sitting outside in the cold, knowing there's a warm fire blazing inside somewhere, but no one remembered to let me in.

And I'm tired of pretending I'm thankful for Jake. I'm not.

Talking to Jo, however, had brought her up short. Even though she felt a little defensive and somewhat foolish, it had been good to hear the woman put things in such a blaring light. The least she could do was release Jake before she started pursuing someone else. And even that sounded selfish, and childish...and very, very Renee-ish.

Renee. She had so much to do this week in preparation for the Wine and Dine Gala. Renee wanted all new window treatments hung in the Country Club Garden Room, which was crazy enough in itself. But they would all come down as soon as the event was over, and Renee didn't care what happened to them after that.

"We won't ever use them again, you know. They're like an evening gown for the windows. You can't wear the same thing twice, right?" The theme was *The French Garden in Winter*, and Renee had Nora ordering a ridiculous amount of custom iron pieces for centerpieces, décor, and more. Her order for silk plants was the largest Nora had ever placed, but Renee wanted unique and high-end items; topiaries, and exotic ferns, all frosted with a delicate sparkle of artificial snow. It would be a great month financially for Nora when it was all over, but she would be working hard for every penny of it.

"So much for quality family time tonight," she grumbled as she sat in the car waiting for Felix. She would have to go back to the office tonight. Maybe they could just go out for dinner; some place the kids would like. That might appease everyone, including her frazzled nerves.

FIFTEEN

Jake glanced up at the clock for what seemed the tenth time in the last half an hour. The laundry was done and even put away, and so were the dishes. His Blazer sparkled in the sun after its bath and waxing at the car wash, and the yard was raked into submission, the few leaves left on the sweet gum tree quivering on their branches, afraid to let go. His desk was organized, the paperwork in three piles; incoming, outgoing, and to file.

The incoming held one sheet of paper in it, a notice for renewing his Inspector's license. He really wanted to talk it over with Nora, whether or not to continue in his line of work, but he knew what she'd ask him: What would he do if he wasn't doing inspections?

He didn't have an answer for that question, and until he did, he couldn't talk to her.

Everything in his life seemed to be in limbo these days. He had little or no work, he didn't spend much time with the kids, and being alone with Nora happened only between the hours of midnight and 6 a.m. He didn't know how on earth she was surviving the pace she was setting. The holidays were almost upon them, and he knew Nora's work load typically nearly doubled with the season's events. He wondered how she would manage.

His phone rang and woke him out of his reverie. It was Nora. "Hey, Babe."

"Jake. It's me, Nora."

He knew it was her. He didn't call anyone else Babe.

"I'm just calling about dinner tonight and wondering if you'll be home. Because I was thinking we might go out someplace fun for the kids. It's been a long day, and it'd be nice not to have to cook. I thought it might be nice just to do something a little special with the whole family, just because. What do you think?"

It was the longest string of words he'd heard come out of her mouth in weeks. "I'm fine with that. Or I can cook tonight. You can come home and put your feet up, or soak in a hot bath." He glanced around the house, glad now that his nervous energy had kept him busy making the place shine. She could come home to peace and order, and relax a little. Surely, she would like that. "Maybe we could rent a couple movies. We haven't seen *The Great Pumpkin* yet this month. I'd even tolerate a chick flick if you'll snuggle with me on the couch."

He heard her intake of breath through the phone, and realized with a grimace that he'd just made some very misguided assumptions. She had no plans to take the evening off, and dinner out with the family was her token peace offering.

"I can't, Jake. I mean, dinner and a short movie with the kids sounds fine, but after they go to bed, I need to head back to the office. Renee is in charge of her Country Club's Wine and Dine Christmas Gala, and she's just given me a to-do list that makes my head spin. I have to get things in the computer, and place my orders as soon as possible, or stuff won't get here in time. Besides, you'll just fall asleep anyway, and I'll be left crying alone in my hot chocolate." She was trying to make light of the situation, he knew, but it didn't sit well with him.

"I don't understand. Okay, so we don't have to snuggle on the couch, but I thought you weren't going back to the office these days. I thought you were working from home in the evenings again. At least you'd be here with us, even if you couldn't join us. And you can use my office if we're too loud. You know how much I hate thinking of you locked up in that building, all alone, late at night."

"I have too much to do, Jake. I won't get enough done at home. Like you said, I don't do this often anymore, but tonight, I'm asking you to keep the kids while I work here at the office. I'll be back before you know it."

He really didn't have much say in the matter. "Will you wake me up when you get home?"

"I always do."

There was a short, stilted silence that followed her comment. Then she spoke again, her words overly bright. "I need to get off the phone. Felix and I are parked a bit farther out than usual, and Leslie can't see us. We'll be home soon, okay?"

"Okay. I really wouldn't mind cooking, you know. It might be nice just to stay home and—" But the line was dead in his hands.

To Jake's surprise, everyone opted to have him cook after all. Nora and the kids had stopped by the grocery store on their way home and picked up fixings for Chicken Alfredo, a family favorite, some soft French bread, a salad, and *The Great Pumpkin*. Les and Felix had even convinced her to buy microwave popcorn, a rare treat in their household, along with the first carton of eggnog of the season. It was sizing up to be a fine night.

Dinner went smoothly with the kids talking about their days, and Nora regaling them with tales of Renee's outrageousness, albeit she kept the woman's more sordid adventures to herself. Jake had heard enough about Renee that even the thought of meeting her scared him a little. But she had a little dog that was out of control, and she took him everywhere she went, causing all kinds of trouble. She went through landscapers like hotcakes because she loved topiaries, and the young men who trimmed hers always did it badly, inadvertently lopping off leafy heads, or other various body parts.

Jake chimed in when he could, but had little to contribute because his day had been so uneventful. The kids didn't press him for more than a short story about a homeless man he met at the car wash.

"Did you give him any money, Dad?"

"No, but we walked across the street together, and I bought him lunch. We ate burgers and talked about where he came from. Poor guy. He's trying to get in on a Salvation Army program, but he keeps falling off the wagon, so they won't take him."

"What's that mean, falling off the wagon?" Felix asked around a mouthful of pasta. "Sounds like a float in a parade."

"Actually, you're not too far off. He's an alcoholic, Felix, and he wants to quit drinking. Every time he tries, though, he ends up giving in and drinking again. That's what it means to fall off the wagon; first you quit drinking, then you start up again. You either get to participate in the parade of life, or you fall off the wagon and get stuck lying in the dirt alongside the road, watching life pass you by."

"Jake." Nora gave him a raised eyebrow across the table. "I think they get the picture."

Leslie interjected with a question about History, and she and Nora talked briefly about the black plague until Felix wanted to know what the plague was. When Leslie described in detail the puss-filled boils and the blood coming from all orifices, Jake put an end to it, and turned the conversation to the movie they were going to watch.

"*The Great Pumpkin* is one of my childhood memories, guys. I used to pick one of the pumpkins Grandpa was growing and baby that thing up until the night before Halloween. It was always perfectly shaped, a brilliant orange, and huge. I never entered any contests or anything, but I grew some massive pumpkins."

"And you always named your pumpkin Linus. Or Snoopy." Leslie finished for him, grinning good-naturedly at the story their father told every time they watched the movie.

The movie was a hit. So was the popcorn and eggnog. In fact, the whole impromptu family night was a success. After putting the kids to bed, Jake and Nora straightened the living room and kitchen together.

"I'm going to take a shower," she said, heading down the hall toward their bedroom. Jake smiled to himself. Maybe she had changed her mind about going back to the office. Maybe she'd enjoyed the evening so much she'd decided to stay home tonight, after all. With him.

In the kitchen, he pulled a couple of mugs out of the cupboard and put on the kettle to boil, then he hurried to the bedroom to make sure the bed was clear and neat; ready. But when Nora emerged from the bathroom, she wore a pair of jeans and a sweatshirt.

"I've got to go back to work, Jake," she said, frowning when the kettle began to whistle, and she saw the two mugs waiting beside the stove. She reached for her purse and keys she'd left on the end of the counter and headed for the door.

Jake stopped her, pulling her into his arms, accidentally knocking her purse out of her hand. "Are you sure this stuff can't wait until tomorrow? I'll help in any way I can," he whispered. "I don't want to you leave." He pressed a kiss to her forehead then tipped her face up so he could kiss her mouth. She returned the kiss briefly, then pulled away.

"I need to go, Jake."

No. She couldn't leave. Not after he'd convinced himself she wasn't. "Just stay home with me, please. I need you, Nora. I need you here. And I know you need a good night's rest. Don't go." He cupped her face in his hands, not caring that he begged.

"Actually, I need to go so that I *can* come home and get a good night's sleep." She pushed him away and bent down to scoop up her purse. "Don't wait up for me."

Without considering the consequences, he moved around her to lean against the front door, blocking her way. He was suddenly overwhelmed with a sense of urgency to make her stay. "Nor. Please stay home tonight."

"What are you doing, Jake?" She looked at him with raised eyebrows, and he could see she was beginning to get angry. But then, so was he. Why couldn't she take a night off and spend some time with him?

"I want you to stay home. I've asked nicely, but you don't seem to be listening, so this is me being more assertive. I'm not letting you go. You need to get some rest, and I need you in my bed. You're staying home." He threw the dead bolt, latched the chain in place, and turned to eye her defiantly.

"You're joking, right?" Nora's tone was incredulous. "You're going to lock me in the house tonight?" She spun on her heels and headed for the door to the garage.

"Oh, no you don't." Jake was there before her, locking that door, too. A ringing in his ears prevented him from thinking about anything except keeping her here "You're staying home."

"You're crazy, Jake. You're insane. You're freaking me out." She stood in the middle of the kitchen and watched him move around the room, pulling blinds closed, turning off lights, checking windows and doors again.

"Come on. Let's go to bed." He stepped close to her and reached for her hand, but she slapped his arm away.

"I'm not going anywhere with you," she growled as she dug around in her purse for her cell phone. "I'm calling the police; that's what I'm doing. I'm going to file an imprisonment charge against you, you... you freak!"

She dialed 911 and was just about to push send when Jake grabbed the phone out of her hand, appalled at how quickly things had escalated out of control. This was not the way he'd intended this all to happen.

"Stop it, Nora! Just stop it! You're seriously going to call the cops on me for wanting you to stay home with me? Good grief! Go then. Just go. Get out of here. Hope you have a terrific time with yourself." He threw her phone across the kitchen table and into the living room, where it bounced off a couch cushion and landed in the plush carpet, none the worse for wear. Nora glared at him, then she headed out the front door without her phone.

SIXTEEN

"What on earth was *that?*" Nora's mind was spinning, her scalp prickled, and her heart raced She was appalled by her husband's uncharacteristic behavior tonight. Things had been going so smoothly up until she came out of the bathroom and saw the assumption in his eyes. She'd made it inarguably clear that she had to go back to work after their family night, and had even stayed longer than she'd planned. Did he really think his aggression would make her want to spend more time with him?

In the light of day, maybe he would come to his senses and they could talk about it...but then she remembered how she'd felt weeks ago, when she'd been so cruel to him, and he'd wanted to talk the next morning. Well, she simply didn't have time to think about it right now. Renee's list was ridiculously extravagant, and Nora hoped that getting a jump-start on it right now while everything was fresh in her mind, would make for an easier load the rest of the week. She glanced at the clock. Ten-thirty. It was later than she'd hoped, but she set her mental timer for midnight, making herself a goal to be finished ordering the big stuff by the time she came back home.

Half an hour later the office phone rang, and she remembered her cell phone, lying where Jake had tossed it, on the carpet in the living room. She couldn't believe his nerve. She picked up the phone and spoke into it without so much as a greeting. "You are amazing, you know that? You absolutely blow my mind. What are you doing calling me here?"

There followed an uncomfortable silence, then a chuckle that sent shivers up her spine. "First I'm awkwardly stimulating. Now I'm amazing, and I blow your mind. I'm beginning to think you like me, Miss SoNora Decor."

She gulped hard in an effort to regroup and breathe, then she repeated her question, her tone much less aggressive. "What are you doing calling me here?"

Tristan spoke at the same time. "What are you doing in your office at this time of night?" Then he chuckled again and asked, "Okay. Do you want to go first, or shall I?"

"Look, Tristan." She decided to end this quickly with a little honesty. "It hasn't been a good night. I thought you were my husband hounding me about working late again. Sorry I jumped on you, but this isn't good timing."

"I didn't expect to take up any of your time, Nora. That's why I called so late, just to leave you a message. Would you like me to hang up and call back?" His voice was low and husky, as though he was settling in for the night. "Let it go to voice-mail. Then you'll have something to look forward to in the morning."

Something sparked inside her head. Nora took a deep breath and let it out slowly, his words making her bold, and...reckless. "Actually, what are you doing right now?"

"I'm sitting here at my drawing table, watching my *Isolde* move in the shadows. I couldn't help but think of you."

"You're not at home?"

"Yes, I'm at home. My studio is upstairs, remember? Why? What's up?"

"Oh! Oh, I didn't realize you lived there, too." The thought hadn't occurred to her that the rest of the old Victorian was actually a home, *his* home. She'd assumed it had been converted into offices like so many of the old homes in the downtown areas.

As though reading her mind, he explained, "It was apartments when I bought it several years ago—for a steal, I'm proud to say—and I turned it back into a home. Houses aren't built the way they used to be, and I think they need to be preserved, if at all possible. I fell in love with this place the first time I saw it and probably would have bought it, even if it didn't have the turret."

"I feel the same way about the old houses." She smiled, pleased by his sentiment, but she was intent on something else, something she didn't even want to formulate into complete sentences in her mind. "Well, are you planning on going to bed any time soon?"

"These are rather personal questions, Nora," he teased after a brief pause. "Actually, I just got up here. I was planning on putting in a few hours before I call it a night."

Nora opened her mouth and let the words pour out before she changed her mind. "Would you like some company? If I bring my laptop and my pile of paperwork, can I clear a spot in the corner of your studio and do my work? I won't bother you, I promise. I just... I just suddenly don't feel like being here alone right now, but I *must* get some things done, and I can't go home and do it." She couldn't believe what she was suggesting.

Apparently, neither could he. "You want to come here? In the middle of the night? To work?"

She laughed at the incredulity in his voice. "Yes. Go there. In the middle of the night. To work. With you," she added, almost inaudibly.

"Well, then, I'll be watching for you. Are we pulling an all-nighter? Shall I put on the coffee?"

"Oh, coffee would be lovely." She ignored the all-nighter question, but thrilled at the rumble of satisfaction in his voice. "I'll be there in fifteen minutes." Her mind set, she refused to consider the consequences, whatever they may be. Instead, she slipped her laptop into its case, strapped it and her box of Renee's files to a wheeled trolley cart, and turned off the lights. She hurriedly locked up and climbed in her car, her heart racing from the rush, the adrenaline, and the unfamiliar urgency she felt.

Tristan was silhouetted in the turret window, the heavy drape pulled back so he could watch for her. She smiled as she saw him turn and disappear, the curtain falling back in place. A few moments later, he was emerging from the front door. She stayed in the car with the window rolled down until he was close enough to hear her quiet words.

"We have to discuss the rules before I get out." She'd had the whole ride over to think things through. She wanted to come, felt a wild need to be with him tonight, but she wasn't going to let things get out of control.

"Rules? We're playing games? I thought we weren't any good at games." He was teasing her again, but she remained firm.

"I'm serious, Tristan. I'm a little afraid of what I'm doing, okay?"

"Why are you afraid, Nora? I thought you were coming over here to work, so that neither one of us would have to be alone. Give yourself a little more credit; give me a little more credit."

"Even so, I need to put it out on the table so you and I are on the same page." Something about the way he was studying her made her feel like a fly on the lip of a carnivorous plant. She should run...but everything about him pulled at everything about her.

Traps are re—Shut up, Vicky.

"Hm." He crossed his arms and rocked back on his heels, his feet planted wide as he stared down at her. She tipped her head back a little more; she had to force her eyes to stay focused on his face, to keep her gaze from drifting over the rather distracting lines of his large frame. He wore faded jeans that had seen better days and a gray undershirt that pulled tightly across his chest. Work clothes. There was a streak of black paint along the ridge of his left forearm and his hands looked damp, like he'd washed them quickly before coming down to greet her.

"Rule number one." She began, holding up one finger, not waiting for him to agree or disagree. "You can't touch me. Rule number two: You can't kiss me. Rule number three: You can't have sex with me. Rule number four: You can't ask any questions about why I'm here, or why I don't want to be alone, or even why I was rude to you earlier today. You can't ask anything else that will make me feel guilty, okay?" Her voice shook, her palms were damp, and she knew if he reached out and touched her skin right now, his fingers would probably sizzle.

Under the yellow glow of the antique porch light, he looked almost menacing, staring down at her, his eyes narrowed. She took a deep breath to steady her nerves, but her nostrils were assailed by the aroma of balsam and citrus and something else. Turpentine?

Tristan. In that moment, she realized she already recognized the way he smelled.

She didn't exhale right away.

He continued to study her for a few more moments before responding. "Look Nora. I'm not really a rule kind of guy. I'm an artist, remember? I take other people's trash and turn it into masterpieces. My whole way of living is programmed to think outside the box. I can't promise you won't feel guilty for coming over here, because I can see you already do. I hope you're not here only because you're desperate, or because you feel badly about the way you treated me today, because that would really stink." He uncrossed his arms and leaned forward to rest his hands on the rim of the open window, throwing his face into deeper shadows. She could no longer see his eyes, but she could certainly feel the warmth of his gaze. "I'd like to think you came here because you want to be with me."

Her throat felt like it was closing up on her, so she simply nodded.

"Good. And your rules? Well, why don't we compromise? I will respect your boundaries, and I ask that you respect mine in return. I promise I won't do anything you don't want me to do, Nora, and I expect the same courtesy from you. Can we agree on that?"

Don't do it, Nor. Run! Run like mad in the opposite direction! Traps are real, remember? Run!

"Boundaries," she said, pulling her bottom lip between her teeth. Then she looked up at him. "I actually have them, though. Do you?"

Tristan burst out laughing and opened the door when she unlocked it. "Get out of the car, woman. It's cold out here, and I've got work to do. I'm in the middle of creating something, and I'm on a roll, so you'd better be on your best behavior, or I'll send you packing."

"I'm only here to work. I'll be as quiet as a mouse, I promise." Nora climbed out of the car and handed him her box of files. She slung her computer bag over her shoulder and followed him inside, enjoying the confident way he moved. They took the stairs up and he directed her to a big, overstuffed recliner in one corner of the turret.

"That wasn't there before," she noted.

"Yeah, it was. It was piled with junk, but I cleaned it up for you. It's usually my thinking and drinking chair, but tonight, you may honor it by placing your pretty backside in it." He set her box of files down in front of the chair, pulled a TV tray around for her to set her computer on, and turned to face her. "Will this work for you?"

"It's perfect," she whispered, suddenly at a loss, overwhelmed by the fact that she was here. She looked up with a shaky, vulnerable smile. "Thank you, Tristan."

He reached for her then, breaking her first rule, and she went into his arms willingly. She took another deep breath full of his scent, and let it out slowly, savoring the way she felt cradled against him. Then they broke her second rule. And her third.

But no one asked any questions.

SEVENTEEN

"Well, look at you. Don't you look scrumptious with your hair all loose like that!" Renee held her door open for Nora, whose arms were full. "It's been ages since I saw you, Nora, dear."

"Hi Renee. Actually, I was just here three weeks ago, remember?" Nora headed toward the dining room as Renee closed the door behind her. She spread her things out on the table and turned to face her exuberant client.

"Yes, but that was last year!" She laughed at her own childish joke, then squeezed Nora in greeting, her remarkably firm breasts between them making Nora feel slightly scandalized. "And you do look absolutely radiant. What's gotten into you?"

"Thank you, Renee. I guess it's just a new year, you know?"

"The new year? I don't know about that. A new year for me usually just means it's time for a new face-lift." She laughed again, and offered Nora a drink.

"A glass of water would be great." Nora started sorting through things while Renee filled two glasses with filtered water, then they sat, ready to pour over palettes, color charts, and fabric books.

"So what's going on, Renee? You were in such a hurry the other day when you called. Is everything all right?"

"Well, my dear, I'm having you redecorate my bedroom. Does that give you any hint?" Renee gave her sultry look, her platinum Marilyn Monroe hairdo in fat, looping curls, adding to the effect. The last time Nora had been here, Renee was sporting Rita Hayworth hues. She did like those vintage glamour girls, that was obvious.

"Are you... getting married?" Nora could only hazard a guess.

"No, silly! Oh, all right. I'll tell you. I've dropped Freddy like an old cigarette butt, and I want something fresh, fresh, *fresh*, something new, new, *new*. I want you to come up with something wild. Crazy!" She spread her hands in broad arching movements. "Something that feels *free*...but very expensive, if you know what I mean."

"Wow. I'm a little surprised. Back in November you said you were in love. What happened?" She was teasing the woman; in the two years Renee had been a client, there'd been a whole string of men in her life. They came and went almost as regularly as her gardeners.

"Nora, Nora." She said her name as though talking to a slow-witted child. "I *was* in love, darling. But it got old so quickly, this whole affair thing, especially since I had to share him with his family over the holidays. Now that was tough!" She shrugged. "Besides, I really do like Tanya, and I just felt so awkward all the time around her. No man is worth losing friends over, Nora. Don't ever let yourself get fooled into believing that lie."

"I can't keep up with you." Nora laughed, shaking her head. "You're crazy, do you know that?"

"Exactly!" Renee clapped her hands together, clearly delighted by Nora's comprehension skills. "And that's what I want my room to feel like. Impulsive. Crazy. Uninhibited. Wild." She meowed like a jungle cat, ending the noise with a long purr. "I'm working on my animal magnetism."

"You're trying to attract animals?" Nora teased, wide-eyed and innocent.

"Stop it, you naughty thing! No, I'm sending out vibes for my own wild man, my own Tarzan, if you will. The silent, hungry type." She bared her teeth in a seductive growl. "What do you think?"

"Would you like me to find you a four-poster bed with vines?"

"Well, my goodness, Nora! You're thinking like I am now. How am I supposed to shock and offend your delicate sensibilities when your mind is no purer than mine?" Renee stuck out a bottom lip in a pretty pout. "What's become of you?"

Nora leaned toward the older woman and spoke in a soft, sultry tone of her own. "You want wild? I'll give you wild, Renee. You'll have Freddy replaced in no time." Then she tossed her a confident, mischievous smile.

Renee stared at her, eyes narrowing. "Stand up."

"What?" Caught off guard by the command, Nora froze.

"Stand up. Let me see you." Renee waggled her hand in the air. "Turn around. All the way around."

Bemused, Nora did as she was told.

"You look *hot*, Nora." Renee crossed her arms over her ample chest. "You look *really* hot. You look like you're doing something you're not supposed to be doing. I've seen that look in my own mirror enough times to recognize it. What are you up to?"

"Oh please. Can't a woman look hot just because she feels like it?" She felt the flush begin to creep up her chest and neck, and she knew Renee's sharp eyes wouldn't miss it.

"Ah. Answering a question with a question. The first line of defense when trying to avoid the truth. I watch television. That's what all those lawyers say is a clear sign of guilt. Who is he?"

"Stop it, Renee. I'm not like...." Nora stopped, realizing what she was just about to say.

"Oh yes, you are. You're just like me. All women are. We're all looking for someone, or something, who will make us feel alive. Who is he?"

"I don't know what you're talking about. Can we get back to business?" Nora pulled a fabric book toward her and began leafing through it. Renee came around the table and snatched the book out of her hands, sliding it down the table and out of reach.

"Does your husband know about him?"

Nora ignored her and picked up another fabric book.

"Oh my." Renee put a hand on Nora's hand, stilling her movement. "Does he know about your husband?"

Silence filled the room. Renee stood beside her a long time, her hand pressing down on top of Nora's. Finally, Nora pulled her fingers out from under the other woman's, her wedding band catching on one of the many rings on Renee's fingers, and leaned back in her chair, crossing her arms. She ran her tongue over her lips, her mouth suddenly dry. Renee sat down in the nearest chair.

"Do you have anyone to talk to, Nora? I know you're religious, and in light of that, you probably don't think I could possibly understand, but believe me, dear, whether it's religious, social, ethical, or just moral motivations, we all have rules that we feel compelled to follow. And when we break our own rules, well, it's a little like falling off our personally-constructed foundations. I know all about it, and it can feel pretty unsettling."

Nora managed to work up enough courage to look at her client. Renee's fairly objective understanding of the situation was a bit of a surprise. The concern in her eyes was real, and for a moment, just a moment, Nora wondered if she could confide in her. To be able to talk to someone, anyone, who would listen without judging seemed so tempting. But only for a moment.

"Renee, I appreciate your friendship. As different as we are, I really care about you, and I know you care about me, too."

"I do. Quite a bit, Nora, dear." Renee's vigorous nod made her bosom jiggle above the deep V of her neckline, and Nora couldn't help smiling.

"And if I ever need someone to talk to, right now I can't think of anyone else I'd feel more comfortable with."

Renee snorted and said, "Not sure if that's a compliment, but I'll take it anyway."

"I just don't think I'm in need of that right now. I've been dealing with stuff in my marriage, and things aren't great, but we seem to have arrived at some kind of a... a no-fight zone. At least there's stillness, if not peace."

"And that's good enough for you?"

"Of course not. I long for peace, and so much. But I'm coming to grips with the probability that it may not come from Jake. At least not right now."

"Are you sleeping together?" Of course she would ask something so base.

"You mean in the same bed or sex?"

"Well. Aren't you direct?"

"The answer to both is yes. Fairly regularly. He's not being denied his conjugal rights at any rate."

"So this is Jake we're talking about, right? But?"

"But what, Renee? This is way out of my comfort zone, especially with a client." Nora began gathering her things together, realizing this meeting was headed in a completely different direction than she wanted to go.

"Let me see," Renee went on as though Nora hadn't spoken. "You were pink and perky a few minutes ago, like a schoolgirl in love. Then I brought up Jake, and now you're as gloomy as a storm cloud, and you're talking about making love with your husband like it's a chore. Things aren't lining up, that's what."

Nora shrugged. "No, they're not lining up, Renee. But I'm tired of being the one to hold the loose ends together, so I'm letting go. If it all unravels, then so be it."

"Is that what's happening?" Renee placed a soft hand on Nora's forearm and leaned in. "It's unraveling?"

Nora smiled sadly. "We'll see."

A painful quiet surrounded them for a few minutes, until finally, Renee spoke. "Listen, Nora, dear. Leave some stuff here for me to look through. You're in no mood to come up with wild and crazy now, and I take full responsibility for it. Why don't you go do a little shopping or something just for yourself, something that will lift your spirits a bit, okay?"

They agreed to meet again at the end of the week, and Nora stood, adjusting the strap of her purse over her shoulder. Renee hugged her warmly again, then poked her cheek with a finger.

"The new year, ha! You've had a face-lift, sugar pie. You're in love."

She had time. After the aborted meeting with Renee, she had time to surprise him before having to pick up the kids. She slowed down as she approached the exit, her heart racing. She could feel life flooding back into her veins, everything turning pink and perky again.

· · · ● · ● · · · ·

JAKE KNEW THAT NORA was meeting with Renee again, fairly regularly these days. The woman was incessant with her demands on his wife's time, but Nora couldn't have asked for a better client. Renee was heavily involved with event committees for several different organizations, and she used Nora's decorating services almost exclusively. He didn't like that she drove so far for a client, but he also knew that Renee changed her mind often, and she had the bank accounts to fund those changes. That meant that Nora would go the distance, quite literally, to keep her happy.

He also knew that his wife was exhausted. They'd barely survived the holidays, hardly seeing each other at all up until Christmas Eve, but Nora always took the week off between Christmas and New Year to catch up on some much-needed rest and family time, and this year she did the same. Unfortunately, she spent much of that week taking care of things around the house, catching up with friends she hadn't visited with in too long, and shopping non-stop, something she usually loathed, especially during the after-holiday sales. He didn't want to admit it, but he wondered if she was purposely filling her days in order to avoid spending time with him.

As soon as January 2nd rolled around, however, she jumped back into work with a frenzy that hadn't let up yet. There were days when she'd come home, spend time with the kids, cook the evening meal, and clean up the kitchen, all on auto-pilot, her mind a million miles away. She didn't seem sad anymore, he realized, but she seemed more distracted than ever.

And she'd started going back to her office after the kids were in bed again, sometimes not coming home until the wee hours of the morning. She'd slip in bed beside him, trying not to disturb him, then she'd lie there wide awake for some time. Usually, he rolled over and pulled her close, and she came willingly, if not enthusiastically. Her long hours wore her out, but she rarely refused to participate in making love with him. After so many years, they knew how to please each other, and they both seemed to gain mutual satisfaction out of the release. He'd curl around her and drift off to the sound of her shallow, restless breathing.

Jake didn't know if things were better between them or worse. They seemed to have come to a truce of sorts, and he was glad for the reprieve. But really, they'd resolved nothing. She still did most things involving the house and the children, and he still struggled to stay busy with work. They just no longer argued about either one. Was she simply resigned to his incompetence? Or was she trying to help him by freeing him up? He didn't really want to know the answer to that question, so he didn't ask.

The weather had warmed up considerably for March, even for Southern California, and between sporadic showers and brilliant sunshine, spring was in full swing. Jake felt a sense of hope as he looked out his office window onto Nora's little rose garden in the back yard. The bushes were well-established; she'd planted one for each family when they moved in, then added new ones to commemorate different special occasions over the years. Leslie's rose had petals of apricot swirled with red, Felix' was a green rose she'd found at a local family-owned nursery. Nora planted a climbing rose called 'Jacob's Ladder' for him at the entrance to her little garden, and it vined up and over a trellised archway. She used to tell him he was like that rose, covering them, guarding their lives with his own. There was a different rose bush planted for each anniversary they'd spent here, and every one of them was a different color. Nora's favorite rose was called 'Peace' and there were several of them planted intermittently among the others. He like to see them blooming because it made him think of her wandering through the garden of their memories together.

His phone rang and he smiled, recognizing the special ringtone he'd assigned to Nora. Maybe she'd sensed he'd been thinking about her. "Hey." He answered casually, but his pulse quickened.

"Hi, Jake. Look, I have to meet my iron guy out at Renee's this afternoon. Are you going to be around? I need a favor."

Did she want him to go with her? Did she need help assembling or mounting pieces? There was a time when she borrowed his muscles on a regular basis, but it had been months since her last request. Maybe things *were* getting better. "Absolutely, Nor. How can I help?"

"Well, it may take a while because I need to oversee the project. We're hanging a huge chandelier in her front entry, and it needs to be done right. Anyway, I just wanted to make sure you don't have any plans for the afternoon. I need to drop the kids off with you after school."

Jake tried not to let his disappointment seep into his words as he replied, "That's not a favor, Nora. They're my kids, too. Of course I'll be here, especially if it will help you out." He tried desperately to hold his tongue, but the words forced themselves out anyway. "Are you sure you don't need any help with the chandelier? I'm at your beck and call, you know."

There was an awkward pause, and Jake closed his eyes, wishing he could scoop the words up and shove them back in his mouth. He sounded needy even to his own ears, and he was sure she was hearing the same thing. "Never mind. Forget I asked. I'm here. Do you want me to pick them up, too? Would that help?"

"No. I'll pick them up. That way I'll still get to see them this afternoon. I may not be back until late this evening. Once it's hung, all the crystals have to be put up, and Renee is insisting I oversee that as well. There are hundreds of them, Jake. It could be a late night."

"Will you be home in time to eat dinner with us?"

"I'm not counting on it. That's why I called it a favor. You've got to do it all tonight. I may not even be back before their bedtime, so you might get stuck doing that on your own, too." Her voice sounded tight, like she was upset by his question. What was wrong with asking her if she'd be home for dinner? "Is that okay, Jake?" she asked, when he didn't respond immediately.

It wasn't okay, but he didn't say so. She rarely left him with the children while they were awake, so he was already thinking of ways to make the afternoon and evening special for the three of them. He just wished he could plan a special evening for all *four* of them. He imagined her sharing a meal with the bawdy Renee and a bunch of muscled iron-workers, and scowled. It was definitely not okay with him.

"I almost wish we were fighting again," he muttered to himself after he said goodbye. "At least I'd know better what she was thinking." He glanced over at his untouched Bible where it was being used as a paperweight for a stack of leftover door-hangers he'd purchased to advertise his services in some of the nearby housing developments. The book that had once beckoned him, when he was a new believer, inviting him into a conversation with God. Reaching out, he ran his palm over the leather cover, his fingers tracing the lettering that spelled out 'Holy Bible', leaving trails in the dust that had collected there. Guilt made his stomach clench slightly, and he picked it up, wiping the cover clean with the hem of his shirt. "You got something for me today?" He asked the question quietly, not really expecting an answer.

Opening it to the page marked by a black ribbon, he skimmed through a couple chapters in Galatians until he came to a verse that practically leapt off the page at him. "Let us not lose heart in doing good," he read aloud. "For in due time we will reap if we do not grow weary."

He rested his head against the back of his cushioned office chair, and spun slowly, his eyes fixed on the recessed light above his head. "Well, that's what I'm doing, God. I'm doing good to Nora. But shouldn't she be doing the same to me? Shouldn't she be here doing good to me tonight?" Then his thoughts honed in on the last words of the passage. *Do not grow weary. Do not grow weary.* Had Nora grown weary? Was that it? Was she weary of him?

Jake leapt up, his chair rolling away from him across the plastic chair mat, and he grabbed it to keep it from tipping over once it bumped up against the edge of the carpet. He wasn't willing to focus too long on that thought. He would be ready for her when she came home tonight. He would ask how her day had been, he would help her unload her car, he would be kind, considerate, and sensitive to her needs, and most importantly, he would be awake. He would not let himself grow weary.

EIGHTEEN

"Oh, Jo. What am I going to do?" Nora moaned. It was the end of the day, and they were sitting at a table together in a little sandwich shop a few blocks from their building. The waitress came by to refill their coffees a second time, but Nora still had no compulsion to go home.

Jo leaned back in the wrought-iron bistro chair and scrutinized the younger woman. "Nora, I'm going to say this because you already know I'm thinking it, okay? Here goes." She took a deep breath. "I told you so! Why on earth do you not listen to your elders? Didn't your mother teach you anything?"

Jo was the only person she could talk openly to about her crisis, the only friend who knew the sordid details of all that was going on. Renee was a ready and willing alibi when she needed one, but she was too caught up in her own love affairs to care much about the details of anyone else's heart problems. Although Jo disapproved vehemently of the double life Nora was leading, and didn't hesitate to say so, she also understood the emptiness Nora was trying to fill, and was a willing sounding board for her. "You can't keep this up, Toots, being in two places at once. You'll go crazy, I guarantee it."

"Crazier than I already am? Is that even possible?" Nora shook her head. Almost every waking moment was spent keeping track of her story, and her dreams were even more distressing. The more time she spent with Tristan, the harder it was to go home and pretend like she didn't want to be somewhere else. Yet while she was with him, she missed her family, she missed *being* a family. Granted, she could hardly stand being alone with

Jake, but she missed the camaraderie they had once shared, the four of them doing life together. They'd been a family far too long for her *not* to miss it.

"Not in a million years would I have imagined that I would be the one to be unfaithful. I thought it would be Jake, if either one of us was to go down that road, because I've always considered his drinking to be an affair of sorts. He was much more interested in the woman at the bottom of the bottle than he was about me and the kids when he drank." When he quit drinking, the doubts waned dramatically in light of the relief Nora felt, but every once in a while, they resurfaced, usually due to some erratic behavior on his part. In the last few years, she admittedly found herself doubting him more often, wondering what he did with the unaccounted hours in his days. Although she never found evidence to support her fears, neither did they ever quite go away. "Which is why I wasn't surprised when he told me about his little waitress the morning after he came home plastered, back in September."

"Why didn't you leave him then, Nora? Even your church would have supported you back then. But not now. Now you're the bad guy, not him."

Jo's words mocked her somehow. This wasn't a game they were playing; she wasn't trying to one-up Jake, or point fingers. She knew they were both at fault before the waitress *or* Tristan came on the scene. But the truth was that she, Nora Anderson, had always been the rock in their marriage, the stable one, the dependable one, the stalwart enabler, and she was still having a difficult time believing that she, and not Jake, was having a real-life, full-blown affair.

She was even more surprised at how easy it was to lead the double life. At first, anyway. She put distance between her and Jake as a result of his night out, and it worked to her advantage as she indulged in her new relationship with Tristan. The increased time she spent with the children by taking on their transportation needs and extra-curricular activities eased her conscience somewhat, but as Tristan demanded more of her time, she found she was having a harder time juggling everything. Jake was aware of her weariness and frustration, she knew, but he didn't question her when she attributed it to being overwhelmed with work. He willingly helped when she let him, but instead of freeing her up, it just weighed her down with guilt.

The turmoil was affecting her work. She was having a difficult time concentrating and paying attention to details, and some of her customers were beginning to notice, not just Renee. At the beginning of her illicit romance with Tristan, she'd been radiant, glowing with passion about everything from paint colors to bed linens, and her clients were ever so responsive to her suggestions. Now she felt stretched so thinly she thought she might be see-through in some places, just like Jo had said so many months ago, and she sensed her customers' loyalties beginning to waiver. Heaven forbid that Jake, or even worse, the children, should happen to see through one of those transparent places to what was really going on.

"I just can't make myself leave him, even though I know it's not fair to him that I stay." Her voiced cracked as she spoke from her turmoil. "Sometimes I actually hate him for needing me so much, but I'm tired of carrying around his fears. He's afraid of losing me. He's afraid of making me angry. He's afraid of not meeting my needs. He's always, *always,* asking me if I'm okay. I can't stand it!" She felt tethered to him, tied down, a ship held fast by an anchor in the middle of the ocean, never able to make it to any port.

"Huh. Sounds like pretty good reasons to leave, if you ask me." Jo toyed with the yellow fringed plastic on the end of the toothpick that had held her sandwich together.

"You don't get it, Jo. Sometimes, I need him, too. I know what to expect of him, and I know what he expects of me, and sometimes that's exactly what I need." She frowned. "This sounds terrible, but he's like my favorite pair of jeans. I know where his worn spots are, and I'm usually comfortable with the way he fits."

In contrast, with Tristan, everything was an adventure; new, uncharted territory. His confidence and self-assurance excited her, and she was caught up in the whirlwind of his world. The way he abandoned himself into his art, exposing himself in fearless brush strokes and vivid, bold colors, made her heart ache with something she couldn't define.

Guilt and shame warred with passion and self-indulgence, and she was beginning to hate herself for the constant state of compromise in which she lived. "But *what* do I do? How do I get out of this now? I don't want to lose either one of them. I get nauseous when I think of giving up Tristan, and I have panic attacks when I consider leaving Jake. I...I think he might die if I do. Besides, I can't even imagine how it would affect the children."

"If you didn't have kids would you still be with Jake?"

"I've asked myself that question, too, but we *do* have kids so it doesn't really matter what I might or might not do if we didn't."

"Are you still sleeping with him?"

Nora cringed, disgusted even by the thought of it, even more so by the *truth* of it. "With Jake? Yes," she admitted, shame tightening her throat around the words. "It's so wrong, Jo. Sometimes I go from one bed to the other in the same day because I can't say no to either one of them."

"Tristan knows that you go home to Jake, and he's okay with that?" Jo scowled, her disapproval unmasked. The toothpick snapped in two, and she tossed the pieces onto the table between them.

"I don't know that he's okay with it," Nora said. "We don't talk about it. But he knew I was married when we started seeing each other, and he didn't make any demands then. Maybe he just doesn't think about it." She shrugged and stared down into her half-filled coffee cup. "Or maybe he avoids asking because he doesn't want to know the truth. I don't know."

"What kind of guy is okay with screwing you and then sending you home to your husband to be screwed by him?"

"Wow, Jo. Thanks for putting it so delicately." Nora frowned at her friend.

"Hey, I'm not the one warming two beds, Toots. There's nothing delicate about your dilemma, except for the way you have to maneuver yourself through it. You're going to trip up. It's inevitable." Jo wiped her mouth with her napkin, folded it neatly and tucked it under her cup. She smoothed on a fresh coat of lipstick, dropped the tube back into her purse, and began to dig for her keys. "You know how I feel about Jake, that I think your marriage is pretty hopeless, and that I think you deserve so much better."

"You're always so encouraging, Jo." Nora's sarcasm didn't go unnoticed, but Jo pressed on even harder.

"Yep. But the way I see it, your Tristan isn't any better a man. He sounds fun and charming and passionate and all those good things, but he also sounds selfish and immature to me. He's getting his cake and eating it, too, but he doesn't have to pay a penny for it." She reached across the table and put her hand on Nora's arm. She continued in a more gentle tone, but her words were just as harsh. "Of course he's not asking questions or making demands, Toots. Why mess with a good thing, you know? He—"

"Okay!" Nora interrupted, pulling away from Jo's touch and covering her ears with her hands. "With friends like you, who needs enemies?" She grinned wryly, trying to lighten the blow of her outburst, but Jo wouldn't let her off the hook so easily.

"I'm being honest with you *because* you're my friend, and I don't want to see you hurt. I don't want to see you hurt anyone else either. But if you don't figure things out, like I said, it's inevitable. There are going to be a lot of hurting people in this town. You're the only one who can do anything about it. You know that, right?"

They sat in silence for a few minutes before Jo finally spoke again. "You want to know what to do? Really?" She waited until Nora responded with a nod. "Just do the right thing. I know you know what that is."

Nora dropped her eyes to the table cloth, her shoulders slumping, but didn't say anything. Jo stood and came around the table to hug her friend.

"Go home, Honey. Go home until you sort things out."

NINETEEN

EASING HER EYES OPEN, she stared at the moonlight prying its way between the slats of the blinds, slashing the bed covers to ribbons across their bodies. Nora tentatively drew her legs up, curling into herself, turning her back to the sleeping man beside her. *Please don't wake up, please, oh please.* She held her breath, afraid even the tiniest exhalation would stir the air between them, reminding him of her presence.

Why was she here, she asked herself for the thousandth time. Why did she keep coming back when she knew it would just mean more pain, more heartache for everyone? What was it that kept drawing her to him, to his arms, to his bed?

Like a druggie to the needle, like a drunk to the bottle, like a moth to the flame, like a fly to the web, like a.... The taunting voice inside her head paused, running out of stupid clichés to which she could compare herself.

Oh God, where are You? A single, hot tear spilled from the corner of her eye, running down her temple and into her ear where it pooled and tickled. She didn't wipe it away; all she needed now was for him to wake up and find her crying.

Her low back ached from the pressure in her bladder, and she knew she couldn't hold it much longer. Sliding her feet from beneath the covers, she pushed herself up into a sitting position. She waited, afraid to look at him, to see his eyes half open, his hands reaching for her.

But he didn't stir. She took a step away from the bed, tugging her nightgown down over her hips. The floor creaked and she paused, slowly turning to glance over her shoulder at him.

"Mmpph." He rolled onto his side and flung out his arm. It landed on her pillow, and his hand curled around the soft edges, pulling it toward him. She fled the room.

Standing at the sink a few minutes later, she dropped her chin to her chest, and covered her face with both hands. Her tears surprised her as they began to fall in earnest. What was she going to do? How was she going to get out of this? Where would she go? Where *could* she go?

Tap-tap-tap! The punctuated rap of knuckles on the door startled her, and she let out a frightened squeak.

"Nora? Are you okay?" His voice was gravelly from sleep, and she shivered at the rasp of it. "Nora?"

"You scared me, Jake! I'm fine. Just going to the bathroom." She prayed he wouldn't notice the catch in her voice.

"Are you okay?" He knocked again.

"I'm fine, really. I'll be right out." *Please go away,* she silently begged him.

"Are you sure? Do you need anything?"

Just for you to leave me alone. Can't I even go to the bathroom without you checking up on me? "I'm fine, Jake," she said again, hoping the children wouldn't wake up. "Really."

"Are you coming back to bed?"

"Where else would I go?" The words were out before she could stop them.

"What was that?" He jiggled the handle, and she grimaced, thankful she'd had the foresight to lock the door.

"I said, 'Just needed to go,' Jake. I'll be right there."

"Okay." He didn't sound very certain. "Don't take too long. I'll keep the bed warm."

As she washed her hands, she studied her face, the mirror above the sink stark and honest in the glare of the energy-efficient lighting that framed it. She hated those bulbs, preferring the old-fashioned kind with the softer glow. It had been a long time since she'd shed any tears over the condition of her marriage, and she resented the dreams that had her emotions so stirred up without her permission. The puffy shadows under her eyes, and her swollen, red nose, bore witness to both her lack of sleep and her tears. She hated crying. She couldn't hide it to save her life. One look and he'd know.

"Oh well," she shook her head and opened the door, reaching over to turn off the light as she did.

"You're crying." Jake stood there in the hallway just outside the bathroom. This time she actually shrieked.

"Sorry!" He reached for her, pulled her up against him. "I didn't mean to scare you, Nor."

She hid her face in his chest, her heart pounding so hard between them she thought she could feel it reverberating back against her cheek. Why on earth was he standing outside the bathroom door in the dark?

"Are you okay?"

She nodded. If he asked her that again she would scream. And maybe never stop.

"But you were crying."

"Just a nightmare, I guess. I woke up crying." She surprised herself at how easily the half-truths slipped off her tongue these days.

"What was it about?"

"I don't know, Jake." She pushed away from him. "I just woke up sad from it. Which means I probably don't really want to remember it."

"Okay. If you're sure...." He studied her while she brushed her fingertips across her cheeks, wiping away any lingering dampness. Standing this close to him in the narrow passage made her feel ill at ease, and she turned away to gaze across the hallway toward the bedroom.

"Were you waiting to use the bathroom?" she asked, glancing up at him from the corner of her eye.

"Oh. Oh! Yes. Yes, I was. But I just want to make sure..."

"That I'm okay?" She cut him off. "I'm *fine*, Jake. Honest. I'm just tired. It *is* the middle of the night." Nora pressed her hands to the ache in the small of her back that hadn't eased up, even after using the bathroom. She realized her mistake too late.

His eyes dropped to the contour of her breasts now plainly outlined beneath the thin fabric of her nightshirt stretched across them.

He reached up and cupped her curves possessively. "You're so beautiful." He leaned down to kiss her. She turned away slightly, not ready for where this was heading, and Jake's voice dropped to a husky whisper against her ear. "Playing hard to get, are you?" He slid one arm around her and pulled her against him, his other hand skimming up the back of her thigh beneath her hem.

Trapped.

Oh, no, no! Please no. She held her breath as his fingers caressed her flesh, his mouth moving over her face, her neck, her shoulders. His choppy breathing was making her stomach knot, and she flinched as his teeth nipped at her ear.

"I thought... Didn't you say you needed to use the bathroom?" It was a desperate attempt, but that's exactly how she felt. Desperate.

He whispered against her neck; there would be no reprieve tonight.

· · ● · ● · ● · · ·

JAKE AWOKE FROM HIS troubling dreams and peered through half-open eyes at the clock on his bedside table. He sighed, rolled onto his back, and reached over to rest his hand on his wife's thigh. Her skin was warm from sleeping cocooned against him. The familiar rhythm of her breathing was a sound he loved waking up to.

She looked so serene and soft with her long hair spread out on the pillow beneath her head, her mouth relaxed and slightly open, her brow smooth, sleep softening the lines of motherhood, and work, and life in general. But her eyes seemed puffy to him, as though she'd been crying, and he closed his eyes, trying to recall if anything had happened the night before that would cause her pain.

Nothing. He remembered nothing but a certain stillness about her she'd attributed to fatigue. She readily agreed to go to bed when he asked her to, and she readily participated in their love-making before falling asleep beside him, her foot resting against the top of his the way she'd done their whole marriage.

And later—he smiled at the memory and felt his pulse begin to quicken—in the middle of the night she'd come out of the bathroom looking all soft and rumpled, her hair a little wild around her face. She'd cocked her head and peered up at him out of the corner of her eye, posing in a provocative way that drew his gaze away from her face, away from her glistening cheeks....

She *had* been crying. She'd brushed it off as nothing, just dreams. *I'm fine,* she'd said, then let him lead her back to the bedroom.

Jake sighed, berating himself for being so insensitive. He should have paid more attention to her needs and not his own. Something had upset her, and even if it was only her dreams, they'd been bad enough to make her cry. He studied her again in the morning light.

She grew more and more beautiful to him over the years. Her skin was milky white, just a smattering of freckles across her nose, her mouth full and soft, her wide eyes hinting at the Celtic blood that ran through her veins. She wasn't tall, but God had been generous with her in all the right places. She'd gained some weight with her second pregnancy, and she hated it, always trying to lose an extra fifteen pounds. He, on the other hand, didn't mind it at all.

If he was honest with himself, he felt more comfortable with her being a little plump. Men still turned to look at her, but their eyes didn't linger as long as they used to.

He reached over and brushed her cheek with his fingertips, a tiny tremor of doubt tripping through him, the same doubt that had plagued him since that camping trip—was it only a year ago? What if there was something she wasn't telling him? What if there was something she felt she *couldn't* tell him? He wanted to believe her, that everything was okay, but a voice inside his head whispered ugly words of uncertainty. Was she lying to him? Bad dreams? What else would make her cry in the middle of the night?

He wanted her to wake up. He knew it was selfish, but he didn't want to spend the next hour or so alone with his thoughts. If she was awake, she'd assure him that everything was going to be okay, that she would always be there. He didn't think he could survive if anything happened to her, if she was taken from him, or worse, if she ever left him.

He knew these early mornings before she woke were an ideal time to spend in conversation with God, praying and reading his Bible. He used to do so more regularly, especially right after he quit drinking, but lately God seemed distant, and Jake was too easily distracted by his nagging questions about Nora.

He propped himself up on an elbow, debating whether to get up and put on the coffee, or hunker back down under the covers with her. She stirred a little, sighed, and smiled softly in her sleep. He wondered if she sensed him watching her, and the thought made him smile in turn.

"I love you, Baby," he whispered.

· · · · ● · ● · · · ·

I LOVE YOU, BABY.

Nora rushed to the surface of awareness, her heart pounding. *Tristan!* She almost said his name out loud. In her dream, the two of them had been together, a family, along with her children. They were sitting by a pool on a brilliant summer day, the kids splashing and shouting in the water, while she and Tristan looked on. The next moment Tristan, Leslie, Felix, and Jake were waving goodbye to her as she reached through the bars of her jail cell. Tristan turned and said, "I love you, Baby," then herded the others out the door ahead of him. She cried out for them to come back, not to leave her there, but they couldn't hear her. No one could hear her.

She held her breath, afraid to open her eyes until she was fully awake. Her pulse slowed as disappointment and frustration, coupled with relief, washed over her. She was in her own bed. The words that sounded so much like Tristan's had come from Jake who lay awake beside her in the subtle light of dawn.

She could feel him watching her, and she tried desperately to stay relaxed, as though still asleep. She snuffled and rolled away from him, turning onto her side.

"Nora?" He said her name quietly, tentatively.

She didn't respond, and he must have assumed she was still in dreamland. She felt his fingers touch her hair, brush along her shoulder, and down her arm. She tried not to flinch. The mattress shifted beneath her as he got up, then he quietly left the room.

She buried her face in her pillow, her body curling slowly into a tight ball of misery. How much longer could she go on like this? Love, hate, need, obsession, manipulation. Lies, lies, lies. It was like being torn apart from the inside out, and Nora couldn't help wondering if there were already rifts in her body, little fissures, tiny striations in her skin. She ached for Tristan. Thoughts of him consumed her almost every waking moment, nearly suffocating her at night. When she wasn't with him, she worked until she couldn't even prop her eyelids open, then came home and went straight to bed. But the minute she closed her eyes, she saw him, his face, his hungry eyes. When she did finally fall into an exhausted slumber, her sleep was anything but peaceful. Her dreams were haunted by hide-and-seek games with Tristan, Jake, and herself. Renee often appeared, trying to keep everyone and everything organized, and the kids dashed in and out, sometimes oblivious, sometimes looking haunted and empty.

Jake maneuvered carefully around her most of the time. He didn't avoid her, he just handled her with kid gloves. He was deeply affected by her suffering, and in response, tried way too hard to make her feel better. But in his attempt to comfort her, he only suffocated her, in being sensitive and tender toward her, he only seemed the bigger fool to her. If he only knew why she was so miserable, he'd want nothing more to do with her.

Last night. Her stomach recoiled as she remembered. Over the last several months, she'd become so skilled at separating her mind and body, that sex was more of a performance than anything else. Jake knew how to make her physically respond, but she rarely stayed engaged mentally during the act itself. She played her part well—she knew he thought highly of their sex-life—but all she really wanted was for him to leave her alone. *Don't touch me, don't coddle me, don't try to comfort me, don't ask me if I'm okay. I'm not okay, but I'll keep lying to you, and telling you that I am.*

TWENTY

TODAY, JAKE NEEDED HER. He didn't know why the urgency coursed through him, but he needed to hear her voice, to feel her softness up against him, to smell her hair, her skin. He felt sullen and ill-humored, like a pouting child, but he didn't know what was getting him down. He had to have her in his arms, to be able to whisper in her ear that they were going to be okay, and have her assure him that indeed, they would be. He dialed her number, hoping she was finished with Renee and would answer.

"This is Nora with Sonora Décor. I'm either with a client or out of my office. Please leave your name and number, and I'll get back to you as soon as I am able. Thanks for calling and have an inspiring day."

He listened to her recording, trying to ignore the disappointment settling around his shoulders. "Hey, Nor. It's me. I just called to tell you I'm thinking about you. I love you. Call me."

Did that sound too wimpy? He sighed, certain it did, or that she would perceive it that way. Needy, she called it. She'd only said so once, maybe twice before, but that was enough.

"Maybe I'll surprise her this afternoon when she picks up the kids," Jake decided out loud. He'd make it about the family, not just her. They could all get an after-school treat together, maybe watch a movie or go to the park. How could she choose work over family time?

He had plenty of time to get there, at least an hour, and he decided he'd let Nora know exactly how much he was thinking of her. He changed his shirt into the one she'd given him for Christmas, brushed his teeth, and splashed a little of her favorite cologne on his neck and jaw. Stopping at a flower stand along the way, he picked up a bouquet of yellow roses that were sure to make her smile. Things didn't take nearly as long as he'd expected, and he drove slowly toward Felix's school. He'd wait in the parking lot, he decided, and watch for her. Maybe she'd get there early too, and he could surprise her with the flowers before Felix joined them. The potential was there for a very romantic moment, if all went well.

Jake pulled into the parking lot and drove slowly around the loop, looking for a strategic place to park where he could see every car coming or going. He didn't want to miss her. He was just backing into a spot when he saw her car parked in the next row. And she was sitting in it, too.

Certain she hadn't seen him, he grabbed the flowers, and ducked around the van parked beside her. He got close enough to realize that her window was rolled halfway down, and he could hear her talking quietly on the phone. He smiled to himself, imagining her face when she saw him.

"You know I can't do that, Tristan. It's not fair to even ask me that." Nora's voice rippled through him, stirring something terrifyingly familiar deep inside of him. The tone. The way her voice caressed each word. The way she said the name Tristan. It reverberated in his ears like a long-forgotten song suddenly remembered.

She used to talk that way to him.

"Of course I *want* to go. I just can't."

Jake felt his feet moving. He looked down and saw the pavement slipping away beneath him, he felt the rhythm of his own footsteps, but he didn't quite realize his intentions until he was standing outside her window, staring in at her soft, sultry expression.

"You can't go where?" He asked, watching his startled wife's face change into that of an incredulous, angry creature. She covered the phone with her hand.

"What are you doing here? You scared me to death!" She didn't yell, but she might as well have. Jake actually cringed.

"Excuse me just a moment," she said into the receiver before covering the mouthpiece again. She thrust her head out the window toward him and snarled, "What do you want?"

Wordlessly, Jake held up the bouquet of flowers.

Nora stared at the roses with half-closed eyes, then looked back at his face without even acknowledging them. His mind was spinning out of control as he tried to process everything that was happening.

"I'm on a phone call with a client. I can't talk right now." She rolled up her window.

Jake just stared at her. Did she really think he was so foolish as to believe she was talking to a client that way? When he didn't move, she rolled the window back down, and said, matter-of-factly, "Excuse me. Do you mind?"

He'd been dismissed.

Reeling inside, he backed away from her car. Not knowing what else to do, he returned to his truck and climbed in. He sat there, his stomach churning, his thoughts careening around in his head.

"Liar. She's a liar." He said it again, a little louder. "She's a liar." She was lying to him, he knew that without a doubt. Tristan. *Tristan.* The way she said his name. *Oh Lord, help me, please. The way she said his name!* He closed his eyes and leaned forward to rest his forehead on the steering wheel.

"I need to go. Before the kids see me. I need to get out of here," he muttered, trying to motivate himself to move. He opened his eyes and looked up to see Nora crossing the parking lot toward him.

I could turn this baby on and drive right over her. The thought charged through him, and was immediately pursued by guilt and shame so intense that he just sat slumped forward, waiting for her. His hands still gripped the steering wheel, holding on for dear life.

She tapped on his window. He made her do it twice before he acknowledged her by rolling it down.

"Hey. Sorry I freaked out. You just scared me, Jake. I wasn't expecting anyone to come banging on my window, and you startled me." Her voice was full of false cheer.

He couldn't look at her—he'd only end up believing her. "I didn't bang on your window."

"Semantics, Jake. You did sneak up on me." She crossed her arms.

"Actually, no, I didn't. I walked up to your open window. You were so absorbed in your conversation you just didn't see me. I wasn't sneaking up on you." Her accusation was like knives in his stomach, because technically, she was right; he had meant to surprise her. But she was right for all the wrong reasons.

"Well, it sure seemed like you did." She chewed on her bottom lip and looked away. He watched her from the corner of his eye, wondering what she was thinking about. *Who* she was thinking about. She turned back and caught him looking at her. "I wish you would respect my privacy. It was pretty obvious I was on a phone call, wasn't it? Were you spying on me?"

"Geez, Nor. You think I came here to spy on you?" She sounded so childish. *Spying?*

She looked away again without answering.

"Do you really want to know why I came here today?" When she didn't answer, he continued. "I came to surprise you and the kids. I thought the four of us could to go to the park or the movies or something. I thought it'd be a good way to spend a Friday afternoon. Together, as a family." He picked up the bouquet of flowers lying on the seat beside him. He might as well go for broke. "And I brought these for you, because I was thinking about you, and I was hoping to catch you before the kids got out so I could give them to you." He thrust them through the window at her.

She hesitated before taking them, and he felt his blood begin to boil. "Take them, Nora! They're for you!" What was wrong with her? What woman wouldn't be swept off her feet by a surprise visit from her husband, bearing flowers no less?

A woman who wishes her husband was someone else.

The little voice inside his head was so loud, he wondered, just for a moment, if she'd heard it too, but she had her nose buried in the bouquet. Someone else. How could it be? Who was Tristan? He shook his head, refusing to accept it.

"That sounds like fun, Jake. I'm sure the kids will be thrilled to see you." His thoughts had wandered so far he almost didn't remember what she was talking about. Then he realized what she'd said. The kids will be thrilled. Was she thrilled? That's who he really wanted to impress; her, Nora, *his wife.* He wanted Nora to be thrilled to see him. He wanted Nora to be excited about spending the afternoon with him. He wanted Nora to be happy to see him; not suspicious, accusing him of spying on her.

"But you're not."

"I am, too, Jake." She rolled her eyes. "You surprised me, that's all."

"As I intended to do, remember? I just expected it would be a good thing." He was suddenly tired, weary beyond reason.

She didn't try to placate him, nor did she defend her reaction. Instead, she looked at her watch, then toward the school yard where the kids would be gathering in the next few minutes.

"Actually, I'm taking the kids to my mom's for the night. I have a new development showing tomorrow morning, and I haven't finished preparing for it." She glanced back at him for just a moment, then away again. "I'm sorry. I wish you had said something sooner. We could have planned things better."

"A new development showing? Did I know about this?"

"Yes, a new development showing. And I didn't know I needed to keep you informed about every client of mine."

"Sorry. That came out wrong. I meant about the kids going to your mom's for the night. Did I know about that?" This couldn't be happening. It was all coming at him too quickly to process.

Nora shook her head, still watching the empty playground. "No. I just arranged it. I was going to try to finish the presentation up at home tonight, but this is a really important client, and I need to be sure things are right. You know how hard it is to concentrate at home, especially on a Friday night when the kids stay up late." She buried her nose in the flowers again. "That's who I was talking to when you surprised me."

"Your mother? Since when do you call your mother Tristan?" Jake couldn't keep the venom out of his voice. It was the lamest lie he'd ever heard, and she had the decency to flinch when he said that name.

Now she did look at him, her eyes narrowed. "I call my mother 'Mom.' Tristan is my client. Anything else you're confused about?"

From bad to worse. Out of the frying pan, into the fire. "Well, since you asked, where can't you go with your *client*, Tristan?"

Nora stepped back, letting the bouquet fall to her side. "Tristan is hosting a dinner for his employees and asked if I could attend."

"Have you, by any chance, told him you have a husband?" Jake knew he sounded defensive and suspicious, but he actually *was* defensive and suspicious, and he didn't feel like pretending otherwise. Right now, he felt like he was fighting a losing battle, and he wasn't going to go quietly.

"He knows. I told him."

"And?"

"And what, Jake? What else do you want me to say?"

"I don't know, Nor. I just can't help but think there's more to this than you're letting on. I'm not a fool. I heard the way you were talking to him. You sounded awfully familiar on the phone with him."

"This is ridiculous. I *am* familiar with him. I've been working with him for months now. And believe me, this isn't the first time I've been included in the invitations to company dinners, and I'm sure it won't be the last. He's hoping that eventually I'll say yes."

"And I'm hoping you won't."

"Don't be such a jerk. I said 'no,' remember? You were *listening*." She held the flowers up. "By the way, how much did I pay for these? Another three hundred and seventy-two dollars and change?"

It was Jake's turn to flinch. The exact dollar amount on his tab at Friar Puck's last October. The night that changed everything.

Just then the buzzer went off across the school, and children poured out of every classroom. The school yard was instantly overrun by miniature people, and Nora turned and walked away.

"What about this afternoon?" Jake called out. Watching her purposeful steps, he suddenly noticed she'd lost weight. Her curves were more pronounced by the anger in her posture, and she looked terrifyingly sexy to him.

"You're a free man, Jake. No kids, no wife, no work. The day is yours to do with what you will." She called over her shoulder, but she kept walking, the flowers swinging upside down at her side, leaving a delicate trail of leaves and tiny white petals like confetti in her wake.

He watched her open the trunk of her car and carelessly toss the bouquet inside. The flowers lay in a forlorn heap on top of a small suitcase he recognized as one they'd bought together for a weekend away a few years ago, a garment bag, and what looked like a pair of hiking boots.

TWENTY ONE

Spring had run its course and was doing its best to hold summer at bay, but a heavy heat settled over all of Southern California. Bees buzzed lazily from blossom to blossom, butterflies bobbed along on the warm breeze, and shimmering dragonflies ducked in and out of the brush, never flitting too far from the little decorative pond behind Tristan's house. They sat together on the bench swing on his patio, letting the late afternoon sun lull them into a bit of a stupor.

Nora was weary of the secrecy, the lies, the games, and she was especially unsettled by Jake's appearance at the school this afternoon. She was sure he suspected something, and after today, there was no reason for him not to. Hearing her lover's name on her husband's lips made her stomach flip-flop, and she cringed even now as she remembered. It was almost as if it made things real in a way they hadn't been before, and she could no longer convince herself she could pull this off, that her new life with Tristan was just a fantasy. She turned to look at him, and wondered again what on earth she was going to do.

She knew this was wrong. She knew it went against everything she believed was right. She even knew that being here was a choice, that she was allowing her feelings to dictate her actions. But she also knew that feelings of guilt and shame, pride, and obligation had kept her in a disastrous marriage for far too long. So which feeling should she obey? Which one should she let dictate her path?

She studied Tristan's profile as he rested his head against the back of the swing, his eyes closed, a half-smile on his full lips. He could always tell when she was looking at him. His shaggy hair fell back away from his face, and she reached over to touch the sandy streaks sweeping over his temples. Chocolate brown eyes in deep sockets were fringed by sooty lashes, and his cheeks were a warm hue. He had single-handedly designed and put in the landscaping in his back yard, and his skin responded well to the sunlight, turning his face and upper body a beautiful, California bronze. Everything about him seemed relaxed, untethered, carefree.

Tristan opened his eyes and turned to meet her gaze. He grinned, his full features close enough that she could see the pin-pricks of facial hair shaved close around his mouth and jaw. He was always so tender with her, never pushing her for details of what was going on inside her head. He didn't ask about Jake, even though he knew she went home to her husband almost every night. He didn't push her to leave her family, even though he made it clear he wanted her with him. He did ask when he was going to meet her children, but only when she brought them up, and he accepted her reservations, not pushing her in that area either. He seemed to find satisfaction in just being with her, and took full advantage of what little time she did have to offer him; an hour, an afternoon, a weekend, or just a quick phone call across the miles.

In public, he was very respectful of the fact that she was still married. Not too long ago, they ran into each other at the big home and garden depot near her office. Uncertain of how he'd behave toward her, she'd at first been terrified that someone she knew would see them together. He didn't even try to touch her, though, but gallantly offered to help her load her things into her car. In the parking lot, he'd assaulted her senses with an extremely graphic proposition while standing several feet away from her. She thought she might just melt into a blushing puddle right where she stood. His knowing, smug grin didn't help. But he never touched her.

It was exciting, and stimulating, and fulfilling in so many ways, but she was exhausted. She hardly slept anymore. She still did everything for the kids, the normal, everyday stuff, as well as attending all the end of the year school functions. She was back working long nights at her office again, not because her clientele was growing, but because she was spending so much time with Tristan.

She was modeling a lot for him these days. It was a huge hurdle for her to leap, to accept his constant scrutiny, his sudden inspirations, but she was beginning to enjoy sitting for him. Sometimes he'd have her sit for hours in front of a window as the light changed, just so he could capture the effects of the shifting shadows on her face. More often than not, though, he didn't paint an image of her at all. Much of his work was very surreal, more emotion and color than identifiable images. "This is the feeling I have when I watch you," he'd say. It was always a little disconcerting to her, but she was growing to love his work, the way he expressed himself, the way he used his art to communicate. She loved the smells that filled his studio: the different paints, the glues and epoxies he used, varnishes and other chemicals. She'd claimed a short counter along one wall, and set up a work space where she had a virtual office, and she loved working there, even when he wasn't around. Everything about the place was Tristan, and she felt enveloped in his world up there.

She breathed deeply as Tristan pulled her close to his side and laid his cheek on top of her head. She loved the artist, too, she was certain, but she didn't know how to keep everything together. Something had to change.

"What was that sigh all about?" His voice rumbled in his chest against her cheek.

"Just glad to be here," she said. "Can't think of anywhere I'd rather be right now."

"I'm glad you're here, too. Can't think of anywhere I'd rather you be right now either."

Nora closed her eyes. If everything was so perfect, why did she suddenly feel like crying? When one tear escaped down her cheek where it rested against his shoulder, he pulled away.

"You're crying," he stated simply, but he was obviously curious. She was a little surprised herself. Something had happened to her the night Jake started drinking again. Except for those rare moments in the middle of the night, it was as though the well of her tears had all but dried up. It was great to not have to carry around a tube of mascara everywhere she went, but she was sure there was some underlying psychological issue that was being ignored. She used to cry over everything. Not anymore.

She covered her face, embarrassed, commanding herself to stop. He'd never seen how horrible she looked when she cried. "Ignore me. I guess I'm just a little hormonal today."

He wrapped one large hand around both her wrists and pulled her hands away from her eyes. "Are you going to tell me what's going on?"

She shook her head and tried to look away, but he reached up and took her chin in his hand, forcing her to face him. "What's making you cry, my Isolde?" He'd started calling her that around Valentine's Day after gifting her with a painting of the statue, but with her face, shifting light spilling across her upturned features. They'd hung it in his room over his dresser where he would see her first thing each morning.

"I'm not crying. It was just one little tear." She swiped at her cheek. "I can't... I don't...." Why couldn't she get this out? *Maybe because you don't know what you really want,* she answered herself. "I... I wish I knew."

Tristan brought her left hand to his lips. He kissed each finger, then each knuckle, then finally the inside of her wrist before he began toying with the wedding ring she wore. "Does this have anything to do with your one tear?"

Why did he have to be so nice about everything? It only made it more difficult for her. *Oh God, are You there? Do You still listen to me? Help! What am I going to do?*

If he was demanding, or jealous, or petty, or even whiny, things would be so much more cut and dried. But Tristan acted like he would wait forever to make her his, if that's what she asked him to do.

Suddenly, Nora stiffened as the thought replayed itself. He would wait forever to make her his, if that's what she asked him to do.

He would wait forever.

A veil lifted from before her eyes, and she could suddenly see clearly. Tristan, her tender lover, her gifted artist, her no rules man, *would* wait forever for her.

And while waiting, he was willing to share her with another man. No, even worse. He was willing to let another man have the responsibility of her, while he got the good stuff, the fun stuff, the easy stuff.

"You all right, Baby?" Staggering a little under the impact of her epiphany, his concern seemed somehow false.

"I... I...." She took a deep breath. "Let me start again. Are... Are you okay with where this is going, with what you're getting out of this relationship? I mean, what do you want from me? What do you want for us, Tristan?"

"What do I want? Well, what do *you* think I want from you?" Renee's words about avoiding truth by answering a question with a question ran through her mind.

"I don't think I know, Tristan. That's why I'm asking. What do you want for our future?"

"Really? Well," He hesitated, considering his answer. "I want you." He flashed a boyish smile at her and wrapped his fingers around the back of her neck, massaging, stroking, soothing.

"You have me," she quipped, trying to remain impervious to his touch.

"Not all of you. I want all of you."

"But what does that mean to you?" She wasn't going to let him off that easily.

"I love you, Isolde. I wish you were my wife. I wish I knew your children. I wish we could make this real, that I didn't have to act like I don't know you when we meet in public." Obviously, he thought often about their chance meeting in the home and garden shop, too. "I wish for a lot of things, but I fully understand why I can't have things the way I want them."

"And all that wishing is okay with you?" She pulled away a little, folding her hands in her lap. "I mean, how long are you willing to wait around for me? Is it really okay with you that I can only give you an hour here and there, a day or two once a month, maybe a weekend now and then?"

"I'm not exactly sure what you're getting at, but all I can tell you is that I understand your situation, and I'm glad for any part of you that you can give me." He was frowning now, his broad forehead furrowed above his eyes. "I'm willing to wait, if that's what I have to do. It's not like I'm going anywhere. You know where to find me." He leaned over and kissed the tip of her nose. "If this is working for you, well, I'm not going to rock the boat. I know a good thing when I find it, and believe me, Baby, you're a good thing."

Nora shook her head. That was *not* what she wanted to hear. "Wait. Stop placating me with clichés." She pushed him away as he tried to move in for another kiss. "This *isn't* working for me, Jake. I have to—"

"Tristan. My name is Tristan. Not Jake."

She brought her hand up to cover her mouth. "I'm so sorry. It just slipped out. I'm sorry." Nora was mortified. Nothing about this conversation was going well.

"It's okay, Nor. I understand." He intentionally used Jake's name for her.

"No, it's not okay. And this is exactly what I'm talking about." She waved her hand between them, indicating the uncomfortable name exchange. "None of this is. I guess that's what I've been trying to say all along. I can't keep this up. I can't do this to you. To Jake. I can't do this to my children. I have to make some decisions, Tristan." She took a deep breath and hurried on before she lost her courage. "I'm leaving him."

Tristan was quiet for so long she wondered if he'd even heard her. Finally, he spoke. "What are you going to do?"

Now it was Nora's turn to be silent. He had just said 'you,' not 'we.'

"I mean, do you have some place to go? To live?"

"I guess I, um, thought that you... that you and I... well, we'd be together." She couldn't believe she was stuttering.

"Do you think that's a good idea?" He was still lounging in the seat beside her, but she sensed a tension in his body, the muscles in his forearm bulging slightly, his artist's hands making slow, sweeping motions on his thighs. "I mean, your kids are going to need time to adjust to you being in love with someone else, you know? I don't know that it would be the healthiest thing to force feed them to me so quickly after you bail on your marriage, do you?"

Nora almost laughed. Now he was telling her what was healthy for her kids? "Wow. You're singing a different tune all of a sudden. I thought you were dying to meet them, to make them a part of your life."

"I am. I really am. I just know how tough this kind of transition can be. My folks were divorced when I was eight, and my dad moved right in with his girlfriend. It wasn't cool, you know? It really screwed me up for a long time." Tristan stretched his legs out in front of him and leaned his head on the back of the swing again, staring at the outdoor ceiling fan spinning lazily above their heads.

"I don't think Dad ever knew what he wanted. He moved from one woman to another his whole life, leaving a trail of broken hearts in his wake.

A few broken bones along the way, too. He got drunker and higher and meaner as he got older." He smiled ruefully, his eyes still closed. "I swore I'd never be like him. That's probably why I'm almost forty and still not married. Holding out for the perfect woman." He turned his head toward her and winked, his impish grin turning lecherous. "Can I help it if she happens to be someone else's wife?"

Nora stood up quickly, something akin to panic beginning to rise up inside of her.

"Isolde?" He sat forward, watching her. "What's up?" He reached for her hand, but she shoved it in her jeans pocket. "Hey. Don't be like that. Come here, Baby."

Nora couldn't look at him. If she did, she'd never be able to resist him. His timbered voice, the coaxing hunger in his eyes; he was like the pied piper to her heart, and right now, she needed to use all her untried defenses with him.

He pushed up off the swing and swept her up against him, nuzzling the side of her face with his mouth, whispering gruffly in her ear. "Let's go inside. I'll turn down the air conditioner and we can light a fire."

"Stop it, Tristan." She put both hands on his chest and shoved, hard. "Stop it!" *What on earth am I doing here?*

"Isolde, baby. Calm down. You're hot enough to light a fire yourself. And I think I like it." He smoothed her hair back, then he cupped her face in his hands. "We're good together, you and I, and that's all that matters. We'll figure the whole kid thing out when it happens. For now, we've got this weekend. Let's not blow it with all this talk about the future."

Nora stepped back. Her heart was pounding so hard it almost hurt inside her chest. "I can't do this, Tristan. Suddenly, I can't do this. I... I need to go."

He grabbed her hand. "You always say those words to me, Isolde. Don't go. Not this time." He brought it to his lips and pressed a kiss into her palm.

TWENTY TWO

What if she wasn't here? What if she was? What did he plan on doing either way?

He pulled into the secured parking structure next door to her building, using the numerical code she'd given him when she first began renting the office there. He was almost surprised when the bar rose, allowing him in, having considered the possibility that she might change her pass code without telling him. He drove slowly through the nearly empty lot, looking for her car.

There it was. Parked right up against the wall, her silver Nissan was nestled in, safe and sound, present and accounted for. Then he saw her, in the front seat, looking over her shoulder, watching him as he drove past the back of her car.

Jake said a few choice words, things his family would be appalled to hear come out of his mouth. He considered looping around again, just to see if she was okay, then thought better of it.

Caught. How would he explain this? He'd seen the look on her face. He knew how she'd interpret his checking up on her. He could already imagine the argument they'd have about this, the accusations, the anger, and it eliminated any relief he had in finding her there.

Go home, man. Just go home. You've done enough.

Jake drove slowly, taking the side streets instead of the shorter route via the freeway. He needed time to think, to process things before defending himself to her. Even though he hadn't admitted it to himself before, he'd believed, deep down, that she had somewhere else to be. Finding her car, and then seeing her in it, had significantly altered the way he was dealing with this night.

When he finally pulled into the driveway, she still was not home. He wasn't surprised, but then, he didn't think he'd be surprised at anything anymore. None of it made sense to him. He'd seen the suitcase in her trunk. He understood the convenience of having her mother take the kids overnight without consulting him first. He even thought she'd cleverly taken advantage of his surprise appearance at school in order to orchestrate a fight with him, so she would have an excuse for not coming home tonight.

So why was she where she said she was going to be?

He wanted a drink. He *needed* a drink.

The house was dark, silent, and a little unsettling to come home to after his excursion. He'd eaten out, not wanting to dine alone in the empty silence of their home, went to see the latest spy movie in theaters just to take up time, then drove around in circles, until making the decision to go to her workplace. Now he wished he could rewind things. Why didn't he just go home after the movie? She was probably just getting ready to come home herself when he'd pulled his stupid stunt. Now who knew where she'd go?

Going through the garage, he schlepped into the family room, dropped down on the oh-so-familiar sofa, and sat there, toying with his keys, for what seemed like ages before he heard the sound of her own key in the lock at the front door. He stayed where he was, sitting there in the shadows, watching as she came in and turned on the entryway light.

Oh yeah. She was angry. Then he took into account the things she was carrying. The strap of the overnight case pulled heavily against her shoulder, and her garment bag was sloppily draped over one arm. She dropped her boots just inside the door, obviously not at all concerned that there might be questions about why she'd had them in her car. They hadn't gone hiking or camping in ages, and they didn't have any plans to do so in the near future. At least none that he knew of.

He must have made a sound. She glanced up at him, narrowed her eyes, and proceeded to drop the rest of her things in the entry right where she stood.

"Good. I see you've already figured out the sleeping arrangements for the night." She headed down the hall, slammed their bedroom door behind her, and he could have sworn he heard her drag something heavy up against it.

After several minutes of silence, he got up and crossed over to the heap of her things. She'd obviously had plans of some kind this weekend. He bent over and picked up the garment bag, unzipped it, and peeked inside.

A blazer, a long skirt. His favorite black dress, the one she'd worn when she took him out to tell him she'd landed the Heritage Center contract several few months ago. She'd looked so classy and elegant, so proud of herself, and he'd never thought she looked more beautiful. She'd been distant, even in her obvious happiness, but he'd chalked it up to nerves in anticipation of the job. Now, he wasn't so sure.

Against his better judgment, he opened the small suitcase. He rooted around a little, then slipped his hand into the zippered pocket on the lid. Cool, slippery fabric met his probing fingertips, and he brought out a fistful of lacy lingerie, things he'd never seen before.

A vile, black emotion reared up inside of him, and with a growl, he upended the whole bag, spilling its contents on the floor. Something in a blue glass jar labeled "Allure" rolled across the tile and skittered to a stop in the corner. Her things that had been neatly folded and precisely packed, scattered as he pawed through them, trying to find more evidence of his wife's deception.

He dumped out her bathroom kit, make up and accessories skittering across the floor. A second cobalt container tumbled out and broke, spilling its intoxicating fragrance into the air, something he realized she'd just recently begun wearing. He scooped up a handful of her shirts, bringing them to his nose, smelling the scent over and over again, torturing himself with the suspicion that this new sensual perfume of hers was for someone else's taste, someone else's pleasure.

Jake finally stood, his stomach clenching and twisting, and he stumbled back to the sofa. He sat, his face turned away from the mess in the entryway, breathing in through his mouth so he didn't have to smell her betrayal. He fought to keep his reaction under control. He clutched the edge of the couch cushions, rocking back and forth, clamping his jaw shut as he tried to hold everything in. But a sob wrenched its way up from his gut, tearing through the band around his throat, and another, then another, until he was weeping, his whole body quaking in the violence of his anguish.

When she emerged from their bedroom just after seven the next morning, he was sitting up, coffee in hand. He watched her as she made her way from the bathroom to the kitchen, passing the pile of her things with only a brief, acknowledging glance. She poured herself a cup of coffee and sat down on one of the stools at the counter.

She looked almost as bad as he did, he thought. Her eyes had dark circles under them, they were puffy and bleary, as though she'd been crying too. Her hair was tangled, there were long, angry marks on one cheek from where she'd lay on creases in the pillowcase, and she still wore the same jeans and top she'd had on when she came home the night before.

"Are you leaving?" He asked.

"Probably."

"When?"

"As soon as I can figure something out."

"Have you told the kids?"

"No."

"I want to be there when you do."

"Okay."

"Okay." There didn't seem to be anything left to say. Well, maybe one more thing.

"Who is he?"

TWENTY THREE

"Who is he?" he asked again when she didn't answer; louder, more demanding this time.

"It's no one, Jake. There's no one." Nora didn't look at him. She just sat on the stool, her ankles crossed, her hands wrapped around the mug on the counter in front of her. She hadn't even taken a drink. She didn't look like she was lying this morning.

"So you're not seeing anyone?" Why was he so quick to hope?

"I'm not seeing anyone." Then she turned lifeless eyes to him and added, "Not anymore."

Jake felt his heart stop, then suddenly jerk back into action. It pushed up against his throat until he thought he might explode. He leapt up and began pacing the floor. *Not anymore. Not anymore. Not anymore.* Her words throbbed inside his head to the rhythm of his footsteps.

"Stop pacing, Jake. You're making me crazy."

"Making you crazy?" He stopped marching back and forth and stood, his feet apart, his arms akimbo at his sides. "I'm making *you* crazy?" His voice was trembling with rage. He could hardly believe she was making this about her.

"Don't yell at me." Even her voice sounded lifeless. She turned away and gazed out a window at the overgrown backyard. He wondered if she noticed that he'd neglected mowing it for a few weeks.

"Stop pacing. Don't yell. Be quiet. All you do is give me orders, Nora. You know what? You have no right to tell me what to do. None, whatsoever. In fact, this is me telling *you* what to do. Get out." He walked over to her pile of clothes, kicked at a tube of mascara with his bare foot, then bent over and started shoving things back into the suitcase. "I'll even help you pack."

His hand swept through the lotion that had spilled last night, and he realized too late the broken pieces of glass were still there, too. "Ouch!" he roared, angry at himself for not paying attention, frustrated that even while trying to be tough, he would appear weak and wounded to her. He carelessly pulled a large blue shard from his palm, then grabbed an item off the top of the pile in her bag, and pressed it against the bleeding wound. The silky fabric of the negligee slithered against his hand, and rather than absorbing his blood, it seemed to repel it. He tossed it away from him, repulsed by the sensation. It made him think of snakes.

Jake looked up and found her watching him from her perch, unresponsive to either his anger or his injury. "Are you just going to sit there?"

Nora turned away again without answering him.

"Hello! Are you in there?" He raised a fist and knocked his knuckles against an imaginary surface. "What is *wrong* with you, Nora?" He stood up and kicked at the pile of clothes, scattering the things all over the entry again. "How could you do this to us? How *could* you?" Now he really was yelling. His voice broke embarrassingly, and he stormed down the hall toward the bathroom to wash his hands.

More than the blood, he wanted to scrub the stench of her affair off his hands. The sultry fragrance suddenly turned rancid in his nostrils, and he barely made it to the toilet before he started gagging.

He bent over the bowl as everything left from the night before came up, including the coffee he'd been drinking for the last two hours. Even when there was nothing more, his body continued dry-heaving, his hands clutching the vanity on one side and the edge of the bathtub on the other, leaving bloody hand-prints all over the white porcelain. His empty stomach still churned and growled, but straightening, he rinsed his mouth with water from the sink, the coppery tang of his blood mingling with the acid taste in his mouth. Then he slumped to the floor, his back to the wall, and looked down at his palm. For such a little puncture, it sure bled a lot. And hurt a lot. Or maybe it was just the gaping hole in his heart projecting pain to the wound in his hand.

"Oh God, help me. Help me. Help me, Jesus." They were the only words he could come up with, and he repeated them over and over again. Finally, he stood, washed his hands with soap and hot water, relishing in his pain, taking extra care to make certain he no longer smelled like Nora. Then he cleaned up the bloody prints he'd left all over the tub.

By the time he emerged from the bathroom, Nora had returned all her things to the suitcase. It stood upright, propped against the open front door, her garment bag folded neatly in half, resting on top. The broken glass and lotion were gone, even the aroma seemed to be dissipating out into the world, although not quickly enough for him. Her boots were nowhere to be seen. Neither was Nora.

Jake could see her car parked in the driveway, so he knew she was still here somewhere. He didn't know whether to look for her, or sit and wait for her to show up again. Apparently, she wasn't going to get out as he had demanded, and he didn't know if he had it in him to force her out. He headed down the hall to their bedroom for a change of clothes, but as he pushed open the door, the smell of her perfume assaulted his senses and he felt his stomach roll.

She'd slept in their bed while her body was drenched in her lover's stench.

He backed out and pulled the door closed behind him. He couldn't get away from it.

As he made his way back down the hall, he glanced into the kids' bedrooms. Nora was lying on Leslie's bed on her side, her face turned toward the wall. She didn't act like she was aware of him, but he knew she was. He hadn't made any attempt to walk through the house quietly.

"So does this mean you want to talk now?" His voice dripped with sarcasm as he taunted her from the doorway. "It's a little late for words, Nor."

"What's there to talk about?" she responded, not looking at him.

"Um. What's there *not* to talk about? Like what are we going to do with the kids? What are we going to do with the house? What are we going to do about the bills?"

"Really, Jake? Do we have to hash all this out right now?" She brought her legs up to her stomach, as if the idea of dissecting their lives was repugnant to her. How did she do that so smoothly, turning words around to make the sharp edges point at him? Fine. Then he'd push from the other direction.

"I don't know what we're waiting for. The kids are gone, you're already packed, and we're both here. What better time than now?"

"I'm not going to talk to you about this right now, Jake. I don't think either of us is in any condition to think clearly about our future." She still didn't look at him.

"I disagree. I really don't know what good waiting will do. Conditions aren't going to change any time soon. Stop making excuses; I'm ready to talk right now." He wasn't about to let her control how this was going to go down. Right now, he had the upper hand, even if just slightly, and he wanted to keep it that way.

"Leave me alone."

"I will *not* let you off the hook so easily! You don't *get* to make the calls around here anymore. You relinquished that right when you... you... spread your legs for some stranger. Get up and behave like a woman with at least a modicum of decency, even if you have to fake it! Or get out!"

Nora rolled over and pushed herself up to sit on the edge of the bed. "Fine. I'll go." She slipped her feet into the fuzzy slippers she'd removed, and stood up. "I have to get a few things, first." She waited for him to step aside, then she walked by him out of the room.

There was that sickening smell again, and he nearly gagged. His anger surged and he followed her, reaching for her just as she opened the door to their bedroom.

"What is that stuff you reek of?" he snarled, his face so close to hers, he could see the tiny flicker of something—fear?—in her green eyes. He had her pinned against the door, his hands wrapped around her upper arms. "Is that something *he* gave you? Because it makes me want to hurl."

Nora didn't look away. "Jo gave it to me."

"Well it smells like sex. And it makes you smell like a...like a whore." He leaned forward and sniffed at her neck, and she trembled slightly when he tightened his grip on her arms. His blood was pumping hard, adrenaline surging through him, and he groaned deep in his chest. Before he knew what he was doing, he was kissing her neck, her face, her mouth, roughly, possessively, both angry and terrified at how close to the edge of insanity he felt. "You are mine," he ground out against her lips. "Mine. And I will not share you."

He wrapped one arm around her, pinning her arms to her side, and buried the other hand in her hair, pulling her head back so he could have better access to her face. He could taste tears but he didn't know if they were hers or his... and he didn't care.

Whore! The toxic, black voice growled in his head.

My whore, he responded, just as blackly.

TWENTY FOUR

Nora lay on her side, her back to Jake whose body was curved possessively around hers. She could hear his breathing begin to slow as he slipped into the heavy sleep of a spent man. She didn't dare move for fear she'd wake him.

She wasn't afraid of him; not anymore. She no longer had any reason to be. Maybe he'd forced himself on her, but she didn't really resist. Her body ached, though, in places where it shouldn't, not after love-making. His behavior this morning was reminiscent of his drinking days when he'd come home intoxicated, and demand his conjugal rights. Granted, he'd never been quite so rough with her, but she didn't think it was because he was a kinder, gentler Jake back then. No, he'd just been too drunk to be anything but sloppy, and she'd been too miserable to refuse him. This time, however, she was fairly certain that to resist would have only made things worse for her.

She still wasn't afraid. He didn't mean to hurt her, she knew, not physically, anyway. He wanted to break her on the inside the way she'd broken him. The things he called her, the words he used while having his way with her, even the way he pushed her physically without causing any real damage, it was all evidence that he didn't want her bleeding on the outside. She understood. That was why she didn't stop him. Maybe pain would fill the dead, emptiness in her heart, at least for a while.

She didn't want to think about anything; divorce, children, guilt, or the apologies that he was certain to heap on her head when he came to his senses. He would attack her character, all the while beating himself up for forcing his way on her, for wanting to be with her at all. She would watch him with empty eyes, fully knowing what to expect, because he was so predictable. He would rant and rave at her, asking her why, why, why, and she would say nothing, knowing there was no way he could, or would, even try to understand her actions.

If she stayed, he would do it all again and again, and she would let him, knowing it was his way of staking his claim on her, of proving his manhood to her, to himself, and in some sick way, to Tristan. He would apologize after, she would hold him, and tell him she understood. Because she did. The sudden clarity that had opened her eyes to her own destructive behavior, gave her a strange and removed sensitivity to what Jake must be going through.

Eventually, if they chose not to divorce, living together might be possible again. It might get easier, but this would always be between them, always lurking in the shadows of the photo albums, the family videos, the memories.

She eased her body out from under his heavy arm and scooped up her scattered clothing off the floor. Her left inner thigh was already beginning to shadow, and she winced when she touched the teeth marks above one collarbone. The skin wasn't broken, but it was raised and red. This was no teenage love-bite she was now sporting.

"Jerk," she muttered almost inaudibly. "How am I supposed to cover that up?"

She crossed the hall to the bathroom and turned on the shower. There was no amount of hot water that could wash off the way she felt, but it might help her relax enough to take stock of the situation. She had a long day ahead of her, and she still didn't know where to begin. "If nothing else, maybe I can wash the whore smell off of me. Jerk," she said again.

By the time she was done in the bathroom, she was feeling irritable and cantankerous, rather than calmer and more collected, but at least she'd made a few decisions about the immediate future.

Jake was back in the living room pacing the floor, and that irritated her. He had changed his clothes, but he still looked rumpled and out of sorts... and that irritated her, too. He waited until she had crossed the room to the kitchen before he spoke.

"I made fresh coffee." It sounded almost like a peace offering, but she didn't acknowledge it, or him. She filled the tea kettle instead, and put it on a burner to boil. She desperately wanted another cup of coffee, but she wouldn't admit that right now for the world.

"What time do you have to be at your presentation today?"

"I don't," she replied. "There isn't one."

"Oh. What happened?" Jake stood with his thumbs hooked into his pants, looking like a little boy who was pretending to be brave and unaffected by the bully's unkindness.

"Nothing happened. There just isn't one."

"As in, there never was one, or it's been canceled?" A slight edge crept into his voice.

"There never was one." There wasn't any reason to lie to him. He knew the worst, and now the details seemed insignificant to her. He obviously felt differently.

"What do you mean? So this was all a set-up? You *lied* about it so you could spend the weekend with your lover? Where were you planning on going? What if I'd asked questions? Like which development you were going to be at?" His voice became louder and louder. "How did you expect to get away with it?"

As if echoing his emotions, the tea kettle began to whistle, softly at first, then more shrilly as steamy water sputtered out the top of the spout. She didn't move until he shouted, "Would you get that stupid thing? Can't you hear it?"

Nora turned the burner off, poured the hot water over a couple of mint teabags in her porcelain teapot, and readied a cup and saucer for when it had steeped the way she liked it. She stood at the counter watching the steam puff cheerfully out of the teapot spout, trying to be objective and honest with herself.

Was she purposefully goading him? Was she intentionally antagonizing him, trying to get a reaction out of him, so that he would be the bad guy? She snorted softly and shook her head. *I don't care*, she thought. *I don't care that I'm the bad guy.*

In fact, the more she thought about it, the more she realized how freeing it was to shoulder the blame for the failure of their marriage. She was so accustomed to being responsible for making everything succeed, that the cloak of blame settled comfortably around her, like an old friend. If she was responsible for her actions, then she would be responsible for the repercussions as well.

"I'm going to find a place of my own, Jake,"

"You're not taking the kids," he cut in, crossing his arms. She could see his chest rising and falling, his breathing fast.

"I'm not taking the kids. But I'm going to say this once, and just once, so listen carefully." She didn't miss the flush that crept up his neck from beneath his shirt. "If you so much as have a sip of wine-vinegar dressing, and I find out about it, you will have hell to pay. I will not have you endangering their lives. Is there any part of what I just said that you don't understand to be a threat *and* a promise?"

"Got it loud and clear, Nor. Anything else?" Sarcasm dripped from every word. The morning's debacle in the bedroom, and the guilt he must have felt, were apparently forgotten, and Nora was relieved. She didn't want to hear his apologies. She came around the counter and sat down at the dining table, her hot teacup held between both hands. She looked across the back of the couch at her husband, making sure he was listening to her.

"I will still take them to and from school every day. We will come home in the afternoons, I will feed them, help them with homework, spend the evening with them in some semblance of normalcy, and after they're in bed, I will go to my own place to sleep. I will be back in the mornings to get them up and make them breakfast. Until school is out, my new place, wherever I end up staying, will be my new workshop as far as they are concerned. I will not, nor will you, ruin the last of this school year with our sordid affairs."

"*Your* sordid affair. I'm not the one who screwed around."

"Excellent. Glad you're on board." Nora rolled her eyes, then took a sip of the strong tea. The mint would help settle her stomach, she hoped. "When school is over, we'll tell them what our plans are, because hopefully, by then, we'll actually have more permanent plans to tell them about."

"Wow. You've got this whole thing figured out, haven't you? Did you come up with all of this in the shower?" Jake sneered at her. "Did you find a place to live while you were in there, too?"

"Grow up, Jake. Someone has to figure things out in this family, and it never *has* been you, so why are you acting so surprised? Yes, I came up with all of that in the shower. And yes, it's the way things are going to be. If the kids ask questions, we'll just deal with them as carefully as we can."

"You mean, lie to them." It wasn't a question. Nora rolled her eyes again.

"Call it what you want. There are some things better left unsaid until the right time."

"Like the fact that you're screwing another man? What's the matter, Nor? You worried about how that will go over with our precious children?" He was kicking the corner of the sofa without realizing it: *thunk, thunk, thunk.*

"Just don't make this any harder on them than it needs to be. You can say your mean little things to me, you can call me names, you can rape me if you need to, but don't take it out on them."

"I did *not* r—rape you, Nora!" He practically choked over the word. "I might have been a little rough, but I did *not* force you to do anything you didn't want to do."

"Call it what you want, Jake," she said, tugging at the neckline of her top so that he couldn't miss the marks he'd left at the base of her neck. "Just keep your attacks between us, you understand? This has nothing to do with the kids."

"I can't believe that you're accusing me of r—rape—raping you!" He could hardly get the word out, but he was staring at her shoulder, his cheeks flushed with guilt. "You came in here all proud and... and *alluring*." He drew the word out to emphasize his distaste. "You baited me; *seduced* me! What did you expect would happen?"

"Like I said, Jake. Call it what you want." Nora stared down into her nearly empty cup. Even knowing how blind he sometimes was, she couldn't believe he really thought she'd set out to seduce him. Because she didn't scream bloody murder when he pinned her to the door? Because she clamped her mouth shut around the pain as he shoved her, twisted her, bent her in ways she didn't know she could bend? Because she didn't cry when he bit her, squeezed her, forced his way inside her unreceptive body? Because of this, he assumed she *wanted* him?

Jake charged across the room, gripped the edge of the table with one hand, and leaned forward so that he was looking down his nose at her. She took note of the rage he wanted her to see, as well as the fear and shame he was trying desperately to mask behind his snarl. He pointed a finger in her face. "I'll tell you what I call it. I call it just rewards. I got what I wanted—a long, overdue release—and you got what you wanted—some wild and crazy sex with a complete stranger. You've never met this side of me before, doll, so you'd better pay attention. Don't, for one second, think that you're calling the shots around here." He pounded his fist on the table to emphasize his point. "I'm not the one walking away." He jabbed his finger at her again, nearly taking one of her eyes out. She closed them, just in case, but didn't flinch. "*You*," he growled, "are the bad guy this time, Nora."

She almost smiled as she heard her own guilty verdict being spoken aloud. But she *was* going to call the shots around here. And he was just going to have to deal with it.

"Do you have a better plan then?"

"How about this? You tell our kids the truth about yourself, then get on with your sorry life. I'll pick up the pieces of their broken hearts."

"And you'll put a roof over their heads?" She snorted softly. "You'll make sure there's hot water for their showers, and bread in the cupboard and milk in the refrigerator for their cereal? You'll pay the phone bill so the school can call you when you forget to pick them up? You'll mow the lawn without having to be reminded every week, like a child?" She looked pointedly out the window at the scraggly back yard. "Are you actually going to go out and get a real job, Jakey?"

"Ah. The claws are out." He straightened and crossed his arms over his chest again.

"Why don't you sit down. Maybe we can talk this over like adults."

"Hm. I think not. I don't really feel like sharing a table with an adulteress."

"You and Jesus, huh?" She put a finger to her lips and furrowed her eyebrows. "Wait a minute. That's not how I remember the story. There was something about being without sin and throwing the first stone." Nora shook her head and shrugged her shoulders. "I must have misunderstood what I was reading."

"Shut up, Nora."

TWENTY FIVE

JAKE SAT ON THE sofa all morning, getting up only to refill his coffee, then to urinate it out again. His stomach ached, and the high doses of caffeine and coffee bean oils did nothing to settle it, but he found strange pleasure in the self-inflicted discomfort. It was better than dealing with the pain in his chest, he decided, as he brewed another pot around noon.

Nora had been gone for over an hour now. She took only her purse, so he knew that even if she found something right away, she'd be back for her things. Besides, what was she going to do about Leslie and Felix? Her ridiculous plan didn't address weekends when the kids were home all day and up late at night. Did that mean she'd be sticking around the house all weekend long? And if so, where did she plan on sleeping? He shivered at the thought of her in their bed beside him, his body betraying him while his mind was repulsed by the thought of being with her.

He couldn't help thinking of this morning—he'd been going back to it over and over. Yes, his anger had gotten the best of him, and yes, he'd been forceful with her, but how could she accuse him of rape?

"She reciprocated, I know she did. It wasn't like she just lay there." He dropped his head in his hands, running his fingers through the hair at his temples. "I didn't force her. Things just got a little rough." He felt like he was arguing with himself. "She certainly didn't seem to mind."

He shuddered, imagining Nora giving herself to someone else in the same way. Responding. Going back for more. Coming home to him. Responding to him. Then going back.... How long? Days? Weeks? Months? It couldn't be years. It wasn't possible.

The countless late nights at the office when she didn't come home until two or three in the morning. Mornings when she'd left dressed in loose, flowing dresses, or jeans and t-shirts, quite a departure from her normal classic attire of suits or blazers. Then there were the long weekends she'd taken. They were rare because of the kids, only two that he could remember, but both were home conventions she insisted she needed to attend.

How convenient for her that he trusted her.

How convenient for her that she was such a good liar.

Granted, her first trip away, he hadn't been so innocent himself. She'd made arrangements for the kids to go to her mom's house, and he'd spent the first night in front of the television. Before he made any concerted effort to be careful, he was watching a late night show that was beyond borderline pornography. With no one around to hold him accountable, he'd watched the whole thing, indulging in self-gratification at its basest. When the show was over, he called Nora, hoping to have an intimate phone call with her in order to ease his guilty conscience, but she didn't pick up. He even left two sexy voice mails asking her to call him back. She never did, and he'd gone to bed feeling both alone and lonely, and called her back in the morning, leaving another message apologizing for his inappropriate requests.

She, on the other hand, was apparently participating in things about which he was only fantasizing, and now it made him cringe as he considered what a pathetic loser he'd been. When she returned home, he assumed her air of discomfort and stand-offish attitude were because she'd guessed the reason behind his sick phone calls. Now he knew better.

The next time she'd gone away, however, he'd been a model husband and father. Jake went out and bought new sheets, putting them on their bed himself. He and the kids spent all day Saturday cleaning up both the front and back yards, then he bought two dozen roses and divided them into vases throughout the house. They were a soft, velvety coral-pink that made him think of her lips. The night she came home, he'd scattered rose petals on her pillow, and had a bottle of her favorite Moscato chilling in the fridge. But she was late. The disappointed kids were already asleep in their beds, and Jake was nodding off on the sofa, a half-full cup of coffee in his hand. When she stumbled through the door with her things, the noise startled him awake, and he had spilled the remains of his mug all over the carpet. She was obviously exhausted, and now thinking back on the night, it occurred to him that she looked like she'd been crying. By the time he cleaned up his spill, however, Nora was sound asleep, the petals in a pile on her bedside table.

The amber bottle with its elegant label was still somewhere in the back of the fridge, he was pretty sure. Well, he decided, that would be the first thing to go. He would take great pleasure in destroying the evidence of his ignorance and stupidity.

He found it lying on its side behind the large milk and juice jugs on the bottom shelf. Taking it out to the garage with him, he pulled out a locked case at the back of the highest cupboard, and lifted out his dad's old Browning 20-gauge shotgun. It had a brutal recoil from some mishap his dad had with it, something he'd always intended to get adjusted so he could use it, and someday train his kids with it. Well, today, he'd just have to deal with a bruised shoulder. He had some shooting to do, and he couldn't wait for a gunsmith to pamper him.

It was a beauty, his daddy's gun. It felt manly just to hold it in his hands. Weighing in at just a little over six pounds, it bumped solidly up against his shoulder. It had been a long time since he'd fired this baby off, but it would be well-worth the effort it would take to get it ready.

He'd get only one chance. The neighbors would call the police if he took more than one shot. People's ears might only perk up at the sound of one loud blast, but two or three would have them picking up their phones.

When the gun went off the first time, the kickback was considerably stronger than he remembered, and he clutched his shoulder as pain shot through his collarbone and down his arm. It took several minutes to recover enough to realize he'd completely missed the bottle he'd set on the low wall separating Nora's flower garden from the lawn, but one of her rose bushes lay on its side, shredded by the blast. Lucky for him, he'd thought to put an extra slug in his pocket. He reloaded, relishing the sound of oiled metal sliding over metal, took aim, and pulled the trigger. Let the cops come. Let them arrest him. He didn't care. This time, the butt of the gun skittered off the top of his shoulder and slammed into his jaw just below his ear. He dropped the gun, cupping the side of his face, bent over double, in so much pain his vision blurred.

"Argh!" He growled against his fist as he straightened up to see if he'd been successful this time. The remains of the bottle were scattered all over the yard, and he'd taken the tops off a few more of Nora's bushes, but he realized too late that the kids would not be able to play out here until he cleaned up the worst of the glass. The flowerbed, on the other hand, was her problem, and he was looking forward to seeing her face when she noticed the devastation he'd wrought.

"You're an idiot, Jake." He clutched at his throbbing right shoulder; he was seriously hurting and wondered if he'd broken something. He needed an icepack and quickly. The glass would have to wait. "At least I hit it," he grunted.

Back on the sofa, ice packed around his pulsing collarbone and swollen jaw, he let himself sink into the pain he was feeling. Why was destruction the way to deal with this? Even injured, all he wanted to do was go out and destroy something else. He thought about methodically breaking each piece of the pink Depression glass she'd been collecting since before they were married. He considered driving down to her office and downloading a virus onto her computer. He even contemplated accidentally driving her car off a bridge, but he couldn't think of one close enough to make it worth his while.

What he really wanted to do was to find out where this guy lived, and beat every last ounce of manhood out of him. He'd even be willing to take another hit to the shoulder if he could use the gun. He was sure it was that Tristan guy he'd caught her on the phone with yesterday—was it just yesterday?—and if he could find out anything about him, the Browning might just get a little more use. At least he knew he could actually hit his target.

The police never showed up, and Jake finally fell asleep after giving in and taking something for the pain.

· · • · • • · • · • ·

THE TINY COTTAGE WAS a gift, one she knew she didn't deserve. The little stream running along the edge of the river rock patio made her think of water sprites and pixie hollows, and she was able to lay aside her cloak of guilt and her longing for what she couldn't have when she sat beside it, her feet dangling in the chilled water.

Whoever had lived here before her had spent some time in the little yard. There were perennials under the trees, rose bushes in the flowerbed under the kitchen window, and a honeysuckle vine twining with a star-flowered jasmine grew up and over the tiny entryway, forming a lacy arch leading to the front door.

It was really just a box; one large room, a tiny bathroom, and a galley kitchenette that looked out onto the patio. By using folding panels and furniture groupings, she was able to convert the one room into several designated areas, and it suddenly became a miniature home. It was perfect in every way.

Oh, she knew it was temporary. They couldn't do this forever. At least she couldn't. She was having a difficult time falling asleep at night, and the early mornings were beginning to take their toll on her. Yesterday she didn't get to the house until after Leslie was up and in the shower. Jake, much to her surprise, had covered for her.

Every time she saw Jake, he seemed different to her. Sometimes he was moody, angry, and said incredibly horrible things to her. Sometimes he seemed distant and unaffected by her presence. Still other times he couldn't stop touching her; the back of his knuckles following the curve of her shoulder, his fingertips smoothing the hair away from her cheek, his body brushing against hers as he passed by. Sometimes he even rested his hand on her low back as they walked together.

They spent very little time alone, and they never spoke of important things. Their conversations revolved around the daily activities of their children, meals, and the house. They didn't even discuss work, although it was pretty obvious they were both busy. Jake seemed to have tapped into a new source for referrals, and was heading out the door on most mornings, just as she was leaving with the kids. She didn't ask for details, and he didn't offer any. The bank account, still jointly-owned, reflected his increased income, and she was honestly happy for him.

School would be out in two weeks, and Nora felt the pressure of anticipation. She knew the day was coming when they would sit down with Leslie and Felix and tell them the truth—or at least a version of the truth she and Jake thought the kids could handle—and life would permanently change for their little family. She dreaded it and longed for it at the same time, afraid of what was to come, but needing closure, too.

Tristan called repeatedly the first several days. She finally agreed to meet with him somewhere public so they could talk.

"I miss you, my Isolde. You're breaking my heart." The words sounded cliché to her ears, but the pain in his voice seemed very real. He sounded terrible, and she was overwhelmed by guilt for all the lives her choices were affecting so terribly.

They met at a busy sandwich shop about halfway between their homes. He didn't wait for an invitation. Cupping her face in his hands, he bent and kissed her sweetly, intimately, thoroughly.

She pulled away while she could still stand upright. "Please don't do this, Tristan. Please. I can't take it."

"Come back to my place. I don't want to do this here. I thought I could, but it's not right asking me to behave like you're a stranger, knowing how we feel about each other. Let's get out of here."

Nora knew it wasn't fair—none of this was fair to anyone, anymore—but she also knew exactly what would happen if she went back to his place. She couldn't let things pick up where they'd left off. "I can't. I don't trust myself. I don't trust you."

"You can trust me. I love you, Isolde. I need you." He pulled her close again and bent his head to whisper against her hair. "Just let me touch you. Let me hold you; kiss you the way you need to be kissed. I'm aching for you."

The whole public setting thing backfired horribly. Tristan's powers of persuasion had her faltering, wavering, and then giving in all together. He wouldn't stop touching her and looking at her like he might devour her.

Once on his own turf, he quite literally swept her off her feet, destroying any last vestiges of her defenses, and she cried bitter tears of defeat, mingled with sweet relief, as she lay in his arms at the end of the evening. It was where she wanted to be more than anything in that moment. She felt covered by his big body, both physically and emotionally, and she was having a hard time remembering why she'd left him in the first place.

"Why are you crying now, my Isolde?" He murmured softly against her hair. "Although I admit I'm almost afraid to ask."

She turned in his arms to face him, smiled sadly, and wiped the tears from her face. "I missed you, Tristan."

"And I missed you." He replied matter-of-factly. "You're not leaving again, you know." He ran his fingertips along her hairline, down the column of her neck, following the curve of her collarbone. Suddenly his fingers stilled.

"What's this?" He propped himself up on one elbow and pushed her hair away from the bruise that was still visible at the base of her neck. "Are those teeth marks?" His incredulous tone made her flinch, and she reached up to cover it with her hand.

"It's nothing, Tristan. Leave it alone."

"This is *not* nothing. Someone bit you! Did your husband do that to you?" He sat up and flipped the sheet back, exposing her whole body to his scrutiny. "What else did he do to you? And you'd even *consider* choosing him over me?" His hands ran along the contours of her body, and even though she tried to push them away, he was persistent. "Look at these bruises!" He was livid. "What did he do to you? Did he rape you? I'll kill the little...."

"Stop it!" Nora sat up, yanking the covers back over her. "No one is going to kill anyone. You guys are all alike. All you want to do is go out and kill something. What will that solve?"

"First of all, we guys are *not* all alike," he growled, his voice ratcheting around her. "I would never mark your body like that. Never. Do you hear me?" He waited until she nodded. "And I'll tell you what it will solve. If I kill your husband, he'll be out of the picture, and you'll be freed up to take on a real man."

"Except that you'll be sharing your room with a cellmate, Tristan." Nora interjected sarcastically.

She knew he didn't like her sarcasm, and his devil-may-care response confirmed it. "That's only if I get caught. There are plenty of ways to do away with a body, though."

She stood up and began putting her clothes back on. "You know what? This is ridiculous! Why on earth did I come back here?"

"You weren't complaining a few minutes ago." He lay back against the pillows and flashed a wide and cocky grin at her. "Where do you think you're going, woman?"

She dressed quickly, angrily, and he just watched, until she stood, hands on her hips, glaring at him from the foot of the bed. "I don't know what I was thinking coming here. How could I be so stupid? I'm leaving. For good this time. I don't want to cry anymore. I don't want to lie anymore. I'm tired of running around like a chicken with my head cut off, trying to figure out what I want out of life. I'm tired of me! I, I, I! That's all I do anymore—look out for me."

She was spinning out of control, no longer caring that the tears were pouring steadily from her eyes, her voice rising as she voiced thoughts she'd never given air to until now. "What about my husband? So what if he's got issues. Doesn't he have the right to expect his wife to come home to him every night? To be faithful? And my children? Don't they deserve a mother who puts them first, who would sacrifice her own life for theirs?"

She pointed at him. "And you. What about you? Don't you deserve a woman all to yourself? Don't you *want* that, Tristan? How can this be okay with you, sharing me with another man?"

She spread her arms wide and stomped her foot. "I have wounded every person who is precious to me, including you, and I'm tired of it. I'm a self-centered, self-absorbed wretch, and I will only make you miserable." She hiccupped and sobbed at the same time, as if emphasizing her point.

"You only make me miserable when you leave me." Tristan spoke quietly, pushing himself upright, the sheet settling around his waist. "I love you, and I want you to be with me." Oh, he was a beautiful man, with beautiful words.

"Love? Love is not enough." Nora shook her head. "It's not enough, Tristan."

"Well, what more do you want from me? You have my heart, you have my home, you even have my studio, and that's more than I've ever given to any woman. You're already a part of everything in my life. I'll take your kids, too, if that's what you're waiting for me to say. You just surprised me the other day when you talked about them moving in here so suddenly. But I've thought about it, and I know we can make it work, the four of us. Come on. Let's give this thing a chance, okay?"

"No, Tristan. I'm not staying. I can't stay. It isn't me here, not the real me, anyway. The one plugged into your world is a fantasy. You have no idea what it means to be a dad – you don't even know my kids. And I don't want you to just "take" them so you can have me. That would be horrible for everyone, especially you. It can't work."

"Why not?" He was frustrated, hurt by her words. "People make it work all the time and I'm more than willing to try. What else do you want?"

"Oh, Tristan. It's just not right, that's why. It's not right. It's not right. Oh, God, I hope it's not too late." Her voice faded, and she bowed her head, wrapping her arms around her ribcage, as she began to weep quietly.

"My Isolde. Come here." He reached out for her, but she stepped back, shaking her head. She spoke so quietly that he had to lean forward to hear her.

"I... I miss God, Tristan." Saying the words brought a sense of stillness like she hadn't known in so long. "I miss God. I've conveniently left Him out of our relationship, but that's what else I want, Tristan. I want God back. He's not in this thing between us." She waved a hand between them. "I can't have both of you."

"I can take you to church, Nora. Why didn't you say so in the first place? We can be a church-going family." He chuckled as if the solution was something so simple.

"No, Tristan. That's not how it works." Nora smiled ruefully and shook her head. She turned and dropped to the edge of the bed, her legs no longer able to support her. She let him slide down next to her and take her in his arms, but her mind was made up.

"I'm sorry, Tristan. I'm sorry for not being the right person for you. It's not you, it's me. I—I can't stay with Jake, either."

She was completely moved into the cottage by the end of that week. The kids watched her and Jake with wide eyes, but took their cues from the adults, and avoided any discussions about the reasons behind the changes that were going on in their home. It was a tense, difficult time, but everyone seemed to be on their best behavior, and trying extra hard to get along.

Nora cried herself to sleep alone in her antique, wrought-iron trundle bed almost every night, the stream outside weeping along with her. She suffered a complete and utter misery, but was somehow relieved to find that the tears were back. The well had not run dry, after all.

TWENTY SIX

THE TIME HAD COME. School had been out for a few weeks and the children were beginning to ask questions.

"When are we going camping? It's already the middle of June and it's going to be too hot to fish if we don't go soon." Leslie, a natural when it came to stream fishing, could hardly wait to get out into the wild, and Nora couldn't help but wonder how many more years she'd be this excited to spend time with her family. *Once we drop the bomb, we may get zip, zero, none more years.*

"I need to go shopping, Dad. My fishing vest is too small. I can't hold everything in it." Felix dug his vest out the first day of summer vacation every year and practiced wearing it; "breaking it in," he called it. "I'm making plans to catch the biggest fish this summer, and I have to get into character."

"You're going up against a champion, bro. Ain't gonna happen." Leslie was justifiably confident. Even Jake rarely outdid her at the river.

"Just wait and see, Lester, my snarly sister. Just wait and see." He wiggled his eyebrows at her and nodded his head, as though he had some secret weapon he was keeping mum about.

"I'll wait and see, all right. I'll wait with baited breath so I can see you go down in flames again."

"All I can tell you is this...," he paused for dramatic effect. "Just wait and see."

The kids had finally gone to bed, much later than usual, even for a Saturday night during summer vacation, and she and Jake sat in the living room across from each other, sharing a few rare moments of peace between them. It was dark, and the world was settling into stillness outside. Tomorrow was Sunday, and Nora was looking forward to the day off. She'd worked with a new client that morning, Sandra Madison, and knew it wasn't going to be an easy week. The woman was demanding and entitled, but with their uncertain future, Nora was afraid to turn down any work at this time.

"Maybe we should wait until after we go camping, Nor." Jake didn't look at her when he suggested it, as though he was measuring the words as they came out of his mouth. "There's probably never going to be the perfect time to talk to the kids about us, but this trip is pretty important to them." Then he did look at her, a wry grin on his face. "If you think you can handle being with me twenty-four-seven without killing me."

"I'm more worried about you being able to handle being around me without killing me," she chuckled, trying to keep the mood light. "If you're up for it, then I'm game, too. I'd love to do it one more time as a family. You know, one last huzzah."

She wondered if she sounded too callous, but she couldn't help it. She knew they were just putting off the inevitable, that no matter when, or even what, they told the kids, life would forever change for them. But she really did want one more sweet memory to tide them over. "Do you really think we can pull it off?"

Jake turned away from her to look out the window, not acknowledging her question. She saw a flicker of something cross his face, and had the grace to be ashamed. She didn't want to cause him any more pain; she was so tired of hurting people. She set her teacup down and lay her head back on the couch cushions behind her, blinking back the emotions welling up inside her. Suddenly, she was beyond weary, and unable to resist any longer, she closed her eyes and tears slid silently down the sides of her face and into her hair as the stillness stretched out between them.

"Stay here tonight. I want you to stay tonight." He spoke softly, gently. She didn't respond. She didn't need to; all she had to do was *not* leave.

"You don't have to sleep with me. That's not what I'm asking. I just want you to stay here where I know you're...close to us."

She opened her eyes and found him watching her, leaning forward in the big chair he was in, elbows on his knees, empty coffee cup held between his two hands. She could see his bare toes curling in the carpet under his feet; his toenails were neatly trimmed. It suddenly dawned on her that he wasn't asking her if she was okay, that he hadn't asked in weeks, and that made her cry even more.

"Look, Nora. I don't know what we're going to do. This whole thing terrifies me. I don't like admitting to anyone that things are broken, but they are, and I think we need help." He took a deep breath and let it out slowly, his next words coming with obvious effort. "Will you go talk to Pastor Rob with me before we make any final decisions?"

Still she said nothing, but for different reasons. She hadn't been to church in nearly six months, and she knew Jake still showed up every Sunday on his own, taking the kids to Sunday School. Once or twice he'd tell her that someone had asked how she was, but most of the time no one seemed to even notice her absence. Their small group had moved to a home on the other side of town after the first of the year, and they'd stopped going to that altogether, her long hours their excuse. Only one of the ladies had called Nora, but that was to ask for prayer because the woman's husband was struggling with his pornography addiction again, not to ask about their absence.

She simply didn't feel like talking to a pastor. She didn't feel like talking to anyone, really, but a pastor who would give her formulaic answers with no understanding of the situation was more than she could handle. Even Vicky with her 'pray first' therapy put her off. A lot of good *that* had done. In fact, praying for her husband had sent him right out to the bar and into the arms of his waitress. No, she wasn't interested in talking to a pastor.

She wanted to talk directly to God, but only if He would talk back, and He seemed nowhere to be found.

"I don't know, Jake. It's been months and no one even notices we're gone. Not that I'm waiting for them to notice or take care of us, but we've been members there for sixteen years. You'd think someone would start asking questions. You'd think someone would notice that you show up alone every Sunday. You'd think someone would bother asking if things are okay. Pastor Rob married us, for goodness sake. We saw him every single week, and I'm assuming you still do. Doesn't he even notice that I'm not there?"

"I don't know, Nor. I don't know why no one asks. Everyone is too busy with their own issues, I suppose. But I don't want to give up without a fight, and I think we have to talk to someone. Do you have any other suggestions?" Jake was staring down into his mug as if looking for options there.

Nora shook her head slowly, once again considering and then ruling out Vicky. The woman had faithfully called her every week all through March, then Nora had politely, but firmly, asked her to take her off of her call list. Vicky had agreed, encouraging her to call if she ever needed to talk. She promised to continue praying for her and said goodbye. To Nora's relief, the woman had remained true to her word and not called again. Whether or not she continued praying for her seemed irrelevant at this point. "I don't know. Let me think about it for a couple of days, okay? Maybe talking to Pastor Rob would be okay, but I just need to think about it. In the meantime, if you want to, feel free to call him and talk to him yourself."

"I don't want to go alone." Jake looked up at her, his eyes wide and frustrated. "What good will that do?"

Before she could stop herself, the words were out, but she wasn't sure if she was more frustrated at her husband, or about the church family who didn't miss them. "Man up, Jake. You don't need me there holding your hand. Go alone. Tell him the truth about us, about yourself, about me. I don't care."

Jake got up and headed toward the kitchen. Nora sat for some time before she, too, took her cup to the sink. "I'm going home."

"This is home, Nora."

"Whatever, Jake."

"This is home, Nora," he repeated. His fingers curled into a fist, and although he didn't do it hard, he thumped his knuckles on the counter beside him in time to his words. "This is your home. This is home." His voice rose as he spoke more adamantly. "This is your home, my home, our children's home. This is our home. Why are you trying to destroy it?"

Nora picked up her purse and walked out. Would things ever get easier for them?

· · · · ● · ● · · · ·

The entrance to the cottage was lit by the white stringed lights she'd tacked up under the eaves of the little patio. It looked inviting and peaceful to her weary soul, and the sound of the water gurgling close by made her feel undone in a good way. Here she could let down her guard. No thinking, no deciding, no faking, no worrying. She could simply shut down.

As tired as she was, she knew it would be a long time before sleep rescued her from her plight, so she showered, put on some comfortable pajamas, and put the kettle on for tea. She tried to read while she waited, but she couldn't focus on the words, so she just sat, staring out the window into the darkness outside.

Alone in her little sanctuary, isolated and lonely, bitter and frightened, she sat, while out there beyond the boundary line of her little plot, others were hurt and wounded and in turmoil because of her. Maybe if she just stayed here forever, they'd eventually forget about her. The honeysuckle growing along the front porch would creep slowly up and over the cottage, the jasmine filling in the empty spaces. The stream would, over time, overflow its banks and wear away at the river rock foundation, and bit by bit, the little house would float away, taking her with it.

"Oh, good grief, Nora. Snap out of it." She grabbed a quilt off the slipper chair she'd been sitting in and headed out to sit by the water, hoping to be soothed into a more relaxed state.

She listened to the sound of the night creatures busy with their lives all around her. Anywhere there's water, there's life, and her little section of the stream teemed with it. Critters rustled in the vines covering the opposite bank and ambling up over the fence beyond it. There was a chittering in the branches of the mulberry tree arching over her head, and she could see the silhouette of her neighbor's cat as it sat near the water's edge, focusing intently on something in the shrubs close by.

Nora reached over and let her fingers trail in the water, closing her eyes as she imagined once again being swept along this little stream. What would it be like to just float away and disappear into nothing? She wasn't really entertaining thoughts of death. She just had an overwhelming desire to stop living for a while, at least until the things she'd messed up so badly were set to right again. Then she could just step back into life and pick up again where she left off. Was that too much to ask?

"God? Are You there?" She whispered, knowing she couldn't be heard by any human ears, not above the sound of the water. "Is that too much to ask? Can you just let me hang out here, in the shelter of the rock, until everything is back to normal?"

He didn't answer in words, but something in the music of the brook seemed to shift subtly. A sighing breeze swept a few leaves across the rocks at her feet and she waited, listening for something else, something more specific, but that was all. She had to smile at her overactive imagination; even so, she felt comforted in some small way.

TWENTY SEVEN

T̲he̲ ̲next̲ ̲morning,̲ ̲she̲ awoke to a pressure between her temples that pulsed against the backs of her eyes. She sat up groggily, her head weighing a thousand pounds.

She had the morning to herself while Jake and the kids were at church, so she took another shower, hoping the steam would open her sinuses and wake her up, but it didn't help much. She poured herself a glass of cold soda water, afraid to even try coffee, and took some pills to combat her headache. She couldn't remember what the plan was this afternoon, but the way she felt, it wouldn't matter. Whatever they did would be torture for her.

After locking up, she fumbled in her purse to find her shades, the sun like daggers in her eyes. She sat in the car for a few minutes, actually considering calling Jake and telling him she couldn't make it, but after the way things had ended last night, her guilt overrode her misery. Surely the medicine would kick in soon.

Jake was out in the garage when she arrived, fiddling with the lawn mower. He glanced up as she pulled up in front of the house, acknowledged her with a wave, and bent over his task again. She was greatly relieved when he didn't rush out to meet her; all she wanted to do was lie down again. There was a bomb ticking away inside her head, and she felt flushed and chilled at the same time. She hoped the kids were in the back yard, or at least uncharacteristically calm.

She dropped her purse on the coffee table and curled up into the corner of the sofa, dragging the throw from the back of the couch around her shoulders. Several minutes went by before she heard the front door open and close, and Jake's footsteps approaching.

"Hey."

"Hey," she replied, not opening her eyes.

"What's up with you?" It wasn't kindness in his voice, but at least he wasn't ignoring her.

"I think my head is going to explode. Not feeling so well today." She cracked one eye open and peered up at him, unable to read his expression.

He stood looking down at her for such a long time that she finally closed her eye again and pulled the throw up over her face. She heard him walk away and sighed heavily, wishing for all the world that things were different.

"Nora?" He was back with a glass of water in one hand and something cupped in the other. "I brought you some medicine."

"Thanks." She didn't know how much time had passed since she'd taken the pills at the cottage, and she murmured from under the blanket. "Just put them on the end table."

He sat down on the coffee table in front of her and waited until she poked her head out to look at him again. Apparently, he wanted to talk, so she pulled herself a little more upright, bringing her feet to the floor for balance.

"Mmm," she moaned quietly. She was feeling worse by the minute, not better.

"I'm sorry about last night." Jake spoke without preamble, straightforward, and to the point. "I was out of line trying to pressure you to stay here, but I still want you to consider going to see Pastor Rob with me. Will you think about it?"

"I have thought about it, Jake. I think you should go to him yourself for now. I'm just not ready. I don't care what you tell him. You can tell him everything and anything. I mean it. I'm not interested in hiding anything; I just don't feel like talking about it myself." She leaned her head back on the cushions behind her and closed her eyes again. "If you think he can help you sort some things out, then I absolutely encourage you to go."

Jake didn't speak. She could sense his physical closeness even with her eyes closed, and she drew her legs back up on the couch, tucking them under her. She wasn't put off by him; she just didn't want to be touched by anyone right now. Her skin felt like every nerve ending had worked itself to the surface and was just waiting to be stimulated, to cause her discomfort.

"I think I need to go back to bed," she muttered. "Where are the kids?"

"They're next door at the Buckners. Their grandkids came home from church with them, so I let Leslie and Felix go over there to play until lunch. Do you want me to call them?"

"No, that's all right. I think I should just go back to my place and rest some more." She sat forward, trying to work up the energy to stand. "Can you tell them I'm not feeling well and that I'll be back tonight?"

"Sure, but you look pretty awful. Are you okay to drive?" Jake stood and offered her his hand. She took it, finding momentary comfort in the way her hand felt so familiar in his, and pulled herself upright. He didn't resist when she pulled away.

"I'll be okay. I just need to go get some more sleep." She found her sunglasses in the top of her purse and slipped them on as he followed her out the front door to her car. "I'll call you when I wake up. Stop worrying," she said when she saw his look of concern. "I'll be fine."

Jake stood on the curb watching as she pulled away, but she didn't pay too much attention. She needed all her efforts focused on the road in front of her.

She barely made it in the front door and raced to her bathroom where she vomited what little there was in her stomach. She hated throwing up. She hated the uncontrollable violence of it, the way her body felt like it was going to turn inside out, and especially the way it seemed to increase the pressure in her head. What was wrong with her?

Nora exchanged her jeans for baggy sweats, slipping a pair of thick socks on her feet. June was as hot as ever in the middle of the day, but a fever was making her teeth chatter and her skin goose-bump. She burrowed beneath the covers of her bed and waited to get warm.

Her throat hurt, but she wasn't sure if it was from the fever or from vomiting. Every inch of her body was hypersensitive to touch; even the sheets rubbed against her painfully when she moved, and every single muscle group ached inside of her.

"I'm so sick," she whispered pitifully. There was no one to hear or care. She was truly alone in her quiet little sanctuary.

•••••••••••

Jake sat at the kitchen table, his coffee cup empty before him, staring at the wood grain beneath his fingertips. He'd been sitting there for almost an hour, listening to the silence of the house around him. The kids would be back soon for lunch, but he couldn't stop thinking about his wife.

If he didn't know any better, Jake would have thought she looked hung over. Nora had her favorite wines, but she never drank more than a glass or two in a sitting. She didn't like not having control, and inebriation to her was the epitome of no control. She hated throwing up—he'd learned that with her first pregnancy when he'd found her in the bathroom one night, weeping and clutching her stomach, desperate to keep from vomiting.

But if she wasn't hung over, then Nora really was sick. And if the suffering on her face this morning was any indication, then she was *really* sick, indeed.

Should he call her? Should he offer to help?

His initial desire was to go to her and take care of her. He could make her hot tea, chicken broth, make sure she drank her water and took her pills. But why? Why should he do *anything* to help her feel better? She should suffer, and suffer, and suffer some more, until everything inside of her was torn to shreds. Why was he even considering it? Besides, she hated being rescued and she'd told him so many, many times. Oh, she didn't use those words. No, she called him clingy, and smothering, and suffocating, but all he'd ever wanted was to make her happy.

"Ah. Let her rot over there in her little hovel," he growled, shoving his chair back as he stood. "She doesn't need a knight in shining armor. She needs a poison apple." He wrenched open the refrigerator door and began pulling out ingredients for the dishes he'd planned on cooking for their Sunday lunch together, then slammed it with even more vehemence, as he laughed scornfully at himself. On the counter was everything necessary for her favorite Italian meal. He'd even taken the kids to Panelli's Market Saturday morning for some authentic Calabrian sausage and another bottle of Moscato. Maybe he should just get the gun out again. Maybe he should use it on himself. What a *fool* he was!

In fact, she probably wasn't even sick today! She was so good at faking things, maybe she was faking that, too. His mind reeled, spinning out of control. Maybe she was going to see Tristan. Oh God, no. Oh please, no.

Jake had to lean against the counter for support, the thoughts coming at him like flying fists. How could he survive? How could he endure yet another day with this much pain? This morning, he sat in church listening to Pastor Rob speaking from John 15 about what it meant to lay down your life for your friends. He explained that laying down one's life was not about being acknowledged, it was not about expecting a life in return, but about loving unconditionally. Yet, it all seemed so unrealistic to him. Sure, he'd heard this message before. He'd even taught on it during their Bible Study. In fact, up until now, he always thought he lived out what it meant to love unconditionally. But he never really considered how things might change if Nora didn't love him unconditionally back.

What was she doing right this very moment? Was she with him? Was he there with her? He pressed the heels of his palms into his eyes, desperate to squeeze out the images behind his lids. He couldn't take it another moment. He picked up the phone, and when the neighbor answered, he made things up on the spot.

"Hi, Mrs. Buckner. I have a huge favor to ask. Nora is at work today, but she isn't feeling well and needs me to bring her some medicine. Can I leave Leslie and Felix with you just a little longer? I shouldn't be gone too long."

Edie Buckner agreed readily. "In fact, why don't you take her some lunch and I'll keep Les and Felix here. The kids are making hopeful plans for a picnic as we speak, so I know they'll be thrilled."

Jake thanked her and shoved everything haphazardly back into the refrigerator.

He didn't care that she'd given him strict instructions to call first, that he wasn't allowed to simply show up at her cottage unannounced. He was going over there to find out what she was up to. In fact, once the decision was made, he found the idea rather invigorating. Suddenly, he wanted more than anything to meet this Tristan. He wanted to see first-hand what he was up against.

By the time he pulled up outside her little place, Jake had worked himself into a rage. He burst out of his truck, slamming the door behind him, and charged up to her front patio. He'd already used his fist to pound on the door, before it occurred to him that hers was the only other car there. It didn't slow him down too much, though. She probably picked the guy up and brought him home with her.

"Nora! Open up!" He thumped a few more times before trying the door, and was surprised to find it unlocked. He threw it open so that it banged against the wall behind it, and stepped inside her secret lovers' hideaway.

It was shadowy and cool inside with all the blinds drawn and the lights off, and it took a few moments for his eyes to adjust. He'd only been in here two other times before, both during the week she'd moved, because she needed his truck and manpower to move her furniture. He'd left everything in a pile in the middle of the floor, so the artfully arranged room made him pause as he looked around at all her stuff. Everything here was uniquely Nora; her trinkets, the artwork she loved, the fabrics, the colors. And the fragrance. There was that erotic fragrance again.

"Jake? What is it?" Her voice, quiet and shaky, came from behind the two-paneled divider separating her sleeping area from the rest of the room. "The...the kids?"

He heard the pain in her voice, and he stood, suddenly uncertain, suddenly deflated.

Suddenly wrong.

"Jake? Is something wrong?"

Peering through the space between the divider's panels, he could see the outline of her form huddled beneath the blankets on her bed.

"I... I came to check on you, Nora." He cursed himself inside for where his mind had taken him, and now for having to lie about it. "You looked terrible when you left. I was worried."

She didn't say anything in response, and he added lamely, "Sorry I didn't call first."

When she still didn't respond, he began to feel defensive. "Come on, Nor. Don't give me the silent treatment. I was just worried about you, okay? Geez."

Then he heard the sniffle. She was crying. He'd blown it again. Jake turned around and walked out, pulling the cottage door closed quietly behind him.

He crossed her little river rock patio and gazed down into the water, wishing it would wash away the last half hour. She really was sick. And he really was ridiculous, as Nora so often said, charging over here like a bull in a china shop, barging in on her like that, making all kinds of false accusations. Even though he hadn't verbalized them, he was pretty sure she'd heard his thoughts in the way he knocked on the door and hollered for her. She knew him well enough to know that he wasn't over here checking up on her out of concern for her well-being, and he knew her well enough that he *should* have known she wasn't faking the dark circles under her eyes and the bright pink fever splotches on her cheeks.

"Why should I believe her, though?" he asked himself out loud, trying to justify his behavior. "Why should I believe anything she tells me? She doesn't deserve my trust." But his reasoning didn't make him feel any better, and the fact that she actually was sick, and now crying in there, made him feel even worse.

Swallowing his pride, he headed back inside and poked his head around the screen. Nora was sitting up on the side of her bed blowing her nose, her blanket pulled tightly around her shoulders. "Go away," she mumbled between sniffles.

"I'm sorry, Nora. What can I do to help you?" Her skin was so blanched, she almost looked blue to him, and he was becoming quite concerned. "Have you taken anything? Do you need some water?"

"I can't keep anything down, not even water. And pills just come back up with the water." She rested her forehead in her hand and closed her eyes again. "My head. It's in a vice. I can't think. I need to sleep but it hurts so much."

The way she spoke in choppy sentences around long pauses scared him, and he reached out and pressed the back of his hand to her neck. "Oh, Baby, you're burning up. I'm getting you a cold washcloth." He hesitated briefly, not really comfortable digging around her domain. "In the bathroom, right?"

"Oh no, please. I'm so cold."

"Nora, you need to break that fever. It's really bad. I can feel your heat from a foot away."

"I just need to sleep." She lay back down, groaning as she pulled her legs back under the covers. "Go home. Tell the kids, okay? I'll see them tonight. Or tomorrow."

Jake stood undecided for another minute, then made up his mind. "You need to come home, Nora. You're really sick, and I'm not leaving you here alone." He found her sandals by the door and brought them back to the bed. She still didn't respond, so he slipped his hand under the blankets and reached for her feet. "Come on, Nor. Let's go." She didn't resist when he pulled her feet out and took her hand to pull her back up to sitting. She even let him slip her sandals on.

"Thanks, Jakey." She croaked, then patted him on the head. "I don't really want to die alone."

"Don't joke like that. Not cool." He stood up and pulled her with him, not caring that she'd called him Jakey today. In fact, it was the most tender she'd said his name in a very long time. He tucked her blanket more tightly around her, scooped up her favorite pillow, and shuffled her out the door, grabbing her purse and keys on the way. He helped her up into his truck and settled her in, grimacing at the thought of blankets in the ninety-five degree weather.

She sighed pitifully. "This heat feels so good. I'm freezing." He left the air conditioner off, and by the time they reached home, his back was drenched in sweat against the seat cushion. She was curled in on herself, her burning cheek against his shoulder, sound asleep.

Jake helped her to bed, then he made her take more pain killers with some hot tea he brewed for her. She managed to keep it down this time, and fell asleep with a hot water bottle on her stomach and a cool washcloth on her forehead.

He headed to the neighbors to fill them in on Nora's condition and was relieved when the Buckners asked if the kids could go with them to a matinee movie. That would keep them busy for the afternoon, and Nora could sleep undisturbed for a while.

Back at home, he made himself a quick lunch, then he returned to check on her. She was still asleep, but seemed so restless. He sat down on the edge of the bed and gently stroked her hair away from her face. She murmured something unintelligible and turned on her side, curling her body around him where he sat. She opened her eyes briefly, peering up at him from behind a haze of sleep, and smiled sweetly. "I love you, Jakey."

TWENTY EIGHT

Nora tried to open her eyes, but it felt like her lids were weighted down by sandbags. She moaned as she turned onto her side, every muscle resisting her with pain, but she felt certain she was over the worst of it. She'd been in bed for nearly a week, getting up only to use the bathroom. Jake made sure she always had fresh water, cool washcloths, and something for her headaches on hand. He brought her hot tea, and chicken noodle soup when she could handle it. Otherwise, he left her alone.

She preferred it that way; it was another way they were so different. When Jake was ill, he lay on the couch where he could be surrounded by people he loved, and be loved on in return. She, on the other hand, holed up when she felt poorly, rarely showing her face until she was ready to get back to real life. This time was no different in that respect, but she knew she'd been sicker by far than she could ever remember, at least as an adult, and she was glad Jake had made her come home so he could take care of her.

Jake slept on the couch all week, converting the bedroom into a sick bay. The kids poked their heads in periodically, but he usually made them keep their visits brief. He fielded her work calls, rescheduled everyone in her appointment book, and called Jo to ask her to check on things at her office. Nora let him call the shots on just about everything except taking her to the doctor. She refused to go anywhere, certain that this was nothing more than a bad case of the flu, complicated by her overly-stressed immune system.

It was Friday afternoon, and even if it killed her, she was determined to take a shower, wash her hair, and go sit outside in the sunshine. Maybe Jake would help her change the sheets and air out the room. She desperately needed some fresh air herself, but even more, she wanted a cup of coffee. That was how she knew she was on the mend.

She sat up, closed her eyes and waited until the room stopped spinning, then carefully made her way across the hall to the bathroom. The shower was sheer heaven this time, and she ran it so hot that she was rather wobbly by the time she stepped out. Undaunted, she dressed slowly, brushed her teeth twice, and headed out to the kitchen in search of caffeine.

Instead she found Jake, Leslie, and Felix, gathered around a map of the Sierra Nevadas spread out on the table. She smiled at the endearing sight of her little family making their summer plans. "Hey guys," she said quietly, not wanting to startle them.

"Look! Mom's up!" Felix clambered off his chair and came running at her.

"Don't touch her!" Jake yelled at him, causing him to pull up short, shocked at his dad's tone.

"Jake!"

"Dad!" Nora and Leslie spoke at the same time, their appalled tones melding into one reprimand. A vibrant silence settled around them for just a moment, then Felix burst into tears.

"I'm sorry, Mom. I wasn't going to hurt you." He took one more tentative step towards her and stopped, completely undone. "I didn't mean to."

Jake hurried to him and put an arm around his son, pulling him close. "Felix, Felix. I'm so sorry. I didn't mean to scare you. I just didn't want you to knock her over with all that love." He turned and reached a hand toward Leslie who was still hovering near the table. "You, too, Les. Come here. I'm sorry I scared all of you." Leslie ducked under his arm and ruffled Felix's hair. Jake looked over at Nora. "And you, too, Nora." He waited until she was close enough, then he pulled her into his embrace with the kids. "Group hug. Mom's alive!"

They hugged and giggled and Felix's tears dried up quickly. "Do you feel better, Mom?" He still seemed a little afraid to touch her, but she smiled and assured him that she did.

"I am really shaky right now, though. I think I need to sit down. I haven't eaten much in too long, and if it hadn't been for your dad pouring chicken soup down my throat, I might have come out of that room as your *mummy* instead of your mommy." She raised her hands over her head and let her eyes roll back as she stumbled stiffly around the coffee table, moaning, "Come hug me. I'm your mummy." Then she dropped into Jake's overstuffed easy chair.

Jake and the kids piled onto the couch, and all three stared at her. "What?" she asked, feeling a little awkward under their scrutiny.

"Was Daddy a good nurse?" Leslie asked, her eyes hesitantly hopeful, before she looked down at the purple polish she was picking off her nails. Nora waited until she looked up again and smiled at her daughter.

"Yes, honey, he was a most excellent nurse." She knew Jake was watching her, but she couldn't bring herself to meet his gaze. She continued for his benefit as much as for Leslie's. "I don't know what I would have done if he hadn't taken such good care of me. I was pretty sick, you know. I don't think I could have taken care of myself." She leaned back and closed her eyes, relishing being out of bed.

"And Mom is still getting over this, kids. She's pretty weak still, and probably will be for a while. When you're that sick, it can take some time to get back to your old self, so just be gentle around her, okay? No charging bulls, Felix."

"Okay. I'll be careful around you, Mom, I promise." Then Felix giggled. "Do you remember what you said on Monday when I came in to see you?"

Nora had to smile at his obvious delight, but she couldn't remember one day from the next of the beginning of the week, and had no idea what he was talking about.

"Oh Mom! You were kinda smiling so I thought you were awake even though your eyes were closed so I came closer to talk to you but when I got close I could tell you didn't really know I was there so I started blowing raspberries to see if maybe you were just joking and you laughed so then I thought you were just joking so I did it again and you smiled but you didn't open your eyes so I asked you why you were laughing and you told me that you were turning your shirt buttons and the buttons were tooting." Felix giggled uncontrollably throughout his diatribe. He was notorious for his run-on sentences when telling stories. Like a windup doll, once he got started he just kept going until he ran out of steam.

Leslie called him the Conjunction King.

Felix considered it a compliment.

The kids went on to regale her with some of the more humorous moments of her fever-induced stupor, and they all enjoyed a good laugh at her expense. While Leslie and Felix talked, Jake sat quietly and smiled, looking content and at peace in the moment. Finally, he stood up, interrupting yet another tale of Nora talking in her sleep.

"Would you like some tea?" he asked her.

"Oh, Jake," she shook her head. "I don't know if I ever want tea again. I would love to go sit outside in the sunshine and have some coffee, though. Is there any left from this morning?"

"I'll put on a fresh pot. I have some work I need to finish up, so you kids take your mom out to the back yard and treat her gently. No tether ball competitions today, Nora, you hear?"

"Yes sir!" She grinned and nodded.

• • • • • ● • ● • • • •

By EVENING, NORA WAS back in bed with a low-grade fever and a nagging headache. She didn't feel horribly, but she had to admit that perhaps she had pushed things a little too quickly. That afternoon, she pulled the dirty sheets off the bed herself, not wanting anyone else needlessly exposed to her germs, and put everything directly into the washing machine. Felix dutifully and generously doused the room with antibacterial spray, while Leslie opened the windows and turned the ceiling fan on high. After an hour or two, Nora realized she was running out of steam, so while Leslie and Jake put clean sheets on the bed, she made herself a piece of toast with peanut butter. It was delicious, but her stomach wasn't used to digesting anything solid and balked. She kept it all down, but only by sheer will power.

Jake insisted that she stay at the house until she was well. She resisted briefly, but only out of a sense of obligation rather than a desire to go back to the cottage alone. She wanted her own bed, their bed, and as she lay shivering in the darkened room, she realized that she wanted Jake there with her. She wanted to feel his arms around her, pulling her snugly up against him, whispering that he loved her one last time before drifting off to sleep.

Tears began to fall as she thought about all the things she suddenly wanted. She wanted her marriage to be fixed, she wanted her children to no longer look at them with eyes full of questions, she wanted her heart to stop hurting when she thought about this last year.

When Jake slipped in to check on her once more before going to bed himself, she somehow worked up the courage to whisper his name.

"Sorry," he murmured from the end of the bed. "I didn't mean to disturb you. I'm calling it a night. Do you need anything before I crash?" The light from the hallway was enough for him to see his way around, and he was trying so hard not to make any noise.

"You didn't disturb me; I was awake already." She was still whispering, so he moved around to stand on his side of the bed, and leaned over the bed toward her. It was almost as though he was intentionally keeping some distance between them, and she wondered if he was feeling drawn to her, too. She turned onto her side so she didn't have to look directly up at him, and reached out for his hand where it rested on the mattress. The words she used were his from just a week ago. "Stay here tonight, Jake. I want you to stay."

He stood so still for so long that Nora began to dread his response. Finally he turned and walked out, leaving her alone in the shadows, her pulse racing, distraught and embarrassed, her stomach flip-flopping for reasons that had nothing to do with the flu. Why on earth had she put them both in such an awkward situation? Why must she be so selfish? Of course he didn't want to stay with her! For one thing, she was still sick, and he certainly didn't want what she had. For another thing, she was making plans to leave him, so her request was selfish and unfair.

Jake returned carrying his pillow and blanket and the glass of water he always kept at his bedside. After warning her to shield her eyes, he switched on the lamp on his nightstand just long enough to get situated for the night. Before turning it off, he glanced over at her and grinned. Then the light blinked out.

"Slide over here, Sicko. You're shivering." He eased an arm under her shoulders as she turned toward him, and put his hand on her head where it rested on his shoulder. When he felt the dampness from her tears, he asked if she needed a tissue.

"No. I'm okay now. I just thought... I just figured...." Now she was embarrassed. "Never mind. I'm glad you're here."

Jake laughed quietly. "Did you really think I'd say no to sleeping in my own bed? That couch is comfortable enough for a nap, or even an emergency, but given the choice, I'll take the bed any time, hands down." He kissed the top of her head and squeezed her carefully. "Especially since you're in it, Nora."

She sniffled and sighed contentedly, her eyes, heavy with fatigue, finally closing. She was beginning to drift when he spoke again; barely a whisper. Maybe she imagined it.

"Do you still love me, Nora?"

TWENTY NINE

Jake lay listening to her breathing, waiting for an answer, then sighed when he realized he wouldn't get one. She obviously hadn't heard him before she drifted off, or she simply wasn't ready for that question.

But he wanted an answer. He *needed* one as he lay there in the dark, holding his wife the way he used to when he didn't have to ask her if she loved him.

How sweet this was, being here with her, but how messy, how muddy, how uncertain. He knew tomorrow was coming just as it always did, and he knew the stark reality of day would completely unmask the slippery promises of night. He knew she'd soon be too well to put off making decisions about their future. He didn't want to think about tomorrow; only now, this moment, with her in his arms where she belonged.

He'd met with Pastor Rob before asking Nora if she'd go with him. The man had agreed that it would be best if she came, too, to go ahead and ask her to join them, but for Jake not to get his hopes up.

"You need to understand something. Nora isn't firing off a warning shot. She's been doing that for years. Son, this is the real thing. Your marriage probably won't survive this cannon blast."

The pastor leaned forward in his seat and put a hand on Jake's knee. "Your job now is not to try to win the battle. Your job is to get home alive. That means getting on your knees, Jake. That means working on you. You need to stop worrying about her, stop asking questions, stop wondering if she'll stay or go, and you need to get back to the dock where you can be rebuilt and restored by the Master Shipbuilder. You have to let Nora go."

Jake shook his head, resistant to what he was hearing. "But how am I supposed to just accept all of this? How could she do this to us? She doesn't even act like she's done anything wrong. In fact, she makes me feel like this is *my* fault!"

"This is exactly what I'm talking about. You are wasting time trying to figure out how to change her, how to make sense of the way she thinks and behaves. All you can do is choose to change you, and you must let the Lord do that, because you, Jake, will fail miserably."

"But I'm not the one out there screwing around, she is! She's the one that needs to change, not me. The least she could do is acknowledge what she's done. She won't even talk to me about it! She won't tell me anything about him. I want to know *why.* I want to know what was so wonderful about this guy that was worth destroying our family for. I want to *know*!" Jake beat a fist on his chest to emphasize his point.

Pastor Rob was silent for several moments while Jake's words tumbled in the air between them, and the longer no one spoke, the more petulant the words sounded. Jake hung his head and asked again, his voice cracking with vulnerability. "Don't I deserve to know what I'm up against?"

"It wouldn't change anything. It still happened. You're still where you are today, no matter what this guy looks like, sounds like, acts like, no matter what they did together, and no matter why. You can't change any of that, or any of Nora's part in it. All you can do is change you today, and you tomorrow, and the next day, and the next day. If Nora chooses to come back, then we can talk about what you can expect from her, and what she can expect from you. Until then, you can only work on you."

"Argh! That just doesn't seem fair! Besides, what if I don't want her back?" Jake knew he sounded childish, but the man was making unrealistic demands on him.

"Do you want your wife to come home, Jake?" Pastor Rob cut right to the chase.

"Actually, no. Yes. Not really, not the way she is now." He paused for a moment, then his shoulders fell. "I don't know. I think I do."

"Then you need to work on becoming someone she wants to come home to. You need to get back to the Shipbuilder and have him restore you, put you back together with new parts. That's the only way to get through this, do you hear?"

"How do I do that?" Jake felt beat up, knocked down, and overwhelmed.

"I have four rules you must follow. Only four, but they're tough." He said it like he thought Jake might not be man enough to handle them.

"What are they?" Jake asked sullenly.

"Rule Number One. You ready?" Jake nodded. "Pray. Start on your knees. Get up in the morning, and before you do anything else, get on your knees and pray. Ask God to direct your footsteps, your hands, your mouth. Do it in secret, not where everyone can see you, but in private, where you can speak freely and openly with God. And when you pray, don't complain about Nora. In fact, don't mention her at all except to pray blessing over her. No exceptions. Can you do that?"

"No." He thought it was a stupid rule. He couldn't even talk to God about Nora's betrayal?

"Good." Pastor Rob continued as though Jake had readily agreed. "Because they only get harder. Second rule. No sex."

"What?" Jake sat up a little straighter.

"No sex. No sex with Nora, or anyone else for that matter. This is not a competition, and her unfaithfulness does not give you permission to go and do the same. No masturbation. No pornography. No sex of any kind."

"I don't want to be with her anyway. She disgusts me."

Pastor Rob nodded noncommittally, then continued. "Number Three. Get—"

"Wait a minute," Jake interrupted, holding up a hand. The pastor nodded patiently, as though he'd expected Jake to argue. "For how long?"

"For how long what?" Pastor Rob raised his eyebrows.

"How long? How long do I have to deprive myself of sex?" Jake wasn't so sure he was okay with Rule Number Two after all. "And what about Nora? Does she have to go without, too?"

"Deprive yourself, Jake?" Rob's voice was quiet, but there was no criticism or rebuke in his tone. Jake heard how self-serving and ugly it sounded anyway. "Are you sleeping with her now?"

"No." Jake looked down at his hands. "No," he said again, shaking his head.

"Have you slept with her since finding out about her affair?"

"No," he responded too quickly, then admitted the truth. "Well, actually, yes. A few times. But it's been a while since the last time." He didn't meet the pastor's eyes. "It was just...just release, you know? Sexual tension. It wasn't because I wanted her."

"Did you force her to have sex with you? Manipulate her in any way? Punish her? Rape her?"

"No! No way! I'm not that kind of a guy! I would never do that to anyone, especially not my wife!" Jake felt the flush creep up his torso, and his heart began to race. What would make him ask a question like that? Had Nora talked to him already?

"I see. So let me get this straight." Pastor Rob pressed his fingertips together, and pursed his lips as if contemplating some universal mystery. "You used your wife's body for self-gratification, even though she disgusts you, but you aren't the kind of guy who would rape her. I don't know, Jake." He shook his head, not convinced. "It doesn't make a whole lot of sense to me. But then, that's why I'm giving you Rule Number Two. When it comes to sex, it is impossible to not get it tangled up with emotions, especially betrayal and anger. A man's anger can blind him, particularly to his own actions. I wonder what Nora would answer if I asked her the same question."

Jake had nothing to say, but tried anyway. "Go ahead and ask her. I don't care. I don't rape." He only ended up embarrassing himself.

Pastor Rob held up both hands to make Jake stop speaking. "You don't have to defend yourself, Jake. I'm not asking for that. I'm asking you to commit to taking sex out of the relationship for a while so you can look at what's left over a little more objectively. Let's agree on one month, okay? Four weeks, can you do that?"

"Four weeks?" Jake grimaced. It had only been two months since learning of her affair, and he found his body reacting to her all the time. He tried to convince himself that he was repulsed by her, and when he thought about the whole situation, he was. Even so, his revulsion rarely overruled his physical desire for her. Then he ended up disgusted with himself, too.

"Four weeks. And then we determine if you need to go longer."

"I'm not sure I understand why, though. She's my wife. The Bible says her body is mine, and mine is hers, and that we're supposed to give them to each other so we don't get tempted into sin."

"Ah, yes. The Bible does say that, doesn't it? But like so many who read that and misuse it to demand their conjugal rights—is there such a thing?—you're not getting the big picture. A marriage license isn't a license for carnality, even if it is just between the two spouses. Just because both husband and wife agree to watch porn together doesn't make it right. This passage isn't talking about your right to own and have access to your wife's body. It's talking about giving of yourself to the one you love in a way that's pleasing to the Lord, in a way that builds one another up. So, answer me this. Do you feel like the sex you're having with your wife right now is wholesome and pleasing to the Lord? Do you believe it's the way God designed it to be, or do you think that perhaps it's carnal, and self-serving, and motivated by lust and anger and lack of self-control? Do you think—"

"Okay, okay. I get it. Wow. I'm totally screwed up." Jake dropped his head in his hands. "Four weeks it is. What kind of torture is Rule Number Three?"

Pastor Rob chuckled sympathetically. "Rule Number Three. Get a job."

"I have a job." He hated how defensive he sounded.

"Okay. Let me rephrase that. Get a job that makes you some money. And before you respond to that," Pastor Rob held up his hand, palm out, stopping the words that were erupting from Jake's mouth. "Let me explain where I'm coming from." He picked up the worn, leather-bound Bible from his desk and opened it before reading from it.

"In his first letter to Timothy, this is what Paul says in chapter 5, verse 8. But if anyone does not provide for his own, and especially for those of his household, he has denied the faith and is worse than an unbeliever." The pastor turned the Bible around so Jake could read it himself.

It burned, seeing those words in front of him. He was working so hard at making things happen, but it just hadn't panned out into any money yet. Did that mean he wasn't providing for his family, though? The fact that he was *there* for them was so much more than many men gave their families. And he still believed his business would take off at some point; he just hadn't reached that point yet.

"It doesn't matter what it is, Jake. Find work that pays, even if it's not enough to pay all the bills. Start looking as soon as you leave my office." Pastor Rob's voice brooked no argument.

Jake's eyes skimmed the page, trying to find anything around verse 8 that would support his stance. When he read back two verses, the burning turned to molten lava in his veins. "Wait. What about *this?* What about what *she's* doing?" He jabbed his finger at the page, then sat back in his chair, his hands clenched on his knees. He wanted to leap up and punch something; the wall, the door, even the man in front of him for being so calm.

"But she who gives herself to wanton pleasures is dead even while she lives." Pastor Rob read the verse out loud.

"Yes! According to the great and mighty apostle Paul, my...wife is a walking dead woman." Jake choked on the word, his mind tormenting him with visions of her giving herself to wanton pleasures in someone else's bed.

"You're right, Jake. However, you're not here to fix Nora. You're here to work on you. This brings us to my fourth rule."

"I don't want to hear it." Jake leaned forward, elbows on his knees, and dropped his head into his hands, shoving his fingers through his already disheveled hair. He wasn't sure what he was referring to; that he didn't want to hear the sounds his mind was conjuring up, or that he didn't want to hear what Pastor Rob might say next.

"Pay attention to this, son." The man waited, and finally Jake looked up at him.

"I'm all ears," he muttered, sullen and defeated. This was not going at all the way Jake had thought it would. He'd come here needing someone to tell him he was right, that he was the good guy, and he deserved to be angry. He thought Pastor Rob would at least call Nora out, demand she come see him. Sure, Jake knew he had some things to work on, but so did she.

For some reason, though, he was pretty sure this last rule wasn't going to have anything to do with her.

He was wrong.

"You must protect Nora's reputation at all cost. Do not speak of this to anyone without prayerful consideration. Do not discuss this situation with anyone who will not respect both you and Nora, and hold your confidences sacred. If you are serious about even the possibility of a restored marriage, then you will do all that is in your power to protect your wife's name. In a full-circle way, you will also be protecting yourself and your future. If you go spouting off and badmouthing Nora, if you air all your hurt and pain and anger to the world, she will know that you are not safe, and she will have no reason to come home to you. Do you understand me, Jake? Do you realize how important this is?"

"I don't know." The pressure sitting on Jake's chest at that moment had him clutching at the front of his shirt.

"Then you'll have to trust me. Can you do that?" Jake studied the man sitting a few feet away from him. His graying hair was combed neatly back from his face, and his wire-rimmed glasses sat perfectly straight on his face. A button-down shirt and khaki slacks made the guy look the epitome of trustworthy.

"I guess so." The words fell from his mouth like stones.

"Good. Go talk to Nora, invite her to be here, but whether she chooses to come or not, I want to see you back here in a week. We'll see how many of the rules you've broken by then." Pastor Rob smiled kindly, but Jake realized he wasn't really kidding. Somehow, that made him determined to do his best to keep all four rules. They prayed together, Pastor Rob laying his hand on Jake's head in blessing, and Jake had to hold his breath to keep from breaking down and weeping.

He'd met with him again just yesterday, proud of himself and his efforts to be the kind of husband Nora wanted to come home to. He told Pastor Rob about her illness, about caring for her, about how he was praying faithfully, every day, for wisdom, and that he already sensed a change in the spirit of their home.

Now here he was, not even twenty-four hours later, and he wanted to make love to his wife so badly he thought he might die if he didn't. And for the first time in weeks, it seemed like it might be for the right reasons. He wanted to love her, he wanted her to love him. No anger, no jealousy, no uncontrolled lust, just acting out physically what he hoped for emotionally and spiritually. She felt so soft and lovely in his arms, so right.

Three rules out of four was pretty good, wasn't it?

THIRTY

THE SUN WAS POURING in the window when she awoke, and she was feeling much better, but Nora decided to stay in bed and rest anyway. She would take it a little slower than she had yesterday. Jake was up early as usual, and gone before she was even conscious, so she turned over and brought his pillow to her face, breathing in the lingering aroma of her husband. It was something she did often right after they were married, when he left the house long before she did in the morning. The act now stirred up fiery tendrils of desire in her. Last night, falling asleep in Jake's arms, his body warm and familiar behind her, had been like coming home. She brought her knees up, curling her body around his pillow, as a deep ache filled her, a longing for what once was, for the wide-eyed hope they'd once shared. How far they'd come from the star-crossed lovers they'd been. What was to become of them?

A soft tap on the door interrupted her spiraling thoughts. "Come in!" She hoped she sounded brighter than she felt.

Jake pushed open the door, two coffee cups in his hand, and a gentle smile on his face. "Good morning," he greeted her.

"Good morning, sir." She sat up and propped her pillow behind her so she could lean comfortably against it.

"How are you feeling?" he asked, as he crossed to her side of the bed and held out one of the cups to her.

"Much better, actually. Thanks." She accepted it, and took a careful sip of the hot brew. "Mm. Yum. Coffee." For some reason, she felt almost shy around him this morning. "How about you? Did you sleep okay, or did I keep you awake with my sleep-talking?"

Jake, still standing, looked down into his coffee. "I'm fine," was all he said.

"Come," Nora said, patting the bed beside her. "Sit down. Make yourself comfortable. It's too late to try to avoid getting sick."

Jake went around and sat down on his side of the bed beside her, his back against his own pillow, stretching his long legs out on top of the comforter. Considering the consequences, and throwing caution to the wind, Nora nestled up close to him, and rested her head against his shoulder. "Thanks for being so nice to me this week, Jake. You've been a real trooper."

He smiled and put an arm around her. They sat that way in silence for a while, drinking their coffee, lost in their own thoughts, until Nora took his from him, set both cups on her nightstand, and turned so that she was pressing into him.

"Jake," she whispered, her heart in her throat. "I miss you."

• • • ● • ● • • • •

"The kids will be up soon, Nora. We have to talk." They were snuggled close together under the covers, her head tucked under his chin, her fingers toying with the wiry hair on his chest.

"Yeah."

"We can't do this anymore, not until we figure stuff out. I can't. It hurts almost worse afterward, because I know it doesn't fix anything. Although it should," he vehemently declared. "The way it feels, it should fix everything."

Nora smiled sadly, understanding that her week at home, her sabbatical from her confusing and painful life, was officially over. "I know," she murmured. "I know." She stretched up and kissed him tenderly on the cheek, appreciating the scratchy burn from his unshaven face, then began searching for her discarded clothing. "Can we just talk in here until they wake up? They'll find us." Nora didn't want to leave the sanctuary of their room, not yet. "You get us some more coffee, and I'll make the bed."

They sat side-by-side on the floor, facing the door, their backs up against the footboard. "I've been meeting with Pastor Rob," Jake began.

"Oh. Well, good. I'm glad." She wasn't sure what else to say.

"He wasn't very encouraging."

"Oh. Well, that's not good. Maybe I'm not glad."

"No, it's all right. He was encouraging in a different way than I expected, that's all." Jake set his cup down on the floor beside him and turned so he could look at her face. "I told him that I would stop having sex with you for a while." He looked sheepish. "I didn't do so well, did I?"

"Stop? As in, none at all? What does 'a while' mean?"

Jake laughed. "You sound like I did. Kinda. Four weeks, he's asking. And then we'll decide if we need to go longer."

"Wow."

"Yeah. Wow."

"Then I guess we should avoid bedrooms and other places like this." She tried to make light of it, but her heart was doing odd things inside her chest. She didn't want to avoid places like this. And it wasn't about the sex, not really. She was relishing in this new version of Jake. He seemed more stable, somehow more secure in himself, someone she might be able to lean on, and count on.

"Yes," he agreed. "We should. His reason, though, is good. He wants us to figure out all the rest of the stuff, and he says sex prevents us from being objective and really seeing things clearly. It kinda blurs the lines."

"I guess I can see that." And she could, but she didn't know that she fully agreed with it. If they could manage to make love like they had an hour ago every time, she didn't know how that could possibly be a hindrance toward a better marriage. Her body and spirit still hummed from the euphoria of it.

"Yeah." Jake laced his fingers with hers, his thumb rubbing back and forth over her wedding ring. "Me, too. I don't like it. And this morning reminded me just how much I'm not going to like it." He grinned ruefully, and brought her hand over to press his lips to the back of it.

"So. We should probably talk about our plans." She sighed, hating that word. Plans. It sounded so flippant, so lightweight for such a heavy thing. Future plans. Big plans. Short-term plans. Long-term plans. What kind of plans were they going to discuss today?

"Okay. I'll go first. Do you—well, I.... Okay." Jake laughed nervously and shrugged his shoulders. He reached for his coffee cup and took a sip. "Maybe a little caffeine."

"You're doing great so far," she teased him, patting his knee reassuringly.

Jake took a deep breath, squared his shoulders, and started again. "Nora, I don't want a divorce. I want you to know that up front. If there's a way we can fix things, I want to find it. I don't want to give up without fighting for us." He didn't look away this time, but held her gaze, looking into her eyes as if hoping she could read his mind. "Will you stay and fight with me?"

Nora giggled, and Jake rolled his eyes. "Okay. That wasn't quite what I meant to say, but I'll even take that if it's the best we can do for now. But I really want you to stay and fight for us with me."

She drew her legs up and crossed her arms on her knees, resting her chin on her forearms. "I know." She'd thought about this all day yesterday as she sat in the sun listening to her little family doing life around her. She'd thought about it this morning when he brought her coffee in bed. She'd thought about it in the aftermath of making love, and even now as she listened to him speak so vulnerably.

She squinted at her unpolished toenails so she wouldn't have to see his reaction to her words. "Oh, Jake. I don't want to fight for what we had. It's not enough." She turned and looked at him then. "Is it really enough for you?"

Jake's expression was almost unreadable, but she saw the flicker of pain at the back of his eyes, and she knew her words had hurt him as badly as she thought they might. But she continued anyway, needing him to understand. "I don't want to hurt you anymore, but I know I will if I settle for just getting back what we had."

Jake shook his head, slowly at first, then more forcefully. "What makes you think I want what we had? Why would I want a wife who isn't satisfied with me? Why would I want to fight to be little more than your utility man again?"

"My utility man? What is that supposed to mean?" Nora cocked her head to one side, beginning to feel a little defensive.

"That's how I feel, Nora, like your utility man. I'm the boring old stand-by guy. I clean your house, take care of the kids, wash your clothes, pleasure your body. They're all things I want to do, don't get me wrong, but I feel like I'm just the 'meet your basic needs guy,' the utility man. When you decide you want the deluxe version, the extra flare, the super service, you look elsewhere, because no matter how much I do, or how hard I try, it's never enough. I'm not enough for you."

Nora didn't know quite how to respond. First of all, she'd never thought of him as serving her before, but if she was honest with herself, she could understand why he might feel that way. Yet his assumption that she went looking for more because he wasn't enough, turned her into a fickle, shallow, selfish animal of a woman. Was that how he thought of her?

"Help me understand, Nora. I can see you pulling away inside your head. I don't want to lose you, so help me understand what you need." He reached over and brushed a finger down the length of her forearm.

"I don't want a utility man, I know that much. I don't want to be served and maybe that's been the problem for a while. I want a partner, not a servant, Jake. But if that's how you see yourself, then how am I supposed to see you any differently? That's a role you took upon yourself. I never asked you to serve me. Never."

"Then what do you want from me? How do I be your partner?" He was getting frustrated, she could tell, and she could sense the weapons being sharpened in the background of their conversation

"I want you to be a man, that's what I want. I want you to be strong on the inside, a man I can depend on, who will be there to support me and encourage me, so that I can support and encourage you. I want you to be a man who will not make me lead, but will lead me in such a way that I will want to follow you anywhere. I want you to be a man I can honor and be proud of." She paused a minute, remembering something her father had once said to her about choosing a husband. She spoke quietly, tentatively. "I want you to be a man who loves the Lord more than you love yourself. Or me."

Jake stared at her for a long time without speaking. Finally, as though making up his mind about something, he stood up, putting several feet of space between them. "Okay. So let me ask you something." He crossed his arms over his chest, and Nora tensed, sensing things were not boding well for either of them in this conversation. "Is this... this Tristan all that? Does he love God more than he loves you? Is he strong on the inside? Dependable? Is he honorable?" His sneer became more pronounced with each question.

Nora took a deep breath and pushed herself up off the floor so she was at least on equal footing. "No, Jake, he doesn't love God at all. And he isn't dependable or honorable. That's why I'm not with him. But then, the same goes for you." She shrugged slightly and tried to look unaffected, but she knew she was having a hard time pulling it off. She heard his voice in the back of her mind, "There was this waitress...."

"Well, what about you? Are you honorable? Dependable? Are you a woman I can be proud to claim? Are you a woman who loves the Lord more than you love yourself? Let me see." He held up the fingers of one hand and ticked them off one by one. "Honorable? Nope. Dependable? Nope. Make me proud? Nope. Love the Lord? Not that I can tell. Zero for four, Nora. Not a very good score."

"Don't be such a jerk, Jake. You asked me what I wanted. Now you're beating me up for answering your question. Wow." She leaned her hip against the footboard, her still recovering body beginning to tremble. "I need to lie down. Can you take me back to the cottage?"

"How convenient. Now that the conversations get sticky, suddenly you're ready to run off to your little hideout again. I *hate* that place."

Nora sat on the edge of the bed feeling overwhelmed, despair washing over her at how quickly their little love bubble had imploded on them. Yesterday with the family had been so sweet, and sleeping in Jake's arms, waking up with his familiar scent still on his pillow. Then their tender love-making this morning; how could she not feel despair over the way it was all coming undone?

"I'll stay if it will help. I'm not trying to run away. I just need to lie down, and I thought it might be better if I got out of your room, that's all. I feel like I've stayed too long."

"*Our* room, Nora. It's our room. This is our family you're breaking up. This is our home you're moving out of. This is our marriage you're walking away from. This is our bedroom you no longer want to share. I'm not asking you to leave. You're choosing to abandon all of this."

"Stop! Please stop, Jake. The kids will hear and be worried." Nora could feel the tears coming, and she was afraid of how he would react when he saw them.

"Well, maybe it's about time they did hear the truth. They're already worried, Nor. Can't you see it in their eyes? Don't think for one second you have Leslie fooled. Maybe Felix, but not Les. She knows your cottage isn't an office. Why do you think they haven't wanted to come visit you there?"

Nora was appalled that he was bringing the kids into the argument. "They've never really wanted to come visit me at any of my offices, so why would they want to come to the cottage? Why would they think it's anything else besides another office? What have you told them?"

"Nothing! I've told them nothing! Even when they ask me, I tell them nothing. I keep waiting until the timing is right for you, Nora. How does Nora want it? When does Nora want it? What does Nora want to say? How does Nora feel? It's all about you, isn't it? It always has been." He turned and headed toward the door, but stopped before he opened it. "Maybe you should leave after-all. I'll go start the truck." He left the room, pulling the door closed behind him.

Wiping away the few tears that had managed to escape, Nora glanced around the room for any of her belongings. There was little to take back with her; she'd come wrapped in a blanket, wearing only her pajamas and a pair of sandals, and carrying her pillow. She grabbed her pillow, stripped off the case that was part of the linen set on the bed, scooped up the blanket she'd neatly folded and stored in their closet, and slipped her feet into her sandals. Jake still had her phone and purse, and she shook her head as she thought about all the responsibility he'd taken on this last week.

He had already scribbled a quick note for the still sleeping kids, and Nora added to it. "I love you, and I'll see you later today after I get a few things done around the office." She hurried outside to find Jake sitting in the truck, windows rolled down, the music too loud to converse over. She climbed in her seat without his help, holding everything piled on her lap. Her purse was already on the console between them.

They made it back to the cottage in record time, and Nora hadn't been that glad to see it since the week she moved in. Jake did get out to help her carry her things, but he didn't say a word until she was inside. He stood on her welcome mat, unwilling to cross her threshold, and said, "Call before you come over."

"Okay. Is my phone in my purse?" She hated this. She hated seeing the hurt and anger on his face, knowing that she'd put it there. She hated the hollow feeling in her belly at the thought of him leaving her here. She hated that she couldn't figure out how to bridge the gap between what they wanted from each other and what they really were.

"Yes."

"Thanks for covering for me this week, Jake. I know some of my clients aren't easy people." She was so sad and so weary. "I really do appreciate everything you've done this week. I don't know how I would have survived without you."

Jake nodded and turned to leave, but she stopped him with her words.

"I'm glad you made me go home with you, and I'm glad you took such good care of me. You're a good man, Jake, worth fighting with. And for what it's worth, I want you to know that I know it."

THIRTY ONE

Jake stood in the frame of her open doorway looking in at her forlorn figure still holding her pillow and blanket. *If I'm such a good man then why am I standing out here watching you getting ready to shut me out of your life? If I'm such a good man, then why can't we figure this out? If I'm such a good man then why don't you want me?* He opened his mouth to say something profound, but only her name came out.

"Nora." Then tears came, and he buckled around the ache in his gut, pressing his hands to his knees, sobs wracking his body. "Oh God, oh God, oh God." He moaned over and over as he stood there, breaking into pieces right in front of her. What must she think of him? What kind of man came undone like this? He was the biggest loser on the planet. Why had he ever thought she would choose him?

But oh, how he loved her. In spite of her treachery, in spite of her betrayal, in spite of his broken heart, he loved her beyond measure. How could he just let her go?

"Jake? Please come inside, honey." Her hand rested lightly on the back of his bowed head, her fingers moving through his hair ever so gently, soothing, calming. She drew him inside, and he followed her meekly to the dainty slipper chair near the window. She handed him a box of tissue, then waited in patient silence for him to get his emotions under control. After blowing his nose and taking a few deep breaths, he braved looking over at her where she sat cross-legged on the floor, leaning against the wall. There were tears on her face, too, but he felt so ashamed over his lack of composure. She wanted a man she could lean on, not the other way around. She wanted a man who would support and encourage her, not burden her with his own meltdowns. No wonder they were where they were. He and his fear and his insecurity had brought them here.

"I am so sorry," he said gruffly, his voice cracking a little around the words. "I'm sorry for this."

"Stop apologizing." She said it so gently that he didn't feel reprimanded.

"I just don't know what to do, Nora. I'm lost without you, but I can't seem to figure out how to win you back. I'm a fool and a failure, so I can't blame you for not wanting me, but I love you, and I would do anything to make you love me again." He was so broken, and so exposed already, that he no longer cared how desperate he sounded. "I can't give up, I just can't. I need you. The kids need you. And you need us, I know you do. I just have to figure out how to make you see that. Please just give me a chance to find a way. Please."

"I'm not going anywhere, Jake. I know I need you—if this last week didn't make that very clear to me, I don't know what would. I...I know I love you, too," she stammered a little over the words, and he tried not to wonder if she really meant what she was saying. "I really do. I just don't love the marriage we've created, and I can't go on pretending it's okay."

Jake started to protest but she raised a hand to stop him. "Look. Let's give things a little more time before we make any big decisions, okay? We seem to do all right together when we're not trying to make the hard, fast plans, so let's put that off and just work on things one day at a time, at least for now." She toyed with the braid she'd put in her hair that morning after making the bed. "Keep seeing Pastor Rob, Jake, and I'll make an appointment with Vicky. She's a counselor I was seeing last year before everything happened. I know she's been praying for us and would love to help us figure this out. Maybe I'll even work up the courage to call Pastor Rob myself."

Jake had to look away lest she see the eagerness in his eyes and get scared off. Her words rocked through him, giving life to the desperate hope inside his heart. Vicky. She'd called him by accident after his night out. A counselor. Nora had been seeing a counselor.

"I want to go camping with you and the kids, and I don't want that trip to be tainted by fear or doubt or ugly arguments between us. Maybe we'll figure things out when we stop trying so hard to figure things out, you know?" She looked up at him, her eyes wide, then she crawled across the short distance between them and laid her head on his lap.

"Oh, Jakey." Her voice was hoarse with emotion; he was beginning to like the way she said his name. "Please don't cry like that anymore. It's too much to bear." He put his hand on her head, and they sat that way for several minutes.

Finally he spoke. "I need to get home to check on the kids. I told them I'd cook them a big breakfast when I got back, and you know how they are about Saturday morning breakfasts." He smiled as she looked up at him, and he brushed her cheek with his fingertips. "Why don't you rest for a while, and then I'll call this afternoon to see how you're feeling. If you're up to it, you can come with us to the Sports Depot for fishing supplies. If you're not, well, we'll all survive I guess, but you'll miss out on all the fun, and we'll miss out on the fun of having you with us."

"I wouldn't want to be anywhere else this afternoon." Her words settled around him; still waters after a storm.

"I want you to come home tonight, Nor. I can sleep on the couch again. I'd feel better knowing you were there in case you needed anything."

Nora was in bed and settled before he left, after making certain she had everything she needed within reach. She lay on her side watching him as he moved around her little place, tending to her few immediate needs, until he ran out of reasons to stay any longer.

"Is there anything else before I head out?" he asked from the doorway.

"You've done more than enough, Jake. Go feed our babies." She smiled and blew him a kiss; he caught it out of the air and pressed it to his cheek the way they did with the children at night. He slipped out, closing the door behind him.

Jake rolled down the windows and let the rushing air buffet his face still flushed with emotion. The drive home wasn't long, but it gave him time to think a little more about what she'd said. In the aftermath of his meltdown, she'd been lucid and calm, and it made him feel all the more inadequate. He'd done so well all week, keeping his feelings at a distance, focusing on getting her well. Now that the worst of her illness had passed, however, he felt weak and weary and as though, having served his purpose, his role was once again dubious. Yet he also found hope in her words, in the fact that he agreed to them whole-heartedly, albeit not without reservations. It was easier to put off making any definitive plans, but the lingering doubt remained that they were just putting off the inevitable.

How could they love so sweetly one minute, then fight so bitterly the next? He retraced each moment of the last few hours, savoring the memory of waking up with her in his arms, of coming back to the room to find her soft and yearning for him—for him! The transition from joy to full-fledged battle happened so quickly, so *fluidly*, it still left him reeling as he remembered how angry he'd become, how his perception of her changed so drastically, how she went from lovely creature to deceiving seductress in a matter of moments, right before his eyes. He couldn't stand it, the way his thoughts shifted around her, the way he always felt so out of control these days. He hated feeling helpless and foolish as he waited for her to make up her mind about them, about him. He wanted to draw a big, black line in the sand and dare her to cross it...but he knew, somewhere in the back corner of his mind where he didn't want to go, if he did that, she would cross it, never to return. And oh, how he wanted her to return.

And oh, how he *hated* himself for wanting her back! He hated himself. Why, why, *why* couldn't he hate her instead?

"I hate you, Nora." He said it quietly, testing, tasting the words out loud for the first time. "I hate you, Nora." Louder, firmly. "I hate you, Nora Anderson! I hate you!" He was yelling now, the anger and pain building up inside him until he could no longer form words, and he roared at the top of his lungs, the rushing air whipping the sound around his head and out into the world. He raged with unintelligible noises until his throat felt like it was being torn to shreds, until he broke down coughing, gasping, choking on his emotions. "I hate you, Nora," he rasped again, but he knew it was still a lie.

By the time he pulled into the driveway, his throat was raw, but it felt good to him; tangible evidence that he was waging a battle. He may not be winning yet, but he had determined that he wasn't ready to give up. He wanted his family back. He wanted his family whole. And somewhere between Nora's cottage retreat and the home she was retreating from, Jake had drawn a line after all. Maybe it wasn't big and black, maybe it wasn't even something she could or would see, but he knew it was there, because he'd drawn it for himself. He wasn't going back. He was crossing the line and never going back to the old Jake.

"Do You hear me, God? You'd better show up. I'm ready to fight, and I'm expecting You to be here, leading the charge. I'm expecting You to stand by me, to help me fight for what's right, for what You gave me. For *who* You gave me." He leaned forward and rested his forehead on his hands where they gripped the steering wheel, suddenly longing for communion with Christ. "Jesus, I've failed miserably. I've failed her. I've failed my kids. I've failed you. I need your help. She's right. This marriage sucks the way it is, the way it was. I don't know why I couldn't see that. How did I become so blind? When? Show me what it means to be a man. Please, God, let her see that I want to change. Help me be the man You want me to be so that I can be the man she needs." He could feel his shoulders drop, the tension easing out of them, as he sat in stillness. He grimaced as a new thought struck him. "And if You need to break me even more...." He hesitated just for a moment, then continued bravely. "Then break me more. If You think I can handle it, bring it on." He lifted his face, though, and declared a little defiantly, "But You're responsible for keeping track of all the pieces and remembering where they go when it's time to put me back together again!"

• • • ● • ● • • • •

"You don't need to apologize anymore." Vicky touched her knee, stopping her flow of words. "I'm not going to reprimand you or make you do push-ups or penance of any kind. I'm just glad you're back and that's all I'm going to say about it, okay?" When Nora nodded, Vicky continued. "So tell me how you've been."

Nora snorted in a rather unladylike manner. "Now there's a loaded question."

"Hm. I figured as much. Well, all we can do is begin at the beginning. Do you remember my rule?"

"Yes." Nora rolled her eyes. "No bad-mouthing my husband."

"Then he is still your husband?" Vicky asked.

"Yes, he is." Nora's dubious tone made Vicky raise her eyebrows in question.

"That's good, right?"

"Yes, I think it is." Nora shrugged. "I'd like it to be. I'm hoping it can be good again. It's just not so easy right now. A lot has happened since the last time you and I met, and I think Jake and I are just hanging on because we don't know what else to do."

Vicky just nodded encouragingly.

Nora took a deep breath and blew it out in a huff. "I had an affair," she said bluntly. "And yes, Jake knows."

"Ah. I see. Well, that does change things." True to her promise, Vicky's eyes didn't darken with judgment or condemnation. If anything, Nora thought she saw compassion on her face. She continued, doing her best to be completely honest.

"I don't know how I feel about it all. I'm confused that things aren't clearer to me, more black and white. I know it's selfish and wrong, but part of me loves Tristan, and leaving him feels like dying. But I also love Jake. Is that possible? And leaving him feels like dying, too. I feel like I'm being made to choose how I want to die. Except that I want to live." Nora shook her head and shrugged again. "See what I mean? I feel inside out and outside in all the time."

"Are you still seeing this man?"

"Tristan. His name is Tristan." Nora felt a sharp need to make him real to Vicky, to make him more than just a nameless entity. "And no, I'm not still seeing him."

"Are you in contact with Tristan in any way?" Vicky emphasized his name. "By phone? By email?"

"No."

"Has he tried to contact you?"

"Yes."

"But you haven't reciprocated?"

"Only once right after I left him. That was a disaster."

"Does he know where you live?" Vicky's one line questions were coming at her quickly, but Nora appreciated them today. She wanted to purge, to get the details out on the table. The counselor, in her black skirt and yellow top, with her hair pulled back in a large barrette, looked no different than she had a year ago. Even though Nora felt changed through and through, it was good to come back to familiarity with this woman.

"No, he doesn't. And by the way, I've kinda moved out. Or at least I've moved into a place of my own."

Vicky frowned. "Is that your decision or Jake's?"

"Mine. When I left Tristan, I kinda left Jake, too."

"What does 'kinda' mean? You keep using that word." Vicky asked.

"Huh. I do, don't I? It usually drives me crazy when Jake uses it; like he can't decide one way or the other about things." She snorted. "Which makes it apropos for me to use it in this case. 'Kinda' means that I have my own little place where I sleep most nights, but I'm still home after school and in the evenings with the kids. Then after they're in bed, I go to the cottage. It's just for now, until we figure out what we're going to do." It sounded pitiful to Nora's ears.

"But you're not seeing Tristan? Even at your little place?" Although Vicky mimicked Nora's words, it didn't sound like she was being unkind.

"No. I told you he doesn't know where I live. It's not a little love shack, Vicky. Just a one room cottage on the edge of town where I can be alone. Alone being the key word."

"Are you sleeping with Jake?"

"Not regularly."

"So... kinda?"

"No. Yes. I guess." She shrugged noncommittally.

"Ah."

Nora frowned at Vicky's response. "What does that mean?

"Why are you sleeping with Jake and not with Tristan? According to you, you love them both, right?"

"What kind of question is that? Jake is my husband and Tristan isn't." Nora resisted the desire to cross her arms. "Look, I'm not interested in playing psychological games here, okay? I left Tristan because it became very clear to me that it was what I was supposed to do, like it or not. I'm hoping there's enough good in my marriage to make it worth saving. Jake is willing to work on things with me, and I'm willing to work on things with him. That's all we have right now. Can you help me without trying to trip me up, or should I go somewhere else?"

Vicky sat quietly for several moments, long enough to make Nora even angrier. "Fine. What would you like me to say? Yes, I suppose I love them both. I sleep with Jake because he's my husband, and I owe it to him. I don't sleep with Tristan because if I do, he'll think that there's hope for our future together and there isn't."

"Why do you owe Jake sex?" Vicky kept verbally punching her.

"I don't know. I just do. I feel badly for how I've hurt him. I feel guilty about Tristan. I know I can make Jake happy with sex, at least temporarily. It makes him feel good. You know, manly."

Vicky leaned forward, the sadness in her eyes growing more intense. "Nora, those are horrible reasons for having sex with someone, even with your husband. In fact, I think if Jake knew you were sleeping with him because you feel like you owe it to him, or out of guilt, or because you felt sorry for him, he'd be pretty upset, don't you agree?"

"Well, believe it or not, sometimes I actually *want* to have sex with my husband. It's not all obligatory." Now she was feeling defensive.

Vicky smiled. "Good. I'm glad to hear that. Now," she said, eying Nora to make sure she was listening. "I'm going to ask you to stop. Stop having sex with Jake until you're able to do so for the right reasons. Biblically, your body belongs to him and vice versa, and so the two of you need to be in agreement on this. Which means you'll have to talk to him about it. Do you think you can do that?" She waited for Nora to respond.

"Why? I'm not arguing. I'm just wondering why."

"Do you really want your marriage to be restored?"

Nora nodded slowly, already sensing where this was leading after what Jake had shared with her about his sessions with the pastor. "I think so."

"Good," Vicky repeated. "Then we're going to learn to prioritize. Nora, you and your husband rate sex too highly in your relationship. Don't get me wrong. It's an incredible thing when it's right. God knew what He was doing when He put all those nerve endings in the right places and connected them to our emotions. But the world has taken lust and disguised it as love. They've taken sex and disguised it as intimacy. They've taken commitment and disguised it as a prison. They've twisted everything until it's all inside out, and then we wonder why everyone is so confused about relationships.

"The thing is, Nora, a marriage in God's eyes is the act of two becoming one in every way. Yes, sex is one of those ways, but it should be a reflection of the bigger picture. In Mark chapter ten, Jesus tells us that two become one flesh. No longer two, but one. And He goes on to say that whatever God has joined together, we're not to tear apart. Think about the choice of words Jesus used. Tear apart. Not a neat incision. Not a clean, surgical procedure. A brutal, ripping and tearing act; like what animals do to their prey.

"It's not just graphic and cool imagery, you know. When you shared yourself with Tristan, you tore apart the flesh that God joined together. But even more importantly, I want you to understand this. It's not like you cut off your arm and gave it to Tristan. A body can go on living without an arm or two. No, you tore out the heart of your marriage and handed it over to him as though it was yours to give. But what happens to flesh when the heart is removed?"

She paused, and Nora answered compliantly. "It dies?"

"It dies," Vicky repeated, nodding vehemently. "Nora, there is no hope for your marriage right now. None. Until you get your heart in the right place, your marriage is doomed. It doesn't matter how much you and Jake *want* to work on things. It doesn't matter how willing you are to try to save your marriage. What matters is where the heart of your marriage is, and that starts with getting your own heart in the right place first.

"You and I are going to try to unravel things a bit, and see if we can't put things in their proper places. Maybe, and this is what I'm banking on, in the process of working on you, we'll uncover some treasures in your marriage that you've lost sight of over the years." Vicky leaned over and took both of Nora's hands, squeezing them hard. "You've taken the first step toward restoration in choosing to end your affair, and I can see that it wasn't easy. But you and your heart can't hang out in this in-between place. You must keep taking steps in the right direction. Coming here today is good. It's another step. You should be proud of yourself."

Nora took a deep breath and forced her shoulders to relax. "Why don't I feel better then? If this is the right thing, why do I still feel so torn up about it? I actually feel guilty for not feeling guilty."

"One step at a time, Nora. Let's not wait around for your feelings to line up with your actions. That would be hanging out in the in-between place, and we're not going to do that, remember?"

Nora nodded.

"Okay. Here's your next action step. I want you to make a list."

Nora rolled her eyes. "Here we go again. What is it with you and lists, hm?" She smiled to soften her words, but she wasn't anticipating Vicky's request.

"Lists help us with perspective. We are reasoning creatures by nature, but we are also easily deceived and distracted. Lists are a simple way to organize our thoughts and keep us focused on the tasks at hand. They aren't the end all solution for everyone, I readily admit, but I have yet to meet anyone who can't benefit from making a list or two, now and then. If nothing else, it's a good place to start." She folded her hands in her lap and leaned back in her chair. "Are you ready for your assignment?"

THIRTY TWO

THEY'D BEEN ARGUING A lot these days. In the long-suffering tone of a martyr, Jake explained to her how Pastor Rob had instructed him not to ask questions about Tristan. So he didn't. Instead he casually let slip the things that he *would* ask if he was *allowed* to ask, and then left awkward silences in hopes that she would fill them with the information he wanted. Disgusted by his manipulative attempts to garner information, and the accompanying guilt trips he tried to dump on her, she goaded him with juicy hints, but no real details. He called her names, she called him names. It was destructive and unproductive and exhausting.

The outcome of the battle to save their marriage looked bleak, indeed.

This morning, though, they maintained a truce of sorts, carefully treating each other with something like respect. By the time she left for work, Felix had eaten his bowl of cereal and was sprawled on the floor watching cartoons. Leslie was in the shower, catering to her teenaged awareness of personal hygiene. The day was off to a good start.

By the time she arrived at her office, things were unraveling quickly. Her phone was ringing as she walked in the door, and she hurried to answer it.

"I have been trying to reach you for an hour, Nora, and I'm appalled that you have taken so long to answer the phone. I have rearranged my day in order to deal with this unacceptable situation, and I do not appreciate being made to wait."

"Excuse me," Nora responded guardedly. "Who is this?"

"Sandra Madison," the clipped voice replied. "Where have you been all morning?"

"My office hours vary greatly, Sandra, because of the nature of the work I do. It's unfortunate that you felt you had to wait for me, however, I don't officially open until ten." She glanced at the clock on the wall across the room. "It is only 9:15 now."

"I'm well aware of what time it is. I'm the one who's been waiting, remember?" Sandra Madison was not happy. "So does this mean that you'll be unable to help me for another forty-five minutes?" Her sarcasm oozed through the phone, and Nora had to resist the urge to hang up on the woman.

"What's the problem, Sandra? Perhaps we can resolve this without any more misunderstandings."

"How quickly can you be here? I have a catastrophe on my hands, and I want it fixed immediately."

"What is the problem?" Nora asked a second time, her face flushed with temper at the way she was being spoken to.

"It isn't a problem, Nora. A problem can be resolved. It is a catastrophe, and you will not be able to address it over the phone with me. I am not one of those silly little trophy wives who can be so easily put off or appeased by empty promises. I insist, no, I *demand* that you come and see for yourself. When can I expect you?"

"Listen, Sandra. My day is booked, however, if I know what the problem is, perhaps I can figure out how to best shuffle appointments so that I can deal with it today." This was not getting any easier.

"No, you listen to me. You just admitted that you have forty-five minutes until you are officially open. My assumption, then, is that you have no appointments until ten either. I see no reason why you can't come now. No schedule changes required." The woman's arrogance was remarkable.

"I'm sorry, but that won't be possible. Please tell me what's wrong so I can figure out how best to help you." Sandra Madison had been nothing but trouble since the day Nora took her on. She wished now she'd paid more attention to her gut feelings about her, because after the last four weeks of dealing with her, Nora was at the end of her rope.

Sandra finally explained that the men who came to install her new draperies the day before, had left a thick layer of dust on everything, including her grand piano, and had scratched her hardwood floors in several places with their ladders.

"But Sandra, the men you used were not mine. You insisted on hiring your own installation people, because you couldn't wait until today when my crew was available to come. I can't do anything about their quality of work because I did not hire them, you did. You need to contact their management immediately and get this resolved with them."

"No, this is not my dilemma to solve, it is yours. If you were sufficiently staffed, I would not have had to hire someone else to come in and complete your work for you. And you should have been here anyway. I told you what time they were coming to install these drapes, and I expected you here to oversee the work. You never showed and now look at the catastrophe we have on our hands. I suggest that *you* call their management and arrange for them to come out and take a look at the abuse my home has taken from these imbeciles."

"Okay." Nora took a deep breath and blew it out slowly, holding the phone away from her mouth. "Here's what I can do, Sandra. I was planning on taking a short lunch break around one on my way back to the office from the west end of town. I can stop by your place briefly then, and see what needs to be done, and how much I can do about it. I cannot call those men before I see it. Will that work for you?" She hated feeling like she was catering to the woman, but the conversation was going nowhere, and she really didn't feel like talking to her any longer. It was a horrible way to begin a day.

By noon, things had not improved. Two of the three clients she'd met with in the morning were reconsidering their projects, although both assured her it had nothing to do with her. One was dealing with a child's emergency medical needs, and the other had been invited to join a group of friends on a safari in August. She thought a safari might be a better use for the money she had planned to spend on redecorating her master suite this summer. "My bedroom will always be here, you know, but a safari with the girls? Well, that might only come once in a lifetime!" How could Nora argue with that reasoning? She rather wished she could go, too; just disappear for six weeks into the wilds of Africa. Maybe a hungry lion would eat her and she'd never have to return.

"Okay, Miss Crabby Pants. Snap out of it. Being eaten by a lion can NOT be a fun way to go." Nora tried to pep talk her way out of her doldrums, but she was having a hard time mustering her nice girl attitude as she pulled into Sandra Madison's perfectly manicured horseshoe driveway. She turned off the engine and sat in the stillness of her car for a few minutes while she uttered a prayer.

"God, if You're still hanging out with me, this is going to be tough, I already know. In fact, I'm actually thinking the whole lion thing might be a good alternative after all. Would You mind just making her keep her claws sheathed until I'm outta here? And it probably wouldn't hurt to have You help me keep mine sheathed, too. I'd really appreciate that."

Nora rang the doorbell. She could hear the deep tones like distant church bells gonging. It was such a tranquil sound, that when the front door flew open, Nora jumped.

"You're here. Come in." Sandra didn't greet her, nor did she wait for any niceties in return. Assuming Nora would follow, she marched through the polished granite foyer, her expensive workout shoes squeaking militantly with each step.

Nora tagged along, feeling like prey being ushered into the lion's den, then she pulled up short behind her client as they entered the formal living room. Her breath caught with pleasure. Although she'd decorated the room piece by piece, she had yet to see the finished product because of her busy schedule. She would have come with her installation crew had Sandra given her an extra three days. Regardless, the window treatments pulled everything together, as though dressing the whole room in royal attire.

It was magnificent. The furniture, a deeply stained mahogany, polished to an almost lacquer finish, the upholstery in bronzes and golds, shot through with brilliant red threads, were glorious complements to the black grand piano, the focal point of the room. Oriental rugs strategically placed, ancient Chinese urns, some exquisite replicas, some authentic, tastefully positioned around the room, it all declared opulence and class. The windows were dressed with hand-painted shades, intricate brushwork depicting cherry blossoms and lotus flowers falling dreamily into the room as though a soft breeze carried them in from outdoors, and red shantung silk panels framed each of the six windows, puddling in excess on the dark wood floor. But Nora's eyes were drawn, as intended, to the huge and ornate mantle that dominated one whole wall. Mounted above it was one of Tristan's most intense paintings, in reds and blacks, wild plums and brilliant greens. It was a mesmerizing whorl of color, not oriental in any context, but the passion and mystery in its swirling depths echoed the intrigue of the ancient culture she'd worked so hard to capture here, while sweeping the whole room into the 21st century.

Nora felt her eyes tear up, but forced her emotions under control. She would not cry in front of this woman, lest she create any more reason for Sandra to doubt her capabilities. The room was everything and more than she had hoped it would be, and she wasn't going to be bullied into admitting otherwise.

"Sandra, this room is spectacular."

"A spectacular mess, yes." Sandra crossed to the piano and stuck out a French-manicured finger. "Look at this!" She swiped it across the padded bench-seat, leaving a faint line behind. "Cleaning this instrument requires a professional, someone who knows how to care for it and who will not scratch it or mar it in any way. Those men didn't even bother to cover it when they started drilling and screwing the drapery hardware on the wall. I just had this thing cleaned, and now the man is going to have to turn around and come right back to do it all again. It's simply unacceptable."

It was all Nora could do to keep from giggling at how ridiculous the whole situation was. The room truly was breathtaking, a jaw-dropper, and Sandra couldn't see it. She was so consumed with what was wrong with it that she couldn't relish in its beauty.

She led Nora over to one of the windows and moved aside the puddle of red silk beneath it. "Look at this! Look what they did with their ladders. And they didn't even bother telling me. I had to find it myself." She pointed the same long finger at the floor. Nora looked, then looked again, then turned questioning eyes to her client.

"Can't you see that? Are you blind?" Sandra crouched down so she could run her finger along the wood floor. "Look at this long scratch!"

Nora leaned closer, finally realizing what the woman was pointing at, then stepped back again. She moved the curtain a little further out of the way and smiled politely. "Sandra, I know you're concerned about this room, and the great expense and effort that you've put into making it beautiful. Your taste is exceptional and I'm so glad you love this wonderful era, because I've always wanted to decorate a room like this. I'm sorry about the dust, and I would like to offer you a complimentary cleaning. You arrange it with your piano man, and I will take the cost of his services off my bill. Drilling into these plaster walls always stirs up a little dust, and it could very well have happened with my installers, too. Will that work for you?"

Sandra stood, her hands on her hips, and pursed her lips tightly for a moment. "All right. Hopefully Brandon can come sooner than later. If he can't come sooner I may have to look for someone else, and there's no guarantee that I'll be charged the same price that Brandon charges."

"That's all right. It needs to be done, correct?" When Sandra nodded, Nora continued. "Then you get someone over here to do it and just send me a copy of the bill."

"What about the scratches?" Sandra asked, still trying to maintain some of her indignation. She'd obviously prepared for a fight and wasn't so sure how to proceed from this point.

Nora kept the gracious smile pasted on her face as she tried to explain. "Sandra, I don't think the installers made that scratch. Look from over here, from this angle with the light shining on it." She reached for Sandra's hand but the other woman flinched. Nora ignored it and grabbed her hand anyway, pulling her gently around to stand beside her. "Do you see how there isn't a scratch in the top coat, the sealer? Do you see how the groove is actually sealed beneath the finish? I can absolutely understand why you might think it's a new scratch, especially if you've just noticed it for the first time, but from here it looks like just part of the wood grain. Oh Sandra," she gushed, as though the woman had not just made a complete fool of herself. "This is some of the most beautiful flooring I've ever seen, and part of its beauty is its unique grain pattern. It really takes a sharp eye to find something like this, you know, and I'm so glad you chose this one. You obviously are one of those people who appreciate the value of beauty." She cocked her head, secretly wondering if she'd gone too far with that last comment, then opted to jump in with both feet anyway. "I'm even wondering if we should redesign these drapes *not* to puddle so that more of this flooring will stay exposed."

Sandra was quiet for a long time. They both stood staring at the spot on the floor until Nora couldn't take it any longer. She turned to look at the other woman, prepared to suggest that they bring in the flooring guy and have the section replaced, when she saw Sandra's expression. There was no anger, no embarrassment, no ridicule or superiority in her eyes. Instead, Nora thought she read a depth of defeat that worried her. She reached out to touch Sandra's arm.

"Are you all right?" she asked tentatively.

Sandra straightened, nodded briskly, and pulled away from Nora's touch, placing a safe distance between them. The vulnerability in her eyes was gone. "I'm fine, yes. You're right, of course, the flooring is beautiful, and I do appreciate beautiful things. I don't think that scratch is part of the grain—it's too deep—but I do see now that it was done by someone besides the drapery installers. I'm glad we didn't call those men and give them an excuse to be condescending toward me. I can't stand it when I see that 'stupid little woman' look in a man's eyes." She frowned, apparently disgusted at the thought, and when she began to rearrange the fabric over the spot again, Nora helped.

But her mind was racing with unasked questions. What was it with all these women she worked with? Where were the men in their lives, the real men? Sandra had spoken of her husband only once in the weeks they'd worked together, and that was to indicate that he was in France, she didn't expect him back until the middle of September, and that he wouldn't even notice the changes she'd made to the room. Nora couldn't imagine anyone *not* noticing the differences, but she held her tongue because of the scathing tone Sandra used. She now wondered if Sandra's meanness wasn't directly related to how her husband treated her, or mistreated her, or possibly didn't treat her like anything at all. What was wrong with men these days?

"Is there anything else I can do for you, Sandra? I'm sorry to have to rush, but I do have an appointment in half an hour and I must get back to my office first."

"Of course. No, you've taken care of everything." She began walking towards the front of the house and Nora followed, not sure what else to do. She glanced once more over her shoulder at Tristan's painting and had to bite her bottom lip to keep from making a sound. The pain in her heart made her glad she didn't have to come back here to photograph the room for her portfolio. Although she was extremely proud of the way it had turned out, Sandra refused to allow photos of it to be displayed, for fear someone might take note of some of her priceless possessions and rob her.

When Sandra opened the massive front door and stood aside to let her out, Nora took a deep breath of relief. She started to say good-bye, but Sandra spoke first.

"Listen, Nora. I do appreciate you making time in your day to see me. I know that I wasn't very flexible with you this morning." She paused briefly, then flapped one hand in the general direction of town. "And thank you for sparing me the embarrassment of making a fool of myself in front of those men. That would have been unbearable." She took a breath and didn't let it out right away, as though she wanted to say more but wasn't quite sure what.

"Well, I'm glad I could help," Nora spoke into the silence. "Just let me know when you have your piano cleaned, all right?"

"Oh no. Don't worry about that. I'll take care of it. I'm sure some of that is normal dust that builds up anyway. As my husband always says, 'Once again, Sandra dear, you've gone and opened your mouth simply to find a place to park your foot.' And he's right. That's exactly what I've done." she shrugged, a hint of the earlier defeat on her face again.

Nora smiled kindly, not sure what to say. "Call me if you need anything else, okay?"

"I will. Thank you. Goodbye now." Sandra closed the door slowly, but firmly.

Nora got back in her car, pulled out of the driveway, and headed back to her office. The whole encounter was distressing. "Kill her with kindness," she muttered, shaking her head. She was grateful that it had all been resolved with no loss of life or limb, glad that claws had been sheathed on both sides, but she struggled to understand the misery that she'd seen in Sandra's eyes. Were all marriages doomed to such an end?

THIRTY THREE

THE REST OF THE afternoon passed without any more major hang-ups. Jo poked her head in at one point to ask if Nora needed anything from the office supply store. Their relationship was a little strained, but she understood. Although Jo was glad she had stopped seeing Tristan, it wasn't because she thought Jake was any better of a choice. Jo firmly reminded her that she'd been making plans to leave Jake even before meeting Tristan, and her concern was that the problems in the marriage hadn't changed, that Nora's affair had only added to them. Even so, she often poked her head in for a quick hello or a short chat, and she always welcomed Nora when she crossed the hall in Jo's direction. They just didn't have any long visits anymore, and Nora wondered if Jo missed her as much as she missed Jo.

By the end of the day, Nora was starving, having skipped lunch to meet with Sandra. Her arms full, she backed out the front door of the building, and tripped over the doormat, landing on her rear end. Embarrassed, but not surprised after the day she'd had, she thanked the group of teenagers walking by who helped her gather her things. She finally got herself home, anxious for the reprieve it promised. But when she walked in, things were not as she'd expected. Leslie was in her room, the door closed, and Felix was sitting on the sofa, sullen and frowning, an open book unread in his lap.

"Hi, Felix." She didn't ask him what was wrong; she wasn't quite ready to open the floodgates of Felix's mouth. "Where's Daddy?"

"His office," came his stilted reply.

"Thanks. I'll be right back." She placed a kiss on the top of his head and hurried towards Jake's office.

Her husband looked up from his paperwork and smiled tightly when she entered the room. "Nora."

"Hey. What's going on around here?" She didn't like the way he greeted her; it sounded foreboding. She closed the door behind her and leaned against it.

"Well, let's see." Jake's voice was falsely bright. "Les is in her room crying, Felix is on the couch mad, and I'm in here trying to figure out what else I can say to further destroy our children's lives."

"Sounds like great fun. Shall I join in on this activity? Maybe I can pour a little rain on everyone's sunshine." She tried for levity, but Jake just scowled.

"Unfortunately, you already have." He sighed heavily, and leaned forward, his elbows on his desk. "Les and Felix asked me if we were thinking about splitting up. They wanted to know why you have your own place." Jake didn't look at her. He ran his fingers through his hair and stared at the flickering cursor on his monitor.

"What did you say?" Nora could feel a band tighten around her chest, squeezing the air out of her lungs. She straightened and crossed her arms, suddenly feeling defensive.

"I told them that things weren't easy for us, that we were working on stuff, but that you just needed some space right now."

"Oh no." Nora groaned. "You told them I needed space? Jake! Do you realize how selfish that makes me sound?" She couldn't believe he'd said those words, probably the most often used line in the history of all break-ups. No wonder her daughter was in tears.

He shook his head, grim lines forming around his mouth. "You know, I wasn't thinking it at the time, but I suppose you're right. It does make you sound selfish." He shrugged one shoulder and held her gaze, his blue eyes glittering with frustration. "But what else should I have said? It's the truth, isn't it, I mean, the whole needing space thing?"

"Oh please, Jake. Now you're just trying to make me feel rotten, too. I never said that, and you know it." She closed her eyes and leaned her head back against the door. "Why didn't you wait for me? It would have been much better to have both of us here."

"I didn't choose the time, they did. They came to me when you weren't here. Don't make me out to be the bad guy, Nor."

"Oh, right." She brought her hands up in surrender. "God forbid you should be the bad guy in any of this."

"Hey, you're the one who had an affair, remember? You're the one who chose to move out." Jake snapped back at her.

"You know, life didn't start a year ago, Jake. A lot happened before my affair, *remember*?" Her face burned with indignation as she mimicked his tone. "In fact, if I recall—please correct me if I'm wrong—the majority of problems in this marriage have been brought in by you, *remember*? Drinking, porn, women, spending money we didn't have, not working, forgetting that you have children, a wife, responsibilities, *remember*? Do you remember any of this? The foundation of my affair was laid by you, Jake," she pointed at him. "By you!"

He stood up and took a step toward her, his fists clenched at his sides. "Are you actually trying to say that your whoring around is my fault?"

"I didn't whore around!" Nora cried out. "Why do you insist on using that vile word? Does it make you feel better about yourself?" She was sick to her stomach, anger and hunger churning up the acids and making her feel shaky and weak. She still hadn't completely regained her strength since being so sick, and the continued stress of trying to work things out with Jake wore her down. "And no, I am not blaming you for my affair. But I am blaming you for your part in the breakdown of this marriage. For sixteen years, I bent over backwards trying to hold things together. I covered for you, I cleaned up after you, I supported you, I encouraged you, I cheered for you. For sixteen years I devoted myself to you. In return, you always chose something or someone else. Always! That doesn't make what I did right, but by God, it sure makes it understandable, whether you want to admit it or not."

Jake glared at her, and she could see his Adams apple bobbing in his throat like he was trying to get words out past it. Finally, he spoke, his voice tight. "You, my dear, are amazing. I have no rebuttal." He backed up and leaned against the edge of his desk, still facing her, his hands resting loosely on either side of him. "I stand corrected. You win. You always win."

"I win? I *win*? Why do you always say that?" She could feel tears beginning to form, but she didn't want to cry. "I almost wish you had just told them the truth. At least things would have been out on the table for real, and they wouldn't be out there with more questions than they started with."

"And what would you have had me say to them, hm? You're the master wordsmith. How do you think I should have put it to them? 'Well, kids,'" he opened his eyes wide, tipped his head to one side, and spoke in a chipper tone. "'Your mom has had an affair and can't decide whether she wants to come back home to us or not. Meanwhile, I wait around like a beat dog, trying not to beg for any morsels she'll throw my way.' Is that what you're looking for?"

"Very nice, Jake." The tears evaporated in the heat of her anger. "You want words? How about this? Maybe you should have said, 'Your mother has moved out because I am a self-righteous, suffocating, condescending jerk, and I can't stand the thought that she might not have been blissfully happy with my asinine qualities, so I refuse to stop beating her up with scathing remarks about her personality, calling her inappropriate and degrading names, and dropping unfair hints of her betrayal around you children. I am squeezing her so tightly that she has been forced to find an alternate air supply just so she can breathe.' How long, Jake? How long are you going to do this to us?"

"Me? Do what to us? You're the one who can't decide whether you're coming or going, Nora. You're the one calling the shots around here. You're the one with all the options. Which door will it be, Nora?"

"This one!" She cried, tearing open the office door, then slamming it again behind her.

Felix sat still as a stone, with wide, frightened eyes. She had no doubt that even if he hadn't heard the words, he'd heard the angry tones coming from behind the closed office door. She leaned over and kissed the top of his head again.

"I love you, little man," she reassured him. "Let's find something to eat, shall we? I'll grab Les."

"She won't come out. She said she's staying in her room until you move back." His words were so quiet she had to bend down to hear them.

"Hm. I guess we'll just have to see about that, won't we? You wait here. Maybe I'll try to find that tickle spot just behind her left knee." That got a small grin out of Felix, but Nora noticed the smile didn't remove any of the fear from his eyes.

Nora knocked on Leslie's door but was greeted only by silence. "Les? It's Mom. Can I come in?"

Still no answer. Nora quietly opened the door, thinking that maybe her daughter had fallen asleep.

"Get out! Did I say you could come in? Get out!" The anger in Leslie's voice shocked her, and she stood just inside the door, not sure what to do. Leslie was lying face-down on her bed, her arms up under her pillow.

"Can we talk?" Nora finally asked.

"I don't want to talk to you, *Nora*." Leslie lifted her face to glare at her mother across the room. "Why don't you just go home?" Nora sucked in air like she'd been punched. This was far worse than any pain Sandra Madison or a hungry lion combined could inflict on her.

"Go home!" Leslie yelled this time, her voice breaking into sobs. "Go home," she repeated mournfully, as she buried her face in her pillow again. Nora quickly crossed the room and sat down on her daughter's bed. But when she reached out to stroke her daughter's shoulder, Leslie flinched the same way that Sandra had earlier, and this time, Nora withdrew her hand.

"This won't fix things, Les, not speaking to each other. I want to get things figured out as much as you do, honey."

"Oh please!" Her response was muffled into her pillow, but Nora knew sarcasm when she heard it. "You don't want to figure anything out. You're just going to run off and make your own life. A few problems and you're just going to cut and run."

"Daddy and I are trying...."

"Don't you *dare* bring Daddy into this!" Leslie pushed herself up to a sitting position, her back to her headboard, pulling her pillow up against her chest and hugging it to her. She turned her puffy red face on her mother, eyes filled with rage and accusation. "He's not the one leaving, you are! If you think that leaving is the way to figure things out then you're stupid. Stupid!" Leslie pressed her face down into her pillow again, her body trembling as she tried to control her anger and tears.

"I'm not leaving, Les." Had she been listening outside the office during her parents' argument?

When Leslie didn't respond, Nora tried again. "I'm not leaving. The cottage is a place where I can spread my stuff out and work on things. It's a place where I can be alone. It's like your room, honey. Like right now. You came in here to be alone, to a place that was yours, to deal with all the thoughts in your head without having to explain everything to someone else."

"Alone. That's right."

Nora bit back a frustrated sigh; she felt on the verge of collapse. She needed food, rest. Little pinging sounds kept going off in her throbbing head. She continued anyway. "Well, I don't have my own room. In fact, I've never had my own room. I shared a room with Aunt Cass my whole childhood, up until Daddy and I got married, then I moved right into his room. I need my own room right now, Leslie. It's not because I'm leaving, though. I think it's so I can figure out how to make staying work better."

Leslie didn't respond.

"I'll be honest, Les. Daddy and I are struggling right now, that's true. Sometimes, we don't really like each other very much; that's true too. But I do love him, just like when you and Felix fight and you still love him."

"Felix isn't my husband."

"No," Nora relaxed a little, sensing a softening in Leslie's muttered response. "He's not. And I'm relieved to hear that, because it would be really weird if he was." She paused, and smiled when Leslie poked her in the hip with a toe. It was a little rough, but Nora understood. "But I think you know what I mean. I love your Daddy, Les. I just don't feel like I know how to show him right now."

"And I love your mom, Les." Jake slipped into the room and slowly approached the bed. Nora could read the pain on his face, and she knew that it must have taken a lot of courage for him to come in to support her after hearing her speak so candidly to their daughter. "I'm sorry I wasn't more careful with the things I said to you earlier. I should have chosen my words better. Your mom is right, things are hard right now. But neither one of us is willing to give up. We won't give up on this family, do you hear me?"

Leslie lifted her head a little but didn't look at either one of them. She finally nodded in acknowledgment. Then she asked, "You two were pretty loud in there. Has it been hard for a long time?" Her voice shook in a way that broke Nora's heart.

Jake and Nora exchanged glances and he responded first. "Yes, for a while. We should have started working on things long ago, but I didn't want to admit that there were problems. That's my fault, and I take full responsibility for letting things get to this point. Your mom was brave enough to take action even when I didn't. She kinda woke me up, and I've been really grumpy about it."

Leslie still didn't make eye contact, but she nodded again, listening to every word he said. Nora too, sat silently, drawing circles on the sheet with her fingertip, listening to words that sounded so different from anything Jake had spoken before. It was clear he'd heard her back in his office, even through his anger.

"I don't really like being awake, I have to admit." Jake chuckled in a self-deprecating way. "I don't like facing what's been going on while I was sleeping. But not facing things would just be pretending again, and I'm not going to do that to this family anymore. Leslie, I love you very much, and I'm proud that you're my daughter. It certainly helps that you can fish the way you do...." His voice trailed off and Leslie snorted quietly, a small smile beginning to curve the corner of her mouth up. "Your mom loves you, too. I know that without a doubt."

"Is camping going to be totally weird with you two?" Leslie's question caught them both by surprise, but Jake's comment about fishing might have triggered her concern.

"Camping is always weird in this family," Nora said with a smirk.

"Yeah, but is it going to be weird in a normal way or weird in a weird way?"

"Normal weird," Jake assured her. "We promise."

THIRTY FOUR

Jake watched Nora as she regaled the kids with the tale of her terrible day. They were appropriately shocked at Sandra Madison's behavior, envious of the woman going on the safari, and they all laughed at Nora's expense when she told them about tripping in front of the group of teenage boys outside her office. They had all stopped to help her and were very polite and courteous, but she could tell they were trying desperately not to laugh at her, at least not until they walked away.

"I'm telling you, my feet just went right out from under me. Both my bag of folders and my purse went flying, and my cell phone actually hit one of them in the leg. I sat there on my butt, trying not to cry, while they scrambled around picking things up for me. See what happens when you try to do too many things while talking on your cell phone?"

"Oh, Mom!" Leslie was mortified for her. "What if you see them again?"

Nora laughed. "Hopefully, for the sake of my pride, I never will."

Jake enjoyed listening to his girls talking, their two voices blending so sweetly. Leslie was growing up; her voice was beginning to have the same rich timbre as Nora's.

His girls. Leslie was long-legged and lanky, still a little awkward in her growing body. Her eyes were too big for her face, her elbows were usually black and blue from banging into things. But she had a softness to her that defied her angular lines, a promise of things to come. Nora, on the other hand, was fully woman. Her curves were all in the right places, and the softness hinted at in Leslie was in full bloom in his wife. He knew every inch of her body, every freckle, every dimple. He loved the fullness of her mouth, especially when she smiled just for him, the way her eyes, big and bold with excitement, or slanted and deep with passion, watched the world around her.

The dark thought suddenly launched itself out of nowhere. Is she really yours? Maybe he thinks she's his. He's also looked into her bold eyes as she smiles up at him. He's also rested his hands on the curves of her body. He's probably counted the freckles on her skin.... In an instinctual effort to stop his train of thoughts, Jake shoved away from the table so abruptly that everyone stopped talking to look at him in surprise.

"What's the matter, Daddy?" Felix asked, caught in the middle of a laugh. "Are you okay?"

Jake quickly recovered, looked around at the three faces of his family, and smiled a little too brightly. "I'm fine. Just thought I'd check to see if we have any ice cream and got a little too excited over the idea. You know me and my ice cream."

"You're an addict, Daddy. We all know that." Leslie rolled her eyes good-naturedly and went back to telling them about an embarrassing moment of her own. Jake glanced at Nora's face and wondered if she could read his mind. The look in her eyes made him think perhaps she could. He pushed his chair back under the table as quietly as possible, and headed for the refrigerator.

He had to stop. Stop thinking about him. About them. He pulled open the freezer door and leaned forward a little, relishing the brisk air on his face. He reached for the tub of vanilla ice cream but had to set it down on the counter to keep from throwing it against the wall. Pressing his hands to the counter top, he leaned forward a little, bowing his head. *Oh Lord, why isn't this getting any easier?* He just kept getting blindsided.

"Jake?" Nora spoke his name, a question in her voice. "Do you need help?" She was asking about more than ice cream..

"I got it," he said, smiling over his shoulder at her. He could see the concern on her face and for some reason it irked him. "Maybe you three can clear the dinner dishes."

Nora nodded and stood up, prodding the children to help her. Within minutes, the table was clear and Jake filled four bowls with ice cream, while Nora made a small pot of coffee.

Somehow, they made it through the rest of the evening. Together, they put the kids to bed and reassured them again with hugs and kisses. The two of them spoke briefly about what still needed to be done before the camping trip, then Nora left.

Jake could not bring himself to go to bed just yet. In fact, he was beginning to dread their bed. It had been twenty-three days, and fifteen hours, give or take a few minutes, since he'd last made love to Nora there, since she'd last slept in his arms, and every time he even thought about going to bed, his body reacted with desire for her. If he was being honest, it really didn't take much these days. When she walked in a room, when he heard her voice on the phone, when she passed so close he could smell her perfume. Something new, he realized. She was wearing something earthy and still a little spicy, but softer, more subtle. It suited her perfectly. And then he thought about smelling her skin, about pulling her close enough to breathe her in....

"Stop!" He spoke out loud, trying to get his thoughts under control again. How on earth was he supposed to last a whole month without being with her? Or more, if Pastor Rob had his way? Nora told him Vicky had requested the same of her, and he was glad that it wasn't just some form of torture or punishment being inflicted on him. He often lost sight of why they were abstaining, though, especially since they were trying to work things out. Sex had always been an effective way to end arguments between them; or to at least lay things to rest for a while. Without it, they were stuck dealing with their seemingly unresolvable differences with no reprieve.

Sometimes it seemed like sex was all he thought about now that he couldn't have it, and he was certain that wasn't the point of the exercise. He couldn't help but wonder how Nora was coping, but he was too afraid to ask her, lest it open up the doors to temptation and they gave in. He knew better than to talk about it with her—more than once, he'd caught her looking at him with something potent and raw in her eyes. It made him want to launch himself across the room at her like some crazed animal.

And how on earth were they going to keep their hands off each other during their camping trip? It was part of the thrill of their time away, making love beneath the blankets out under the stars, the soft glow of the fire illuminating his wife's sensual features.

He stood up and began pacing the floor. Why was he worried about the camping trip still a few weeks away? He didn't know how he was going to get through this night!

What was she doing over there in her little sanctuary? Was she being tortured with thoughts of him, too? Was she pacing the floor, her throat tight, her muscles tense, wanting him with every fiber of her being?

Maybe she's wanting Tristan.

He stopped pacing as his imagination kicked into overdrive.

"No!" He shouted, then covered his mouth, surprising himself with his own vehemence. He was not going to let his thoughts control him. Not again. Desperate, he scanned the room. Where was his Bible? What was that verse in Corinthians about taking captive his thoughts, about not letting his thoughts control him? Shouldn't he be able to decide what he was going to think about and be able to do away with all the other thoughts?

"Where is my Bible?" he asked out loud, searching the room more earnestly. He was sure he'd left it on the coffee table after the last time he'd read it, but it was nowhere to be seen. Spotting Nora's Message Bible on the bookshelf across the room, he began flipping through it until he reached the New Testament letters Paul had written to the different churches. In 2 Corinthians 10, verses 3-6, he found the passage he was looking for. After reading it in Eugene Peterson's paraphrase, he thought that perhaps he hadn't fully understood the passage until now.

The world is unprincipled. It's dog-eat-dog out there! The world doesn't fight fair. But we don't live or fight our battles that way—never have and never will. The tools of our trade aren't for marketing or manipulation, but they are for demolishing that entire massively corrupt culture. We use our powerful God-tools for smashing warped philosophies, tearing down barriers erected against the truth of God, fitting every loose thought and emotion and impulse into the structure of life shaped by Christ. Our tools are ready at hand for clearing the ground of every obstruction and building lives of obedience into maturity.

Demolishing. Smashing. Tearing down. Clearing the ground. Those were words he could understand! Fighting words. Loaded Browning 20-gauge shotgun words. Warrior words.

If he was willing to let Christ shape him into a holy warrior, then he would be equipped with some pretty powerful God-tools. He didn't have to sit around waiting in defense mode, ducking and dodging thoughts and feelings as they came flying at him. Demolishing, smashing, tearing down, clearing the ground; charge! He might even paint half his face blue and get a claymore.

That's how he wanted to live. He wanted to be battle-fit, a warrior ready to fight for his life, for the lives of those he loved, for truth, God's truth. For freedom. This back and forth, loving then hating, kindness then cruelty, it all had to stop.

"So show me, God, please," he cried out in frustration. "Show me how to use Your weapons. I need Your help. Teach me how to be Nora's hero. You gave me this woman, this marriage, and I have not fought well for either, but I want to. I want to know how! Shape my life into a warrior fit for Your army. Help me to smash and tear and clear away the thoughts that are not truth so You can build me into a man of obedience and maturity." He read the scripture again and again as he prayed the words. "Help me to fit every loose thought and emotion and impulse into its rightful place so that if it doesn't line up with a life shaped by You, then it has nowhere to take root."

That meant putting sex in its rightful place. That meant manning up and practicing self-control, when all he wanted to do was throw her down and take control. That meant paying attention, being sensitive to Nora and her needs, and not making it all about what he wanted. That meant being a real man, and not settling for less than what was good and wholesome and right between them.

Boy, he had his work cut out for him.

"Break out the big guns, God. We've got us a real battle ahead, and I've been badly trained and poorly equipped until now."

He closed the Bible and got down on his knees in front of the sofa. It was an awkward posture, one that still made him feel like a child, but he'd been doing it faithfully since talking to Pastor Rob. He'd been getting up early every morning, getting down on his knees before God, and as foreign as it felt, it seemed right somehow.

THIRTY FIVE

Nora slumped low in her chair, feeling churlish and crabby, her notebook lying open in her lap. She tapped the end of her pen lightly on the blank page, trying to motivate herself to start this new list. She didn't want to think of anything good about anyone. She didn't want to think of anything bad about anyone, either. In fact, she really didn't want to think, period. She'd prefer to just sit and stare out the window at the stream meandering along the edge of the patio, and think about nothing at all.

Things had been bittersweet since the confrontation and ensuing talk in Leslie's room a week ago. Felix was brought in at the end of the conversation, and Jake prayed for all four of them. It was strange, that prayer. They always prayed with the kids before bed, and as a family over their meals. She and Jake used to pray over the needs in their Bible Study group. But she couldn't remember ever having prayed intentionally over their family the way they had that night. Jake, with a hand on each child's head, asked God's forgiveness for not being a better father, a better husband, for not being a better son to his Heavenly Father. He asked God to protect them, to help them fix the parts that were broken. He reached over and cupped Nora's face briefly and prayed that God would bless her, his wife, and that they would grow in love and learn to understand each other better.

Now, alone yet again in her little cottage, she replayed his petition over and over, wondering if it was really possible. Was there hope for them? Could they get the heart of their marriage beating again? Could Jake be trusted? Could she be trusted?

Could God be trusted?

And there was the real question, she realized, as she stared down at the blank page labeled *Things I Love About God*. It was due tomorrow for her meeting with Vicky, but every time she'd start on it, she'd wind up listing what God had done for her or what He'd given her, like her beautiful children, her job and the joy she got out of helping people feel good about their homes, the cottage, Jake. But she couldn't, for the life of her, come up with one thing she honestly loved about God, Himself; about His nature, about His character. And suddenly, she understood why.

She wasn't so sure she loved Him anymore, and a lot of that had to do with the fact that she wasn't so sure she could trust Him with her love.

"Just like all the other men in my life," she muttered.

Frankly, it had been a long time since she'd really trusted God. Oh, she knew He was who He said He was. She knew He was real and present and aware. But that was what made her afraid to trust Him. If God was real and present and aware, then why didn't He ever respond to her?

Why would He just stand back and let all this stuff happen to her? Why didn't He keep Jake from drinking? Why didn't He motivate her husband to be a better man, to be responsible, to not be so needy? Why hadn't He kept Tristan out of her life, especially when she was so terribly vulnerable? Why didn't He at least help her resist the temptation Tristan offered? The questions kept chasing round and round in her mind.

"Don't you see, God? All those years of waiting for You, asking for You, listening for any tiny piece of evidence that You cared a single iota for me? And You just stood back and watched me stumble around in the darkness. Where were You, God? Where *were* You?" She spread her arms wide, her hands trembling, hating how completely and utterly alone she felt. "Is this all part of Your plan? This?" Her voice caught on an angry sob. "Do You hate me so much?"

He responded to her with silence.

Finally, Nora closed the notebook with its still blank pages, and crawled in bed, expecting sleep to whisk her away from this heavy day. But as she lay there listening to the busy nightlife at the little stream outside her window, she became more and more awake. Frustrated, she punched her pillow a few times, rolled onto her side, and burrowed down a little deeper under her comforter.

"Comforter, ha!" She growled to no one as she threw off the ineffectual article a few minutes later. By the dim glow of the twinkle lights she always left on outside the kitchen window, she poured herself a glass of juice, and slathered a piece of toast with cream cheese. Still grumpy, and now even more frustrated because sleep was eluding her, she headed out into the summer night in her nightgown to join the masses at the stream.

Everything went still except the water as she arranged a lounge chair and small table at the edge of her patio. All the creatures watched, waiting to see what this morose monster was going to do, but they soon realized she was no threat to them, and started up their chirping, scritching, buzzing, and rustling again. The night, even after such a warm day, had cooled pleasantly, and Nora sighed and leaned back in her chair, stretching her legs out in front of her. She gazed up at the night sky through the lacy branches of the mulberry tree overhead. It really was lovely out here beside the waters.

"He leads me beside still waters," she murmured quietly, not sure what had stirred the memory of the old Bible verse up. The water wasn't still, but it was soothing, its constant motion a massage to her nerves. The verses played out in her head. "The Lord is my shepherd, I shall not want. He makes me lie down in green pastures; He leads me beside still waters. He restores my soul." It seemed like she'd known the twenty-third Psalm her whole life, but like the stuffed animals that had been so alive to her as a child, the Scriptures had become just as ineffective at soothing her spirit.

"But I desperately want, Lord," she whispered. "I want You to restore my soul, my marriage, my family, but You just don't seem to have it in Your heart to do it."

She sat there for a long time, listening; for what exactly, she didn't know. In the rhythm of the water, she thought she heard a song, and she strained her ears to it, but it remained just beyond her grasp, elusive and mysterious. Her thoughts drifted aimlessly back over her day

Renee. So full of life, vivacious, charming. She wanted only to love and be loved. Wasn't there a man out there who appreciated those qualities in a woman, who would nurture her heart without taking advantage of her vulnerability? What had happened to convince Renee that short term romances and shallow indulgences were better than deep intimacy and real commitment?

And Jo. Tough, hard-working, confident; Jo was the quintessential modern woman. Men were, to her, a necessary evil. She needed them, but did not trust them. She was attracted to them, but did not like them. As far as she was concerned, there were very few good men left in the world, and those few had already been snapped up by a few lucky women. Nora never met Jo's ex, but he must have been cruel in his passivity.

Sandra Madison and the ugliness behind her perfectly coiffed and manicured world. The woman's husband obviously had something to do with her anger and bitterness. His absence was a blaring sore spot in her life. Was it like that at the beginning of their marriage, or had they once spent every waking moment together, star-crossed lovers with eyes full of hope, and hearts full of dreams for their future together? Nora pictured again how beautiful the new room looked, but how Sandra, in her bitterness, could only see the negative things, even finding fault where there was none.

"And then there's me, complaining about my husband needing me too much," Nora said. "Am I like Sandra? Only seeing the negative when there's so much good in him?" But she knew that a needy man was just as destructive to a marriage as an absent man; she'd experienced it firsthand. A man whose woman had to fight his battles for him was no better than a man who abandoned her to the fight altogether. A woman didn't just need to be pursued; she also needed to be covered. She needed a partner, a protector, a champion. And she needed to know that her champion would fight for her.

She thought about Tristan and his stoic acceptance of her leaving him, yet again. Yes, he'd tried to contact her, but when she didn't return his calls or respond to him in any way, his attempts dwindled to nothing but a missed call now and then. "You never fought for me," she whispered into the night air. "I thought you were my knight in shining armor rescuing me from the dragon's lair, but you never picked up a sword, not once." Tears welled up as her heart twisted inside her. She'd been swept off her feet by a fraud, by a coward, not a warrior. "You, Tristan, you *were* the dragon."

Oh, what a fool she'd been.

As understanding washed over her, she thought of what Vicky had said. "The world has taken lust and disguised it as love. They've taken sex and disguised it as intimacy. They've taken commitment and disguised it as prison. They've twisted everything until it's all inside out and then we wonder why we're so confused about our relationships."

She opened up the emotions inside her and examined them for what they were. Maybe something had grown out of the self-indulgence of her lust for Tristan, out of feeding her physical reaction to him until it became something more, but only because she chose to do so, with eyes wide open. Temptation, yes. Chemistry, sure. Passion, absolutely. All extremely powerful feelings.

But love? She shook her head slowly, her thoughts perusing another passage she'd learned from the Bible long ago; a list she was certain Vicky knew too.

Love is patient. Love is kind. Love is not jealous. Love does not brag and is not arrogant. Love does not act unbecomingly. Love is not self-serving. Love is not easily provoked. Love does not keep record of wrongs. Love does not rejoice in evil, but in truth.

Love bears all things, believes all things, hopes all things, endures all things.

Nothing about her relationship with Tristan qualified as that kind of love. Absolutely nothing. Truth be told, nothing about her behavior toward Jake qualified as love, either, except for perhaps the enduring part, but that was probably negated by her remarkable ability to keep record of his wrongs.

A record that she'd decided entitled her to no longer be patient or kind, but arrogant, and easily provoked. A record that gave her the right to act unbecomingly and self-serving. A record that she'd turned into a weapon, one she'd wielded relentlessly in the tearing out of the heart of their marriage. A record so terribly different than any list Vicky had asked of her.

Although admitting it brought shame that sickened and curdled her innards, Jake, on the other hand, patiently waited for her to come home, giving her the time and space she selfishly insisted on having. He'd been kind to her when she was so sick. He faithfully cared for the children and their home while she abandoned them all. He endured her terrible and unappeasable anger over his night out, he'd stepped up and gone to the pastor for counseling, because he hoped and believed their marriage could be saved. Time and time again, he'd done exactly as she'd asked—no, demanded—of him...because he truly loved her.

Overwhelmed and a little frightened by this indisputable evidence of how wrong she'd been, both about herself, and about Jake, she muttered childishly, "He's *definitely* jealous, though."

But then, wasn't she giving him every reason to be? Leaving Tristan wasn't some grand and noble gesture on her part. How on earth had she convinced herself that it was? She'd almost believed she was some glorious Isolde, denying her heart's desire and sacrificing her lover to return to her husband, as though their affair was something honorable and eternal, good and pure....

And all along, she'd blamed God for being standoffish. She'd blamed Jake for being needy. She'd even blamed Tristan for making her an adulteress.

Her circumstances, her pain, her struggles, she'd made them all someone else's fault.

She'd been fooled by the world, blinded by her selfishness. She'd fallen for the disguise, and she'd been swept up into the duplicity and confusion that comes from trying to justify wrong, from embracing sin and denying truth.

"Oh, Lord Jesus, what have I done?" she moaned, burying her face in her hands. "What's to become of us?" She drew her legs up to her chest and rocked back and forth as the tears came again, pushing through her in great waves of emotion. How she longed to hear God's voice right now, to have Him take her in His arms and comfort her, protect her, fight for her.

No one will fight for you, a small, pouting whisper prodded her spirit. Not after all you've done. Not even God. And if Jake were a real man, he'd kick your sorry backside to the curb. You'll just end up on your own again, as usual.

Nora reached down and dashed her hand into the water, splattering the stone patio and her bare feet with cold glittering droplets, breaking the hold the voice had on her. She lifted her face, twisted by misery. "Help me. I'm so sorry. I've been so wrong. I've been so arrogant and proud. I don't know how to fix this on my own. I need You. I need You so badly. I want to believe in You, God. Help me believe."

I don't want to give up without fighting for us. The words floated into her consciousness, like a song sung over the rhythm of the water. God had given her and Jake to each other, joined them as one flesh. Why wouldn't He speak to her now through Jake's awkward and tender appeal?

Will you stay and fight with me?

THIRTY SIX

"Hey, Jake." Nora ducked her head around the office door. "I'm here. Do you need any help packing?"

"Hm?" He didn't look up until he'd finished answering the question on the form in front of him in the best way possible. But he'd known the moment she arrived. He'd heard the kids' voices raised in greeting, the quick footsteps of her approach to his office, her light tap on the door, and it took every ounce of concentration to stay focused on the task at hand.

The way she said his name these days made his skin flush. Something had changed. Something had altered, either in the way he perceived it, or in the way she projected it, since that night they'd talked and prayed with the kids in Leslie's room, and it made his pulse quicken.

Nora crossed the room and peered over his shoulder. "What are you up to?" He smiled a little to himself at the curiosity in her voice.

"Hey Nor." He turned around in his chair and looked up at her, giving her his full attention. "Sorry. What was that?"

"What do you have there?" She tried again to peek at the paper on his desk, but he covered it with the flat of his hand.

"Well, aren't you nosey?" But he winked at her so she would know he wasn't offended. "Actually, I'm applying for a job. You know Scott, from church? Well, we were talking last Sunday, and I asked him how work was going. He started telling me how busy he was and that he was thinking about hiring an assistant in the near future because he was feeling a little overwhelmed. I told him he needed me, that I could do the job. He agreed, and asked me to fill out one of these." He lifted his hand so she could see the application he'd just completed.

"Is it inspections? What does he do again?" Nora propped one hip against the edge of the desk. Even the interest she showed in his work was sincere and encouraging, without an ounce of disdain. "Doesn't he work for the county?"

"Yeah. He's contracted with Public Works. His company oversees the "Get Smart" programs. Get Smart About Water, Get Smart About Fire, Get Smart About Gardening, you know, all those reduce, reuse, and recycle programs. Anyway, he needs someone to monitor the presentation sites all over the county so it's inspections of a kind. It's a new position he's just created so he's starting it out part time. He thinks it will eventually go to full time, but for now he can guarantee me at least three days a week so far." He laced his fingers behind his head and grinned up at her. "They have to post it publicly because it's a public works related job, but Scott assured me it's mine."

Nora's eyes were bright with what he hoped was appreciation. "What are the presentation sites? Is that like that place at the park where they teach the community about composting and recycling and stuff?"

"Exactly. Scott's constructed almost thirty of them in public parks all over the county, and it's just getting to be too many to keep track of on his own. He has a crew to do the maintenance and upkeep, but he needs help overseeing and managing the care. That's what I'll be doing; going from site to site making sure everything is in order. I know I'll have to learn a little more about the whole program, but as far as I can tell, it's mostly about teaching good sense when it comes to watering and planting and caring for your little piece of earth. I think it'll be a good fit for me." He studied her for a minute, toying with the pen in his hand. She looked really good, like she'd slept well. She had on a pair of shorts, an apple green V-neck top, and a pair of old school Vans in a checkerboard pattern. Her hair was pulled back in a ponytail and the only makeup she wore was a pale pink gloss that made him want to taste her lips.

"What?" She smiled self-consciously and tipped her head to one side.

He stood up and stretched, then slipped his arms around her, drawing her toward him.

"Smooth, Jake. Really smooth," she giggled. "The old stretchy snake move from high school."

"Stretchy snake? That just sounds wrong."

"You know what I'm talking about. At the movie theater. The guy pretends to stretch, then he casually drapes his arm around the unsuspecting girl's shoulders. Next thing she knows, he's snaked his arm over and is trying cop a feel."

"I have absolutely no idea what you're talking about...but does it work?" He grinned, then dipping his head, he breathed in the smell of her hair, her skin, and gently pressed his lips against hers. "So what do you think?"

Nora leaned back in his arms and looked up at him, a sparkle in her teasing eyes. "Of the kiss or the job?"

Jake covered her mouth with his again, this time with more intensity, and felt the tremor of his rising pulse as she sighed against his lips. When he lifted his head, she smiled, her eyes soft, her cheeks flushed. "Now that, my husband, was amazing."

He grinned, pleased with himself for making her look so satisfied. "And the job?"

"The job sounds amazing, too, Jake." She cupped his cheek with one hand and took a deep breath. "I didn't know you were looking for something other than inspections."

He didn't let her go, but turned them so he was leaning against the desk with her facing him, standing between his legs. He let his arms relax a little around her waist, keeping his hands clasped at the curve of her low back, enjoying the way she fit tucked into him like she was. She rested her hands on his biceps, toying with the cuffs of his sleeves. Her touch sent small currents up his arms, making his scalp tingle with pleasure, and he flexed for good measure, making her eyebrows shoot up in response. He just grinned, feeling cocky and playful and on the right track.

"I've been working on a few different things, trying to come up with some alternatives to doing home inspections. My license is due to be renewed this month, and it seemed a good time to consider what I'm really doing with it. I'm not yet ready to give it up all together, because I like doing inspections. But I think I have to accept that it's more of a part time business, at least for me, because of my strengths and weaknesses." He leaned forward and kissed the tip of her nose. "I just do better when I know where I'm supposed to be, when I'm supposed to be, and what I'm supposed to do, and I'm okay with that."

"I don't know what to say," she acknowledged. "It sounds like you've really processed through some things."

"Yeah. It's been a big help, talking to Pastor Rob. He's encouraged me to think outside the box, to talk to other men, get involved in guy stuff at church. The whole 'iron sharpens iron' thing. But it's making me realize how much I've been leaning on you all these years, Nor."

She didn't respond, and for a moment, he felt the usual trepidation rising up, the fear of her criticism, but he stopped his thoughts from spinning out of control with a blast from his spiritual shotgun, and continued, suddenly wanting to tell her everything in his heart. "Nora, I've been so wrong about you, the way I've had you up on a pedestal. It's like some form of sick idolatry, because part of me always expected you to fall; almost like I've been waiting for it so I could point my finger at you and say, 'See? I *knew* you weren't perfect!'"

He felt her tense, her body shifting in his arms, as though gearing up for another skirmish. "No. Don't pull away from me. I need you to listen, to hear me out. Please." He waited, silently willing her to stay, to trust him.

She didn't meet his eyes, but she nodded and relaxed her stance a little, her hands sliding over to rest against his chest. He could feel the warmth of her palms through the thin fabric of his shirt.

"I love you, Nora. I love everything about you. But I've been putting you, in both good and bad ways, ahead of everything else and everyone else in my life, especially God. I don't want to do that anymore." He leaned forward to put his forehead against hers. "I want God to come first. It just doesn't work any other way, does it?"

"No. I don't think it does."

He released her and leaned back so he could read her face easier. Taking her hands, he brought them both up and kissed her fingertips. "As for the job, I'm excited about it. I hate to admit this to you, because it makes me sound like a schmuck, but it's almost as though when I finally admitted that I didn't have to compete with you, the Lord opened doors in a whole different direction for me."

Nora nodded encouragingly, her voice soft, but rich with emotion. "I think the Lord opens doors all the time for us, but we have to keep our eyes open to see them and be ready to walk through them. You seem like you have your eyes open, Jake."

"It's like I told you and Les the other night; I really do feel like I'm waking up." He shrugged. "I'm seeing things differently; myself, you, the kids, our future. I want you to be proud to call me your husband, not because I'm all that and a bag of chips, as Les would say, but because I'm the man God created me to be. I know I've sold us all short too often. I know it's going to be tough to reinvent us, Nor, but I also know that's what I want to do." He turned her hands and held them pressed tightly to his chest again. His heart was beating hard against his sternum and he hoped she could feel it under her palms.

"I know I'm going to fail miserably on a regular basis, and that I'll let you down again and again." He grimaced slightly. "But if I can convince you that my heart is yours, and that God gave you to me to love and protect, then I will have succeeded in fully waking up."

Tears welled up in Nora's eyes and he was thrilled at the sight of them, no longer afraid of what they meant.

"Oh, Jake," she murmured, and his name on her lips was like a cool drink to his parched soul. She leaned forward and buried her face in his neck. He could feel the dampness on her cheeks. "Jake, I'm so sorry. I'm so sorry." She whispered again and again. "I'm so sorry. I was so wrong."

He wrapped his arms around her again, enfolding her like a child. He stroked her back, brushing his fingers along the soft curve of her neck, not saying anything at all. Words and emotions welled up inside of him until he thought he might burst, but he kept them in, setting aside his own feelings, wanting to be only what she needed him to be. This is how it feels to be a man, he thought. This was what it means to be a hero. *Lord, teach me.*

Finally spent, Nora reached over his shoulder and grabbed a couple of tissues from the box on his desk. He waited quietly while she blew her nose and sniffed a few times, then he cupped her chin, turning her to face him. She resisted at first, but he knew it was only because she hated the way she looked when she cried.

"I think you're beautiful," he said gently. "Look at me."

She finally lifted her glistening eyes to his, and he smiled, his heart overflowing with love for her. "I love you, Nora. I forgive you. And I need you to forgive me, too." He put both hands on either side of her face when she tried to turn away, his thumbs brushing away the few tears that still collected in her bottom eyelashes. "I have been a rotten husband to you."

Nora shook her head, but he wouldn't let her speak. "No. I need you to listen to me. I have been the worst kind of man, Nora. Even as I put you on a pedestal, it was because I didn't want the responsibility of taking care of anyone but me and my needs and my desires. Then I lashed out at you in the cruelest of ways, because you didn't want a selfish man like me." He closed his eyes briefly, then opened them again, wanting her to see into his heart. "I'm sorry for the things I've said to you, the horrible names I've called you, even for some of the things I've thought about you. You are my beauty," he repeated. "I don't want you to doubt that, ever again. Can you forgive me?" He paused and waited for her response.

"Yes." It was only a whisper, but he needed to hear it before he went on.

"And I'm sorry for all those years I drank and acted so selfishly. I know for a fact that I've never really apologized for that. I'm sorry for not being the kind of man you could count on, depend on. I think I had myself convinced that the alcohol was my battle, and the decision to quit drinking was my gift to you, like it was some noble act." He took a deep breath, noticing that her eyes widened as he spoke. "I pompously believed I was sacrificing my desires for you, and that you should be grateful. Can you believe that? I never felt I needed to be remorseful or repentant for those years; I excused my behavior, blaming it on the drink."

He shook his head and swallowed the lump in his throat. Saying these words—finally—felt so different than what he'd feared. So empowering.

"And then last October. Oh Nora, I'm so sorry about going out like that. It was my pride, you know? And now I see that my pride nearly destroyed us. Will you forgive me for those wasted years, Nora, and for that horrible night?"

She was silent, but the way she chewed on her lip made him think she wanted to say something.

"What is it?"

"Your waitress." It came out just above a whisper, her voice breaking over the next words. "I... I don't even have the right to ask this, but what about your waitress? Are you—were you... with her?"

Jake sighed heavily, and closed his eyes, suddenly putting two and two together. "Oh, Nora. No." He hesitated, then forged ahead, determined to be honest and honorable. "But not for lack of trying." He opened his eyes again and looked at her, still holding her face before him. "I wish I could undo it. I wish I could go back and choose differently. I wish I could go back fifteen years, twenty years, and choose differently." He paused. "Is that why you were with... because of me... because of her?"

It was obvious she knew what he was talking about, and she seemed a little taken aback by his question. "No, Jake. No! I didn't intentionally go out looking. It wasn't about revenge. I just got blindsided at the wrong time, and I was in the wrong place, in the wrong frame of mind. Then I said 'yes' when I should have said 'no' and I knew it. And I'm sorry."

He couldn't believe they were having this conversation. It was killing him, but it was like debriding a wound, the cleaning out of things that wanted to fester if they let them.

"Did you love him?" He knew he shouldn't ask, but his self-control was weakening. He was desperately trying to locate his spiritual claymore, but it wasn't happening fast enough to keep up. Part of him wanted her to just pull him close and tell him it was all a bad dream, that they were going to wake up and it would all disappear. But the other part of him needed to know the truth.

She dropped her eyes and he let go of her face, sliding his hands down her arms until they were just holding hands again. He wondered, too late, if his question would destroy the fragile bridge they'd been working so hard to build between them. "At the time, I thought I did, but I was so blinded by my selfishness and anger. I totally understand what you were saying about the whole quitting drinking thing. I felt that way about this. That you should be grateful I'd done the right thing. But the thing is, it wasn't right for me to say yes to him in the first place."

Could he live with that? He tipped his head back and closed his eyes. Was that enough to build a future on? Well, at least she was being honest with him, and honesty, yes, honesty he could work with. He took a deep breath and pulled her close. He couldn't look at her, not yet.

"Do you love me?" She hadn't said that she did; not here, today, in this conversation, and he needed to hear her say it.

This time, she pulled back and waited for his eyes to meet hers. Her gaze was wide, steady, sure. "I do, Jake. I love you."

His breath caught, and he crushed her to him, holding her tightly until his heart began beating again. This, right here, this woman, this wife, he could live with. This was where their future would begin.

"I love you, Jake." Nora's voice trembled as she said it again, but there was a certainty in her tone that made him even braver. He straightened, and turned her around so she was sitting in his chair. Then he knelt down in front of her.

"I promise to always fight for you, Nora. I promise to always fight for us. Because I love you."

She was crying again, tears that made him want to celebrate, and he laid his head down on her lap, peace and joy filling him, body and soul.

THIRTY SEVEN

THE BAGS WERE PACKED and sitting in the driveway, waiting to be loaded in the back of Jake's truck. The morning was nearly over, and they still had a six-hour drive ahead of them to their favorite campsite at Kennedy Meadows. It was much later in the season than they usually went, but with the longer days, they'd have plenty of time to set up camp. They might even get to take a dip in the river before the sun dropped below the mountain peaks, making the water too chilly to enjoy.

Nora stood at the sink filling water bottles, and she smiled as she considered the trip ahead of them. It would be difficult sharing an air mattress with the man to whom she was married, but not because she didn't want to. In fact, she was looking forward to the challenge of keeping each other warm without breaking their commitment to abstinence. They had plans to spend a few days away together the following week, so they could rediscover that part of their relationship, but for now, they were like teenagers again, longing for something just out of reach.

They'd both met with Pastor Rob a little over a week ago. His eyes glistened with unshed tears as he said how pleased he was to see them there together. "This isn't usually the way these things end, my friends. I'm so proud of you for choosing to stay together, for committing to putting this marriage back together God's way." He spoke openly and honestly about the ups and downs of the journey that lay ahead of them, not focusing on the past, but on how to move into the new season together. Some of what he said made her want to bury her head in the sand, but because of his gracious and gentle spirit, she came away from their session feeling better equipped, and with anticipation for the future.

It wasn't always easy. In fact, there were days, just as Pastor Rob promised, when it was excruciatingly painful, when one of them would go under, awash with memories, or shame, or questions that had no answers. When fear and doubt would seep in through the cracks in every door and window. But they were learning how to process through those days, and how to move to the other side of them, too.

They were being careful. They continued to meet with Pastor Rob and Vicky independently of each other. Nora still stayed at the cottage most nights. Not only did it make abstinence easier, but it also gave them the time they needed to work on things individually. But Vicky was beginning to challenge Nora's decision to stay there.

"I think the cottage is in jeopardy of becoming one of those in-between places, Nora. I think it's time to start making plans to move back home. I want you and Jake to talk about it while you're away, and when you come back to see me, I'd like you to have a moving date set, okay?"

Nora began reading her Bible again, and was drawn back to some of the familiar scriptures from her childhood, many of them put to music. She found herself singing all the time these days; one of her favorites was a song right out of the Psalms. "Create in me a clean heart, Oh God."

Nora was drawn to her husband anew, too. She ached for him in every way. She loved looking up to catch him watching her, pride and peace, instead of fear in his eyes. She loved coming home to find him busy with the children, or bent over his own work, instead of leaping up to smother her with his need. She loved the evenings when she was home before him, and seeing his face when he walked in the front door, smiling and content to find his family whole.

Church was a bridge they'd yet to cross, but she knew they'd eventually go back. Still no one had contacted them about their absence, and Nora realized it was possible that no one had really noticed. It wasn't that no one cared, she had to believe, but perhaps because their lives were just as difficult as hers.

And now, as she closed the lid on the old red and white cooler, she couldn't wait to get to Kennedy Meadows again, hoping they'd be lucky enough to get their favorite spot, to hike up to Anderson Hollow again, maybe catch a fish or two with the kids. She smiled as the image of her husband bending over to build the fire, the light flickering off the rugged planes of his face, wandered through her mind. She couldn't wait until the end of the day, when they cocooned themselves together on their blanket under the stars, his voice making her body sing as he whispered sweet promises of tomorrow.

It was always her favorite part about camping.

· · · · ● · ● · · · ·

THEY STOOD IN A row on the stream bank, staring at the place they hardly recognized as Anderson Hollow. The falls was little more than an overflow spilling off the top of the stacked boulders. The pool itself was calm, clear enough that they could easily make out the tumbled rocks lining the bottom, and the water level was much lower than in May, leaving more of the sandy slope exposed where they could spread their towels and other gear.

The kids reacted with delight. "Mom! I'm not afraid of that old waterfall now," Felix declared. "I can probably swim right under it."

"Well, maybe you should let one of the adults try that first, okay?" She wasn't really worried, mainly because she didn't think Felix would actually do it without supervision. Although he was remarkably brave when he had to be, he took his time with things, and he wasn't impulsive by nature.

"You won't even get dragged under now, Mom," he declared, patting her arm reassuringly. Thoughts of the last time they were here, and how she'd taken the game they were playing too far, had plagued her the whole hike up. She'd scared them all, including herself, but something in her still stirred its wild head at the memory. She felt the pull even now, as she watched the sunlight dancing on the surface of the pool, and it had her feeling unsettled and a little afraid to go in, in spite of how peaceful it all seemed.

She shook her head slightly and turned toward Leslie, who stared at the falls in a calculating way. "What are you thinking, Les?"

"Is it just me, or does it look like there's a cave back there?" Her daughter didn't point with her finger—pointing was too uncool—but her eyes never left the thin sheet of water falling into the pool. "I think we should explore."

Nora stared hard at the falls, too, not sure she was seeing what Les saw, but Jake immediately agreed that they should check it out. "Maybe we'll find treasure back there. Mountain pirates; ever heard of them?"

"Daaaad." Leslie spun the word out into about four syllables and flicked him in the arm.

Jake reached down and scooped a handful of water up, splashing his daughter from head to toe, dousing Nora in the process.

"Jake!" she screeched, then splashed him back.

"Oooooh, you're in trouble now, Dad. And I'm outta here!" Felix scrambled up onto one of the large rocks at the edge of the pool to get out of the way. But Leslie, already soaked, stayed in the thick of things long enough to give her father a shove that landed him on his backside in two feet of water.

He yelped from the cold, but when Nora, laughing and shivering, reached out to offer him a hand up, he pulled her down beside him. Leslie ran free of the melee and crawled up on the rock to perch next to Felix.

When Nora tried to get up, Jake wouldn't let her, instead drawing her out deeper to where the water was up to his chest. She clung to him, wrapping an arm around his shoulders, trying to absorb some of the heat from his body, still warm from hiking in the sun. He slid his arms around her, pulling her against him.

"I saw you thinking about this," he murmured near her ear, his breath warm on her cheek.

"About what? You dragging me to my icy death?"

"About going under."

Nora stiffened. How did he know?

"But you're not going under without me, Nor. Are you ready?"

"What? No!" But she saw his intent just in time to close her eyes and take a deep breath in before he pulled her down below the surface with him, his arms still around her.

It was so cold it made her bones ache. But when she opened her eyes, it was to find Jake watching her, bubbles seeping slowly from his nose above his playful grin. Then he crossed his eyes and she kicked away from him, bursting up out of the water laughing. He was right beside her.

They turned and smiled at the kids. Felix was still up on the rock, a goofy grin on his face as he watched them, and Les was gathering tall grasses for raft-building, acting as though she wasn't watching them.

"I think we should always come here at the end of summer," Felix called to them. "It's like a different place! This is so cool!"

Jake held Nora loosely, her back up against his chest, her body beginning to adjust to the cold. He spoke first. "Really? But the fishing is better in May, you know. We're going to be lucky to get the leftovers this late in the season."

Leslie paused in her gathering and tipped her head to the side to study her parents. "We won't know that until we try, Dad. But I think Felix is right. It feels different somehow. Not so out of control, I guess. I like it, too."

Nora considered the significance of her daughter's words. That was exactly how she'd felt last year; like everything was out of control in her life, and this place had resonated with the same thing. The waterfall was a rushing torrent in May, launching itself off the ledge and churning up the pool below; roaring and chaotic, stunning and powerful; but unleashed, sweeping everything in its path along with it.

"In May, the snow is melting off the peaks and filling this stream to overflowing, flushing it out, clearing out the debris that's collected in the fall and winter months. New tributaries are forming, banks are being reshaped, pools are filling, even where there weren't pools before. May up here is a time of change and growth. It's good and necessary." Jake tried to explain, but Leslie shook her head.

"I understand that, Dad. I know the different seasons have their purposes. But maybe it's just not the best time to go in the water, you know? When things are out of control? I mean, I know you didn't really get dragged under last year, Mom, but you did drift all the way across the pool from us without even realizing it."

Nora nodded slightly, moved by the teenager's insight. "Yes, I was pretty shocked when I finally came up for air and saw how far I was from you. I'm sorry I scared you." Jake's arm around her middle tightened, acknowledging everything she didn't put into words.

"I like it when the waters fall like that," Felix stated, pointing beyond his parents. "The pool isn't all dark and creepy anymore. I'm not afraid of it now."

Once again, Jake dashed his hand in the water, this time sending the spray up onto the rock where his son still perched. "Well, what are you waiting for, then? Get in here, you two. Let's go hunt treasure together!"

A NEW BEGINNING

· · · ● · ● · · ·

Have you met Willow Goodhope in *Elderberry Croft: Seasons of the Heart?* If you like to read about love overcoming all odds, then let me introduce you to Willow and her quirky neighbors at the Coach House Trailer Park.

~ ~ ~

On a crisp January breeze, a new girl sweeps into the neighborhood, breathing life into the cottage she christens Elderberry Croft.

The folks at The Coach House Trailer Park can't help but fall under Willow Goodhope's spell as she charms them with her vibrant nature, her elderberry gifts, and her outrageous laughter. But there's something about her, a secret sadness that hovers at the corners of her irrepressible smile, and it has everyone talking.

What brings the mysterious young woman to this dead-end place? From what—or whom—is she hiding?

Doc catches her burning letters in her fire pit, and Myra swears Willow drinks alone out in the moonlight.

Joe glimpses the whispering shadows clinging to the girl's coattails, and Patti doesn't miss the way her husband watches the young beauty.

Eddie and Donny compete to see who can make her smile first... even though both figure she prefers her men with good jobs, good homes, and good teeth.

Kathy is doing everyone a favor by keeping a close eye on the wild child next door. Through her binoculars.

And what she sees doesn't sit well with any of them.

♥♥♥

"I meant to savor *Elderberry Croft* - I really did - but I couldn't help myself and gobbled up each installment in one sitting. Brimming with beautifully flawed characters who will make you sigh, smile, laugh, cry, and hurt over their very real struggles, *Elderberry Croft* is a must read." ~ **Tamara Leigh, The Kitchen Novelist, USA Today Bestselling Author**

♥♥♥

(Keep scrolling for an excerpt...)

FROM THE AUTHOR

Dear Reader,

I pray you found hope and inspiration in the redemptive journey of Jake and Nora in *Waters Fall*. This book was a passion project for me. When my search for grittier redemption stories in Christian Fiction came up short, it occurred to me that maybe God had put the desire in my heart not just to *read* a book like this, but to *write* one.

My favorite people to write about are edge-dwellers; those who live on that fine line where hope and despair meet, where love is the only answer, and grace becomes truly amazing. I met Jake and Nora out there on the edge. I'm glad you found us, too.

Where hope lives and love wins. Every time.
Becky Doughty

P.S. Read more about the cottage where Nora came face to face with God and his plan for her life in *Elderberry Croft: Seasons of the Heart*. Keep reading for an excerpt!

Let's stay in touch! Join my mailing list at BeckyDoughty.com to get news on books, audiobooks, and other fun, subscriber-exclusive content.

EXCERPT: ELDERBERRY CROFT

JANUARY BREEZE

AN EXCERPT...

~ ~ ~

A NEW NEIGHBOR.

Kathy expected her at any minute now. She coughed into her elbow as she peered through the narrow opening of her kitchen curtains at the empty cottage across the driveway. It wasn't much more than a shack, really. The roof needed new shingles, the ancient wooden siding was chipped and peeling where the sun beat down mercilessly upon it, and the roots of a massive eucalyptus tree slowly churned up the river-rock patio. Screens were missing from a few of the windows, and the green front door hung at an angle to accommodate the frame that had been put in with a blatant disregard for plumb lines. Its one redeeming quality, a charming little creek that danced along the edge of the patio and on through The Coach House Trailer Park, seemed slightly incongruous with the rest of the ramshackle structure.

The inside, according to Myra, wasn't in any better condition. She'd stopped by to visit the day before after doing a thorough cleaning of the place in preparation for the new tenant.

"Filthy, Kathy! Horrible! And the carpet! Aiee!" Myra often spoke in exclamation marks, bobbing her head for added emphasis, her dark, chin-length hair doing the cha-cha around her face. "It's disgusting! When I told Eddie that it needed to be replaced, he said they won't do it because it's less than five years old. But that carpet looks more like fifty-five to me!

And the shower!" She went on and on until Kathy interrupted her with a glass of her favorite boxed wine, kept chilled in the refrigerator for just such visits.

"Why are you so worked up? This new one will come and go just like all the others."

Myra took a long sip. "I know, I know. But this one," she shrugged her bony shoulders. "I *want* her to like it." The sweet-tart drink puckered her lips. "I want her to like *us*."

"So? What's new? You want everyone to like us."

Myra left a few minutes later, her basket of dirty rags and cleaning supplies hoisted on one scrawny hip. "Don't let her catch you spying on her tomorrow, Kathy-la. I mean it!"

A few minutes before ten, a truck pulled in, one of those little Toyota pickups that simply refused to die, its once royal blue paint faded and oxidized by the California sunshine. The woman driving wore a pair of over-sized, blue tinted sunglasses, and her mahogany-red hair threatened to escape a clip at the crown of her head.

"Young," Kathy quickly labeled her. "Probably between boyfriends. I give her six months, tops."

Her eyebrows lifted with surprise as the woman maneuvered into the parking space in front of the ramshackle house, giving her a full view of the contents of the truck bed. Plants. No mattresses, no dressers or coffee tables, no boxes covered in packing tape and black marker. Plants in huge clay pots and delicate ceramic bowls, hanging baskets and galvanized steel buckets. Verdant bundles wrapped in twine and burlap to protect them from the brilliant January cold. She shot a guilty glance over her shoulder at the one scraggly philodendron on a plant stand in the corner of the room. Between her irregular watering schedule and the fact that the dogs couldn't resist chewing on the few brave tendrils that managed to creep over the lip of the yellow pot, it was a miracle the plant was still alive. Kathy loved plants, but she spent too much of her time and limited resources in futile efforts to add them to her life.

She turned back to the window just as the woman threw open her driver's side door and started talking, gesturing, and nodding effusively. It took a moment, but it finally dawned on Kathy that she was conversing with the plants themselves, making her way around the truck bed, cooing and smiling, fondling leaves and petals, cheering, and clapping her hands.

Kathy muttered to the old and rather obese Labrador that wandered out from under the table. "She's talking to her plants. Like they understand her or something." She twirled a finger around in circles at her temple and rolled her eyes. "I just don't get some people, Heidi." The dog responded by licking her hand and flopping its tail against her legs.

She turned away from the window and coughed deeply again. She hated the way her lungs felt, as though they were being shaken around inside her chest like a baby's toy rattle, but the cough was something she'd earned after forty years of smoking, and she'd learned to live with it. When she caught the seasonal cold, however, it always frightened her a little. Sometimes she'd cough so long and hard, she feared her insides would fly out of her mouth.

She made her way through the obstacle course of her kitchen to the sofa and dropped into one corner, strategically situating herself so she could monitor both her favorite morning soap opera and the activity outside the window. Heidi clambered up onto the cushion next to her. "That's all we need, huh, little girl? Another crazy neighbor." She sighed loudly and leaned her head back on the cushions behind her. Heidi blinked once and sighed, too.

She woke with a start, her open-mouth snoring loud inside her stuffed-up head and peered up at the clock again. She'd been asleep for over an hour! Heidi stood at the front door, scratching to get out, and fat, little Trixie waddled out from the tiny bedroom to see what was going on, her stubby tail wiggling frantically. Bella Basset let out one deep woof from where she lounged on the end of Kathy's bed. Kathy sat up, massaged a crick in her neck, then turned to check on her new neighbor.

She could hardly believe the transformation that had taken place outside her window while she napped. She forgot all semblance of subterfuge and pulled the sheer panel back to see more clearly. Squinting, her eyes bleary from sleep, she struggled to comprehend what she was seeing. She turned and snatched up the set of binoculars off the end table beside the sofa. They still technically belonged to her ex-husband, but he'd never been back to claim them, so she put them to good use keeping an eye on the comings and goings in the park. It was rather convenient that the park's laundry station was practically outside her front door.

On the stoop of Space #12 sat a huge terracotta pot overflowing with fluttering yellow honeysuckle—in flower!—that stretched its tendrils up to the roof and along the low eaves. It formed a natural archway leading to the front entry of the house, and it looked like it'd been growing there for years. Delicate clusters of pink and purple flowers fire-worked out of a wire basket hanging from a decorative hook mounted on the wall below the porch light, softening the askew lines of the door frame. She thought they might be nemesia, or some kind of salvia, but she wasn't certain.

On the patio, in huge pots, red, pink, and white petals hovering over dark foliage had to be cyclamen. Kathy recognized them because they grew right outside her own picket fence, but the only time she'd seen them look so healthy and bloom so enthusiastically was on the shelf at the home improvement center where the plants were all on steroids.

Troughs of bushy geraniums were just on the brink of flowering, what looked like a huge camellia was in full bloom, and were those yellow blossoms African daisies? In January? An old-fashioned hydrangea and a spike-leafed aloe vera odd-coupled in a pedestal urn that was dark with the patina of age and countless waterings. Begonias, blue forget-me-nots, and frilly ferns were tucked into shady spots all over the patio and nestled among the roots of a mulberry tree that spread its branches over the little creek.

In the flowerbed beneath the front window, thick-leaved jades—standard issue in most rentals in Southern California—showed off the last of their winter blooms. Some quick and aggressive weed excavation had uncovered the two rose bushes that had somehow survived over the years and exposed a few saucy snapdragons and a blanket of alyssum the weeds hadn't choked out completely. The roses had been hacked back to sticks, and Kathy wondered if the woman realized it was way late in the season for trimming roses.

Wind-chimes and friar bells hung in the rafters of the porch, their various tones creating harmonies in the breeze, while sun-catchers sent rainbows of light dancing across the tiny yard. She looked over at the clock on the wall for the third time, feeling a little like Rip Van Winkle waking up from his hundred-year snooze.

"How the hula did she do that?"

• • • • • ● • ● • • • •

HEIDI AND TRIXIE WERE snuffling and scratching with renewed fervor, and Kathy realized she had a perfect excuse to spy on her neighbor more openly. "Oh, all right. Let's all go outside for some fresh air."

She pushed open the front door and was nearly bowled over as the dogs scampered past her and out into the yard. "Hey!" she cried out, unprepared for their exuberance.

"Are you all right?"

Kathy's eyes flew to the gate, even more unprepared for the woman who stood there. "Oh! Oh my! You scared me!" She pressed a hand to her chest and took a few deep breaths. "I have a heart condition, you know." Her words came out more gruffly than she'd intended.

"Oh dear. I did *not* know that. I didn't mean to startle you. I just came by to introduce myself; I'm your new neighbor." By now the dogs were snuffling and pawing at the gate, trying to get out. Heidi was actually up on her two back legs, her front paws resting on the crossbar as she leaned her head into the woman's stroking hand. "Hello, pretty girl. You are a lovely old dear; yes, you are."

Kathy frowned. "Careful. They don't really do well with strangers."

"Of course, they don't. Neither do I. I mean, strangers are so strange, right?" She gave Heidi one last scratch behind the ear, reached over and ruffled Trixie's mop, then held aloft the rectangular twig basket she carried. "This is for you. And your pups, of course."

"Oh. Well. Thank you." Kathy fumbled for words. Oh dear. What would Lucy say when she saw treats for everyone but her?

"And I don't want to forget this." The woman withdrew a small drawstring pouch from her pocket and tucked it inside the basket. "This is for your kitty. She came by earlier and fell in love with it. When she wandered this way, I guessed you were her person."

Kathy made her way down the two steps and across the small yard to the gate. She thought she smelled vanilla and cinnamon, and her mouth began to water in anticipation. The image of a large kitchen, a small boy, and the floury aftermath of several batches of Christmas cookies flashed through her mind, and she smiled at the memory. She would have to call her Makani tonight. She wondered if he was eating well.

Her neighbor thrust an open hand over the gate. "I'm Willow. Willow Goodhope."

Of course, Kathy thought as she took the proffered hand. *Even her name sounds organic.*

"I'm Kathy. And welcome. I was going to come over and see if you need anything. Or any help. I mean, moving can be so much work. But... well, I...." She was flustered again, at a loss for polite excuses.

"Work? On a day like this?" Willow waved a hand dismissively. "Oh no. This is a day for doing absolutely nothing. In fact, I'm going to go put the tea kettle on, curl up with a good book, and revel in my new home. I just had to make sure the plants were settled in first. But the rest? Well, moving in will take care of itself, you know?"

"How *did* you do all of that so quickly?" Kathy jutted her chin in the direction of the cottage. "It just doesn't seem possible." She didn't intend to sound rude, but she really wanted to know. She loved her little yard and put hours into it every week, but she'd lived here over ten years now, and she couldn't remember it ever looking so lovely. Somehow, this Willow Goodhope had turned the preexisting eyesore across the way into a greeting card. In little more than an hour!

"The plants? I know! They just settled right in, as though they belong here." Willow held up her hands, palms facing Kathy. "God's incredibly creative, isn't he? And he gave me green thumbs, so I get to participate." She beamed, as if that explained everything.

The hands she held out for examination were roughened and callused, dirt under the nails. It seemed inconsistent with everything else about her, but it made perfect sense, really. The plants didn't climb into those pots on their own volition.

"Well, thank you again and... welcome. Again." Kathy patted the basket, then snapped her fingers at the dogs. "You girls stop sniffing the neighbor!

Go on inside, now. Go!" She looked up, a little embarrassed by their exuberance. "I'm really sorry. They usually just bark at folks, then run away."

"It's fine. They're just curious. Yes, you are, aren't you?" Willow reached down, gave Heidi's ear a gentle tug, and turned to leave. "Don't hesitate to visit, Kathy. I mean it. Anytime, okay?" She fluttered her fingers in the air and headed back across to her own place.

Kathy stood for a few moments longer, watching the woman's long, full skirt sweeping along the ground behind her. What an odd cookie, she thought. Remembering the promise of cinnamon sugar cookies, she glanced down at the basket in her arms. She lifted the cloth that covered the contents and studied them, perplexed and delighted at the same time. The Christmas cookie aroma was gone.

Nestled in the folds of a currant-colored dishtowel was a set of two oriental-style mugs with no handles. Inside one was a small honey bear bottle; in the other, two old-fashioned tea balls on chains. A muslin drawstring bag was stuffed with something crinkly and lumpy, and a stitched-on label gave a description of the contents in pretty, scrolled handwriting.

Elderberries, flowers, ginger, and lemon zest,
Add a dollop of honey and you'll be sure to get some rest.
Colds, coughs, fevers, and malaise,
They'll all flee, and the flu will fly away.

The bag for Lucy held a stuffed crocheted ball on the end of an elastic string. Kathy could smell the pungent catnip, and something else earthy and pleasant, and she had no doubt Lucy would, indeed, appreciate the toy.

The basket also contained a wax-paper packet of peanut-butter cookies, the telltale crisscross pattern on top of each one. She lifted them to her nose and wondered if perhaps she'd been mistaken—maybe it was these she'd smelled earlier and not cinnamon sugar cookies after all. She tore open an end of the package, pulled a cookie out, and took a bite. Not very sweet. In fact, they were almost a little salty, but the peanut butter flavor was rich and robust, making up for any other minor defects the crunchy cookies might have. They'd probably taste better dunked in cold milk.

She lifted the edge of the towel, searching for the promised pup treats, but the basket was empty.

"Oh!" she exclaimed, realizing her mistake. "These must be for you!" Her dogs still sat pining at the gate for the neighbor who had disappeared inside her little home. Kathy, on the other hand, was greatly relieved that Willow hadn't been there to witness her *faux pas*.

"Come on, you naughty kids. Look!" She waved a cookie above their heads and laughed out loud. "I have treats for you. And I have to admit they're the best doggy treats I've ever tasted!"

Pick up your copy of *Elderberry Croft: Seasons of the Heart* today!

• • • • ● • ● • • • •